Sour Milk in Sheep's Wool

by Helen Lundström Erwin

Copyright Notice

Published in the United States by Powersimple LLC, New York

ISBN 978-0-9862666-4-5

Cover design by Helen Lundström Erwin and Ben Erwin, which includes, with permission, a press photo from Gothenburg, Sweden 1918.

Thank you to Pia Johansson for letting us photograph her vintage milk can and small barn for the front cover.

Thank you to Leif Lindholm for his photo of resting cows for the back cover.

Also by Helen Lundström Erwin

James' Journey

For Children
Officer Helga Hedgehog Meets the New Neighbors

Thanks and Acknowledgements

National Museum of Science and Technology, Sweden

Alfred Grimlund, for answering my questions on early telephone history and Anders Lindeberg-Lindevet for answering questions about indoor plumbing in southern Sweden in the 19th and 20th centuries.

Luleå University of Technology, Sweden

Josefin Rönnbäck, History Department of economics, technology and social sciences, for answering my questions about women's suffrage in Sweden.

Lena Lennerhed, History and Contemporary Studies, Söderturn University, Stockholm, Sweden, for answering my questions about Elise Ottesen-Jensen.

Dan Marcus

Rev Dr. R Guy Erwin for help with proper Lutheran English terms.

Rob Flynn for help with Lutheran church history.

Lina Redestig, for answering questions regarding Swedish oxen and cow breeds.

Thank you to my family, especially to my husband Ben Erwin, and sister-in-law Marcia Carter for their unequivocal belief and support of me.

To my dear friend Sandy Saunders for her invaluable support and friendship.

Praise for Sour Milk in Sheep's Wool

"A timely and poignant look into her own history, Lundström Erwin's weaving of these women's stories serves to remind us that we modern torchbearers of reproductive rights owe an insurmountable debt to the women who came before us. Women whose cages had no bars but were prisons none the less, whose consequences were often disastrous and often fatal. And while today we fight to hold on to the choices we have, we must always remember those who have none."
– Megan Shelby, Women's Health Volunteer

From The Swedish American Museum, Chicago
"A well written and interesting historic drama which paints a vivid picture of the challenges an unmarried young mother could face at the end of the 19th century. The way Helen Lundström Erwin depicts the life, struggles and meager pay of "statare" in rural Sweden makes you understand why so many opted for a more uncertain future across the Atlantic."
– Anna Engström Patel

"I was drawn into the story from the very first page and could not put it down. Erwin makes history come alive through a beautiful portrayal of ordinary women, their struggles and desire for change.
– Angelica Farzaneh-Far

"It only took me a second and I was brought into the situation of Anette and then Hanna. I very much like Helen Lundström-Erwin's writing style and she paints the picture so you feel like you are part of the story. She describes both feelings and surroundings with great detail which is very engaging."
– Karin Abercrombie

From the American Scandinavian Association, Washington, D.C.
"This moving tale of women living in the 19th century drew me into the world of Anette's and Hanna's experiences, which resonated with me on many levels. I was drawn into their world through the descriptive narrative woven by Helen Erwin."
– Barbara Friborg

A Note to Readers

Dear Readers,

Some of the places, names, and abbreviations are in Swedish. You may choose to take a look at the glossary at the end of the book to see what they mean. But a word of caution, doing so may give away some spoilers. Mostly the words are street names etc. and shouldn't give you too much trouble. You may want to save the glossary until the end.

"I dream of the day when every newborn child is welcome, when men and women are equal, and when sexuality is an expression of intimacy, joy and tenderness."
- Elise Ottesen-Jensen.

8

For my great-grandmother Anette, whose name I carry.

PART ONE

Chapter One

Lund, Sweden 1889

Anette

Anette knocked and waited for the door to open, taking a deep breath to calm her racing heart. There were no voices or steps inside, indicating that someone had heard. She knocked again. Nothing.

She exhaled slowly. The parson's wife, who had helped her find the safe house so she could have her baby in secret, had assured her she was to show up at this address at 3 p.m. Maybe the mothers were putting their babies down to nap and couldn't come to the door. Relief washed over her at the thought. She could delay the unavoidable, if even for a moment.

Picking up her bulky valise, she walked back down the steps and out the front gate in the fence surrounding the property, turned, and looked up at the red wooden house. It was enormous, three stories with four windows on each. She would spend a good part of a year there, sewing for her upkeep until she had given birth and weaned the baby. Her belly pointed straight out, round and firm. There wasn't any way to deny it anymore. As soon as she stepped inside that house, she would be an unwed mother. Straightening her skirts, she looked down the cobblestone street and the homes along it, feeling foolish for having felt relief when no one opened the door. When leaving home this morning, she had tied a scarf over her hair so people would think her a married woman, but it surely wouldn't deceive anyone seeing her standing outside of this house. What if the headmistress disapproved, thinking it a lie as sinful as having a baby without being married? The thought sent a wave of nausea up her throat, burning it. She swallowed it down. Time ticked by but the house remained silent and dark. A couple entered the street up ahead and headed in her direction. The woman was looking right at her. Anette retied the ends of the headscarf under her chin and pushed a loose strand of hair under the fabric. Her hands were shaking, but she kept herself straight and didn't avert her eyes. Then they made a sudden left and disappeared down a side street. Anette gasped with relief and grabbed hold of the fence to steady herself as her breathing slowed. Perhaps it had never been their intention to walk down this way after all. She had to try not to panic every time she saw someone, no one knew her here. As if to affirm her resolve, she heard the clip-clop of hooves and a carriage laden with sacks of potatoes and firewood came around the same corner. The horse headed straight toward her at a steady trot and stopped in front of the house. A heavy-set middle-aged woman wearing a large brown hat festooned with feathers sat next to the driver. She climbed down and waved as he drove off.

"You must be Miss Lundström. I'm Miss Andersson, the owner here," she said and gestured toward the house, then reached out to shake her hand.

Miss Andersson's gaze was open and searching, not unkind, and she didn't seem to notice her scarf. Anette shook her hand and hid a small sigh of relief.

"You don't look too large yet, but you're at seven months already?"

"Yes, soon."

"I hope you weren't waiting too long. One of my girls had her baby today, and we had to take her to the hospital. Complications."

Anette felt a wave of panic at the word. "Is she all right?"

"She lost a lot of blood, but she'll be fine. I have four other girls living with me now, but they're all out on the town this afternoon."

"Oh, we're allowed to go out?"

Miss Andersson looked surprised for a moment, then frowned. "What did you think, that I'm running a prison?" She didn't seem offended, just genuinely puzzled.

"No, of course not, I just meant…" Anette blushed, wishing

she had kept it to herself but wondering how the other mothers felt being out in public. Weren't they all there to hide their pregnancies?

"Well, as you'll soon see, you girls have a strict schedule during the week, but on Saturday afternoons and Sundays you have time for yourselves. Here, get your things and follow me."

Miss Andersson opened the gate in the fence and then the front door, and led Anette into an airy hallway. "You can set your valise down here for now." She removed her feathered hat, revealing a mane of curly red hair. "I'll show you where you'll be working with the other girls. Then we can have something to eat."

Anette smiled, pleasantly surprised at the gesture. It wasn't dinner time for a few hours yet. They walked through a living area to a large room at the back of the house.

Miss Andersson spoke without turning to face her. "This is the sewing studio. It's where you'll be spending most of your time. We have, as you can see, five lockstitch machines. The table is strictly for cutting and mending," she turned to face Anette, "not for eating or drinking coffee. I keep our material in the storage room near the kitchen. The first Tuesday of every month the women's temperance group meet in there. You girls are responsible for setting up the chairs and removing them afterward."

"I understand," Anette said, even though she wasn't sure of what a temperance woman was. Her eyes went back to the lockstitch machines. They were very large and intimidating, and she hoped they wouldn't be too loud.

Miss Andersson noticed her gaze. "We'll teach you," she said. "Most of the girls learn quickly. You'll be sharing a room with Jenny, one of my best workers, and she'll be happy to help. I'll help you get settled upstairs. But first, let's have sandwiches and coffee before the others come home."

Anette nodded gratefully; she had been too nervous to eat before leaving. Now she was ravenous.

The kitchen was sizable, with a real stove and sink and a huge antique table in the middle of the room surrounded by chairs that didn't match. At its center was a ceramic pot spilling over with wildflowers.

Miss Andersson pulled out a chair for Anette, sat down across from her, then got right up again, remembering the sandwiches she had promised. She pulled out a loaf of bread, a brick of cheese, and liverwurst from a tall cupboard, cut the bread in to thick slices, and brought it to the table on a tray with the coffee kettle, plates, and two cups.

"Now tell me how you ended up in this situation," she said and sat down.

Restraining her eagerness to eat, Anette placed a slice of bread on her plate as Miss Andersson poured them coffee. The direct question surprised her, but maybe Miss Andersson had to ask it to make sure she really needed her help.

"I'm from Hardeberga. You may have heard how small it is, everyone knows everyone else."

"I haven't, but I can imagine," Miss Andersson said.

"My father is a blacksmith, and one day Julius came with his horse to shoe it. He said he came from Dalby and was on his way to Malmö when the shoe came off."

"Julius? Is he the father of your baby?"

"Yes." It felt intimate hearing it spoken of so matter-of-factly, and she blushed, forcing down an overwhelming need to cry. "At first, he seemed shy and didn't speak to me much, but he stayed in Hardeberga for several days and kept coming by the smithy. He always had items that needed mending, and we talked more and more." Anette picked up her cup, then put it down. "I'm eighteen and he said he was twenty-three, but now I don't know. He said he wanted to marry me, said that we could move to Malmö and that he had a job and a house there. We… we only… it was only one time. The next day he was gone." The heat in her cheeks burned deeper. Maybe she shouldn't have told her that part. Miss Andersson must think she was overly naive. "I was such a fool," she added.

"Maybe so," Miss Andersson said calmly. "But no one judges the men, so why should women be judged? The only reason we're made to feel ashamed is because we can't hide what happened."

A load heavier than the baby in her belly melted off Anette's shoulders, and she couldn't hold back her tears anymore.

Miss Andersson reached across the table and patted her hand. "Do call me Helga."

Anette met her eyes silently as the harsh mistress she had imagined dissolved along with her tears.

Helga handed her a handkerchief from her own pocket and waited a moment, then pointed to the bread on Anette's plate.

"Eat Anette, I'll call you that now, if you call me Helga." She poured herself more coffee and nodded when Anette added butter and a piece of cheese to her slice. "I'll explain how we run things here. You girls live here in the House, as we call it, while you're pregnant or nursing. Everyone receives room and board in exchange for work. And if it's needed, I try to find homes for the babies."

#

Anette soon learned that she was far from being the only one who had fallen into trouble as the parson's wife at home had called it. Regina, six months pregnant, didn't say much, but the other women were chatty and spoke openly about their experiences.

Jenny, who was only fifteen, and eight months pregnant, came from a wealthy family in Stockholm. The father-to-be was just a boy, not much older than she was. His parents pressured him to claim that the baby wasn't his, even though he had told Jenny that he wanted to marry her. It was no coincidence that her parents found a safe house for Jenny so far from Stockholm; it was to keep the lovers apart.

Malena, the woman who had her baby on the day Anette first arrived, and who had to go to the hospital, had a boyfriend somewhere. They would get married, she said but didn't explain why they hadn't already.

Then there was Ida, who was nursing a two-month-old. Someone raped her on the way home from the mercantile where she worked, right here in Lund. Her boss became furious when he found out. Not with the rapist, but with Ida who he said was flaunting herself in front of the customers. The horrid man who had done it continued coming into the mercantile openly, as if he had done nothing wrong.

Anette was too embarrassed to tell them of her own experience. Surely, they would think her stupid if they learned how she had been seduced by a man who was just passing through her village. It didn't matter that they had spent days together, she should have known better. She blushed every time she thought of how Julius had brought her to their neighbor's abandoned barn. He had a blanket there, wine and food. She hadn't even thought to question where he stayed while her father finished all those things he brought to the smithy. But he probably slept in that barn. Who did that right after Christmas? Likely he didn't have a house in Malmö either. She had known it too, but hadn't listened to herself. Instead, she had fallen for his kind words and his flattery, telling herself that he was sincere. Her father and Mother Anna, her stepmother, had been upset and disappointed when she told them she was pregnant, but never angry, not even when the parson warned them of the disgrace they would face. Despite his warning, they agreed to raise the baby as their own. Compared to what Jenny and Ida faced, she was fortunate. She could stay here in Lund and find a job, even a husband. No one ever needed to know the truth about her past. Those were the words of the parson's wife. Going back home afterwards would not be an option, she said. Hardeberga was too small, and the stigma would destroy both Anette and the congregation, which would surely disperse and find other churches. Or worse, the congregants might stop attending church altogether. Surely, she wouldn't want that on her conscience.

#

Helga had established a schedule where each girl was responsible for meals on different days, and on that day, it was her only responsibility. At first Anette thought she would welcome a day to herself away from the constant chatter and the clanging of the sewing machines, but being alone gave her too much time to think about the coming birth.

Truth to be told, she was terrified, scared that even if she survived the birth, she might die later just like her mother had after giving birth to her youngest brother. She kept hearing her grandmother's voice echoing in her head, telling her to never use one of those new midwives but to trust in the wise women as mothers-to-be had always done.

When she mentioned her grandmother's warning to Helga, she dismissed it as nonsense and pointed out that the midwife would be a friend of hers who had birthed all the women in the House and there had never been any problems. Except for Malena then, but she didn't dare to remind her Helga of that.

Chapter Two

Hanna

Hanna looked at her reflection as they walked past the glove maker's large window. She turned her hat a little to the left, hoping that she would look proper and wouldn't be mistaken for one of the unwed mothers who lived in the House. Magnhild, walking beside her, raised an eyebrow at her, but she pretended not to notice.

She had met Magnhild at a women's reading circle a couple of years ago while they were discussing A Doll's House by Ibsen. As soon as Magnhild started talking, she knew she had to become friends with her. The play, Magnhild said, only represented upper-class women, the ones who had maids to help with everything. It didn't mention the women who did everything themselves, cooking, cleaning, taking care of all the children, and who may even work themselves. The other women in their circle, including the host, had been aghast, which only encouraged Magnhild.

It had prompted such a heated discussion that Magnhild was told to leave and not come back. Hanna had been so impressed with the way Magnhild stood up for herself and with what she said that she followed her out and decided not to go back either. They had been best friends ever since.

Last year they both attended the famous, or infamous, depending on your political leanings, women's meeting in Denmark where Emilie Rathou spoke about the importance of husbands staying sober so their wives could reason with them. Impressed, they joined the Good Templars and organized a small group of friends to meet once a month. At first, they gathered at each other's houses, but with husbands and other family members around it was difficult to discuss women's issues freely. Then Bengta, who was a midwife, arranged for them to meet in the storeroom of Miss Helga Andersson's sewing workshop, which doubled as a home for unwed mothers. It was a godsend.

"Will Bengta be there tonight?" Hanna asked as the House came into view.

Magnhild nodded. "Yes, she'll be bringing a friend."

"Good another member! I hope she told her that Helga reminded us to slip in quietly and avoid interacting with the residents. She's worried it could cause problems if rumors start that we're trying to convert them to our cause."

Magnhild threw her head back and laughed. "Right. You can't be too careful with women like us around."

Hanna grinned. "It's not as if this place isn't controversial already."

#

The women hadn't taken their seats yet except for Bengta and her friend, who got to their feet as soon as they entered. Bengta's friend was stylish, wearing a dark blue dress and a pearl broch. Hanna got the impression that she was a little nervous.

"Hanna, Magnhild," Bengta said. "I'd like you to meet Mrs. Von Gier."

"Please, call me Vanda," the woman said. She extended her hand, shaking first Magnhild's, then Hanna's hand.

"I hope you don't mind our humble storeroom?" Hanna asked, gesturing toward the stacks of fabric at the back of the room.

"Not at all, it's lovely to be surrounded by all these rolls of soft cloth. The colors are so festive, especially the pastels."

Hanna threw a glance at Magnhild who was following Bengta as she made her way back to her chair, then smiled at Vanda. "We're glad to be here. It's small, but private. Thank you for joining us. Please sit here next to me," she said and sat down, patting the seat of the chair beside her.

"My pleasure," Vanda said and exhaled. She really seemed somewhat nervous.

Hanna nodded, trying to look encouraging. "We felt that meeting privately among women would give us more than just going to general Good Templar meetings." She smiled, adding, "I love your brooch, the pearls are beautiful." They shimmered in the lamplight and looked like milk with honey that was just slightly stirred.

"Thank you, a gift from my husband."

There was something with the way she said it that was awkward. Hanna nodded uncertainly.

Then Bengta called out, "We're about to begin. Did everyone bring their paper and pencils?"

"I did," Magnhild declared proudly.

Hanna chuckled as Bengta gave Magnhild a look of mock exasperation before resuming. "Last time we discussed how to reach more people. Grete, I believe you had a suggestion."

"Yes, I did. We're so fortunate to have the university here. I'd like to suggest that we make flyers and distribute them on campus. We may influence these young people even before they begin to drink."

"We'd better pass the flyers out in the lower schools if that's the goal," said Lova, lifting her eyebrows. Everyone laughed.

Hanna raised her hand with a grin, looking at Vanda. Maybe their merry mood would make her more comfortable. "Going to Lund's University campus is a splendid idea…," she began, only to be interrupted when the door opened, and Helga popped her head in.

"Bengta, you're needed. One of the girls has her time. We just helped her upstairs to her room."

Chapter Three

Anette

The midwife began by scrubbing her hands and nails, then washed her arms all the way up to the elbow in a bucket of soapy water as Helga came in with a new bucket containing more water. She repeated the entire procedure five times as Anette looked on in disbelief. Didn't she know what to do? How would she tend to her if it took her that long to wash her hands?

When she finally finished, she sat down on a stool by Anette's feet. "I'm Miss Pålsson," she said as she placed a neat pile of folded towels at the foot of the bed.

Anette nodded. She felt a dull ache in her lower back. It wasn't as bad as she had imagined, but constant.

"You must open your legs, Miss Lundström. I need to see how long we have to go."

Anette did what she asked and felt her face flush with embarrassment when Miss Pålsson's fingers prodded and squeezed.

"It feels just right, Miss Lundström. You have nothing to worry about. It'll be a while yet."

Anette leaned back. Helga had given her two extra pillows and kept adjusting them behind her head as if she wasn't satisfied with the way they looked. It was annoying, but she decided not to say anything. She lay there for what seemed like a long time and drifted off despite the ache in her back. Suddenly a sharper pain snapped her awake. She gasped and stared wide-eyed at Miss Pålsson, who just nodded calmly.

"There, you're getting your contractions. Breathe deeply and you'll be fine. You're not open very wide yet, it'll take some time. Just try to rest as much as you can between the pains." She took Anette's right hand in both of hers; they felt warm against her own, which was clammy and cold.

Miss Pålsson turned to Helga, who was still standing by the bed. "Why don't you go downstairs and warm up a cup of apple juice and mix it with some rum for her."

Helga left right away, and once they heard her footsteps on the stairs, Miss Pålsson squeezed her hand again.

"My dear Miss Lundström, isn't there anything I can do for you that would make you a little calmer? Don't hesitate to tell me, I know it can be frightening the first time, but you're a strong young woman. This will soon be over."

There was so much to say, but she just shook her head. How could she possibly tell her she didn't want her there?

Helga reappeared and handed Anette the drink, then left. It tasted sweet, and the rum did calm her a bit.

But it wasn't over soon. It felt like the baby was lying incorrectly inside of her. As if it was folded on the bottom of her womb trying to get out sideways. The searing pain was constant now and had her lower back and belly in an iron grip that was shooting down her legs. Anette could hear her own voice shrieking louder and louder, and when Miss Pålsson stood up and leaned over her, she grabbed her shoulders with both hands.

"I want a wise-woman to help me... someone with the old knowledge. This isn't right, it's taking too long. Have you found a place to bury the afterbirth? Women can die if it's not done. I know, it's how I lost my mother!"

Miss Pålsson gently pulled Anette's hands off her shoulders and sat back down on her stool.

"Dear child, I'm very sorry to find out about your mother. I wish you had told me. No wonder you're so scared. Let me ask you something, when did this happen?"

"1875," Anette said, glaring at her. She knew she looked angry but couldn't hide it and blushed from the shame of it. Miss Pålsson had been kind, offering condolences.

"That would explain it. Did she get the childbirth fever?"

"Yes. How did you know?"

Miss Pålsson smiled gently and reached for her hand. "Back then, it wasn't known how important it is to wash our hands before we tend to a woman. Doctors believed women got sick because of foul air and dirty sheets. Even though your mother was birthed by an oath-sworn midwife, if those hands were not clean," she paused and looked at Anette somberly, "it can cause severe disease. The tissue swells up and then the fever comes. Many, many women died needlessly. Out in the villages, some wise-women insist to be present during labor along with us midwives, often contradicting us. You've been misinformed, that's all. You're not the only one."

Anette stared at her for a moment, relieved and embarrassed, but too exhausted to think of what to say.

Shortly thereafter, the pain changed. Miss Pålsson sat up straighter and smiled encouragingly, placing both her hands on Anette's inner thighs, looking intently between them. "It's coming now. Push."

Anette screamed as something strong and fierce inside of her took hold of her body and squeezed. There was a sucking sound, and she heard him cry.

"You have a healthy, sturdy boy, Miss Lundström."

Miss Pålsson cut the cord and immediately stood and left the room, cradling the baby.

"I knew it was a boy," Anette whispered.

She must have blacked out because when she came to, both Miss Pålsson and Helga were standing next to her. Miss Pålsson carefully placed the tightly swaddled boy in her arms. His little face was red, and his eyes were tightly shut. Tiny pimples dotted his nose, and he was so small and warm. Anette touched his check and felt something hot in her chest. It hurt, and she closed her eyes, pushing feelings of pure joy from her heart. He would never be hers.

It was Friday, October 4, 1889, and she named him Carl Frans Julius.

Chapter Four

Hanna

After the meeting, Hanna, Magnhild, and Grete decided to go to a café to continue the conversation. Hanna asked Vanda if she wanted to join them as well, but she declined and said she had to go home and make dinner. A light rain was falling when they stepped outside, making the wet cobblestones shine in the light from the streetlamps. They could see the lamplighter on his ladder halfway down the street. If he only knew what had just taken place in the House, Hanna thought and opened her umbrella, stepping aside when Grete opened hers.

"Let's go to the café near the cathedral," Hanna said and pulled Magnhild in under her umbrella. As usual, she hadn't brought one.

They walked briskly, spurred on by the cold damp air, and soon found the place. It looked welcoming in the darkness with its warm light glowing behind the paned windows. The café was in one of those small cottages from the old days, and they had to hunch to get through the doorway. Magnhild had to take her hat off.

A waitress wearing a striped apron held the door open for them and took their umbrellas. She didn't look older than seventeen.

"Welcome. I apologize for the entrance. I know it's small. Please have a seat and I'll get you something hot to drink. Coffee or tea, perhaps?"

"I think we'd all like hot cocoa," Hanna said as they sat down at a table near the window.

They were alone except for a man sitting with his newspaper across the room. Each table had a vase with a single rose beside a thick candle. A potbelly stove in the middle of the room made the air comfortable but caused the windows to fog up.

Hanna wiped a pane with her glove and peered out. "It's raining harder now. It seems fitting with the mood. That poor girl was screaming so loud. Is it always like that?"

"That's what Bengta says, childbirth is an awfully painful endeavor. I'm glad it's not in the cards for me," Magnhild said and exchanged a glance with Hanna.

Last month, after making her swear to never ever tell anyone, Magnhild had confided in her that she and Bengta had a romantic relationship. Hanna was still getting used to the idea that they weren't just unmarried women living together. Did they kiss? Take their clothes off? It was a little hard to imagine.

Grete lowered her voice and changed the subject. "What do you think? Will we women get voting rights in our lifetime?"

"Voting rights?" Magnhild looked at her incredulously. "Nah, I know there's been talk, but not even all men can vote. I doubt they'd let *us* do it," she added.

"Well," Grete began, but was interrupted by the waitress arriving with a tray full of steaming cups and a plate of cookies.

"Here you are, ladies. The cookies are on the house. Can I get you anything else?"

"Thank you, very kind. No, we're fine," Magnhild answered for all of them.

Grete waited until the waitress had sat down with her book behind the counter before she continued. "Some women can vote now if they're wealthy enough."

"But only in certain local elections," Hanna said. "And only if they're not married."

"Yes," Magnhild agreed, stirring her cocoa, "there are definite advantages to spinsterhood."

Hanna laughed. She didn't dare to look at her, but felt her gaze and imagined her eyes glinting.

"Anyway, my husband believes that all men should have the right regardless of their status. And if they let all the men vote, why not women?" Grete asked.

"All women, you mean," Hanna reminded her.

Magnhild cleared her throat. "There was some talk of it at Miss Rathou's meeting in Denmark, but honestly, as much as I'd like to support it, I don't think it's wise. People already think we're crazy."

"I don't know," Hanna said. "I'm mostly concerned with women being respected as our own persons, not just as someone's daughter or wife. That we can pursue professions and have them respected. Asking too much may cause a backslide." She glanced at the man with the newspaper.

Grete followed Hanna's eyes and lowered her voice. "I can see your point, and it may be more effective to take one thing at a time."

"Yes, the drinking is still the most important thing to focus on for now I believe. Think of all those drunk men using up their household money on alcohol and throwing themselves on their wives who can do nothing to stop them. We have to work for sobriety first. If we do that, women can control the spacing of their children, have saner husbands and would be able to focus on issues like voting," Hanna said. She took a warming sip of her cocoa, feeling proud of her answer, and glad she had studied the literature. It made it much easier to know what to say.

"It's certainly something to keep in mind for the future Grete," said Magnhild, then startled at a loud crash. The man with the newspaper had slammed his chair into the table as he stood up.

"You women should know better than to sit around talking about such unnatural ideas. It's a disgrace!" With that, he stomped out, cursing as he hit his head on the low doorsill.

The waitress rushed over to see if he was all right, but he was already out on the street. They heard his umbrella open and felt the bracing cold air from the open door.

"My dear Lord," Grete exclaimed. "What can be so terrible about three women talking? Was it the voting or the sobriety?"

Magnhild raised her eyebrows. "I told you they'd think us crazy. Did you hear the bang when he hit his head? He'll have a large bump tomorrow. How is he going to explain that to his wife?"

"He can't," Hanna said dryly, then smiled at Grete who was covering her mouth to stop herself from laughing.

The waitress approached, wringing her hands. "I must apologize for the rude behavior of that gentleman. I don't know what got into him. He comes here almost every day to read his paper, and I've never seen him shout at another customer."

"Don't apologize," Hanna said. "Didn't you hear what we were talking about?"

"No, miss, I'm not accustomed to eavesdropping on my customers."

"Well, that man apparently was. We're Good Templars you see, and we work for the rights of women," she added, noticing Magnhild looking at her approvingly.

"The Good Templars? I don't think I've heard of them."

"Simply put, we believe many wives are victims of abuse in proportion to how much their husbands drink, and we encourage people to abstain."

"Truly? I didn't know there was an organization for it. My cousin drinks too much and he is always horrible to his wife when he's drunk. I feel terrible for her."

"I'm so sorry," Hanna said. "It's very common, which is why we feel so strongly about it."

Magnhild nodded and pulled a calling card from her handbag. "Here, please take this. If you're interested, you're welcome to attend one of our meetings."

The waitress took the card and curtsied, looking a little flustered. "I apologize again for the disturbance. Can I get you anything else?"

Magnhild turned to Hanna and Grete and asked, "Another cup of hot cocoa, ladies?"

"Why not," Hanna said, then smiled to herself. If she could talk her father into it, she would open her own café. And if she did, they could meet there instead of at Helga's home for unwed mothers.

Chapter Five

Anette

Carl burped as Anette held him tightly to her breast. Stretched out on her bed, Jenny giggled at the sound. Her own baby was sound asleep in his basket. "I got a letter today from my parents," she announced. "I'm allowed to come home."

"Oh, that's good news," Anette said. "I'm so happy for you." But no sooner had she finished speaking than she felt a pang in her chest; she had heard nothing from her parents, even though she had sent a letter as soon as Carl was born. Not a word to see how she was feeling, or to tell her they were happy that there was a little boy for them to love.

"Yes," Jenny went on, "they've found a family to take the baby. It's a friend of my mother's cousin. They have no children of their own and nobody knows of them, they live far away from us, all the way up in Dalarna."

"What about the father, your boyfriend?"

"Oh, I don't know. He'll do what he always planned to do, finish school and go to university. I could never marry him. My father doesn't find him suitable."

"I'm sorry," Anette said, not sure what else would be appropriate.

At least Jenny could go back home. Anette shifted Carl so he could nurse from her other breast. While he suckled, his gaze immediately went to hers, piercing her with his beautiful light blue eyes, just like her own. She looked away, focusing on the naked wintry trees outside the window.

It was time to think about what to do when this was all over. Maybe she could find a position as a seamstress. Or perhaps she could work in the chocolate factory in Malmö, like her older brother Gösta did, and even share the room he rented. She had written him when she first came to the House and several letters after that, but he hadn't replied to any of them. If women weren't allowed to work there, why hadn't he just told her that? Was he angry and ashamed of her? Or had something happened? It would be Christmas in a couple of weeks and still not a word from anyone.

Helga had remarked that the temperance women had started a collection so they could have a nice dinner on Christmas Eve. All the residents were to spend a few days beforehand cooking and baking. No one would be sewing. If only she would hear from them by then, so she at least wouldn't feel abandoned on Christmas.

Sighing, Anette glanced down at Carl. He was sleeping now and had stopped nursing. Gently she got to her feet and placed him in his basket, relieved that another feeding was done. She dreaded each one. The little sucking noises he made when he ate tore at her heart, and the stillness made her think too much. Carl was so small, so warm and snug. He trusted her so and didn't know she would betray him. At least she didn't have to give her baby to the orphanage as Karla had done just before Anette came to the House. Karla couldn't afford to pay to leave the baby there, so she had to feed it in, meaning she had to breastfeed both her baby and the orphans until she had earned her own baby's keep. There must have been something wrong with the baby, or she would have stayed in the House so Helga could find a home for it.

It sounded so sad, but maybe it made it easier to say goodbye; maybe you would feed so many babies that you would forget which one was yours.

"Is Carl sleeping?" Jenny asked, then slid off the bed and peered into the basket. "He is so cute."

"Thank you, Jenny, isn't he?" No, he's ugly really, really ugly, Anette told herself, but it was no use. She didn't think him ugly.

"Let's go downstairs," Jenny said. "We have more sewing to do before dinner."

The chatter of the women and the pounding of the sewing machines was overwhelming after the quiet time with Carl. They had two new girls already. One of them, Alma, looked as if she was about to cry as Helga showed her how to handle the fast-moving needle. Anette sat down at her own machine and continued what she was doing before she stopped to nurse.

#

Anette was sitting at the mending table, embroidering blue bells on an order of handkerchiefs when Helga entered. She looked flustered and carelessly threw her hat on a chair.

"Anette, wouldn't you know I've gone and lost my purse? I can't believe it. I've retraced my steps, thinking perhaps I left it at the baker's or at the fishmonger's but it's not there. I even went back to both places twice, just to be absolutely sure."

"It's on a little table with pillbox displays," Anette murmured without thinking.

"My goodness, I forgot! I also stopped for a moment at the pharmacy." Helga frowned, then turned on her heels and left the room. Anette heard the front door open and close. Her hat lay forgotten on the chair where she left it.

Anette bent down over her work, face burning. How could she have been so careless? Helga would think she was putting on airs, or worse, the purse would be gone when she arrived and then Helga might think she had just made it up. Why couldn't she have kept her mouth shut? She eyed the pile in front of her, praying that that there was enough time to finish them all before Helga came back so she could move to another task. If she wasn't still sitting there when Helga came back for her hat, maybe she would forget.

But she had ten unfinished handkerchiefs left, when twenty-five minutes later, Helga strode back into the sewing room, purse in hand. Wiggling it in the air, she pushed her hat aside and sank down on the chair.

"Anette, how did you know I had left it by the pillboxes in the pharmacy?"

"I just knew."

Helga opened her purse in Anette's direction. "Look at this, everything is in there, my money, my hairpins and my mother's necklace that I always keep in there. I know I shouldn't, but it brings luck, and it doesn't fit around my neck. The pharmacists hadn't noticed. Anyone could have taken it if it hadn't been for you. Thank you, Anette. Thank you so much." She leaned across the sewing table and squeezed her hand.

"I'm very relieved to hear that it was still there," Anette said. "But how did you know?"

Anette threw a quick glance at the other women, but they were sitting by the lockstitch machines, oblivious.

"I sometimes have the sight." She held her breath, willing Helga not to cross herself.

"The sight? Are you a spiritualist?"

Anette felt her cheeks burning again, wishing she didn't always blush. "What do you mean by that?"

"Are you able to talk with the dead?"

"Lord, no, it's nothing like that. I just see things sometimes."

Helga was studying her face intently. Then she smiled. "It's a gift, child. I want us to talk about this more. For now, finish your sewing."

With that Helga stood up, plucked her hat from the chair, and went upstairs to her room.

Anette exhaled, at least it didn't scare her.

#

By the time summer came, Anette had become so used to living in the House that she sometimes pretended that nothing would change. Carl was a gurgling, content baby now with his own personality, crawling and getting into mischief, and laughing at her antics. She had given up on trying not to love him.

Then one morning, Helga handed her a letter. She pulled it from her fingers, then ran upstairs with Carl on her hip, and tore it open.

Dear Anette,

We received your letter and we have heard from Gösta that you are doing well. Your father and I will pick up Carl on Friday the 20th of June. Take care of yourself,

Mother Anna

She sank to her bed, her heart racing so fast, she was afraid she would faint. Gösta had received her letters then, seen fit to write to them about it, but not bothered to reply to her. Her vision blurred, and she grabbed a tighter hold of Carl. He gazed up at her and tried to catch the tear sliding down her cheek.

Chapter Six

Hanna and Anette

Hanna hurried into the storeroom and took her seat. Grete, Lova, Bengta, and Magnhild had already arrived. Vanda probably wouldn't come. It was rare that she did.

"There you are, Hanna! We were waiting for you," Bengta said as both she and Magnhild looked at her questioningly. They knew exactly what was on her mind.

She confirmed their silent question with a nod, trying to hide an excited grin.

"We have some good news today. Hanna, why don't you stand up," Bengta suggested.

"In this small congregation?" Hanna teased and got to her feet. "Well then, as Bengta said, I have some news." She paused for effect and smiled. They were all staring at her now, and she felt a flurry of excitement in her stomach. "Everything has happened as I hoped it would. Since unmarried women are now legal adults when they turn twenty-one, my father has finally agreed to help me open my own café. He was hoping I'd find a husband first. Luckily for me, I didn't." She winked at Magnhild.

"I'd take a café over a husband any day," Magnhild said, and squeezed Bengta's hand.

Hanna laughed.

"Are you going to bake yourself?" Lova asked.

"No, I'll hire a baker. I already have the space. It needs renovation and painting, a new oven and…"

"A café?" Grete interrupted, looking stunned. "I knew nothing about this. I'm so happy for you. I… if only…" Her chin started quivering, and then she lowered her head and burst into tears.

Hanna's heart sunk. Why in the world was she crying, if only what?

"I'm sorry, Hanna, It's just that you're so lucky and independent. I can't come here anymore. Albert won't allow it."

"I'm so sorry," Bengta said. "Tell us about it."

Grete dried her eyes and took a deep breath. "Albert says I'm embarrassing him. He says he's fearful for my health, that he spoke to a physician who claims a woman can damage her nervous system if she dabbles in politics and reads too much."

Hanna frowned and sat back down. Hadn't Grete been telling them what her husband thought of politics and that she felt women should be able to vote. What had changed?

"Grete, why don't you let Bengta speak to him? She can assure him that you're not in any danger," Magnhild offered.

"It wouldn't work. He'd never listen to a woman, not even a midwife."

Hanna stared at them. Everyone seemed to have forgotten about her café. And to think she was about to suggest that they meet there instead of here. She got to her feet again and cleared her throat. If they looked up, she would tell them the rest. But they didn't, not even Magnhild. She was leaning forward, supporting her elbows on her knees, and was still telling Grete about Bengta's expertise. Hanna swallowed her disappointment, deciding to go out for some air.

No one noticed when she snuck out. Quietly, she closed the door behind her and walked through the kitchen, then the sewing room. The evening sunlight was coming through the curtains, casting slivers of light on the wood floor. The lockstitch machines were covered and work had been put away for the night. She quickened her steps and passed through the vestibule and out the front door.

Anette's clogs pounded the cobblestones as she hurried back to the House. Helga had invited her to her room for what she said would be a pleasant evening of conversation and told her to run down to the store before it closed to pick up a bottle of wine and something to eat. It sounded very formal, but she was looking forward to it, and felt honored. None of the others had been invited to Helga's private rooms.

She had just started up the steps to the front door when it swung open, and a beautiful woman wearing a brown, expensive-looking dress and an elegant matching shawl draped over her shoulders, walked out. She seemed preoccupied. It was one of the temperance women! Anette stepped aside, suddenly feeling awkward and unkempt. She probably disapproved of her, knowing why she was living there.

"Here," the woman said, "let me help you with the door. Your hands are full."

Anette had already begun to shift everything to her left hand so she could open the door with her right, but as she fumbled her sausage fell out of her bag, rolled across the landing, and came to a dead stop underneath the temperance woman's skirts.

"I'm so sorry," Anette blurted, then froze. She couldn't possibly stick her hand beneath her skirts to retrieve it, could she?

The woman just laughed, took a step back, picked up the sausage, and handed it over with a gleam in her eye.

"Thank you, miss," Anette mumbled and quickly slipped inside.

Hanna stood outside the door for a moment, chuckling to herself, before deciding there was no point now in going for a walk. That poor unwed mother, she had looked utterly crestfallen, but the way the sausage ended up under her skirts really was funny. It put her in a better mood. Maybe she was just being selfish after all. Grete must feel terrible that she wasn't allowed to be with them anymore. Even if they didn't notice her come back in, she wouldn't say anything. Her café could wait.

But the others turned as soon as she opened the door to the storeroom.

"What happened, dear?" Bengta asked. "Are you all right?"

"I just needed some air."

"I'm sorry about earlier, Hanna," Grete said. "Please tell us all about your café."

"Yes, I never got to say congratulations," Lova said and started clapping.

Magnhild did the same, smiling approvingly.

Bengta put a finger to her lips. "We have to be quiet, ladies. Someone might hear us."

"I wouldn't be too concerned," Hanna said and grinned while pointing to the ceiling. "The women above us are drinking wine as we speak. I saw one of them coming back with a large bottle."

"You did not!" Magnhild exclaimed, her jaw dropping. "Are you sure?"

"Yes, I even spoke to her."

Bengta looked stunned. "I can't believe they're drinking up there. I wonder if Helga knows about it?"

Chapter Seven

Anette

Anette stopped in the hallway on the second floor to wait for her cheeks to stop burning so Helga wouldn't ask questions. The temperance woman must surely have seen the wine. They were against drinking Jenny had explained, and she could only imagine what they thought of unwed mothers. But she had such a kind face and very warm eyes and didn't seem upset at all. Still, there was no reason for her to mention it to Helga. She touched her cheeks with the back of her hand. They felt cooler, they would have to do.

Helga took the bottle from Anette along with the bread and sausage, filled two glasses, and handed one to Anette. "Please, sit down." She gestured toward a cushioned armchair beside a small table and sat down in the matching chair facing it. "Is Carl asleep?"

"I don't know. Jenny is watching him for me. He probably is, though. He usually sleeps soundly at this time of night."

Anette looked around. The low table between them was covered with an embroidered tablecloth set with two plates, linen napkins, and silverware. Beneath it was a Turkish rug. A table under an open window held a neat stack of books. On each side was a pedestal with a large green fern. The walls were unadorned except for a clock and a framed portrait of the royal family. Mother Anna had the same portrait back in Hardeberga.

"It's very cozy in here. It feels like home."

"Thank you." Helga struck a match to light the lamp beside her chair. "I need a place to call my own since the house is always full of women and babies. I'm not complaining, but I need my rest now and then."

"Of course."

Anette felt her hair tickling her neck as a warm breeze came in through the window. It was like a caress, and she remembered the time when she and Julius drank wine in the barn. How happy she had been. How could he have disappeared from her life without a word of explanation? If he had known she got pregnant, would he have married her? Maybe she should have looked for him.

Helga took the knife and cut the bread into thick slices. "You seem far away, Anette. Have some more wine. I know it's a trying time. But you're very lucky to have someone you know and love to take care of your baby. Do you know how many women seek the help of an angelmaker?"

"No."

Helga's mouth formed a thin line of displeasure. "Angelmakers, if you don't know, are horrid women, paid by desperate mothers to get rid of their newborns." She poured more wine for them both, even though Anette had only taken a sip, then drank deeply from her own glass. "They wring their little, tiny necks or put them out in the cold in the woods and then bury them, or they try to rid women of their babies while they're still in the womb. They put sticks…" She shook her head. "No, let's not talk about the horror of it."

Anette stared at her. What if she had known and had done this too, to little Carl? Suddenly it felt hard to breathe. The clock ticking on the wall sounded loud in the stillness.

Helga nodded gravely. "It's the reason I'm doing what I do, Anette. My own sister you see, fell victim to one of them. She was five months along. To this day I wish I had stopped her, but I didn't. I even went with her to that murderess of a woman." She swallowed audibly.

Anette instinctively reached out and patted her arm while trying to push the horrific images of bleeding women out of her mind.

Then Helga changed the subject.

"What I wanted to talk to you about, Anette, is your future. Actually, your sight and how you might use it to help people. I have to admit that I'm intrigued. I've never had a psychic girl in the House."

Anette pulled her hand back from Helga's arm, then took a long sip of wine before answering. "I don't know. It's not what you might think. It just comes over me now and then."

Helga nodded and cut off a slice of sausage. Anette hoped it wasn't dirty. She had forgotten to wipe it off after dropping it.

"I understand," Helga said, "but I'd like you to accompany me to a spiritualist meeting, just to experience it at least once. My aunt's friend, Miss Ofelia, is a medium. She holds a séance at her home every Thursday."

Helga pushed the plate with sausage toward her. "Here, have some. It's delicious."

Anette cut off a small slice and chewed carefully. There was no crunch from dirt.

"Have you any ideas about what you might do when you leave the House?" Helga asked.

"I might look for work as a seamstress or a housekeeper somewhere. I was hoping that maybe you could recommend me to someone."

Helga nodded. "I do know of someone, an old woman here in Lund, named Mrs. Engström, who needs some help with household duties. She doesn't pay much, but you'd be able to live there. And beyond that, who knows? You have a gift, Anette. It would be a shame not to look into it. Spiritualism is very popular these days. My aunt said that Miss Ofelia can barely keep up with everyone who wants to see her. Why don't you come with me this week? That way, you'd see how other people with your gift use it to their advantage."

"Oh, I don't know."

"Anette, you knew where I left my purse. Do come."

Anette smiled, that part was true at least, and how could she say no after being invited into Helga's private quarters like this?

"I'll go with you."

"It's settled, then. We'll go on Thursday."

\#

Anette wondered what sort of strange house Miss Ofelia lived in, picturing an oddly shaped cottage on a little side street somewhere. It wasn't so. She lived in a small villa on one of Lund's finer streets. Helga was right, Miss Ofelia did well for herself.

As they approached, a formally dressed young man in a

brown suit opened the front door. Behind him stood three older women in old-fashioned black dresses. One of them nodded at Helga.

"Good evening, Helga. Who is this with you?"

"This is Miss Lundström, a friend of mine. She has the sight herself."

Anette smiled, relieved that Helga hadn't introduced her as one of the House residents.

"Oh, that's wonderful, just wonderful." The woman returned her smile and took Anette's hand in hers. "Dear, I'm so glad you're here. Maybe you can help me find out what my Stellan is doing?"

"Stellan?" Anette asked. Then she understood. All three women were in mourning. Stellan must be the woman's dead husband.

Helga gently patted the widow's shoulder. "We wouldn't want to offend Miss Ofelia now, would we? Miss Lundström is here tonight to observe."

"Of course, you're right. Of course."

"One forgets that even those with their own sight may need some advice from an experienced professional," the young man said and led them through a small but elegant sitting room. On the way, they passed a simple red box with a slot on top.

Helga noticed that it caught Anette's eye. "Donations aren't given until after the session. We always begin with tea once everyone is seated. It gets us in the right mood. Miss Ofelia has a spirit guide who travels in India and throughout the Far East. Tea is what he recommends we drink instead of coffee."

"Oh, I see." Anette couldn't think of anything to say. A spirit guide, she assumed, was someone who was dead. Did she really mean that he was traveling there even if he wasn't alive?

They proceeded into the parlor. There were several people there already, sitting around a large round table with a five-arm candelabra in the center. The candles were unlit.

A heavyset woman wearing a flowing red dress approached. Curly brown hair hung loosely around her shoulders. She threw

Anette a quick glance, then turned to Helga.

"This must be Miss Lundström."

Helga nodded. "Yes, Miss Ofelia, this is she."

"Welcome," she said, but narrowed her eyes when Anette curtsied politely. She seemed weary of her. What had Helga said about her?

Miss Ofelia gestured for them to take a seat at the table and Anette followed Helga who hurried over and pulled out a chair for her. Miss Ofelia then picked up a teapot from a stand behind her and instructed the young man in the brown suit to set out cups and saucers. When he finished, she walked around the table and poured their tea. A woman sitting across from Anette pushed a big bowl with sugar cubes toward her.

"It can seem quite bitter the first time if you're not yet accustomed to tea," she said and added with a wink, "There's cream too if you need it."

Anette smiled and took a sip. It did have a slightly bitter, almost burned flavor, but it wasn't unpleasant.

"Thank you," she said, and received several approving looks when she settled for one sugar cube.

When all the guests had been served, Miss Ofelia sat down and poured a cup for herself. She didn't add sugar. The room was silent except for quiet sips and the sound of cups and saucers clattering.

Miss Ofelia finished her tea, then slowly rose from her chair and went around the room and put out the lamps. Skirts rustling, she glided back to the table and lit the candelabra as she hummed the Lord's Prayer. The candles illuminated the faces around the table but left the rest of the room in darkness. It made everyone look pale and ghostly, even Helga. Anette felt a wave of panic threatening to surface. She shifted her gaze to her cup and tried to breathe calmly, but her heart was thumping so hard she felt it in her ears.

"Please keep your hands steady on the table in front of you," Miss Ofelia prompted. "We're here in peace, wishing to speak to our loved ones. If any spirits are present, please give us a sign that you can hear me." She sat down again. Her body tensed and straightened as if she heard something that startled her. When she spoke, her voice was low as a whisper. "I've been waiting a long time to speak with you." She looked around the table, eyes barely open, pausing for a moment on each face.

Miss Ofelia was pretending. It was just for show. Anette's heart rate slowed, and she exhaled, feeling ridiculous and embarrassed that she had almost panicked.

"Is there someone whose mother's name was Agda, Alma, Anna?"

Everyone was silent.

Miss Ofelia closed her eyes, then opened them again. "Berta? Who has a mother named Berta?" No one said anything, and she continued, "Botilda? Carla? Dagny? Ellen?"

She was going through the alphabet. Anette threw a quick glance at Helga, but she was staring at Miss Ofelia with rapt attention and didn't seem to notice anything awry.

Then the woman who had suggested that Anette use sugar gasped, "Carla is my aunt. My mother's sister."

"I'm not happy here. I need… I need help," Miss Ofelia whispered. Her voice was darker than before.

"What do you need?" Carla's niece asked. "Why aren't you happy?" She was sweating and fanning herself with her napkin.

Miss Ofelia continued, her voice growing louder. "I need you to pray for me, pray that I get to the other side. I cannot find my way home." Closing her eyes, she added, "Someone else is trying to come through. I feel a man, yes, a man. Does anyone know someone by the name of Finn?" She paused, skipping ahead. "Knut? Ludvig? Linné?"

Anette bit her lip to keep from laughing, praying that Miss Ofelia wouldn't get to M or N. If she did, she wouldn't be able to stop herself.

"My father, my father's name was Linné," a man with spectacles said. He looked stunned.

"My son, you need not worry about me. I'm in the Summerland," Miss Ofelia said and opened her eyes. Then in her regular voice, she added, "Please, can someone give me a glass of water. I feel faint."

Anette coughed to hide an escaped laugh, then discretely looked at the participants' faces to see if someone else had realized what Miss Ofelia was doing. But it didn't seem like it. If anything, they looked scared.

The man with the spectacles stood up and left the room. Moments later he was back with a tall glass. Miss Ofelia drank it all down at once.

"Thank you. Did something happen? Did someone come through?"

"Yes, my father, for a precious moment," the man said. Then he motioned across the table and added, "And the aunt of this lady as well."

Miss Ofelia smiled knowingly. "We need to pray that her aunt finds peace. Now does anyone else have something they wish to share about this experience?"

After a few moments of silence, the young man in the brown suit glanced at Miss Ofelia, nodded almost imperceptibly and said, "At first I didn't see anything, but after a moment I felt as if a wind had blown in from the back, giving me shivers up and down my spine." He lowered his voice dramatically. "And there she was. A lady with an old-fashioned blue dress and a gray hat, the kind they wore long ago. She walked toward Miss Andersson and opened her hand as if she wanted to give her something."

Helga inhaled sharply at the mention of her name and stared at Anette, her eyes wide with excitement. Miss Ofelia kept her gaze on the man in the brown suit. They were clearly in this together. How could Helga not notice this?

"I saw the same lady," the widow who knew Helga said. "She was so pretty. I clearly saw her walking across the floor. She looked as if she would tell Helga that she had met my Stellan."

Anette looked on in astonishment as Helga picked up a flask from her purse and handed it to the widow, nodding fervently. "I believe you're right. Had she only felt more comfortable with the living, she would have told me what he said," Helga whispered.

Anette tried to catch Miss Ofelia's eye, but she averted her gaze.

#

Anette walked silently beside Helga, listening to her excited chatter about what they had experienced. This was quite a different Helga than the kind and pragmatic woman who rarely showed her own feelings.

When they turned the corner to their own street, she grabbed the crook of Anette's elbow. "You haven't said anything, Anette. Tell me what you thought."

She wanted to tell her the truth, but Helga was looking at her so intently, and with such hope that she couldn't do it and just said, "I found it very interesting."

But Helga must have seen it in her eyes. "I see. I understand, it's not for everyone." She looked disappointed.

Chapter Eight

Anette hadn't slept much, just laid in bed for most of the night watching Carl beside her. He had grown too big to sleep in the basket and slept right next to her on the bed. When the tears came, she was thankful that Jenny was asleep; her pity would have been too much to bear.

Now there were no tears left. Everything was ready. She had packed a bag with his little shirts and diapers, all washed and neatly folded, along with the soft blanket he liked to cuddle with. Her trying year was finally over, but she no longer wanted it to be.

#

Her heart was beating so fast she felt dizzy when she saw Mother Anna approaching the House, followed by her father, Ola, wearing his Sunday suit. Anette had always thought him so handsome in it, but today it looked old and threadbare. Mother Anna unlatched the gate and rushed up the stairs. "My dear child," she said, her familiar large frame engulfing her, holding her so tight that it was hard to breathe. "You look so skinny. Aren't they feeding you here?" She stepped back and looked Anette up and down. "I see you've made yourself a new dress."

Her father met her eyes. She saw no anger there, just warmth.

"Maybe she also wears hats like the other women we've seen here?"

"I do, Pappa. I have a very nice hat upstairs."

"A modern girl now, a town girl," he said and embraced her quickly, then let her go.

They remained on the steps for a few more moments without speaking. Anette stared at the doorhandle but couldn't bring herself to open the door.

Finally, Mother Anna took her arm. "Dear, is there a place where you and I can have a talk?"

"In the garden," Anette said quietly.

Mother Anna turned toward her husband. "Ola, why don't you take a little walk."

"Yes, yes, I'll do that. You women talk," he said and hurried back out the front gate. There was a sadness in the slump of his shoulders.

Anette took Mother Anna to the back garden, and they sat down in the wicker chairs under the knotty apple trees.

Mother Anna sat straight in the chair. She cleared her throat once but didn't say anything. The silence was heavy, full of unspoken words. Even the wind was still.

Then she clasped her hands together and nodded. "Anette, we're moving. No one will talk to us anymore and Ola has lost almost all his customers." She pursed her lips and shook her head. "The smithy is on its last legs, Anette. People rather go to Stora Råby or Sularp, than have their horses shod by…"

Anette knew what she meant. A fallen woman like her, a sinner. It was just the way the parson's wife had said. But apparently it wasn't enough that she went away, her entire family had to suffer, even though the parson's wife had promised to protect them from rumors. Clearly she hadn't. They were cruel, unfeeling people, that parson and his wife, and they who claimed to spread the message of God.

"We've managed to sell both the house and the smithy and we're relocating to Södra Sandby," Mother Anna continued. "We found a new house. It'll be better for Carl if we start anew."

Anette stared at her silently. Then she understood what it meant, and the relief was so intense, she felt dizzy. If they were moving, there should be no concern anymore, no congregants ashamed of her, no scorn from the parson and his wife. Tears sprayed straight out from her eyes as she laughed and cried all at once.

"What are you doing?"

Mother Anna's voice snapped her out of it and she realized she was standing and sat back down. Mother Anna's face revealed nothing, no expression indicating that she had been waiting to tell her, to welcome her back to them.

"If you aren't living in Hardeberga anymore, then I can move back home with you, can't I, Mother Anna?" Her voice barely held.

But Mother Anna cocked her head to the side, looking confused. "Anette, that wouldn't be seemly. Who would believe it? Everyone would be able to tell."

"How?"

"Anette, I'm not a young woman. Everyone who'd see you would understand. If it's just us, they'll assume I had a very late child, but not if you're there. It's as simple as that."

"Please, Mother Anna, please. I could be his mother now. I *am* his mother. Let me at least come back home."

Mother Anna narrowed her eyes and for the briefest of moments, Anette thought she would agree, but then she shook her head.

"It's better that you stay here like we planned sweetheart; Carl will have a new life. He'll be respected, and no one will ever know that he's actually a bastard."

Bastard. Anette's chest constricted and her cheeks burned. She was right. Carl would be judged for the rest of his life and would never have the same opportunities that he would have if people thought he was born within wedlock.

Anette stood up, and without looking at Mother Anna she went inside and up the stairs to her room.

Carl smiled so happily when he saw her, she couldn't bear it. Without saying a word, she took him from Jenny's arms, not daring to look into her eyes. Then she picked up his bag and started down the stairs. The front door opened before she reached the floor.

He must have sensed that something was about to happen and buried his face in her neck, wrapping his arms around it so tightly that Mother Anna had to pry them off. Then the door closed behind them and she heard Carl screaming for his mother as her heart was ripped from her chest.

Chapter Nine

Hanna

Hanna's father nodded approvingly as he took in the newly painted café. The walls were sparkling white, and the moldings were done in the same light green as the chairs and tables. It was hard to imagine that it had once been his old storage space that he had bought while pursuing one of his many projects. That time to collect slightly damaged inkwells from grandpa's factory and then donate them to the poor and to schools. It hadn't been as easy as he thought. Most of the inkwells were too damaged to give away, and grandpa became worried that it would damage the company's reputation. Thus, the place had been empty for over ten years, half of which Hanna had pestered him to give it to her. It was perfectly situated on a street corner and already had a scullery in the back, now with a large new stove and oven where you could bake several batches at one time.

"Very nice, Hanna, clean and stylish," he said and hummed a simple tune to himself as he walked around the room, touching the windowsills to see if they were dry and pulling the chairs in and out. "How about getting one of Mother's ferns and putting it in the corner next to the register?"

"Would it get enough light?"

"Yes, certainly."

"And it would match, too," she said. "With the green, I mean. That's a good idea, Pappa. All we can do now is wait. I only hope someone has seen my note."

Hanna had hung it in the window announcing that bakers interested in a position should apply between noon and 4 p.m. Her father had insisted on being present. She had been mad at him at first, but finally relented. He did have a point, there would be no way of knowing who would show up. Someone might be a scoundrel, as her mother had pointed out. He sat himself down at a table in the rear and began reading his newspaper, looking very pleased with himself, but trying his best not to seem so important.

She hid a grin.

At precisely noon a man knocked on the door. He seemed pleasantly surprised to see her in charge. As she showed him around, he listened intently and politely suggested a couple of improvements in the way the scullery was organized. She liked him immediately and when he left, she told him she would contact him at the end of the week.

"Pappa, he is very knowledgeable and has years of experience. I should hire him."

"Why don't you decide after you've seen some other applicants? There's no reason to rush things," he said, barely looking up from his newspaper and puffing deeply on his pipe.

"Very well, I suppose you're right," Hanna said and sat down on her stool behind the counter to wait. She had brought a book, but only managed to read a couple of sentences at a time before she felt compelled to look out the window to see if someone was coming.

Two hours elapsed before a second man arrived. He strode past her and went right up to her father who slowly lowered his paper and studied the man, his eyes twinkling.

"You're looking for work, I take it?"

"Yes, sir."

"And you didn't notice your future boss?"

The man looked confused. "I'm sorry, sir. A woman opened the door for me and I saw you sitting here."

Her father nodded thoughtfully and winked at Hanna, but so discreetly that the man didn't see. "The woman who opened the door is the one you should speak to."

"Oh, I apologize, sir. I thought you were the owner. I take it she'll know when he comes in, it's still a little early yet." He pulled his watch from his breast pocket and Hanna heard him mumble to himself.

"It's 2:10 already. The note said from noon to 4 p.m."

Her father now had the paper in front of his face again, but she saw him peer over the edge. He was chuckling.

The puzzled man walked over to Hanna. "Good afternoon,

miss, is the owner expected to arrive soon?"

"Good afternoon, sir." She held her hand out for him to shake, but he didn't take it. Instead, he pursed his lips and studied his watch again. "I thought he would be here by now."

Hanna smiled, almost feeling sorry for him. "But the owner *is* here. My name is Hanna Johansson. Welcome to my bakery."

His expression was blank. She waited patiently for him to say something as the seconds ticked by. It was so silent that she became aware of the sound of hooves and wheels on the street.

"Good day to you," he said finally, walked briskly to the door, replacing his hat crookedly on his head as he stepped out.

Hanna dropped her jaw exaggeratingly while shaking her head. "I can't believe it. I thought *he* would be here by now, *he…* Is the *owner* expected to arrive soon," she mocked. "Did you hear Pappa? He didn't even explain, he just left."

"Oh yes, I heard him. I'm glad I'm here. That man isn't someone you want rummaging around in your café."

"Rummaging," Hanna said and laughed.

#

Three more men came during the week and two women. All seemed accomplished and nice. One man expressed surprise that she was the proprietor, but didn't seem especially concerned about it.

Hanna was particularly impressed with one of the women. She was eager to start and had good references. However, she couldn't stop thinking about Mr. Agnell, the first man who came in at the beginning of the week. Something about him just felt right.

She decided to hire him and sent a run-boy to his home, informing him that the position was his and to arrive at 8 a.m. the following morning.

#

Hanna unlocked the café about ten minutes before the hour, feeling a little nervous. What if he didn't show up? Or what if he was late? And maybe he would treat her differently when her father wasn't there. They would spend hours together in her café, and she hoped it wouldn't feel awkward. Hanging her coat on the back of a chair, she went to stand at the threshold of the scullery and looked inside. She had already moved the worktable closer to the window, and the potholders from the wall above the oven, preventing them from falling down and catching fire on the top burners, like Mr. Agnell had warned against. The potholder suggestion was one of the reasons she felt so strongly about him. None of the others had commented on it. She inhaled deeply and was just about to look at her wall clock when there was a knock on the door. Hurrying across the floor, she didn't bother to look at it anymore. He must be right on time.

Mr. Agnell smiled brightly. "Good morning, Miss Johansson," he said, looked her right in the eye and shook her hand, and she instantly relaxed.

"Good morning. Do come in and make yourself at home."

He entered and took his hat off, nodding approvingly as he looked around.

"My wife and I strolled past here last night, and she says to tell you she loves the large windows, that they make it nice and bright in here. She's right I believe."

"Thank you, Mr. Agnell. A friend of mine is having curtains sewn for me. I picked a dark green color. I want people to get a feeling of sitting outside in the grass, like on a picnic," Hanna said, thinking of Helga's mothers who should have finished the curtains by now.

"Very nice, a woman's touch makes all the difference," he said. It sounded genuine and not patronizing. She smiled and motioned toward a table, feeling confident again.

"Would you like to go over what needs to be done? And before we start, Mr. Agnell, I want to say that you're the expert when it comes to the baking. Please don't hold back on it because of politeness toward me. You can do whatever you feel is necessary as long as you keep me informed and it's something I can afford."

"I appreciate that, miss. May I suggest we start small with a just a few types of pastries and cakes? As the café grows, we can expand."

"That sounds wise."

They sat down for about an hour and discussed everything, then went out to buy the ingredients Mr. Agnell would need. He insisted she accompany him. "It's better if you establish yourself as the owner right away, or they'll think it's me," he said.

At that moment, she knew beyond any doubt that she had chosen the right baker.

Chapter Ten

Today was the day. Hanna woke up early while her parents were still sleeping and went out to the field behind their house, picking an armful of bluebells and cornflowers still wet with dew.

As she opened the door to her cafe, a wonderful, sweet scent of baking greeted her, mingling with the fragrance from the flowers and her damp clothes. She made a note to herself to always remember that combined scent and think of her first day.

Mr. Agnell peeked out from the scullery. "Good morning, Miss Johansson. Those are beautiful blossoms. You're here early, it's not even 7 a.m."

"I couldn't sleep. I was too excited about today."

"I'm a little nervous myself, or I was when I got here at 3 a.m. not knowing if I could get everything done in time." He motioned toward the scullery behind him where she could see rolls, cakes, and several long rows of cookies in different shapes spread out on the worktable.

"What do you think?"

"It's wonderful. Thank you, Mr. Agnell." Hanna exhaled. She hadn't been nervous exactly, but was still relieved. It looked better than she had dared to expect.

Mr. Agnell plucked a braided roll and two small chocolate cookies covered with sprinkled sugar from the table and put them on a plate. "Here miss, try these."

Hanna grabbed a cookie and bit into it. It was still warm, and the chocolaty sweetness melted in her mouth. It was delicious. She truly had picked the right baker. "It's exquisite Mr. Agnell. I'd like some coffee with it, would you like some?"

"Please, I could use a cup. And thank you." He looked pleased.

She glanced around the room. "Let me just put the flowers on the tables first."

"Certainly, I'll need a few minutes. I have one more batch of rolls almost ready to go in the oven."

Hanna nodded, then decided to put a small bouquet on each table and a larger bouquet on the counter. It looked perfect. Helga had brought the curtains over yesterday evening and the combination of green and blue was striking. A summer field, just like she had pictured it. Her stomach fluttered with excitement. Her very own café.

"How do you take your coffee miss, sugar and crème?"

She started and saw Mr. Agnell standing in front of her with a puttering coffee kettle in hand.

"A little of each, please, thank you. I can't believe we open in just an hour. Do you think we'll have any customers today?"

"One can never tell," he said as he placed two cups on the table, took a square box made of wicker from the counter, placed it next to his cup, and sat down. He opened the lid and immediately slammed it shut, his lips forming a silent o.

"My oldest daughter packed this for me, breakfast. Unfortunately, my youngest sometimes decides to help." Frowning, he picked up the basket, calmly walked to the door, opened it, and kneeled down on the doorstep. "There you go, little fellow," Hanna thought she heard him say. What was he doing?

He came back to the table, looking exasperated. "Just like Emily, that tomboy, I should reprimand her for this."

"Mr. Agnell, what in the world are you talking about?"

"A frog, Emily put a frog in my lunchbox," he said, looking nervous, but also like he was trying not to laugh. "On the first day of my new job, can you believe it?"

Hanna's eyes met his, and they both burst out laughing.

After catching her breath, she said, "I'm naming my café the frog. And please, call me Hanna."

"I'm Kurt," he said, smiling with relief.

#

The words, The Frog, were emblazoned across the sign in bold black letters. At the bottom of the G sat a smiling green frog. It was holding a cup of coffee.

"Goodness gracious, Hanna!" exclaimed Magnhild as she watched a workman on a ladder positioning the sign above the door while another hoisted it with a rope from below. "I've never heard of such a name. What does it mean?"

Hanna ignored the question and crossed her fingers, hoping the sign wouldn't smash against the glass in the door. "Do you like it? Fortunately, I'd already picked green for the interior and yesterday I found a large green bootjack in the shape of a frog that I'm going to keep on the floor next to one of my ferns. And Kurt is making frog cookies with a green mint leaf on top."

"I'm impressed, but..."

"So am I. I've had thirty-four customers today already."

"Thirty-four people came and sat down in your café?" Magnhild asked incredulously.

"Well, no, they didn't sit down; only seven did. The other twenty-seven bought pastries to take home."

"Hanna, I'd like to write an article about you?" Magnhild squeezed Hanna's arm to get her to stop looking at the men and the sign.

"Oh? Whom would you write it for?"

"For the People's Paper. Can I please? We could inspire hundreds of women to take their destiny into their own hands."

"Oh dear, it almost fell," Hanna said as the man on the ladder let go of the sign with one hand before it was completely secured. It wobbled dangerously, but he quickly caught it.

The next moment, the man on the ground pulled the rope free and the other man climbed down.

Hanna clasped her hands together and shouted, "Bravo! Look, Magnhild. It's up."

The sign was aligned perfectly between the top of the door and the second-story window where Mrs. Nilsson, an elderly widow, was looking out with interest. She spent most of her days there, keeping an eye on the street.

"I see," Magnhild said. She sounded upset.

"I'm sorry for not listening. Please, let's go inside and you can tell me more about your article. We'll have coffee and you'll be the first person to try the frog cookies."

"Very well, I'll try just one. But there isn't much to tell you yet, I have to interrogate my interview subject first," she said and playfully pinched Hanna's arm, sounding herself again.

Hanna opened the door for her, then stepped back and took one more look at her sign. It looked perfect. She loved the little frog and her coffee cup.

Chapter Eleven

Anette

With her free hand, Helga handed Anette a small package wrapped in newspaper.

"A parting gift, it's nothing much, you can open it when you've settled at Mrs. Engström's. It's a sewing kit. There's a thimble, needles, and a few other things you'll need. You're a talented seamstress, Anette. It may come in handy."

"Thank you, Helga," she said, pleasantly surprised and touched by the gesture. With her chin wobbling from emotion, she leaned forward and kissed her on the cheek.

Helga had been nothing but kind to her since the day she arrived. Never a word of judgment, only support, she would miss her.

Helga nodded, dry-eyed. "If you ever need anything you know where to find me, you hear?"

Then she left the kitchen and started up the stairs.

Anette stared after her, watching the roundness of her back and the heaviness in her steps, picturing her getting inside her room and seating herself in one of her chairs by the little table. She slid the gift into her pocket, then bent to get her valise off the floor.

"Anette."

Letting go of the handle, Anette looked up. Jenny was standing at the threshold with Alma, who was encumbered by her enormous belly and was holding on to Jenny's shoulder for support.

"Anette," Jenny repeated and dashed across the floor, leaving Alma where she was, and pulling Anette into a tight hug. She seemed taller. Jenny hadn't only given birth and nursed a baby, but also grown herself. Clinging to each other, Jenny sobbed loudly as Alma made her way past them and sat down on a chair. Anette tried to smile over Jenny's shoulder, but it came out more like a grimace. Her chest felt tight with unshed tears. She needed this to be over. There was too much sadness in the House. Taking a deep breath, she straightened, took Jenny by the shoulders, and looked steadily into her face.

"Jenny, thank you for being my friend. I'll never forget you."

Then she nodded at Alma, met Jenny's eyes one last time, picked up her valise and walked out.

#

Anette settled into her new position as helpmate to Mrs. Engström. She was a kind, spry woman at eighty-seven, who only needed her help with cooking, cleaning, shopping for groceries, and bringing wood in for the stove. It was easy work. Mrs. Engström's small two-story home was orderly, albeit very dusty, and Anette spent the first week with a feather duster and a wet rag while Mrs. Engström did her best to stay out of the dust cloud.

Unless she was needed, which wasn't often, Anette spent evenings in her little room on the second floor reading the old books on Mrs. Engström's shelf. She had dusted there too, but the books were yellow with age, and smelled so strongly of mildew that each one had to be aired out on the windowsill for a full day before she could read it. The books must have belonged to her son at one point and were mostly adventure stories about travels in Africa or India, but they helped her push thoughts about Carl from her mind. She even told herself that it hadn't happened at all. It was manageable during the day, but she dreamed of his warm hands and soft fuzzy head almost every night and woke up with her jaw sore from clenching her teeth.

Chapter Twelve

Hanna

Hanna flipped through the latest issue of the People's Paper from beginning to end. "What page is it on, Magnhild?"

"Page four."

This time she turned the pages from the back to the front and there it was, a small article in the lower left-hand corner. In thick black letters the headline read, **Visit The Frog and have yourself a frog cookie with your coffee.** Beneath it was a small drawing of the café's sign, frog and all. There was even steam coming out of her little cup.

Hanna's eyes moistened with pride as she reached behind herself for a chair, grasping for thin air until Magnhild grabbed hold of her hand and guided it to its destination.

She sat down without taking her eyes off the page. "Please, Magnhild, call Kurt. He should see this as well."

"Kurt, come in here, please!" Magnhild hollered toward the scullery. "Hanna is in the paper."

Kurt came running into the dining room while wiping his hands on his baker's apron. "Your article is out? Let me see." He put his hand on the back of Hanna's chair, leaned over her shoulder and started to read aloud.

"Miss Hanna Andersson, who is only twenty-one years old, already has a successful business. It's a café called The Frog, a name that came about when the daughter of Mr. Kurt Agnell, the baker employed by Miss Andersson, tactfully packed a live frog for her father's breakfast." He paused and looked at Hanna with a raised eyebrow, and they both chuckled. She knew he would love that, and she liked how Magnhild made a point of saying that he was employed by her.

"At The Frog," Kurt continued, "you will find three tables where you can relax, read the newspaper or maybe a book while you are enjoying coffee, delicious pastries, and the café's signature frog cookies with mint leaves. Miss Andersson has designed the space to give the customers the impression that they are sitting in a green oasis or on a lawn, enjoying freedom and independence. She is a true inspiration for women wanting to start their own business."

Kurt nodded several times. "Now for the most important part, written by Magnhild Svensson."

"It's a wonderful piece. Thank you so much for writing about me like this," Hanna said, smiling warmly at Magnhild.

"It's my pleasure. We're all so proud of you, Hanna."

"I agree with Hanna, it's a very good article Magnhild. And to think that Emily is mentioned in a real newspaper. Now you've gone and encouraged her, there's no account on how many frogs she'll provide us with," Kurt said, pretending to look upset.

Magnhild and Hanna exchanged a glance, and Magnhild threw her head back and laughed.

Then Magnhild grew serious. "I hope you don't mind Kurt?"

"No, of course not, it's how Hanna decided on a name, I can't be upset about that. You'll stay a while Magnhild? I'll get you both coffee and a piece of cake."

"Yes, please."

Hanna followed him with her gaze as he walked back to the scullery. "I really liked how you emphasized that I designed the Frog and that Kurt is my employee, Magnhild. It's subtle, but it's important. I'm going to frame your article and put it there." She pointed to a spot on the wall near the counter where people would see it while waiting in line, picturing a nice green frame around it.

"Really?" Magnhild's eyes creased with pleasure. "Of course, that's why I wanted to write it, it's not only about your café but about your independence as a woman."

Kurt came back with their coffee, plates, and a thick piece of chocolate cake, layered with whipped crème, strawberries, and crushed orange flavored cookies, their newest addition and Kurt's invention.

"You ladies sit, I'll take counter for a half hour," he said, just as a customer opened the door.

Chapter Thirteen

Anette

Anette had fallen asleep in her chair with a warm wool blanket draped over her knees and the newspaper on her lap when she was awakened by a loud knock on the door. Before she could make it across the room, the person knocked again, harder this time.

"On my way," she shouted, refastening her hair into a neat bun.

A man was standing in the doorway, twirling his hat in his hands. "Is Mrs. Engström home?" he asked.

"I'm sorry, but she's napping. May I help you?"

"I'm here to chop the wood, but if the missus is napping, I don't want to wake her. You're Miss Lundström, I take it?"

"Yes, I am."

"I'm Jon Henriksson." He put his hands in his pockets and rocked back on his heels without making a move to leave.

She hesitated. Maybe Mrs. Engström would disapprove if she invited him inside. Finally, she pointed to the wooden bench in the corner of the front garden. "Why don't you have a seat and I'll get you a cup of coffee. I was just about to put the kettle on anyway. If you sit in the sun, it'll be warm enough."

"Thank you, I'd not say no to a cup," he said.

She closed the door on him, and went to make coffee, watching him through the window as he walked across the grass and sat down. He wasn't handsome or striking, but seemed calm and sure of himself. It made him seem very likeable.

When she came outside with their cups of coffee, he moved over so she would have plenty of space on the bench beside him.

"I've been a friend of Fiona since I was just a little boy," he said and turned to face her.

"Fiona?"

"Yes, Mrs. Engström.

"I see, she never told me her first name."

"I used to steal her berries until she finally told me to come and have as many as I wanted on the condition that I help her pick them."

Anette gave him a skeptical look.

"It's true. I'm reformed through work," he said with a sideways grin, motioning toward the currant bushes.

She laughed.

He took a sip of coffee, then put the cup down on the bench. Maybe it was too strong for him.

"How can I be sure you're reformed?" she asked teasingly.

"Ask anyone at Hansson's Glove Factory. I'm the foreman. I have thirty men working under me."

She nodded, feeling shy suddenly. He must be a very kind man to still come and help Mrs. Engström when he had such an important position at the factory.

"Would you like to see an orange peel?" Jon leaned backwards so he could reach into his left trouser pocket, then pulled out a neatly folded piece of newspaper. "It came by train, horse, and boat all the way from America," he said, unfolding it carefully.

She took the peel out of his hand. It was orange on the outside and white on the inside, no larger than her pinky finger and curled into a spiral.

"It's hard as a rock," Anette said as her fingers traced it. The orange outside part was bumpy, but the white inside was smooth.

"My cousin Emil grows them in California. He started an orange grove with the money his father made from the gold over there. Oranges are large and very juicy. That's just a piece of the rind."

Anette studied it closely, then put it to her nose and sniffed it. It was faint, but there was a remnant of something that must have smelled very sweet at one time.

"It smells wonderful," she said, wishing she could try a real orange.

"Yes, indeed," he said proudly. "Emil wants me to move to California. He writes me letters and tells me how much he'd appreciate the help. It would be an opportunity, but I have a home and good work here. I'd hoped to speak to Fiona about it today. She's always good with advice." He took another sip of coffee. This time he didn't put the cup back down.

Anette watched the steam rising for a moment. A sense of foreboding came over her and she felt as if she heard roaring winds. "Something is going on with your cousin's farm. You'd be wise to be certain before you go." She blushed under his astonished gaze, and quickly added, "I'm sorry. Sometimes I sense things."

Just then the front door opened and Mrs. Engström came out with her own coffee cup. "I see you two have met. May I join you?"

Jon narrowed his eyes but didn't reply to Anette, lingering briefly on her face before turning toward Mrs. Engström.

"Please do, Fiona. I came to chop the wood but heard a rumor that you were resting."

She came down the steps, moving lightly as if she was a young girl.

"You shall not listen to rumors, but yes, I was. Miss Lundström takes good care of me and insists."

"I'm glad to hear it, Fiona. You need your rest," Jon said, then stood up so Mrs. Engström could take his seat, handed Anette his cup and set to work on the wood.

When she went upstairs that evening, Anette felt for the first time since she lost Carl that she might be able to live again. She stretched and smiled to herself, then opened the window to get some fresh air. The street was deserted except for a lone driver huddled next to his horse to keep warm. It was foggy and the lanterns in the carriage were barely visible.

Chapter Fourteen

Hanna

Hanna, Magnhild, and Bengta were waiting at the Frog after hours for the rest of the women to arrive. It was the first time they were meeting there instead of at the House. It was also Bengta's first time visiting. She walked around, looking at everything, laughing when she saw the frog bootjack by the door.

"I love the frog theme, Hanna. Your café is darling, I'm very impressed. It's just like Magnhild described it in her article," she said and joined them at their table.

"Thank you," Hanna said, feeling exceedingly happy at the compliment. She had been a little nervous about what Bengta would think.

"Bengta," said Magnhild, "on the way here I encountered Mrs. Bondesson, the fishmonger's wife. You know, they have the shop on the opposite corner. She said that Miss Jonsdotter down the street gave birth out of wedlock. Was it you who birthed her?"

"Yes, it was me." Bengta picked up a cookie from the plate Hanna had placed on their table.

Magnhild nodded knowingly. "She also said that Miss Jonsdotter has a reputation as one who's had many men. She said she heard this one had promised to marry her but didn't."

Bengta took a small bite of her cookie. "I can't tell you anything. You know that."

"Yes, but Mrs. Bondesson is the one who started the rumors, not you. She said she thinks the man went to Finland. There were no other children in the house, but she said Miss Jonsdotter didn't act as if she was expecting for the first time. How long has she lived down the street, Hanna?"

"For as long as I can remember... and I've never seen a child with her."

"No?" Magnhild looked triumphant for a moment. "Mrs. Bondesson said Miss Jonsdotter probably used an angelmaker last time."

"Oh, dear God." Hanna whispered.

"Now, ladies," Bengta said, "I wouldn't betray her confidence, whatever I knew. Besides, mothers don't need to tell me anything since the ruling." She put the last piece of cookie in her mouth.

"The ruling?" Hanna asked.

Bengta took another cookie and pushed the plate away. "The King, Gustav III, ruled back in 1778 that a woman can give birth anonymously."

"Give birth anonymously? That's impossible," Hanna said.

"Not at all, it simply means that a woman can give me the baby immediately after birth and is under no obligation to even state her name. Any information I'm given must be held in the strictest confidence. I would then be required to give the baby to an orphanage and the identity of the mother would remain unknown. Therefore, she could never be charged with abandoning her child."

Hanna stared at her, picturing an impoverished girl calling on Bengta to come assist her in a secret basement somewhere and then sneaking out, pretending she had never even been pregnant. Could she do that? And how would that tiny little baby fare in an orphanage? She let out a breath and turned her attention back to the conversation.

"More than you might guess," Bengta was saying in response to something. "King Gustav's ruling provides desperate unmarried women with an alternative to killing the baby, say, by leaving it out in the cold, or handing it to an angelmaker to do the job."

"Don't you just want to take those babies home Bengta, it would break my heart to give them to an orphanage," Hanna said.

"No, I don't. But yes, it does break your heart."

Magnhild reached for a cookie while nodding in agreement. Then the door was pushed open and Lova entered.

"I love the frog drinking coffee, his little fingers! It's perfect," she cried and sat herself down next to Bengta.

"*Her* fingers," Hanna said, forgetting about the sad babies.

A few minutes later everyone had arrived, including several

new members, Vanda's friend Mrs. Eriksson, Kurt's wife Maria, and their oldest daughter Elsa. Everyone helped put the tables together to form one long table, then pulled the chairs over and sat down. They were all looking at Hanna, who wasn't sure why she was expected to lead the meeting just because they were at the Frog. But it didn't appear that Bengta was about to take it on, so she straightened her shoulders and began as best she could.

"Thank you all for coming. I see new faces here today. Welcome." She wondered if she should explain who Maria and Elsa were, but then decided against it. They were here of their own accord, not just as a wife and daughter. She continued with new resolve. "It brings me to something I've been thinking about a lot. Even though we're active Good Templars, there's so much more we could be doing. And now, when there are more of us, we might be able to expand our efforts. I'd love to hear some suggestions."

Maria nodded enthusiastically. "What if we all become members of the Fredrika Bremer Association? Then we'd be connected to another large organization besides the Good Templars and people would have to take us seriously."

"Isn't Fredrika Bremer a bit too radical?" Mrs. Eriksson asked, then looked around the table to see if everyone agreed.

"The more radical the better, in my opinion," Magnhild said, then nodded approvingly at her own comment.

Hanna threw her a warning glance. Not that she disagreed, but she wished Magnhild would be a little careful with new members at least.

"My husband would never allow me to become involved with them," said Mrs. Eriksson.

"Well, mine will," Maria said and put her arm around Elsa's shoulder. "Both my daughter and I would be willing to join."

Bengta held up a hand to get Mrs. Eriksson's attention, then said, "You may want to tell your husband that the purpose of the organization is to correlate work between experienced women *and* men and agitate for a calm and sound growth of women's rights. That's a quote, I don't remember the rest, but it's not especially radical, at least in my mind." She smiled at Magnhild.

No one said anything. It felt a bit awkward. Then Vanda broke the silence by gently banging her spoon against the inside of her cup.

"I'd like to share something," she said, catching Bengta's eye. "I agree we can do more, but we need to do everything we can to get men to drink less. I..." She looked down at her lap. "We women, especially wives perhaps, are vulnerable. The law says that we have to obey our husbands. But what are we to do if they drink and become unreasonable?" Vanda tugged on her collar to expose her neck, pointing silently to a thick scar on the left side. Then she methodically pulled up her right sleeve.

It took Hanna a moment to register that her arm must have been broken in several places and never set right. She swallowed hard to keep from calling out, feeling disoriented as she tried to reassemble how the arm ought to look, and grabbed hold of the table for support.

Vanda pulled the sleeve back down, lifted her head, and said quietly, "My husband promised me he won't do it again."

Hanna inhaled sharply. No wonder Vanda had seemed nervous that first day she joined them. What would a husband like that think of them?

"Has he made that promise before?" Magnhild asked.

"Yes, many times."

"Then you must leave him," Magnhild said with a quick look at Bengta.

"I have nowhere to go."

"You can stay with us. Can't she?" Magnhild was looking at Bengta again and she answered immediately.

"Yes, of course."

Magnhild gave a quick nod, and Bengta actually looked relieved. Maybe they had helped women before. Would she and Magnhild pretend they had separate bedrooms if she moved in, so as not to reveal their relationship? Magnhild had explained that their love was a crime, punishable by law. Hanna glanced around the room, feeling guilty for thinking of bedrooms when Vanda ought to be her first concern.

Maria and Elsa were sitting stock-still with their eyes glued to Vanda, and Mrs. Eriksson was crying.

"Did your husband do this to you, Vanda?" Lova said and stood up abruptly. "We should call on the constable." She pushed the chair back under the table. "I can go now."

Vanda slowly turned in her direction. "No."

Bengta reached out and grabbed Lova gently by the arm. "Lova, please sit back down. It takes great courage for Vanda to trust us with this. Let's leave the matter for now, then she and I will talk in private. Vanda, I don't think you'll find a better group to support you in your situation than the Fredrika Bremer Organization. As for the rest of us, we'll of course still focus on temperance."

"Tha…" Vanda began, but then her voice broke, and she looked down at her lap again.

Everyone was quiet, waiting to see if Vanda or Bengta would say something else.

When no one did, Hanna said, "I'm going to send my application to Fredrika Bremer tomorrow."

"I'll do the same," Mrs. Eriksson said, touching Vanda's hand. She saw the others looking at her in surprise and calmly added, "What kind of friend would I be if I didn't?"

#

Bengta

No one knew, not even Magnhild, that Vanda had once been one of Bengta's mothers. She had been called upon early in the morning and driven to the Von Gier's stately home on the outskirts of Lund. Vanda's husband was a known pianist, with noble heritage too, as was clear by his last name. Bengta had known none of that then. It had been a midwife call just like any other, but as soon as she set foot inside, she could tell something was wrong.

The house was full of servants, looking nervous, even frightened, not the nervous but happy excitement one would expect when a baby was about to be born. They whisked her upstairs to the bedroom where she found Vanda sobbing in bed with a tiny dead infant in her arms. She hadn't made it in time, not

66

that it would have mattered much, there wouldn't have been anything she could have done. The baby girl wasn't more than six or seven months along, and Vanda was bruised all over. It was abundantly clear who had been the cause of the miscarriage. She stayed with Vanda for two days, protecting her from her husband with the help of the servants, until he stopped with his intemperance for the time being and showered Vanda with apologies. It was then that she invited her to join their women's group.

Today, Vanda was finally leaving him, almost eighteen months later.

Bengta had been waiting in front of the cathedral for over thirty minutes when she finally spotted the carriage coming down the street and crossing the square. She lifted her hand to wave, and the driver pulled the horse to a stop, jumped down, and opened the door for her. He nodded curtly while she explained which way to go, then pointed to a little step below the door to show her how to climb inside. It wasn't the same driver that had picked her up that fateful day.

She sat down next to Vanda, who took her glove-clad hands in hers, patting them.

"Thank you for waiting, Bengta."

"Did you get everything you need? I was getting worried."

"I apologize. I had everything packed, but I found it hard to say goodbye to the servants." She looked down at her hands, still clasped with Bengta's. "I loved that house and I'll miss them all, but it was time."

"It *was* time, Vanda, and you won't be alone."

Vanda took a deep breath and pulled one of her hands out of Bengta's grip and moved the curtain aside so she could look out the window.

Bengta patted her hand, then unclasped her fingers and opened the curtain on her side. The day was gray and overcast, not sunny and clear as she had imagined it would be on the day Vanda left her husband.

"I left a note for him on the nightstand," Vanda said. She

drew a breath. "I told him I want a legal separation."

"Good, that's very good, Vanda."

Bengta grabbed on to her seat as they turned. She wasn't used to traveling like this, closed inside a covered, moving vehicle.

"We'll both have to speak to the parson in our congregation and then apply to a judge. That's correct, isn't it?"

"It is. Once you receive the judge's approval, you'll need to take it to the court, which will issue a letter of separation. That will be your proof that you're divorced. Just know that you can stay with us for as long as you need."

Vanda tried to smile, but her eyes were filled with tears. She looked away as she reached into her purse for a handkerchief.

Then the carriage came to a stop, and they heard the driver jump down. He opened the door and nodded briskly at Vanda.

"We're here, Mrs. Von Gier."

"Thank you, Anton," Vanda said, quickly dabbing her eyes. "We'll help with the trunks. They're heavy."

He pulled down the first trunk and placed it on the ground, then grabbed one end as the women took the other, shoulder to shoulder. Together, they carried it down the little stone path toward the door.

Chapter Fifteen

Hanna

When Hanna arrived, Kurt was working in the back, so she poured them both coffee. Before she had time to bring it to him, he entered the dining room.

"I've put the first batch in. What do you say we have some breakfast before we start?"

She glanced at the wall clock. It showed a quarter to five; they had two hours before she had to unlock the door for the first customers.

Kurt cleared his throat. "Hanna, I have a suggestion to make. Why not have my Elsa come to work with me here in the mornings? You should always be in the front with the customers, not come here so early to help me."

"And here I thought I had become a talented baker," she said, only partly joking. Hiring an assistant had been on her mind for a while, she could afford it, but it hadn't crossed her mind to ask Elsa.

He laughed. "Hanna, of course you have, but I've seen how tired you are in the afternoon."

"Well, that would be an understatement." She sat down and reached for a roll, smearing it with butter that melted as soon as it met the warm fresh bread. "I know she's young still, but does she have experience from home?"

"Some only, but she's a quick learner."

Hanna smiled. "I'm not surprised. She's quite impressive at our meetings. How about she comes in for one month as an apprentice and then I'll put her on a salary?"

Kurt looked relieved and happy. "Thank you, Hanna. That's very generous of you. I'm going to make sure she'll earn her keep."

"I'm sure she will. Thank *you* for suggesting it."

Kurt nodded and took a long sip of coffee. He looked thoughtful. Then his eyes lit up and he smiled as if to himself. "Maria didn't tell you then, did she?"

"Tell me what?"

"We're having another little one in about six months."

"A baby? That's wonderful, congratulations!"

"Thank you. It's a bit of a surprise. Maria isn't young. We never expected… I'm sorry, I didn't mean to be too personal," he said, grinning sheepishly.

Hanna laughed. "I'm going to have to start knitting."

#

The Frog was empty, and Hanna was sitting at the table near the counter reading a book. It was five thirty already, and she closed at six. Since Elsa had taken over the early morning hours, she wasn't so tired in the evenings anymore. It became her favorite time of day. It was quieter and she could sit there by herself and relax. It was winter and dark outside, and the lamps on each table reflected against the blackness of the windows. There was a streetlamp, but it was halfway up the street near the florist and didn't affect the ambience. When it was ten minutes to, she closed her book, got to her feet and went to get the cookie tins and cake boxes so she could put everything away for the night. She had just reached for the square blue tin with stars when the bell hanging from its string on the door jingled.

A man entered, rubbing his bare hands together to warm himself, then lifted his face and smiled, looking straight into her eyes. Her heart jumped, and she realized she was grinning at him. What was this?

"Good evening," he said. "It's so nice and warm in here, it's freezing outside. Is it too late to get coffee? And is Kurt here?"

"I'm sorry, I'm about to close in just a moment. The coffee has gone cold, but I'll be happy to heat it up for you, I won't charge you for it, it's stood for a while," she said, relieved that she sounded like herself. "Kurt leaves early in the afternoon, usually. How do you know him?" Immediately she felt ridiculous. It wasn't for her to ask how he knew people.

"Kurt is my cousin, and I won't say no to you heating coffee for me. As long as it's not too much of an imposition?"

"Not at all, please take a seat."

He took off his coat and folded it over the back of the chair opposite to where she had sat, then sat down. He wore a gray vest with a gold pin that attached to a watch chain that kept his watch secure in his vest pocket. He looked stylish, but not overly so, and hadn't pulled on the fold of his trousers when he sat down. For some reason, it always annoyed her when men did that. She collected the unsold cookies from the display and put half in the tin, then placed a cake in its box and carried it all to the icebox in the scullery. When she came back, she put the rest of the cookies in a small paper bag and brought it and the coffee to the table.

"Here, some cookies for you to bring home. Thanks for coming, I'm glad to meet you. Are you Johannes? Kurt has mentioned you."

"How kind, thank you. And yes, I'm Johannes." He met her eyes. They were dark green, almost brown, and she got the feeling that he was looking at her with genuine interest.

"I can let Kurt know you were here when I see him tomorrow. Shall I leave him a message?"

"No need, I just wanted to see where he works. Kurt has told me so much about this place." He glanced around the dining room and then kept his gaze on the display counter for a moment. "It's very nice. Kurt's father and mine are brothers, by the way. I'm sorry I came so late, I should have realized that he would have left, I know he gets here early to bake."

"It's my pleasure to have you," Hanna said, feeling an unfamiliar flutter in her stomach.

Johannes kept his eyes in hers just a little longer than necessary, making her even more affected. Kurt had never told her that Johannes was so young. When he told her about him, she expected him to be like Kurt who was in his mid-forties. But Johannes couldn't be much older than twenty-five.

"Kurt tells me you're a bird watcher. I am too," he said.

"You are? I've not had much time for it since I started the Frog, but yes, he's right." She exhaled, relieved to have something to talk about.

Their conversation flowed naturally after that. She learned

that they both frequented Lund's Botanical Garden to watch birds. Johannes told her he was an accountant at the university and rented a small apartment on campus, which wasn't far from the garden.

By the time they stopped talking, it was already seven thirty. Johannes waited for her to close and then offered to walk her home. It felt genuine, not just like chivalry. The streets were empty this time of night. Sometimes there were drunks or beggars, and she was glad of the company.

Chapter Sixteen

Anette

It had become Mrs. Engström's and Anette's habit to watch while Jon chopped firewood. They sat on the bench in the garden, wrapped in blankets, and warming themselves with cups of coffee. Jon's cup was waiting for him, covered with a saucer on the seat next to Anette.

Today, Mrs. Engström was quiet and left her coffee untouched.

"Mrs. Engström, should I bring you indoors for a rest?" Anette asked.

"I think it might be best, I've been feeling very tired lately." She yawned and reached for Anette's arm, clutching it tightly as she helped her stand.

Jon threw them a concerned look and stopped chopping.

He was sitting down, drinking his coffee when Anette came back out.

"I made her a herring sandwich and she's lying down for a bit."

"Did she eat it?"

"About half," Anette said as she sat down beside him.

"Do you think Fiona is sick? Should we call for a doctor?"

"I asked her, but she laughed at it. I'll speak to her son tomorrow when he comes to get her for church. Maybe he can convince her."

Jon nodded, then handed Anette his cup.

"I think I'll trim some of the trees and bushes before I go home. February is a good time for it. Would you care to help me?"

"I'll be happy to."

They both stood at the same time. Jon's body felt warm and smelled of sweat and wood. He stepped away and went to get a pair of garden shears he had left in his wheelbarrow.

They began with the apple trees. Jon leaned a ladder against the trunk, then gingerly climbed up and cut unseemly new branches, tossing them on the ground so she could collect them and create a pile for burning.

#

Three weeks later, while Anette was reading the newspaper to her, Mrs. Engström slumped in her chair. Anette stood straight up, dropping the newspaper on the floor as Mrs. Engström's jaw went slack, leaving her toothless mouth open and her eyes staring unseeingly. She was dead. There was no question. From one moment to the next, life had just gone out of her. Anette sat down again, feeling weak in her knees, and unsure of what to do next. Mrs. Engström's tongue looked shrunken and dry. Maybe she had an unusually small one? Anette took a deep breath. This wasn't the first time she had seen a dead person. Her mother's body had laid out for viewing for two days. She would handle this, even if she was all alone now. That's when she remembered how her father had closed her mother's eyes. They would stay staring otherwise he had said. Standing again, she bent forward and touched the top part of Mrs. Engström's left eye. It was still warm, and she was able to pull the eyelid down and then do the same with the other. But it felt too intrusive, as if Mrs. Engström could still feel it and knew what she was doing. What if she opened her eyes and looked at her? Anette called out at the thought, startling herself with the sound of her own voice. It echoed in the silence, as if someone were answering her. She clasped her hand over her mouth and ran out of the room and closed the door behind her. Then leaned her back against the door to keep it closed. Her heart was racing, and it felt as though she had eyes on her back. With a heaving, steadying breath, she moved to the other side of the kitchen, keeping an eye on the door just in case. It was silly, but she couldn't help wondering if Mrs. Engström wouldn't still get up from the chair and go open the door.

Mrs. Engström's son needed to be notified, but he had never given her his address. Nor did she know where Jon lived. Maybe one was supposed to go to the constable. She couldn't remember what they had done when her mother passed. One thing was sure, she couldn't stay in the house with the body. Anette forced herself to walk instead of run across the kitchen floor to the vestibule, knowing she would go into a full panic if she hurried. She made herself get her coat and keys in the same slow manner, then opened the front door and went outside. As soon as her eyes fell on the garden bench, it came to her. Jon worked at the glove factory. He would know what to do.

The factory was a good half hour away, but the walk did her good. She calmed down, realizing that she had been in a state of shock and reacted out of fear.

Two men were standing in front when she arrived, smoking and talking. When they spotted her, one of them whistled and looked at her appraisingly. "You here for work? It's the wrong day to apply, but I can show you around." His voice was mocking.

"I'm not. I need to see the foreman, Jon Henriksson." What if Jon didn't work there and had just made it up?

"What you want with him? As I said, today is not the day." He sounded disappointed.

"There's been a death, I need to speak with him," she said, waiting for the familiar feeling of her cheeks getting hot, but they stayed cool. She didn't blush as much as she used to anymore.

The other man handed his pipe to his companion and came toward her.

"Miss, I'm sorry for your loss. I'll take you to him. May I?" he asked, indicating that she could take his arm. She did, feeling comforted by the kind gesture.

It was noisy and smelled of leather inside. Jon stood bent over a table, pointing at something as he was talking with someone.

The man let go of her elbow and called out, "Mr. Henriksson, you need to come here, it's an emergency."

Jon looked their way, saw Anette and dropped what he was doing. Then in two long steps he was by her side.

"Anette, what is it? Did someone hurt you?"

She shook her head. "It's Mrs. Engström, she just died."

"Fiona is dead? How... what happened?"

"I don't know. She was sitting in her chair and then... she died sitting in her chair," Anette repeated. "I didn't know what to do, so I came here."

Jon looked at her silently, then nodded. "She was 87 years old, it's to be expected I suppose." He coughed several times.

Anette sensed it was so he wouldn't cry. She waited, and then Jon nudged her elbow.

"Follow me to the office, we have a telephone there, and I'll get the operator to connect to her son's home."

They walked across the courtyard to a small building. He held the door open for her so she could enter first, then went straight to the telephone which was mounted on the back wall. She only got a glimpse of it before his body blocked her view. It looked just like the newspaper illustrations. She had thought the voice of the other person would be loud and clear, but that wasn't the case. Jon gave the name and address, and it was silent after that. When he spoke again, it startled her.

"It's Jon, I'm afraid I have bad news. Your mother. She just died." Silence. "Yes of course right away. I have Miss Lundström here." Silence. "At home, in her chair downstairs."

It was very odd to hear just one side of a conversation. Then Jon said goodbye and she heard wood and metal clinking as he put the hearing piece back in place. She wanted to ask him what Mrs. Engström's son had said, but was afraid it would be inappropriate.

They hurried back to Mrs. Engström's home. The first thing she did was to ask Jon to make sure that the body was still where she left it, nervous that Mrs. Engström would have fallen out of her chair and that she would be blamed for it. But Mrs. Engström's body was still in the chair. Anette was so relieved that it brought tears to her eyes.

She made coffee, and they waited in the kitchen until Mrs. Engström's son arrived with several members of extended family. It was very clear that Anette was in the way. The hired help and an outsider. She went upstairs by herself.

Two hours later, Jon knocked on her door, then came inside and stood a little awkwardly with an envelope in his right hand, looking embarrassed.

"Anette, I've been asked to tell you to leave. They need your room for Fiona's nieces. They're going to stay here for a few weeks to take care of things." He handed her the envelope. "This is for you for your services."

Anette took it and put it in her lap. Had she done something wrong? Maybe they were upset that she had left the body alone.

"I'll take you home, Anette. Where do you live? If it's far, I can use the factory carriage."

She stared at him. If she told him she had nowhere to go, he would surely ask why. What if Helga had told Mrs. Engström the truth? Explained that she was an unwed mother who sewed for her upkeep so she could hide her sin. All those times they had been talking together on the bench with Mrs. Engström. She blushed. Had Jon known as well? What did he think of her? It's not as if Mrs. Engström was young, but it hadn't even crossed her mind that there might be an after. She was homeless.

"Anette?" Jon was looking at her with an expression full of concern. "Are you feeling faint?"

"My parents live in Södra Sandby, it's too far. Thank you though for your offer," she said finally, ignoring his question. Part of her wished he would insist so she could see Carl.

"I see, that's about three hours away, I think. I know where it is."

It wasn't quite that far, but she didn't correct him.

Jon looked at his hands for a moment, then he nodded as if to himself. "Anette, I have plenty of room. I have a guest room. You can stay with me."

"Truly?" She was both relieved and disappointed. But he probably didn't know then. Come to think of it, he wouldn't have asked where she lived if he had. "Thank you so much. If you really don't mind, it would be easier while I look for new employment."

Jon smiled. "Of course, I'm glad I can help, it's the right thing to do, you've been so kind to Fiona."

#

Anette could hear Jon's whistle receding as he quickened his pace to get to the factory on time. She put away his coffee cup and plate from his breakfast, then went and sat down on the comfortable couch in the living room. They were in the same house he had grown up in, a small two-story home with a garden on a quiet street. It was very similar to Mrs. Engström's home, except that there were no windows facing the street on the upper floor, and his garden was smaller. Jon's father had died when he was a boy and his mother had moved in with his sister and her family a few years ago.

For the first few days after Anette moved in they had tiptoed around each other, both feeling embarrassed that they lived in the same house as if they were a married couple. But once it became clear that none of his neighbors took any note of anything, Jon relaxed and decided that if someone asked, he would just tell them the truth. Anette relaxed too. On Monday she was going to meet Mr. Engström to get a letter of recommendation so she could look for a new position. Jon hadn't asked her why she wasn't living with her parents. He probably assumed they were too poor. It was a good excuse.

#

Anette was peeling potatoes for their dinner when Jon came home with a bottle of red wine and a gigantic bouquet with pink roses and dahlias surrounded by a spray of green.

She wiped her hands on her rag. "Jon, what's this?"

"These are for you," he said and strode across the floor and handed her the flowers. Without a word, he fished a wine opener out of a drawer and opened the bottle, then left the room. Moments later he came back with two crystal wine glasses that he must have taken from the fancy cabinet in the living room. He threw her a quick smile, placed the glasses on the table and filled them. She watched, sensing what was to come.

"Anette, please sit. I have some news and I need to thank you. You've saved me from making the biggest mistake in my life."

She sat, still holding the flowers, shifting them to her left hand when Jon handed her a glass.

"Anette, my cousin lost his orange farm. An early frost destroyed the whole crop, and he's on his way home. If I hadn't listened to you, I would have arrived while he was getting ready to leave, or he might have been gone already. Not to mention that I would have lost my position as a foreman at the glove factory and sold this house." He made a gesture with his right hand, motioning to the upstairs and the downstairs. "I don't know how to thank you, other than to ask you to become my wife."

She stared at him, overcome with emotion and surprise even though he did exactly what she thought he would, and swallowed the disappointment that it wasn't out of pure love but to thank her. But this might be the chance she had been hoping for, a way to start anew, and begin again.

He met her eyes and held her gaze. "Anette, I think I may have expressed myself wrongly. I'd want to marry you anyway. I was just so astonished when I received the letter. It came today, sent to the factory rather than here. Maybe my cousin was scared that my mother would get it, as if she might still open mail here. I don't know." He reached for her hand, eyes still in hers. "I've had my heart set on you since that very first day when you made coffee."

"I will," she said, before he could change his mind.

Chapter Seventeen

Hanna

Since that first evening, Johannes came to the Frog several times a week. He brought his paperwork and if the table was free, always sat near the window, two tables down from her counter.

Hanna loved having him there, poring over his papers while she took care of customers. Sometimes he paused and looked at her with an inquisitive smile, as if he wanted to know what she was thinking about. It always made her laugh. She was aware of him every minute, no matter how many customers she had, and felt herself becoming more animated with people, even bubbly, when he was nearby. She had to admit it to herself, she was in love. With no one other than Kurt's cousin.

One evening he was there until closing and offered to sweep up and wipe the tables while she tallied the day's receipts.

"It's very kind of you. I'll take you up on your offer. Thank you."

"Kind, I don't know Hanna. I have ulterior motives, I wanted to see if I could take you to dinner at the Altona."

For a moment time stilled while she screamed for joy inside, but she managed to answer in a normal voice.

"Yes please, but I'll go for dinner even if you don't do work for it first."

"I still will," he said with a broad grin, looking so relieved that she realized he had been nervous about asking her. It made her smile.

Johannes set to work, picked up the chairs, turned them upside down, and placed them on the table, fetched her broom and swept the floor.

The inn was packed, but just as they arrived three students, all first-year boys, finished eating and they were offered their table. It had a view of the cathedral across the street. The gray stone looked dramatic in the dark, the light from the streetlamps just barely reaching the walls. Johannes noticed her gaze as he pulled her chair out for her.

"Lund's pride, known all over the land," he said.

"And the dioceses of Lund," said a waiter approaching with menus. "Are you from out of town?"

The waiter thought they were married. Hanna exchanged an amused look with Johannes.

"No, we're Lundeners, Miss Johansson here, is one of our town's businesswomen. I'm sure you've heard of the Frog?"

Very racy. By telling him that, Johannes wasn't only establishing that they weren't married, but that she was her own person.

"No, I haven't heard of that establishment." Neither the tone nor expression revealed what he thought, and she and Johannes exchanged another glance. Johannes grinned and she hid a smile, aware of the waiter standing there.

Hanna ordered flounder with dill potatoes, and Johannes ordered chicken. They both declined the waiter's offer to see a wine list.

"Hanna, I should tell you I'm not a member of the Good Templar organization, and must admit that I'm not much for temperance. Not that I drink a lot, but I want to be honest with you," Johannes said when the waiter had disappeared. He looked serious and a little nervous.

"I understand. And do order wine if you'd like. I'm not an absolutist. It's not the alcohol itself I have such an issue with, it's what it does to people. Especially the way men's intemperance affects women."

"Maria and Elsa have spoken of your passion. I can't say I blame you, Elsa told me about the woman at your meeting."

"She did?"

He nodded. "Yes, I was at their house that evening. Kurt and I are building bird houses for their garden. You should come and take a look. There are several species at their bird feeder that we're hoping would nest. I digress, sorry. Elsa was very upset when she and Maria came home. Understandably so, Maria didn't want to tell us at first, but Kurt insisted. Perhaps I shouldn't have told you. She told me in the strictest confidence, but since you were there too." He stopped, looking apologetic.

"I understand. She's left him, by the way. Finally," Hanna said. Magnhild had told her that Vanda was doing well and would be looking for her own place to live soon. She hoped Vanda had her own money.

"I'm glad. It's a disgrace. He should be in jail." Johannes threw a quick glance around the restaurant and lowered his voice. "I know who her husband is. It's that famous pianist."

"Really, who?"

"It has to be. Elsa said that she took note of the unusual surname when they were introduced, Von Gier isn't?"

"Yes."

"I thought so, Alexander Von Gier, a brilliant musician. He had a concert at the university once. I can't say other than that it was an extraordinary evening. It's an odd coincidence that I was invited." Johannes cut a piece of chicken and ate it. "It's not usual for the administrating wing to be invited to these things, but one of the professors and I are friendly, and he couldn't go, so he offered me his seat. I wouldn't have known otherwise, but I recognized it as soon as Elsa mentioned it. With a name like that, German nobility, I believe." He frowned and took a sip of water.

"You should've seen…," Hanna began, then shook her head, deciding not to say anything about how distorted Vanda's arm looked or the scar on her neck. It was too private. "I can't believe you know who he is. How did he seem? Did you speak to him? Was he drinking?" she asked, picturing him playing with a cocktail resting on the piano.

"No, he wasn't, and he didn't stay for questions or to mingle afterwards."

"Maybe he keeps it secret. Drinking only at home." Hanna shook her head again and added, "Clearly it's something he does quite frequently."

Johannes held her gaze. He didn't seem to have an urgent need to defend himself, or men in general, like most men did when this subject came up.

Hanna cut into her fish and took a bite of potato. It was buttery and delicious.

"I apologize. This isn't the nicest conversation to have the first time we have dinner together. I do hope we'll have more," she said, feeling brave for suggesting it.

Johannes smiled that inquisitive smile of his. "I'd like that very much."

Chapter Eighteen

Anette

If it had felt strange to live with Jon before, it felt even more so now. It wasn't suitable to live with one's fiancé before your wedding day. The proper thing to do would be for her to move back home, but of course she couldn't. Nor could she explain why. Instead, she told Jon a story that was as close to the truth that she could get; her father's smithy didn't sustain them in Hardeberga, so they moved to a smaller house in Södra Sandby to start anew. Space was an issue, and it was one of the reasons for why she had gone to Lund to seek work. She prayed that the new house was indeed small, or he would catch her in a lie. She worried about the upcoming wedding as well, about her own reaction to seeing Carl and about Carl's reaction to seeing her. Surely, he would join them along with the rest of the family. What if he didn't remember her? Or what if he did?

Jon squeezed her hand, moved close to her, and gently kissed her on the lips, then stopped and looked searchingly into her eyes. He was so gentle. Had she met Jon before she had fallen for Julius' charms, she would never have let Julius treat her the way he did.

Anette nodded and kissed him back, feeling him smile under her lips.

They were sitting on the swing sofa in the gazebo behind the house. The gazebo was covered with vines and being in the corner of the garden, and hidden behind the hedges bordering the property, it was completely private.

Their kisses grew more intense, and Jon was breathing heavily. Anette felt a flutter in her stomach and wetness between her legs. It was so different with Jon. She wanted him. With her virginity already lost, what difference could it make? They were getting married. Jon began to search around her waist and around her neck to loosen the buttons. Then he stopped.

"Anette, we should marry soon. I was thinking in the early

fall. It's two months until September, do you think it's enough time to send invitations?" His voice was hoarse, and he kept touching her arms. It made her shiver.

"It should be. Did you send the letter to my father to ask for permission?"

"Yes!" Jon stood up abruptly, making the swing wobble. "I got a letter today, I forgot."

He laughed and ran out of the gazebo, leaving Anette with a tightening feeling in her throat. What if her father had written something about Carl in the letter? She hoped Jon hadn't gone against her wishes and told him they were already living together like in a Stockholm Marriage. Her thoughts were interrupted when Jon pushed his head inside the gazebo, waving the letter in the air, grinning as he shoved it into her hands.

"He said yes!"

She held her breath, noticing that despite her nerves, her face wasn't burning.

Esteemed Mr. Henriksson,

My wife Anna and I are so pleased to hear this. Of course you have my permission. Anette wrote to us about kindly Mrs. Engström and if you were like family to her, then we know your character.

Sincerely,
Ola Lundström

Wiping tears from her eyes, Anette shook her finger at Jon. "You shouldn't have opened it without me," she said, then laughed with relief.

He threw himself beside her and hugged her close, kissing her on her teary cheeks. Remaining there, they held each other in silence until the air grew chilly and the sun set. Then they went inside.

As soon as the door closed behind them, they turned to each other and started kissing. Before she knew it, he had unbuttoned all the buttons in her dress so he could reach her corset.

"I'll be very gentle and we can stop if you want. I promise. We can wait. If you rather wait, we'll do so, we have our whole life ahead of us."

Anette looked at him, then shyly reached for him, and he took her by the hand and led her to his bedroom.

She held her breath when he entered her, scared that he would be able to tell she wasn't a virgin and scared of the pain she felt the only other time she laid with a man.

Jon stopped, lifted on his hands and looked her. "Am I hurting you?"

She shook her head, relieved that he didn't notice that it wasn't her first time, and relieved that it didn't hurt.

#

When her courses came a week later, she relaxed. But even if they hadn't, they were getting married soon. It didn't matter anymore.

The month after that, she was pregnant again. When she told Jon, he was delighted.

#

It was a glorious summer morning when they made their way to a church near Jon's home to apply for their banns. The sky was clear except for small cotton clouds that passed in front of the sun, creating moving patches of shade on the ground. Jon whistled happily and took Anette by the hand. With his other hand, he checked in his pocket for the letter from her father granting permission. She should have afelt as happy as he did, but ever since she woke up that morning, she had a sense that something was about to change.

Her fingers were ice cold and she wished she could run back home. She glanced at Jon, hoping to see the same dread in his face so she might talk him into turning back, but he looked the same as when they set out, cheerful and proud.

He gave her a sideways glance. "My dear Mrs. Henriksson-to-be, you look lovely on this beautiful day. I'm honored to have you accompany me to church for a little chat with the parson." He kissed her on the cheek. "You're so quiet. Is it the baby? It looks fine from here."

"Can you see it that clearly? What if the parson sees it too?"

Jon looked at her curiously. "It doesn't matter if he knows or not. We're getting married."

"You're right, and I'm not showing that much anyway," she said, trying to keep her voice steady. "The reason you see it is because you know it's there."

"Not to mention," he added jauntily, "that I had a little something to do with it."

She smiled, but something was still tugging at her. They walked in silence and soon found themselves in the cemetery adjoining the small, whitewashed stone church. Gravel pathways between the graves led to the parish house beside it. Anette read the inscriptions on the headstones as they made their way across. One in particular caught her eye. Agatha Vester, beloved wife, mother, and sister, 1789-1822. Anette shivered as she pictured this woman who died so young and lived so long ago. How different the world must have been back then. Would someone walk past *her* grave one day and wonder what her life had been like?

"Come, Anette," Jon said and took her by the elbow. "I don't think we should study old headstones when we're about to embark on our new life."

They reached the parish house. Jon knocked and only a moment later the door swung open, and the parson was smiling at them.

"Oh, what a pleasant surprise! Finally, some visitors my own age," he said, even though he was obviously several years older than they were. However, for a parson he did seem rather young.

"Most of my parishioners are older than the church itself," he added with a glint in his eye. "This is pleasant indeed. What brings you to my door at this time of day?"

Jon took his hat off. "We live nearby and we wish to be married." He was bending his hat in his hands but didn't seem aware of it.

"I see, come in then."

The parson led them through a sparsely furnished waiting area into an office on the right. It was modest, with a plain wooden sofa facing a table and chair and an armoire directly behind them. To its left stood a tall potted plant.

"Please, sit down," the parson said and gestured toward the sofa, then walked over to the armoire and pulled out a large brown book. Watching him, Anette felt a little calmer. He seemed nice.

"So, you two want to share your life in holy matrimony?" He sat down in front of them and carefully laid the book on the table. "Let's see if we can arrange to have your banns read, eh?"

"Yes, sir, yes, Reverend," Jon said.

The parson nodded solemnly as he looked at them both, pausing almost imperceptivity on Anette before he resumed speaking.

"You're both members of this parish? You've lived here in Lund all of your lives?"

"Yes, Reverend," Jon replied immediately.

"I moved here from Hardeberga," Anette said.

"And when was that?"

"A couple of years ago."

"I see." He opened the book and turned to Jon. "What's your name, sir?

"Jon Henriksson."

"H, H, H," the parson read aloud, wetting his index finger with his tongue before he turned each page. "Ah, here you are, Jon Henriksson. In fact, there are several of you. What's your address?"

"Tran…," Jon began, but the parson interrupted him with a wave of his hand.

"I see. Not married, very good."

He turned to Anette, raising an eyebrow in question. "Your name, miss?"

"Anette Lundström."

He wet his finger again as he turned the pages. "L, L, L… here we have…" He stopped mid-sentence and gave Anette a sharp look.

"Did you say your name is Anette Lundström?"

"Yes."

"Moved from Hardeberga, July 1889?"

"Yes."

"And Miss Lundström, Mr. Henriksson has forgiven you for your sin?"

Anette stared at him, speechless.

"Her sin?" Jon asked incredulously, his voice crisp. "I'm not sure I understand what you mean." He reached for her hand under the table and clasped it firmly.

"Well, it appears that this woman had a child, born the fourth of October 1889, father unknown. I hope and pray that Miss Lundström has discussed this with you," the parson replied, just as crisply. Then he cleared his throat.

Everything went still, and there was a ringing sound in her ears. The parson's words reverberated and hung as a physical presence in the room, spoken as if she wasn't there. *This woman had a child. This woman. Father unknown.* She blushed.

Jon turned toward her. She felt his eyes burning into the side of her face. He didn't remove his hand, but it had gone limp in hers. She was going to meet his gaze when the parson closed the book and sighed deeply.

"So, I gather she hasn't told you," he said.

She would never forget the sound of trousers sliding on wood as Jon moved away from her. The parson put his hand on his shoulder and led him to the corner of the room. Jon turned to look at her for a moment, then turned back to the parson who was now speaking in hushed tones, but she heard most of it and it was enough.

"I'm sorry… deceived… a sin… she doesn't even know the father… brides are supposed to be virgins, there's a law."

Anette rose to her feet. Without looking back, she moved quickly through the room and the waiting area, pushed the door open, and stepped out into the sunny summer day.

She should have known that all births were entered into the parish records at the time of baptism. And if she had been able to think clearly, she could have told the parson that she had already been forgiven. Helga had brought her to a church north of Lund for

Carl's baptism. Before carrying her son to the baptismal font, she had to be churched herself and forgiven for her sin of giving birth as an unwed mother. They said she was absolved and ready for a new life in the church. If only she had thought to explain that to the parson.

She walked back down the gravel path through the graveyard, pausing when she reached Agatha Vester's gravestone: *Beloved wife and mother.*

Then she looked back at the door, willing Jon to appear. Sure enough, a few moments later he emerged, closed the door behind him, put his hat back on his head, and came walking toward her. He was moving so fast that she thought he would keep going, but he stopped in front of her. His blue eyes narrowed and looked almost black.

"You lied to me. You humiliated me in front of the parson."

"I'm so sorry, I should've told you. I was too afraid. Please don't be angry. Please." There was that same ringing sound in her ears, as if to warn her, and fear gripped her with such force, that she thought she might throw up.

He scoffed. "You lived in my house for several months, and not a word. How many men have you been with?" He was shouting. Anyone walking past the church must be able to hear what he said. "You don't even know who the father is? It's outrageous. Who *are* you?"

She went to him and grabbed his shoulders, almost shaking him as tears of desperation rolled down her cheeks. "I do know. His name is Julius, but I... he left, I..." She stopped. The parson was right. She didn't know who he was, not even his last name.

Jon shook his head slowly, as if she sickened him.

"Jon, please. I was forgiven. I've been churched. It was only one time. He said he would marry me like *you* said." As soon as the words were out of her mouth, she knew it had been the wrong thing to say.

"Like me? I trusted you. You've soiled yourself and I was being so careful with you, even feeling guilty for not waiting until our wedding." He put his hand on her chest and pushed her from him, forcing her to take a step backwards. It was as if he were someone else.

"I can't marry you."

"Jon, please I'm pregnant!"

He stared her, for a moment there was a glint of compassion in his eyes, long enough for her to hope, but then he turned away and began to walk off, shouting over his shoulder, "How do I know it's mine?"

She slipped to the ground. The gravel dug into her knees, but she lacked the strength to get up. This couldn't be happening, not again. It was too much. What was happening to her?

Then she heard footsteps. Was he coming back? Her heart started beating out of control, but when she looked up, it was the parson standing over her. With the sun behind him, his face was in shadow. He grabbed her arm and lifted her to her feet.

"You cannot remain here."

"I have nowhere to go," she said, her voice hoarse and congested from tears.

Sighing, the parson pulled a pencil and a piece of paper from the pocket of his coat and scribbled something on it. "Here," he said, handing it to her. "They'll take care of you." Then he turned on his heels and walked back to the parish house.

She looked at the paper and recognized the address. Lilla Algatan, she knew where that was. He was sending her to the poorhouse.

#

Anette spent the rest of the day wandering aimlessly through the streets. At twilight she found herself standing across the street from the House. The women would have stopped sewing since long at this hour, and were either sleeping or in the parlor, quietly talking while some of them were nursing. Most would be new residents who she didn't know. Should she go in and tell them that they would forever be marked in the church books? Why hadn't Helga warned her? She must have known what waited.

A sudden movement in the kitchen window caught her

attention. Then a lamp was lit, and in the warm glow she saw Helga's familiar profile. Without thinking, Anette lifted her hand and waved, but Helga didn't see her and pulled the curtains closed.

Chapter Nineteen

Hanna

Sweat was pouring from Hanna's face and she felt so thirsty that her tongue was sticking to her upper gum line. Johannes had been inside with her father for over an hour. She was waiting in the shade of one of the large apple trees that lined the edge of the garden, but it was still too hot.

Her mother was out. She played cards with her women friends every Thursday, which was why they had picked today.

Hanna had assumed it would only take a few minutes. After all, Johannes was a respectable professional, and surely her father would be happy for her. Finally, she decided to go ask one of their neighbors for a glass of water and was halfway across the street when she heard Johannes call for her. She saw it in his face as soon as she turned around and without a thought started running toward him. Luckily, there were no carriages in the street.

"My dear Hanna, will you marry me?" Johannes shouted as she flew up the stairs and into his arms.

"I will."

He kissed her passionately and spun her around, then noticed her father standing in the doorway, his face stern.

"Oh, I'm sorry, sir. I thought you were still inside." Johannes' embarrassment was unmistakable, and Hanna tried not to laugh.

Her father's face grew sterner for an interminable moment, then expanded into a merry grin. "I assume from this behavior that my daughter said yes, so please don't address me as sir, call me Roland, and welcome to the family."

Johannes chuckled. "Thank you, sir. Thank you, Roland."

Hanna loosened herself from Johannes' arms. "Pappa, my goodness, what took you so long? I thought I'd die of thirst out here."

"We had a lot to talk about. Johannes can tell you. I'll go fetch mother from her game and we'll pick up a bottle of champagne on the way back. And I don't want to hear any of your

Good Templar nonsense today," he said and shook his finger at her.

Hanna laughed as she watched him walk away. When he was out on the street, looking the other way, Johannes pulled her close.

"I'm sorry it took so long. God, I'm thirsty too."

She led him into the kitchen and poured two tall glasses of water, handing him one. "What did he say? What did *you* say?"

"Well, let me see, he… first he looked surprised. I think he thought I was here on business and couldn't figure out why I came to his home and not his office. When I told him I came on a personal errand, he almost looked frightened, so I went right to the point. Telling him I met you a couple of months ago at the café and that we'd been respectfully conversing ever since."

"Respectfully conversing?" Hanna looked at him in disbelief. "You didn't say that."

"What else should I have said, that we've been renting a room at the Altona?"

"No," Hanna laughed, "you just made it sound so proper."

"And we have been proper. We haven't done anything but talk, and a little of this." Johannes took the water glass from her hand and kissed her on the lips.

"So what did he say then?" Hanna asked when they stopped kissing.

"He said nothing for several minutes. Then he left the room and came back with a tray with a bottle and two whiskey glasses."

"Were they the ones with a running moose etched into the glass?"

"Yes."

"That's a good sign. He wanted to impress you."

"Really?" Johannes smiled happily. "He poured the whiskey and asked me to sit down. Then he bombarded me with questions about my work and my family."

"Oh, dear."

"I answered truthfully, but he seemed to think I'm a good match anyway."

Then he kissed her again.

#

They all drank too much champagne that night, Hanna included. Plans were made for a wedding in Lund's Cathedral the following summer. Hanna suggested they have dinner at the Frog afterwards, but her mother wouldn't hear of it. It was too small, she said, and insisted that the wedding dinner should be held at the Altona. Of course they agreed.

Chapter Twenty

Anette

There was a large inscription above the entrance of the poorhouse. If One Does Not Work, Neither Shall He Eat, it said, and her heart sank. She was exhausted, and weak from hunger, having spent the night on a bench outside, afraid of entering the poorhouse when it was dark.

"Don't worry yourself with those dumb words," someone said behind her, startling her. It was an old man.

"Mr. Bulow at the newspaper also finds them distasteful. And they do feed us here." He patted his round belly with his dirty hands. "None of us are starving. Of course, it may not be the same food that King Oskar eats up there in Stockholm."

He laughed at his own comment, showing his only two teeth, one in the upper jaw and one in the lower. Anette shuddered and unconsciously let her tongue slide over her own teeth, then gave him a polite nod and hurried into the building.

Coming in from the bright sunshine, Anette couldn't see a thing but was struck by the rancid smell. When her eyes adjusted to the dimness, she could tell that she was in a small lobby. The walls had dulled to a grayish-white, and a woman was sitting behind a desk that seemed much too large for the room.

"You've fallen into trouble, I see," the woman said, staring straight at her belly, even though it was barely showing. "Do you read and write?"

"Of course," Anette replied, surprised by the question.

"Very good. I'm the warden here. Come sign your name and I'll assign you a bed." She pointed to an open notebook on the desk, dipped her pen into a scuffed inkwell, and handed it to her.

Anette's hand shook and the result looked more like a scribble than a signature.

A few moments later she was following the warden down a dark hallway. The air had gone from rancid to rank and she heard loud banging sounds from the rooms they passed. A few of the doors were open, but there was no time to look inside. In one room, however, she glimpsed a woman lying with her back turned toward the door, picking at the wall by her bed with her fingernails.

The banging continued, but the warden didn't pay it any mind. She walked briskly in front with her head erect and keys jangling from a chain around her waist.

Leading Anette into a large room with wall-to-wall beds in two rows of five each, the warden pointed to a bed in the corner. As they approached it, an old woman in the adjacent bed sat up and shrieked, "Beware of the wall lice!" Her clothes hung from her bony shoulders like dirty rags from a dish rack. She waved a wooden stick about half a meter long with a round piece of leather attached to one end. In her gaunt, almost skeletal face, her eyes appeared enormous. She extended the stick toward Anette.

"Use this before you lie down." The woman lifted herself out of the bed, her legs quivering as she stood up.

Instinctively, Anette took a step backward and immediately regretted it, feeling ashamed for showing her distaste.

The warden frowned. "No, Kjellgren, I'll give Lundström her own swatter." The old woman nodded gravely and sat back down, then violently slammed the swatter against the wall behind her.

So that's the sound she heard from the hallway. They were killing the lice.

When the warden left, Anette sat down heavily on her assigned bed. It felt lumpy and the mildew hit her nostrils as the straw shifted in the mattress. The walls must have been blue once. Now they were blotched with yellow sweat marks and small red dots, the corpses of crushed flies and lice. It's what the woman in the other room had been picking at. She turned her head away from it so she wouldn't feel sick.

"Welcome to the poorhouse, dear," Kjellgren said, exposing her brown, cracked teeth.

"Thank you." Thanking her felt ridiculous, but what other response could she give?

"It's not as bad as it looks. You'll get used to it and you'll probably move on eventually. Me, I have to stay here forever. They think I'm insane, you know."

Anette understood fully. The lice, the smell, and the despair could drive anyone crazy.

Despite her hunger, she was so exhausted that she lay down and slept. Kjellgren left her alone, and if other residents were curious about her, she didn't notice.

When she woke up, it was dark and quiet. She had slept all day, tired from being awake the whole previous night. She felt numb and couldn't quite believe that she was in the poorhouse. Why had no one told her about the parish records? She was supposed to be able to leave her past behind. Everyone had said it, including her parents and the parson's wife. Maybe Mother Anna and her father hadn't known, but the parson's wife must have. She had lied to her face, surely knowing that there was no chance for her to begin again without telling people the truth. *No one ever needs to know the truth about your past Anette. Go get this over with. Pretend you're taking a sabbatical from your life. It'll soon be in the past.* The words echoed in her mind, especially the sugary tone of her voice.

Anette cried into her pillow so as not to wake anyone. It stunk. Gagging, she sat up and stopped crying, feeling as if she might throw up. No lamps were lit, and she couldn't see if all the beds were occupied but heard snores and coughing. She swallowed the bile. The warden hadn't told her where the outhouse was.

Maybe she could get Jon to change his mind. Apologize for not having told him the truth, tell him she had been advised not to. Beg him to forgive her. He must know it was his child, she had been living in his house. Who else could be the father but him?

She lay awake most of the night, hunger and worry keeping her alert, along with a full bladder.

At precisely 7 a.m. a bell rang and everyone got out their beds.

"It's breakfast, Lundström," said Kjellgren. "We eat in the dining hall. I'll show you."

Anette followed her out into the hallway. She wanted to tell her to call her Anette but didn't bother. A stream of yawning people came out from their rooms and lined up in front of a long table. The old man from yesterday had been right, there was plenty of food. There were two big pots of steaming hot porridge, milk and even a plate with cookies and rolls.

Kjellgren noticed her looking at them. "It's from the Frog, she donates what she can't sell every Friday."

Anette nodded, pretending to know what she was talking about. She grabbed a bowl and instead of sitting down at the table, went to stand against the wall, eating quickly while taking stock of the room. There were twelve people in there, excluding herself. Most were elderly, but there was a young man and woman sitting together. They looked dirty, but not too ragged, and were talking with each other as if they were having breakfast at a restaurant.

Anette finished eating and washed her bowl in a bucket as she had seen one of the older women do. Then she hurried outside. The warden looked up when she passed her desk. "Curfew is at 9 pm. You must be back by then or you'll lose your bed."

"Thank you. Where's the outhouse?"

She pointed out the door and to the right and Anette ran over there, overcome with need. To her relief it didn't smell too bad. Someone must have emptied the latrine. Then she left the poorhouse and hurried to catch Jon before he left for the factory.

Anette knocked on the door to what she still hoped was her home. It reminded her of the first door she had knocked on in Lund. This time it opened immediately, and Jon stood there. He looked so cold and drawn that she almost turned around. But she gathered her strength and placed her hands on her belly.

"Jon, it's your child I'm carrying. I promise you. Please don't abandon me. Please let me explain. I should have told you, but I was afraid of losing you."

There was no feeling in his face, not even sadness. "Anette, I can't, I'm a foreman and a respected citizen. This could ruin me. I have your things here, and some money for the baby," he said, then picked up a navy-blue valise from the floor and handed it to her, along with an envelope. The valise looked spotless and brand new. "Here are your things, and four hundred kronor."

She was so stunned that she took what he gave her and watched him close the door in her face. He must have been prepared, bought a valise for her things and gone to the bank to get all that money. It was a good sum, but an insult, it wouldn't last to raise a baby for long. That he bothered to get a new valise for her and to pack her things seemed almost grotesque. As if he thought he was being nice while kicking her out with his child in her belly.

She walked away. Her chest felt constricted, and her jaws hurt from suppressing tears. How could someone change like this from one moment to the next? A bird chirped and was answered by another. Then a woman opened a window across the street and shook a towel to air it out. The world still looked the same, but her heart was broken.

#

Anette stayed in the poorhouse, hiding the money in her corset during the day and under her mattress at night, saving it for the baby. It felt better after a while, at least she had a roof over her head, even the smell stopped bothering her. People there were just like her, they had tried to make it in life, but failed. She never considered going to the House again. She felt too ashamed. The hardest part had been to write to her parents and tell them that the wedding was canceled. She didn't tell them she was pregnant and pretended to have found new employment. Telling herself that it wasn't actually a lie because the warden had asked her to sew for her.

Her daughter was born on the tenth of December 1891, and she named her Edith Henrika after her father. She considered bringing her to Jon to show him, hoping he might change his mind when he saw his beautiful daughter. But she was too proud and angry, naming her after him, more for Edith's sake than her own. She would have to make something up to tell her one day. This time during the baptism, she looked the parson straight in the eye, the same one who christened Carl, and told him that although she knew who the father was, he didn't deserve to be in his book. If Jon ever got married, she hoped he thought of her when he found that there was no child associated with his good name. And Edith was hers.

She would never let her go.

Anette tried to keep to herself, but the men down the hall, smuggled in alcohol, and cold evenings made it difficult. She didn't care so much anymore either. What difference could a little love do when she was already marked a sinner, at least no one promised her anything.

On February 13, 1894, she gave birth to her second daughter, Ingrid. Who the father was, she couldn't say for certain. But she knew the poorhouse was no place to raise two daughters.

PART TWO

Chapter Twenty-one

Anette

Mrs. Petersson was a woman who donated goods to the poorhouse every month. The Charity Lady, the residents called her. She genuinely cared for them and never said anything to imply that she was better than they were. Anette liked her and enjoyed talking with her.

One day she mentioned that there was a man visiting Lund, asking around for women to milk cows on a farm, and offered to make the introduction. Anette decided it was now or never. She washed herself and changed into a simple but brand-new dress that Mrs. Petersson had given her a few weeks earlier. Then they walked across town to where the man was waiting. He told her his name was Mr. Knutsson and that she would become a statare, which meant that she wouldn't get paid much but would have a place to live in the fresh country air, and plenty of food for her and her daughters. Neither Anette nor Mrs. Petersson mentioned she had lived at the poorhouse for the last four years, and Mr. Knutsson didn't ask where her husband was. He said they would leave early the next morning and arrive at a place called Häckeberga around midday.

Anette roused her daughters, picked up her valise with the few items she owned, and went out into a cold, windy morning. To her surprise, Mrs. Petersson was standing right outside, waiting for her. She handed Edith a piece of sweet bread, then placed a tiny object into Anette's palm and closed her fingers around it.

"*Mrs.* Lundström, I wish you a pleasant journey." She leaned in close until their faces were a few inches apart. "It's better if you're a widow," she whispered. Then, quickly, she turned and walked away, her footsteps echoing on the cobblestones.

Anette opened her hand, then inhaled sharply. It was a gold wedding band. Mrs. Petersson had given her a real wedding ring.

Surely this was too much. She looked down the street, but Mrs. Petersson had already turned the corner. *It's better if you're a widow*, she said… Anette swallowed something thick in her throat. The ring was a ticket to a new life. She had covered her hair, but a ring would do so much more. No one would doubt her now. She could finally start anew. With a quick glance at the windows, making sure no one in the poorhouse was awake and looking at her, she slipped the ring on left ring finger. It fit. She fingered it with her thumb, shifting it back and forth, staring unseeingly at the low buildings across the street. Then she made sure that the shawls tying Ingrid to her chest were secured, took Edith by the hand, and left the poorhouse.

#

"We're almost there," shouted Mr. Knutsson from his driver's perch. Anette smiled at Edith, who laughed with excitement. They sat huddled on the flatbed between sacks of chocolate, fine cheeses, and bottles of wine he had purchased in Lund. She wished she could have some of it, if even just one small piece of chocolate or a tiny chunk of cheese.

A few moments later, they approached a lake. At its center was a small island, and at the center of the island stood a castle. Anette gasped. Mr. Knutsson let out a hearty laugh and looked back at his three passengers.

"Häckeberga Castle, most people have the same reaction when they first see it."

"Is this where the king lives?" Edith asked.

Mr. Knutsson gave her a knowing wink. "Not quite, though the owner might see it differently." He turned toward Anette, and said, "It's his farm we're heading to and his cows you'll be milking."

She stared at him, stunned at his words. No wonder Mrs. Petersson hadn't told him where she met her. What would they think of her? "Is he hard to work for, sir?"

"The owner himself, you'll not see much of. They stay there." Mr. Knutsson jerked his head in the direction of the castle. "I've only seen him and the missus once the whole time I've been here. They have people do everything for them, they don't have to mix with the likes of us."

Anette nodded, feeling embarrassed. It had been a ridiculous question, and Mr. Knutsson made clear she knew her place. He turned forward again and continued driving. Fast-moving clouds dominated the sky over the castle, giving it a dark and sullen appearance, and the wind picked up. She pulled the blanket up over the baby and beckoned for Edith to come and sit closer. Anxiety made her stomach churn.

Knutsson glanced over his shoulder. "It won't be long now," he said and urged the horse to a fast trot. The road led into a shady lane formed by large birches curving around the edge of the lake. There was a wonderful scent of moist earth. As they came around the bend and into the open, she realized the island was actually a small peninsula; there was a small stone bridge leading from the road to the island, but it didn't cross over water as she had assumed.

Mr. Knutsson leaned back, eying her, loosening his grip firm on the reins.

"Mrs. Lundström, you're very quiet."

Anette steadied herself with a deep breath. "Just enjoying the beauty," she said after a moment, and lifted Ingrid a little higher on her shoulder.

"It's impressive, I know, quite different from Lund now, isn't it?" He let go of the reins completely. The horse trotted along on its own.

She noticed his eyes alighting on her new ring. The moment had come to address the issue. Trying her best to sound devastated, she launched into the scenario she had concocted on the way. "I've lost my husband. He was a traveling peddler, bless his soul. But the drink got to him and one night he fell off his bicycle, hit his head, and drowned in a ditch."

Mr. Knutsson's eyes widened. "What a tragedy, I'm so sorry for your loss."

"Thank you. As you can imagine, this is something I don't wish to speak of too much. I'd appreciate you keeping it to yourself."

"Of course."

Anette kept her gaze in his, feeling guilty. Mrs. Petersson surely wouldn't condone this much lying. Mr. Knutsson probably wouldn't keep it to himself, but regardless of who heard the story, having a dead drunk for a husband was much better than the truth. And it was just dramatic enough so no one would question it.

The wagon passed a large barn and stopped in front of a long, red statar building with four doors and a low roof of brown tile. Set behind it was an identical structure and set behind that was a third, each separated by a path of grass between them. As Mr. Knutsson helped them down, doors flew open, and an entire village seemed to pour out. Anette held Ingrid close to her chest while Edith clung to her skirts, grabbing on to her leg so hard that it hurt.

"The new one is here," a woman said, rushed forward and took both of Anette's hands in hers as the others looked on. "We're very glad to have you here, missus, and your darling little ones." Her creased, wrinkled face broke into a wide grin, and she shifted her gaze to Edith. "So you're the big sister, eh?"

Edith curtsied and everyone laughed.

"Where is your husband, ma'am?" said a man with strong muscular arms and a sunburnt face.

"He's passed on, sir," Anette said and looked him squarely in the face.

"My condolences."

She hid a sigh of relief.

Mr. Knutsson cleared his throat and made a shooing motion with his hands, and everyone headed back inside. Anette's heart sank. It was Mr. Knutsson she was going to work for. She thought he had just picked her up, but he must be the boss. Now her question about the owner was even more inappropriate.

"You stay here, Harriet," he called out to a bareheaded woman who appeared to be in her mid-twenties, same as her, with long braids piled up on top of her head.

"Yes, sir?"

"Kindly show Mrs. Lundström her space, will you?"

"Of course."

Mr. Knutsson climbed back up to his seat on the wagon, shook the reins with one hand, and drove off with a tip of his hat.

Harriet picked up Anette's valise and gestured with her free hand. "Come along. You'll be sharing a room with me."

Anette followed her the best she could, holding the baby tightly while Edith was still clinging to her leg. When they were halfway to the door, Harriet turned to her and kneeled down.

"Oh, dear child, come here. You'd better let go of Mamma's leg. Come here, little one." She held out her hand and winked conspiratorially. "Come with me and I'll give you a sweet. I have a whole bowl in here."

Anette laughed when she saw Edith's eyes widen as she practically flew after Harriet.

The room was cramped, but smelled clean, and light was streaming in through the window. A small pot with a pelargonium stood on the sill. To the right was a narrow bed covered with a red and blue quilt. Against the opposite wall was a kitchen sofa and a small table that served as a workbench with a cutting board and a copper bowl.

Harriet patted Edith on the head; she had selected a lemon bonbon from the candy bowl and was chewing vigorously.

"Watch your teeth, Edith," Anette scolded.

"I'm so glad to have you here, Mrs. Lundström. You can sleep on the kitchen sofa. I'll try to find an extra blanket to make it softer. I didn't expect anyone until Slack Week."

"Slack Week?"

"Oh dear, you *are* new. Where are you from?"

"From Lund."

Harriet clasped her hands together. "From Lund? I've always wanted to see it. They say the cathedral is as tall as Kebnekaise."

"Not quite." Anette smiled at the notion that a cathedral could be as tall as the highest mountain in the country. "Though it's tall enough to see from nearly every point in Lund."

"I hope I'll see it, even if only once in my lifetime," Harriet said dreamily. Then she straightened up abruptly. "Oh, I was about to explain Slack Week. It's the last week in October. That's the one time each year that we're allowed to go out and look elsewhere for work if we're not happy here. Other than that, we're forbidden to leave."

"We can't leave?"

"No. We can go places, but with the milking and all what we have to do, there's no time. And as I said, we can't actually leave. It's not legal until Slack Week, you'd get a fine and since there's no pay… you can't pay then… jail."

"We don't get paid at all?"

Harriet shrugged then said, "Not really, we're sometimes given a small token, but nah, it's never enough to buy anything."

"I understand." Anette swallowed hard and looked out the window. The sun was shining again, and it looked beautiful out there. It couldn't be that bad, could it? Where would she go anyway?

#

Anette had expected to fall asleep immediately, but no matter how hard she tried she just lay there listening to her children's quiet breathing and Harriet's loud snores. Finally giving up, she sat up, carefully stepped over Edith and the baby who were sleeping on a little mattress on the floor.

Once outside, she was careful to close the door gently behind her. A faint glow from the night sun could be seen behind the soft, wooded hills in the distance and the cool, moist air was rich with the scent of wildflowers, manure, and wet grass. She walked across the adjacent field, disturbing a group of sheep that ran off bleating in the night.

For a moment, she felt as if she was a young girl back in Hardeberga.

Chapter Twenty-two

Hanna

Hanna squinted and readjusted her binoculars but still didn't see it. Looking over at their guide in frustration, she found Johannes standing by his side, oblivious and looking through his own, and brand new, binoculars. Clearly, he had no trouble.

"Mrs. Agnell come closer this way and you might see it. I think your angle is wrong. The nightingale is resting on that first branch on the left," Professor Karlsson said and pointed.

Ruth smiled at her. "I saw it too Hanna, come over here and you'll spot it."

Hanna nodded, went to stand next to Ruth and lifted her binoculars to her eyes again. And there it was, a female, sitting puffed up and leaning against a branch. Seeing one was supposed to give you luck, but the little female didn't look too well. She should spend time eating, fattening up for her long journey to Africa later in the summer, not resting. Hanna kept her eyes on her until she heard Johannes move around and talking to one of the other people on the birdwatching tour. There were six of them, including her and Johannes, and their guide, Professor Sven Karlsson, who was an ornithologist at the university. It was he who had given Johannes his seat to that concert with Vanda's husband.

"She's beautiful. But I worry for her, she's too puffy," Hanna said as she moved over to the others.

"Yes, Mrs. Agnell, well observed," said Professor Karlsson. "I hope she recovers and doesn't stay the winter, she likely won't survive it," he added sadly, shaking his head.

"Poor girl, she looks so tired," Hanna said, then looked at Johannes. "We ought to head home, we're going to Grandma's tonight."

He pulled out his watch and glanced at it. "Yes, I suppose you're right. We should make it back. Family dinner," he explained to the group.

They said their goodbyes and took their time walking home,

stopping from time to time to look at the birds they saw along the way. They had both been in good moods lately and felt more settled being a married couple without children. They hoped they would come, but had stopped focusing so much on it. It made Hanna too depressed. Bird watching with the professor every Saturday gave them something to look forward to. And just this week they had decided to build an aviary in the sunroom. Hanna looked up at Johannes and smiled at the thought.

"I was wondering if it would be possible to extend it out. That way they'll get fresh air if they choose, in case it gets hot. We could build it by the tree and there would be real branches for them to sit, and more shade. Could you do that?"

"An extension on the aviary? As long as we can close the door to the sunroom part, or we'd lose heat in the winter. That's a great thought Hanna. Let me talk to Kurt and see if he can help."

"Yes! I knew you'd like the idea," Hanna said and kissed him on the lips, while thinking of the birds they would have there. She wanted at least two pairs of parakeets and canaries, maybe finches too. They would have several plants as well, nests so they could lay eggs, and little perches and places for the birds to sit. And birdbaths, she had to include at least one birdbath.

#

"Do you really think it looks all right? I've never had my hair coiled in the front like this."

Hanna was trying to copy the latest hairstyle she had found in a magazine and by the time she was done Johannes was sprawled across the bed.

"You look exactly like the woman in the illustration, only she probably had a hairdresser do it for her in five minutes. You've been standing there for over half an hour. Your cheeks are nice and rosy. Have you put on blush?"

"No. I'm just warm. In fact, I'm dripping with perspiration. I must have been mad to try something like this right before Grandma's dinner party." Hanna looked at her image in the mirror, then at their wedding picture on the wall. She had looked so nice that day. Her black dress, her long white veil, and her myrtle crown were perfect.

Johannes stood up and stretched. "Well, I think you look absolutely beautiful. And if anyone says differently, it'll be my honor as your husband to smack him on the side of the head."

Hanna laughed and turned back toward the mirror. Somehow, her hair now looked just the way it should.

#

After a drink in the front parlor, everyone took a seat around the table. Grandma, Hanna and Johannes, Uncle Henrik, Hanna's parents, and her father's colleague Mr. Kjellberg and his wife. Though it was a small gathering, it was planned as if the king himself were expected. The table was set with the appropriate silver, crystal glasses for the water, wine, and schnapps, and a small statue beside each plate to encourage conversation, the latest rage. Hanna had Joan of Arc beside hers. She smiled to herself, was this intended as a show of approval for her unconventional views or a warning? You could never be sure with Grandma.

Hanna caught Mrs. Kjellberg looking at her.

"Interesting, this fashion of placing statues, isn't it? I love mine. Just look at this little boy watching ducks, it's adorable but I can't for the life of me think of a good duck conversation."

"Neither can I," Hanna said and burst out laughing, receiving a sharp look of disapproval from her mother across the table. She pretended not to notice.

"Listen to yourselves," Johannes said. "These little things did get you talking."

Hanna raised an eyebrow at him, then smiled at Mrs. Kjellberg.

"How is everything going at your café, Hanna?" she asked. "I walked by just the other day but didn't see you, so I didn't go in. There was a young girl behind the counter."

"That's Elsa, the daughter of my baker, Kurt. She works for me. She comes to our women's meetings as well."

"Oh," Mrs. Kjellberg said, looking slightly uncomfortable. Hanna knew she would, but couldn't help herself. Her mother had told her that Mrs. Kjellberg didn't approve, and she wanted to see what she thought.

"Yes, Elsa is a wonderful young woman. And who knows, maybe by the time she's older she'll be allowed to vote. Wouldn't it be wonderful?"

"I'm not so sure," Mrs. Kjellberg said, flashing a look at her husband. "Most of us women don't have time to read the articles in the newspaper. We're busy all day with our homes, our children, and our husbands. If you don't mind my saying, Hanna, women like yourself who have no children couldn't possibly understand the full responsibility of running a household."

Hanna stared at her and felt the pulse in her neck increase. She was insulting her.

"I may not have a child yet, Mrs. Kjellberg," she said, trying to keep her voice level, "but I do run a busy café and I can still find time to read the newspaper. Men work all day and have time to read the paper. Why shouldn't we?"

"Well, my dear, you make an interesting point," Mrs. Kjellberg said, then abruptly turned to speak to her husband.

Hanna shifted her gaze to Johannes across from her and let her jaw drop, but he was talking with Grandma and didn't notice. Then she felt a hand on her arm and turned to Uncle Henrik, sitting on her left. He was rolling his eyes while filling her glass with chilled white wine. She nodded with gratitude and took a long sip. It was delicious. There was no reason to let Mrs. Kjellberg ruin an otherwise fun day, and she had pushed her, she couldn't deny that.

She spoke with Henrik for a while and let him pour her a little more wine, just half a glass. He went into detail about his pains and aches and his latest doctor's appointments. She felt for him, but it was hard to concentrate. Her mind kept going back to Mrs. Kjellberg's insult. It wasn't just what she said, but the way she had patronized her and turned away, dismissing her as if she was a child. It had been very rude, but she had to admit that it was only a few years ago that she hadn't felt sure that it was the right time to work for voting rights either. When there was a lull in Henrik's story, she excused herself and turned back to Mrs. Kjellberg.

"Mrs. Kjellberg, I didn't like the way you dismissed me

before. You don't need to agree with my views, but I'd like to finish our conversation. I apologize if I was pushy, but I believe you owe me an apology as well for insinuating that I don't know what it's like because we don't have children yet." She held her breath. Mrs. Kjellberg looked at her silently and blinked twice, then she put her hand on Hanna's arm.

"You're right Hanna. I do apologize and I'd like to continue as well. Let's go back to sit in the front parlor. Your grandmother will call us when it's time for dessert."

Hanna nodded, the others had finished eating and were engaged in conversation. It would be fine. She followed Mrs. Kjellberg, proud that she had dared to stand up for herself. They sat down on the plush couch, next to Grandma's enormous ferns. Everyone had ferns nowadays. She didn't think she had been in a home without one for several years.

"Mrs. Kjellberg, I think I should give Grandma my ferns from the Frog and replace them with something else. Everyone has them, I should be different."

Mrs. Kjellberg laughed a pearly natural laugh and put her hand on Hanna's knee. She looked so sweet now and Hanna felt warm toward her and was glad she had asked to talk to her.

"Yes, why do everyone have them these days? They're everywhere. Your café is light enough, put in some begonias. I'll bring you some. They'll bloom nicely for you."

"Really? Thank you."

"My pleasure," she said and smiled, then swallowed audibly. "As for voting rights for women, I feel that my pride has been in my children and my household. I did a good job and I feel it was it was my role to focus on it. It's what we're naturally equipped for as women. I was very happy with it and proud. I would have been distracted and felt torn if I was expected to hold down a job and not only that, have to be active in politics on top of it. I raised five children, three girls and two boys."

Hanna nodded. Five children, she wished they could have just one or two. "Thank you for telling me. I understand. I've heard a lot of women say the same. I wasn't sure either when I first learned about our movement, but the way I see it, is that we women are discriminated against and not taken seriously without equal voting rights. Your opinion is important, but it's not heard outside your own circle. If you could vote, and if your daughters could, they could help make decisions that help homemakers as well, precisely because they're women."

"But how are we going to have time? When the children are small, they take up all your time. And I had help, but I was always so tired."

"Some women, many women I should say, have to work in factories or other places, they must be even more tired."

"Yes, then think of how tired they'd be if they also would have to think of politics."

Hanna knew she would say that, but was prepared this time. "Yes, I realize that. But getting involved wouldn't be a must, but a choice. We should at least have the choice."

"You know, you're right about that. I'd like to talk more of it when I bring the begonias."

"Yes please, do come in, I'd love that, we'll have coffee." Hanna smiled. One conversation was all it took sometimes.

Chapter Twenty-three

Anette

Just after sunrise, a work bell clanged outside. Harriet roused Anette and put a kettle on the hearth so the coffee could boil while they got dressed.

They barely had time to drink any of it before the women began filing out of the lodgings, each carrying a milking stool. Anette watched them as they walked past the window and silently formed a long line along the hedge by the road where Mr. Knutsson had dropped her off the day before.

She looked at her babies, then at Harriet. "Can I really leave them here?"

"They'll be fine, Anette. Little Kristina will look in on the children around six. If the baby is awake, she'll feed or change her. Edith can help. That's the way it is here, you can't bring children to the pasture. They could get trampled. Come on now, we'll be picked up any minute."

Anette looked at her daughters one last time and followed Harriet out the door. As she stepped across the threshold, two pairs of black and white oxen came trotting down the road. Each pair pulled a long wagon with a large milk can surrounded by buckets that rattled and clanked loudly.

Harriet moved closer to Anette. "Either one of these beasts could pull a wagon by itself," she said, "but they like to walk together, just like people."

"Mornin', ladies," an old man exclaimed from the driver's seat of the first wagon.

"Mornin'," the women responded. Then one by one, they put their milking stools in the wagons and climbed up with the help of two rickety steps attached to the back of each wagon.

By the time Anette and Harriet reached them, the first wagon was already leaving, and there was barely any room left on the second.

Harriet didn't seem concerned and climbed aboard and held

out her hand to Anette. "Here, grab on."

At the command of the driver, the oxen began at a steady trot and made a sharp left to round the statar lodgings. In front of them, the pasture spread out in the morning mist like a rippling green sea. Anette tugged on Harriet's arm. "It's beautiful!"

Her words brought a wave of gentle laughter from the women sitting nearby.

"Indeed," an older woman said as she shielded her eyes with her hand. "One fails to notice what one sees every day. I'm Alice." Her face was browned by the sun and she looked kind.

"I'm Anette."

"Your hands don't show signs of milking, Anette."

"This is my first time."

There was a murmur of disappointment, but before she had time to worry too much, Harriet answered for her.

"It's no matter. I'll teach her."

"What did you do with yourself before you came here?" a younger bareheaded woman asked, eyes narrowing.

"I took care of my husband and children," Anette lied. Her heart was beating a little faster, but at least she wasn't blushing.

"They lived in Lund," Harriet added.

"Oh, deary, a town person," Alice said.

They all laughed, but it was a good-natured laugh and she relaxed.

The rest of the ride passed in silence, and then the wagon caught up to the first one which had stopped in the middle of the pasture. A herd of black and white cows came toward them. They looked enormous. What if one of them was a bull?

Anette's legs felt shaky, but she managed to climb out without incident. Harriet placed her stool on the ground as a cow ambled over and began nuzzling her on the neck. Anette was about to call out to the others, but Harriet just laughed and shoved the big head away. It left behind a slimy film on her shoulder.

"Here, Anette, come and stand next to me. Tomorrow I'll get you a milking stool. Today you can use mine." Harriet moved the stool very close to the cow, almost underneath its belly, and sat down and leaned her forehead against its side. She then grabbed two of the four teats, one in each hand, and squeezed with her thumbs and forefingers. The milk sprayed down into the bucket with a whizzing sound, the stream from each teat hitting the side in a crisscross pattern.

"Now you come and try," Harriet instructed, swiping at a fly buzzing around her face. "Lean forward and squeeze from top to bottom until the teats are empty. Then you'll need to switch and take the other two."

Unsteadily, Anette sat down. The cow moved its hind legs impatiently as she leaned in. Her hands were shaking. The teats were firmer than she expected and very warm, almost hot to the touch. She tried to squeeze the way Harriet had shown her, and a very thin stream came trickling from the right, then stopped. She squeezed some more. Nothing. The cow moved its hind legs again and turned its enormous head toward her as if to ask what she was doing.

Harriet chuckled and looked at Anette's hands under the cow without taking any notice of its tramping feet. She bent closer and placed her hands over Anette's, guiding her fingers. After a few minutes she was able to create a satisfying stream without help. But by the time she finished and asked for a second cow to work on, the other women had milked them all. She must be such a disappointment. Maybe it had been a mistake to come here. Anette straightened her back with a grimace. It was painfully stiff.

Alice noticed her dismay. "Don't worry, you did well. It gets easier after you've had some practice."

"Thank you, Alice," Anette said, hoping she was right.

The drivers were helping the women climb the wagons with their buckets, which they then emptied into the milk cans.

"Let's go," Harriet said. "It's time to get some breakfast and tend to your children."

"What do we do after that?"

"Whatever we want until it's time for the midday milking. The dairy girls will clean the buckets in the meantime. It's easier when we're driven out to the pasture. In the winter, we have to trudge to the barn and milk the cows there, it's not as pleasant. But no matter what, those cows need to get milked every day."

#

The first week Anette's arms and fingers ached so much that she had to wrap a heated, wet cloth around them before she went to bed, or she wouldn't be able to sleep. Her back hurt too and between shifts she had to lie down for several minutes to stretch it out or she wouldn't be able to walk.

But a few weeks later, she was able to milk ten cows on her own. She still wasn't as fast as the other women and usually had to walk home alone unless Harriet waited for her. It was tiring to walk after milking, but she wouldn't have felt right if she didn't insist on milking as many cows as the others. Once her body got used to the work, she found it strangely relaxing, almost mesmerizing to sit with her head against the rumbling cow stomach and let her thoughts flow as her hands rhythmically squeezed out the warm milk.

After milking, the milkmaids usually sat together outside and gossiped while their children roamed freely between the statar lodgings. Edith had already made several friends and as far as Anette could tell she hadn't said a word about their former life in the poorhouse. Maybe she thought all families lived that way.

The women kept asking her about Lund, and Anette found it surprisingly easy to tell them half truths about her life there. As she milked, she thought up new stories to share, nothing too elaborate, just enough to make it seem credible.

Sometimes she ached to open her heart and tell them the truth, but she dared not. The only ones who knew were the cows. She felt as though they could read her thoughts and she could feel their compassion. Likewise, she could feel their longing for a life where they wouldn't be enslaved to the demands on their bursting udders.

117

Chapter Twenty-four

Anette, Harriet, Alice, and Euphemia, a milkmaid who usually took the other wagon to and from the pasture, were sitting beneath an enormous oak behind the statar rows. It was wide enough for all four of them to sit side by side and rest their tired backs against the rough bark.

Euphemia stretched her arms up and touched the thick, low-hanging branch above her. "This oak must have roots as deep as Yggdrasil herself."

Anette smiled. Yggdrasil, she hadn't thought of that majestic tree for many years now. Her mother used to speak of it when she was a little girl, telling her tales of the three Norns sitting by her roots near the well of wisdom.

"Don't talk of that old tale!" Harriet said, aghast. "It's of the Underworld." Then she and Alice spat on the ground three times to ward off evil.

Euphemia exchanged a glance with Anette and changed the subject. "What do you say, girls? Would you like to come to my place tonight? I've found an onion to go with the potatoes. I'm going to fry it."

"Yes, please," Anette said, then noticed that Mr. Knutsson, or Knutsson like most of the milkmaids called him, was approaching with long, rapid strides. Hastily, she reached for her headscarf, which she had draped over a branch above her. She was still fumbling to fasten it when he arrived.

"Sorry to disturb your rest on this warm late summer day," he said, and gestured toward Anette and Euphemia. "The Baroness needs you up in the castle immediately. Go to the back door. Someone will meet you."

Anette kept her eyes at his chest, not daring to meet his eyes. Surely Knutsson thought of the time he told her she would never see the owners.

"Yes sir," Euphemia said. "We'll go at once."

Knutsson gave a tip of his hat and left as quickly as he had come.

"Oh, my dear God!" exclaimed Harriet. "What are they going to have you do for the Baroness?"

"Don't get too excited, Harriet," said Alice. "We still have our cows to milk this evening." She lifted an eyebrow. "And maybe Euphemia's and Anette's as well."

Euphemia laughed and took Anette by the arm. "Come. The quicker we go, the quicker we'll get back so these womenfolk will only have to milk their own cows."

"What do you think the Baroness wants?" Anette asked as they walked up the road to the castle. Her stomach churned with both fear and excitement.

"Maybe some of the servants are sick and she needs extra help."

"But we're just milkmaids."

Hearing that, Euphemia pulled off her apron and motioned for Anette to do the same. She took a few steps toward a bush along the road. "Let's leave these here. At least then, they won't see milk stains on us." She tossed her apron on top of it, then smoothed her hair under her scarf and retied it. "How do I look?"

"You look fine, Euphemia. But I feel dirty," Anette said nervously and placed her apron next to Euphemia's. "I didn't wash as much as I should have on Saturday." She lifted one foot at a time to make sure she hadn't stepped in cow dung, but her clogs were clean. It would have to do.

The castle was now a stone's throw ahead of them. It was as beautiful as the first time she saw it, but seemed larger so close, almost as if it were looming over them. It made her uneasy. She felt special when Knutsson selected her to go, but the closer she got the more nervous she became, wishing he had asked Alice or Harriet instead. Were they really there to see the Baroness? Or was that just something Knutsson said? It seemed very unlikely that she would personally need them for anything at all. Even if they were short of staff, like Euphemia suggested.

They walked the rest of the way in silence. When they reached the back door, a woman dressed entirely In black opened it. Her face was ashen.

"Come in," she said, "and take off your shoes." She stepped aside to let them into a large, whitewashed room, empty except for a small wooden bench in the corner with a porcelain wash bowl, a bar of soap, and a green towel. "The Baroness' mother has passed on. There are many windows and mirrors in the castle, and they all need to be covered before nightfall. I'm the head maid here. Kindly wash your hands and then follow me."

Anette turned to Euphemia, but she was already moving toward the wash bowl. This explained it then, they needed extra pairs of hands that's all. It was just odd that she hadn't sensed the death on the walk here.

The head maid picked up a lantern from the floor, and led them down a dark, narrow corridor with a staircase at the end, holding the lantern high to aid their steps.

The stairs were also very narrow and cut from the same stone as the surrounding walls. Bright sunlight greeted them when they reached the top, and the head maid opened the latch on her lantern and blew out the candle. As their eyes adjusted, she gestured toward the room with a sweep of her hand.

They were in a banquet hall with six large windows, and light reflecting in tall mirrors that lined the wall on the opposite side. The floor was black and white and resembled a huge chessboard. Anette covered her mouth to stop herself from calling out. It was stunning.

The head maid pointed to a pile of neatly folded black cloths on a chair in front of the mirrors. Beside it were two small stepladders.

"The mirrors must be covered completely. When that's done, draw the curtains and go to the next room. Bring the stepladders with you. In each room with mirrors, you'll find a pile of cloths. Then go down the main staircase and do the floors below and so on. When you're finished, you can go to the kitchen on the bottom floor. Wait for me there."

She started to walk toward the other end of the banquet hall, but stopped and turned around. "My name is Edna if you need to ask for me."

Then she was gone. They could hear the clicking of her heels as she hurried across the floor in the next room. Only barn folk had to take their shoes off, apparently.

"I can't believe we're here alone," Anette whispered and stared at Euphemia who was shaking her head. Her face had gone pale. She was afraid they would break something and then get punished for it somehow, Anette realized.

"Let's do this. We'll be careful with everything, don't worry," Anette said, and picked up her stepladder with her left hand and the cloth with the other.

Standing on their stepladders, they each took a corner of the cloth and draped it over the first mirror, moved the stepladders to the next one and did the same thing there. Lastly, they pulled the thick blue curtains shut to cover the windows.

Anette followed Euphemia into the next room. The curtains there were red and already drawn, and there were no mirrors. Three cushioned chairs and a sofa occupied the middle of the room, and bookshelves lined the walls. Several books lay strewn about on a small table in front of the sofa. It looked so comfortable. She was tempted to sit down on one of the chairs, just to try it out for a minute or two and see what sort of books they were reading.

Just as she thought that, there was a rustling sound in the next room. She stopped in her tracks and grabbed Euphemia by the arm. What if it was a ghost? Maybe they hadn't worked fast enough, and the mother's spirit had already gotten trapped in one of the mirrors. The dead mother might be upset that she had thought to look at her daughter's books.

"Did you hear it?"

"Yes! Is someone coming?" Euphemia looked terrified, but Anette didn't dare to ask if she thought it was a person or a ghost. If Euphemia thought it was a ghost too, she would panic.

"I don't know, but let's hurry."

Euphemia nodded and they both took a deep breath and rushed into the room. There was no one there, at least no one alive. Anette covered a small mirror with her eyes closed, too scared to look.

For the rest of the time, they worked quickly and quietly and didn't hear anything else. The final room before they arrived at the main staircase was empty except for three boxes stapled on top of each other in the corner.

They worked through two more floors before finding another flight of stairs at the end of a library with bookshelves so high that ladders were placed against them at various intervals, each with wheels at the bottom so they could be rolled to one's book of choice. Anette didn't dare to wonder what sort of books they were and was glad that there was nothing for them to do in there.

The stairs led down to an intimate sitting room with a fireplace and carved wooden benches covered with furs along the wall. It looked medieval.

Anette was already at the bottom step when a man strolled in with a tumbler in his hand. He had dark brown hair that was a little too long and curled at the back of his neck. His black suit looked big on him, as if it were borrowed.

He looked at Anette and nearly spilled his drink. "Oh, I thought I was alone."

"I'm sorry, sir. It may be we're in the wrong place. We've finished covering the mirrors and were told to meet Edna in the kitchen before we leave," she said as Euphemia caught up.

"I see. Just go through there," he said, gesturing behind him.

"Yes, sir," they both said at the same time. The man looked amused and raised his glass as they curtsied and hurried down the short hallway he had indicated. There was a door at the end. As they approached it, Euphemia grabbed Anette by the arm.

"Did you see the way he looked at you?" she hissed.

"What way?"

"Don't be silly. You really don't know? I'll just say…" Euphemia stopped mid-sentence when the door opened by a short, round woman who must have heard them approach. She was wearing a white apron covered with food stains of every conceivable color. Her face was bright red from the kitchen steam.

"My dear girls, don't just stand there. Haven't you ever seen a cook before? Come and get a bite to eat and have a seat by the fire. There's a thunderstorm upon us and it looks as if it's going to rain for a while. Miss Edna is with the Baroness." She wiped her hands on her apron and nodded toward a table with bread, several slices of meat, and a large brick of cheese. Anette's stomach rumbled in anticipation. And to think she had been happy about fried onions earlier.

Anette picked up a plate with blue swans in flight painted around the rim. Her hand looked dirty and chafed against the plate's beautiful shine.

The cook looked at them both with a twinkle in her eye. "Would you care for some cognac? I just poured a glass for the Baroness' brother out there and he said to share it with the staff. It's our custom to share in a time of grief."

The Baroness' brother. So that was the man they had just met.

"Go on, girls. Don't be shy. Fill those plates up. Go have a seat by the fireplace and I'll come out with a tumbler for you in a few minutes."

Carrying their plates with caution, Anette and Euphemia walked back out to the medieval-looking room. Anette was hoping the Baroness' brother had left. But there he was, holding his cognac and gazing into the fire. He was handsome in a rugged way. If she had encountered him elsewhere, she would have taken him for one of the workers.

He looked up casually as they walked in. "Please, have a seat."

They curtsied and sat down. After several moments of awkward silence, Anette said, "We're sorry for your loss, sir."

"I didn't know her very well, unfortunately."

"I'm sorry to hear that, sir."

"She was not my mother, you see. Our father remarried when we were older. When my sister married the Baron, they made a tradition of bringing our stepmother here to live with them in the summers. I still live in Switzerland where we grew up. I too usually stay here through the summer and at Christmas."

"Oh, I see," Anette said, trying to focus on her food, and wondering why he was telling them all this.

"My sister is very upset, naturally. For her it's as if she's lost two mothers."

"I'm sorry, sir." She wished Euphemia would say something and not leave her to do all the talking. Or that the cook would come with their cognac and help distract him, but she must have forgotten.

He took another sip of cognac, then gazed once more into the fire and leaned back.

She sighed with relief and threw an eye at Euphemia. She was grinning at her.

Anette hid a chuckle, feeling her cheeks grow hot as she turned her attention to the food. The sliced beef, cheese, and bread looked delicious and at least she could eat without him looking at her. Then, as she was about to take her first bite, he spoke again.

"Do the two of you work together on the farm?"

"Yes, sir," Anette said, feeling embarrassed. Even without their aprons, it was obvious.

He narrowed his eyes and glanced at Euphemia, then shifted his gaze to Anette and held it, just for a moment, before he looked back at the fire. A few minutes later he seemed to be asleep. They could finally eat.

Euphemia was right; he had noticed her.

#

It had stopped raining when they left, but their aprons had blown off the bush and lay wet and muddy on the ground. They shook them out as best they could, but they were too dirty to put back on.

"Anette, I'm sorry if I made you uncomfortable in there. I didn't mean to. You're a widow and must miss your husband."

"Don't worry about it. I do, but Jon wasn't as nice as I thought when I first met him," she said, calling him Jon without thinking. It was no matter, it might as well be him, it was a lie anyway. "And you were right, the Baroness' brother did look at me.

He's handsome too."

They both laughed and Euphemia took her by the arm and started walking.

"Anette, I wanted to ask you how you knew what I was thinking up there," she said and pointed back at the castle.

"What do you mean?"

"You told me not to worry and reassured me we would be careful when I was afraid we'd bump into something and break it. But I never said it."

Anette hesitated, fingering her ring with her thumb. She had just lied to her about Jon. Then she nodded and said, "I could tell you were worried. I sense things now and then."

"You do?"

"Yes," Anette said and looked into Euphemia's face, nervous she would think she was putting on airs, but she met her eyes calmly, and with genuine curiosity.

"Anette, do you mean that you have the sight? Can you tell the future?"

"Yes, I have the sight. I do sense the future sometimes, but not as often as I'd like. It would've been very helpful if I could. I make too many mistakes."

Euphemia squeezed her arm. "It's humanity for you, Anette, we all do. Tell me something you *have* sensed."

Anette smiled, touched by her kindness. Euphemia was nice, she could be a true friend.

"I knew about a fire once, the night before it happened. It was at the neighbors across the street. It was put out before the entire house burned, thankfully. Had I warned them when I thought of it though, I could've saved their kitchen, but what could I have said? They'd think I was crazy." They would never have opened their door to a poorhouse resident, but it was nothing she needed to tell Euphemia.

Chapter Twenty-five

On a bitter cold evening right after Christmas, Anette was hurrying home while the other milkmaids were finishing their day's work. Harriet and Euphemia had offered to take some extra cows so she could get back to Ingrid, who was sick. For nearly a week, she had run a high fever and wouldn't suckle or eat. She coughed constantly. Anette was thinking of making a mixture of honey and warm water to ease her cough, when she perceived movement in the darkness ahead of her, and heard footsteps approaching.

At first, she couldn't make out the figure coming toward her, and froze. If it was Knutsson, he might get upset with her for leaving early. She was about to turn around and head back to the barn when the figure spoke.

"I thought it was you. You're the beautiful woman who sat with me by the fire after my stepmother passed on."

It was the Baroness' brother.

Anette blushed and looked down at her clogs, not knowing how she was supposed to respond to such a compliment from someone like him. What was he doing at the statar lodgings?

"How have you been faring since last I saw you? I never properly introduced myself. My name is Erik, and yours?"

"My name is Anette Lundström, sir."

"Where are you going in such a hurry, Anette?"

"I'm sorry, sir. I know I'm leaving the cows to the others, but my youngest is sick with fever and I...I..."

"Your youngest? I didn't realize you were married."

"I'm widowed, sir."

He looked at her intently. Strangely enough, it didn't feel intrusive.

"How old is the little one?"

"She's almost a year, sir."

"It's dark. I'll walk you the rest of the way."

#

Olga and Agneta stepped out of the barn, having finished

with their cows. Olga grabbed Agneta's arm. "My Lord, who's she walking with? I thought she went home early to take care of the baby."

Agneta squinted. She didn't recognize the man but could see that he was wearing a fine coat and a fur hat. "There's only one reason such a man would be down here at night. This is terrible."

Olga pulled Agneta off the gravel path and onto the grass beside it so as not to make noise and motioned for her to follow. When they reached their statar row, they peered around the corner as Erik followed Anette inside.

Olga gasped. "She could give our babies rickets."

"Rickets? What do you mean?"

Olga threw one last glance at Anette's door as she pulled her own door open. "If a woman lays in the hay with a man she isn't married to and doesn't confess to it, the children around her could catch rickets and grow up bowlegged."

Agneta's eyes widened. "Maybe it's not the way it seems."

Olga looked at her nine-month-old son who was sleeping peacefully in his little bed. "Maybe it's not, but I don't want to take that chance."

Agneta shrugged. "What can we do?"

Olga pulled a chair away from the table and lit a candle. "Have a seat. Do you remember that stick Jan used last year to kill the snake?"

Agneta nodded.

"If we can find it, we can use it to hit Anette, not hard, mind you, just a little tap on the back of her legs. It can be done as if by accident."

"Why would we do that?"

"A stick that's been used to kill a snake has power. If she's having intimate relations, she'll become pregnant right away, and we'd know to keep our children away. Whores are usually too embarrassed to tell the truth; it's the lie that causes the sickness. My mother saw it happen herself when she was just a young girl. Her cousin got the rickets and was very sick, and his legs never straightened. Later they found out that one of the neighbor ladies was an unwed mother."

"I never knew all this, Olga."

"Yes," Olga said, her eyes shining in the flickering light. "It'll be much better for everyone to find out, and better for Anette, too, of course. If she doesn't get pregnant, then we'll know she never laid with him. We wouldn't want to falsely accuse anyone."

#

Anette stepped aside so Erik could check on her hearth. Bad air could cause illness he said, and he wanted to take a look to make sure it worked as it should.

Edith was sitting on the floor with her arms around the baby. She looked at Erik with round eyes and hugged Ingrid closer. He bent down and looked where the chute was, as if he thought it wasn't open properly, which she knew it was.

"As I thought, that hearth of yours isn't in good condition. Some of the smoke is seeping back in and it's too hot in here. I'll talk to my brother-in-law. He'll send someone to have a look at it. Good evening."

Anette didn't even think to say thank you as he left. She just closed the door behind him so Ingrid wouldn't catch a draft, then sat down next to Edith and picked up the baby, opening her blouse to feed her.

"Mamma, who was that?"

"Just a man who came to check on the hearth. Promise me you won't mention it to anybody."

Edith nodded, her round blue eyes revealing a hint of disappointment. Anette pulled her close and kissed her on the forehead. She couldn't help that she was curious.

Ingrid suckled a little harder, and Anette broke into a smile. "Look, Edith, she's eating. You've taken good care of her."

Chapter Twenty-six

Hanna

Sitting at one of the tables at the Frog, Hanna's mother sighed. "You've been married for more than four years now dear, and the café is doing well. You've shown us all that you're an independent woman, but both your father and I feel it's time you concentrate on yourself and a family. To think that I don't have a grandchild yet. It's such a joy to see little ones running around."

"So, you and Pappa talked about this behind my back?" Hanna could hear the sharp tone of her own voice but could do nothing to soften it. She could picture them sitting in the living room with their glasses of wine in the evening, both getting tipsy and talking about her and Johannes, wondering about their private lives. "It's not your business, Mamma. Some women are unable to have children. Have you thought of that?" She stood up. "And what if the Frog is enough to keep me happy?"

"Oh, dear, dear child, I didn't mean to upset you. Please, sit down."

Hanna shook her keys to show her she was ready to lock up. "I have to go home and make dinner."

"Very well," her mother said, taking her time to get to her feet. "I did want to mention before you go that science has come very far these days. Just last week I read about a new treatment for all kinds of female ailments, including hysteria."

"Hysteria! Are you implying that I'm hysterical now, too?"

"Of course not," her mother said, ignoring her tone. "I only mentioned it because the doctors who treat women for hysteria have also had success with barrenness."

"Oh, and what kind of potion or pill is that then? You know how I detest taking medicine in any form. I need to get home." Hanna took her by the arm, gripping it just a little harder than necessary. The way she had said barrenness hurt.

"It is not a pill at all. It's a new kind of massage that's supposed to be quite relaxing. There's a doctor on Kyrkogatan near the pharmacy who's becoming quite well known, Doctor Andersson. He uses a device called a mechanical-massage machine. Aunt Jessica's friend's daughter, I can't remember her name right now..."

"Karin."

"Yes, Karin, she's given birth to two healthy boys since she went to see Doctor Andersson. Twins."

"Twins?"

"Yes, twins, and a lady she met in the waiting room told her how she used to have night sweats and a racing heart and is now completely cured. I really think you should go see him. These treatments are becoming very popular all over Europe. And in Great Britain as well. I wouldn't be surprised if Ramlösa Health Spring has them too."

Hanna sighed. "One thing you should be clear about, Mamma, is that I won't sell the Frog."

"I understand, dear. We can talk more later. Are you sure you don't mind walking home alone?"

"Not at all, maybe it'll relax me." Hanna smiled to herself, noting that her mother didn't catch the sarcasm.

#

Kurt was there when she arrived home, working on the aviary with Johannes. They had already made a door in the sunroom and started on the outbuilding. It instantly put her in a better mood. While cooking, she decided to see if she could find Doctor Andersson. It couldn't hurt just to go see him. If it didn't work, she would have a beautiful aviary soon and the birds would have little babies for her to love

Chapter Twenty-seven

Anette

A man came and inspected the hearths in all the statar lodgings. He cleared the debris from Anette's and Harriet's chimney, and soon Ingrid didn't cough as much.

In late spring, she was already walking, toddling around on the grass to the delight of everyone who saw her. On some days, though, her breathing became labored, and Edith had to pick her up and carry her inside. Her daughters were inseparable, which gave Anette great peace of mind when she was milking.

#

Harriet was up first as usual, making their coffee and trying her best to conceal her grumpy mood. Anette ignored it and smiled proudly at baby Ingrid, wondering how she could be sleeping so soundly with the morning sun shining right on her face.

She got up carefully so as not to disturb her and drank her cup of coffee next to the yawning Harriet. A few moments later they were out the door.

Anette had finished six cows when she glanced up and saw Edith running across the pasture. Where was Ingrid?

Then she understood.

She screamed, dropped the milk bucket so all of it spilled across the grass, her feet, and the cow's cloven hoofs. Before Edith reached her, Harriet and Euphemia were at Anette's side, holding her up.

"Mamma, Mamma, Ingrid won't wake up. She's not moving."

Anette ran, vaguely aware that Harriet had grabbed Edith's hand and that they and Euphemia were right behind her. The cows were pastured closer to the lodgings today, but it still took a long time to get back and she had to stop to walk to catch her breath. She didn't know if the others were still behind her but didn't want to waste time even turning her head to see. When she finally reached the road that led to the lodgings, she broke into a run again and ran all the way home.

She threw open the door, then fell to her knees. Ingrid was lying on her side, her right arm pointing straight out, her little fingers rigid. Edith must have moved her when she tried to wake her up, for she had laid on her back when they left. Her face looked as it did before, peaceful and serene, as if she were asleep. Anette crawled across the floor, her heart hammering, then reached out and put her hand on Ingrid's cheek. It was cold.

In the next moment, Edith came running in with Euphemia and Harriet. Euphemia said not a word, just sat down on the floor next to the little mattress and took Anette's hand in hers. Harriet was wailing, a keening sound that ought to come from herself, but she felt as cold as Ingrid. Cold and numb.

"Is Ingrid dead, Mamma?"

Anette turned at the sound. Edith was standing in a puddle by the door. She had peed herself.

"Yes sweetheart, she is. Come here, sit with me." The sound of her own voice shocked her. It sounded too normal, as if she were asking her to come have dinner. Edith ran over and sat on her lap, the dress' warm wetness soaking through her skirts.

"I will go inform Knutsson," Harriet said. She blew her nose. "You stay here, Euphemia. I'll tell him, and then we'll call on the parson. He'll take care of everything. It's what we did when Bettan died last year."

"Good, thank you, Harriet. I'll stay here, please tell the others to leave us alone. Come back after you see the parson," Euphemia said. Then she stayed there silently, just sitting with Anette on the floor.

#

The funeral seemed like a dream. Anette could only be sure it had occurred when she visited the graveyard and kneeled before the simple wooden cross inscribed with her daughter's name, and the dates February 13, 1894 - June 7, 1895.

Chapter Twenty-eight

Hanna

Hanna stood across the street from the doctor's building, watching as two well-dressed, middle-aged ladies left. Both looked happy and energetic as they hurried down the street. Perhaps her mother was right. The pamphlet she brought to her after their conversation had described the different procedures available. Vibratory treatment and hydrotherapy, it claimed, were very modern and scientific. Each promised relief from headaches, infertility, hysteria, heart palpitations, weak bladders, and weak wombs.

She took a deep breath and crossed the street. The entrance opened into a vestibule with a mahogany chest of drawers and four mahogany chairs. On the opposite side was a large gold mirror that reflected the chairs and chest to give the impression that there was a double set. On the right was a white enamel sign with blue text, Dr. Andersson Second Floor, it read.

Upstairs, a nurse was waiting right outside the door. She was plump with a mass of brown curly hair under her nurse's hat. She smiled when she saw Hanna.

"Good day, Mrs. Agnell," she said brightly. "You're not winded from the stairs, I see, that's very good. We see a lot of women who can barely make it to the top without needing to rest for several minutes on the landing."

"It's only two short flights. I'm surprised."

"Well, many of the women who come here are not very healthy, but by the time they've finished a set of treatments, the stairs are easier. Please come with me."

They walked to the end of a short hallway and into a spacious examination room. The nurse instructed Hanna to remove her drawers, then helped to loosen her corset and had her lie back in a large reclining chair. On the wall facing it was a diploma from the Karolinska Institute and certificates from medical associations in France and Switzerland.

The nurse left the room. A moment later the doctor entered. He was trim, probably in his fifties with a graying beard, and projected an air of calmness and efficiency.

"Good afternoon, Mrs. Agnell," he said. "I understand you would like to conceive."

"Yes, Doctor Andersson, that's correct."

"How long have you been married?"

"Four years."

He nodded thoughtfully and jotted something in his notepad. To her relief, he didn't seem shocked that it had been so long.

"Do you have separate bedrooms or share one with your husband?"

"We share a bedroom."

"And you and your husband are intimate?"

"Yes." What kind of question was that? How else would she get pregnant? Surely no one came here with her problem if they didn't have sex with their husbands.

He just nodded thoughtfully again and made another notation. "Are you prone to dizziness?"

"No."

"Migraines?"

"No."

"Heart palpitations?"

"No."

"Rages?"

"Most definitely not."

"Exhaustion?"

"Not really, I do get tired sometimes after a long day at the café, but otherwise no."

He looked up from his notepad. "You work in a café?"

"Yes, I'm the owner."

"I see." His brow furrowed slightly, and he cleared his throat. "Does this tax you? Exhaustion can also contribute to infertility."

"No, it doesn't. I have a lot of free time. I oversee a baker and an assistant, they give me no trouble," she said, grateful that her mother wasn't there to hear him confirm her suspicions.

"Hmm, well, a woman's womb often becomes congested," Dr. Andersson said as he placed his notepad on a shelf. "This can cause problems with the bladder, migraines, even severe melancholia and episodes of rage. The treatments relieve the congestion by loosening the blockage."

"Will this help me have a child, even if I don't have those symptoms?"

"I think we have a chance to achieve that. As your womb frees up, it should be more open for new life. Shall we get started?"

She hesitated for a moment, then nodded.

Dr. Andersson asked her to lean back in the chair, walked to a corner of the room, and pulled out a small table on wheels. On top was a metal box with several round knobs alongside it. Some were bumpy and others appeared to be smooth. They looked like small cookies.

"This is what I use to massage the pelvic area," he said as he attached one of the knobs to a prong-like device connected to one end of the box. "I assume you've read my pamphlet?"

"Yes." Her mouth was dry. She considered asking for a glass of water but decided not to.

"You understand then that this is a safe medical procedure and there should be no cause for alarm. It may feel a bit unusual at first, but most women don't mind it after a couple of treatments. Some even find it relaxing. You'll hear a buzzing from the machine and feel a faint pressure on the vulva. Just lie back please and close your eyes."

Hanna did so, then felt him lift her skirts. She opened her eyes and looked at him in confusion. Dr. Andersson responded immediately with a reassuring smile.

"I must be able to reach Mrs. Agnell, there is no cause for alarm, I can't see anything, but for it to work properly the skirts can't hinder the procedure."

He was right, her skirts were still covering her and only his hand was beneath them, and he was sitting straight up while looking calmly at her. She nodded and closed her eyes again. A loud buzzing began, and the vibrating apparatus felt cold and odd. Above the sound of the machine, she could barely make out the doctor's voice. "It's best if you don't move around too much, just stay calm."

As he applied pressure, there was an intense burning feeling that suddenly made her sweat. The burn was spreading throughout her groin, getting more and more intense, and she heard herself calling out in surprise. After a few moments, Doctor Andersson turned off the machine, and all was silent except for the sound of her breathing as it slowed down.

He rolled his chair back and placed the instrument on the little table. "How do you feel now?"

"I'm not quite sure." Her face was flushed and she was drenched in sweat.

"What you experienced, Mrs. Agnell, was a paroxysm as your body expelled the congestion. It's perfectly normal, I can assure you. My nurse will see you now and can answer any question you may have. Just make a right when you exit here, and you'll find her door on the right. She'll set you up for the next appointment."

"How many do you recommend?"

"Let's start with twice a week first, then we'll see." He pulled his watch out of his pocket and glanced at it while he stood up. "If you'll excuse me. I have another patient."

Hanna thanked him and got out of the chair and left the examination room. That was that then, it had been fast and efficient. She would keep it from Johannes for now, just so he wouldn't be disappointed if it didn't work. The door to the stairs was open and the nurse was waiting by it when she entered the hallway.

"Please go into the office Mrs. Agnell, there's coffee if you're thirsty. I'm going to assist our next patient and then I'll come see you."

It didn't take long. By the time Hanna had poured herself coffee, the nurse entered and went to sit down at her desk.

"Sit please," she said, pointing to a chair in front of it.

"Dr. Andersson told me to set up another appointment,"

Hanna said and took a sip of coffee, then replaced the cup on the saucer.

"Good. How do you feel? Your cheeks are flushed and healthy looking already. Dr. Andersson said you're here to conceive. We've had several patients with success."

Hanna smiled and felt tears in her eyes, overcome with a sense of real hope.

"Have you really?"

"Yes indeed, you see when the womb is cleared from congestion, you'll make space for a baby. Shall we say Tuesday and Friday next week, at four o'clock?"

"Yes, thank you, that'll be fine."

Chapter Twenty-nine

Anette

Anette walked deeper into the woods than she had ever gone before. Grief sat in her chest like a stone, and she couldn't bear the whispering and sad looks on everyone's face. She had to get away. Even from Edith. Her eyes were always swollen from crying for her sister and she spent most days on the step below their door, hugging Ingrid's hat. It broke her heart to look at her.
It was getting late, and the sun sent golden beams between the thick trunks of the trees. The forest floor was covered with dense green moss and the path was carpeted with brown pine needles so soft that she couldn't hear her own footsteps. It sloped downward toward a small creek that glittered in the sunlight, blinding her for a moment. Then a flicker of movement caught her eye.

Someone was sitting by the water, resting on his haunches, and cupping his hands to rinse his face. His violin lay by his side. It was Näcken!

She gasped aloud, frantically trying to remember if she was wearing anything made of steel. It was the only thing that could protect her from him, or he would push her into the water and drown her. Her grandmother had once stuck a steel pin through her shawls, warning her about him and his dangerous music, but she hadn't worn it in years.

The snapping of a twig brought Anette back to the present and she turned to run for her life. Then she heard the creature speak.

"I didn't mean to startle you."

It was Erik.

"I thought you were Näcken," she blurted out, immediately feeling ridiculous.
He laughed, picked up his violin, and approached her.

"Näcken I'm not. But I wish I were. Then I'd know what to do with this instrument, and no one would think I sound so horrible that I have to practice here in the woods. I never imagined that I could scare a beautiful woman without playing a note."

Anette smiled, knowing she ought to reply with something witty, or at least thank him for his compliment, but she couldn't get a word across her lips.

He looked at her curiously. "What are you doing in the woods? I take it you're not here to practice the violin."

"No, sir, my daughter… she…"

"I heard. I'm so very sorry."

Before she could say anything else, he pulled her toward him and held her close. She didn't even know him; he was above her station and ought not even speak to her. Still, for some reason she felt safe in his arms and broke down in tears.

When her crying eased, he stepped back and studied her face. "Please. Come sit with me. I brought some food from the kitchen."

"I should get back. It's late."

"Nonsense, I wouldn't want you to walk back alone. It might get dark before you get home, and there are bears roaming in these woods. I can scare them off with my violin," he added with a wink.

Anette chuckled through her tears and wiped her face on her sleeve.

She knew she ought to leave. Harriet and Edith must already be worried about her. But it wouldn't be the first time she came home after they had gone to sleep, and she followed him down the little slope to the creek.

Erik sat down on a rock and gestured for her to sit opposite him on the trunk of a felled birch tree. Reaching into his satchel, he pulled out a piece of cheese wrapped in a napkin and broke it into two pieces. Her mouth watered at the sight of it, but she waited until he took the first bite and forced herself to eat slowly as he spoke.

"Your daughter… I'm partly to blame. I should have offered to do more."

Surprised, she shook her head. "You did a lot by having the hearth fixed."

"Well, I could have come back to check on how your little

one was doing. I know how it is to lose someone, and my sister still hasn't recovered from her grief. Though she should be in half-mourning by now, she insists on full-mourning, wearing all black."

"I'm sorry to hear that," Anette said. She didn't own any mourning clothes. What if he thought her inappropriate in her pale green dress?

"Thank you. My sister has even tried to contact the spirits on the other side. Have you ever been to a séance?"

"Yes, I have. I went to a spiritualist meeting once in Lund. And I have the sight, you see." Anette didn't know what made her say that, but the question had been so unexpected that she hadn't had time to think.

"Truly?" His eyes flashed to hers. "Can you tell me how it works?"

Anette kept her eyes in his for as long as she dared, sensing nothing but genuine curiosity from his question. "I was working for a seamstress who had an interest in it. She brought me. That séance though was just for show." Anette shook her head at the memory. "The woman had everyone fooled, but she was just a charlatan."

He laughed.

"I've been able to sense things since I was a child. I can find lost belongings and sometimes know if something is about to go wrong. My husband's cousin had an orange grove in California, and I could sense something wasn't right." She left it at that. It was better not to talk about her supposed husband too much. And why hadn't she been able to sense that Ingrid was going to die? She couldn't stop thinking about that, it was at the back of her mind all the time. She looked down into her lap for a moment, trying to hide the tears that filled her eyes again.

Erik nodded thoughtfully, oblivious. "You know, Anette, I shouldn't be so surprised. There's more to our world than we can understand with our brains. I had an experience once that I've never spoken of to anyone. Do you remember I mentioned my mother, my father's first wife, the first time we met?"

"Yes."

He gazed at the flowing water. "My mother and I were very

close. Not long after she died, I was sitting by myself in our church in Switzerland. Then, all of a sudden, I felt the gentle touch of her hand on my shoulder. When I reached for it and looked up, there was no one there. But I know it was her."

"I'm sure it was," Anette said. She needed to get back to Edith. To be her mother, not sit here with someone who lost his many years ago.

"Anette, I'm so sorry again for your loss. Let me take you home. If there's anything I can do. Do tell me."

"Thank you." She stood, watching when he got to his feet and picked up his violin and satchel. What could he do for her? He was the brother of a baroness, and she was just a milkmaid.

They made their way back. Erik was courteous but mostly silent, which was a relief. She didn't have the strength to keep a conversation going.

Chapter Thirty

Anette wiped her brow and shook her head while the others climbed the wagons.

"I'll walk."

No one said anything. They only nodded as the oxen slowly pulled their wagons over the bumpy grass tufts, their black-and-white spotted flanks glistening with sweat. The poor fellows had a heavy load. It was just as well for their sake that she walked. Besides, she couldn't deal with the women's gossip and giggling anymore. Sometimes she felt like screaming for them to shut up.

These days, she rode to the cows but always made her own way back, even when it rained. The walk through the pasture was healing, with the thick green and red grass, the wide vista of dense forest, and the castle in the distance.

Sometimes on these walks, she imagined Ingrid toddling along beside her. It was a comfort and she felt as if she were smiling at her.

Anette was closing the gate to the pasture when she heard the beating of hooves behind her. It was Knutsson, riding on a small black horse.

"Evening, Anette."

"Good evening, sir."

"You're wanted up at the castle. They need you there right away. Change into something appropriate, but hurry." He tipped his hat and started to turn the horse around.

"Why do they want me?"

"It's the Baroness. She wishes to see you." He kicked his heels in the horse's flanks and rode off. Anette followed him with her eyes as he galloped along the trampled oxen path and disappeared behind the oak by the barn. Erik had probably spoken of her, and now the Baroness must want to offer her personal condolences. Was that common after a death? Maybe because Ingrid had been so small.

As she approached the lodgings, she hoped Harriet was

having coffee with the others so she wouldn't have to explain why she was changing her dress at this hour, but there she was at the hearth, waiting for the coffee to boil.

"Ah, Anette, you're just in time. Everyone's in the back. Edith's out there too, running around with the other children."

"I'm glad of it. She's been doing a little better lately, I think. And thank you, Harriet, but not tonight."

"No? Olga's husband brought a bottle of brännvin to spike the coffee."

"I'm sorry, I really can't."

"You can't?"

"No, I have to change."

"All right, then."

Harriet took the kettle off the flame and headed for the door. Then she stopped and turned to Anette, spilling some of the coffee. "Change? What for?"

"Shh," Anette hushed. "Listen for a minute. Knutsson just told me the Baroness wants to see me at the castle. And he said that I have to change into something nicer."

Harriet's eyes widened and she let out a yelp of surprise. "Why?"

"I don't know. Please just help me get my blue dress on and say nothing to the others. Tell them I went for a walk."

"But why? Do you think someone else died and you have to cover the mirrors again?"

Anette shrugged.

Harriet stepped back into the room and placed the kettle on the table. "Where do you keep your dress?"

"It's in my valise. I'll get it."

The dress looked old and smelled faintly of the rosewater soap she kept in there to keep it fresh. Holding it up to show Harriet, she shook her head. "I can't wear this. Look, you can see where it's been folded."

"Let me see." Harriet grabbed the dress and carried it to the window. "No, don't worry, it's beautiful," she said, inspecting it in the summer evening's light. "Where did you get such dark blue fabric? Is it store-bought?"

"No, don't you remember I worked as a seamstress for a time before I got married. Are you certain it doesn't need ironing?"

Harriet laughed. "I'm certain. And where in God's name would you expect to find an iron?"

"Harriet, where are you with that coffee?" Olga hollered from outside. She must have heard her laugh.

Anette looked at Harriet and chuckled as she freed her arms and upper body and let her dress slip to the floor. Her undergarments were yellow with sweat stains, and she smelled of cow. Quickly, with her old dress still around her legs, she splashed some cold water on herself and soaped her face and armpits. Harriet made her lift her legs one at a time so she could get the dress up from the floor as she washed.

"We have to hurry, Anette. Soon the others will forget about the coffee and start drinking the brännvin by itself."

Once she had the new dress on, Anette hurried out. She could hear them laughing raucously. No doubt they had started without the coffee, just as Harriet feared.

Her heart was thumping harder and harder in her chest, the closer she got to the castle. She tried to take deep calming breaths as she walked to the same door she and Euphemia had entered when they were summoned to cover the mirrors.

A few moments later it opened. Edna's astonishment when she recognized her was unmistakable. She frowned as her eyes scanned the blue dress, causing Anette to lower hers in embarrassment. When she raised them, Edna had already moved ahead, and she had to catch up. Clearly, she had expected a fancier guest than a milkmaid, even if she had been asked to wait by the servant entrance. Uppity snob, thinking herself better for being a head maid.

They passed the stairs they had climbed last time and continued down a long hallway. The walls were painted with a hunting scene, and men on large horses were galloping across a field.

"Extraordinary, isn't it?" Edna said proudly.

"Yes," Anette said.

Then a woman entered the hallway, silhouetted against the light behind her.

"Thank you, Edna. I'll guide our visitor from here."

Edna curtsied and left without a word.

As the woman approached, the dim light revealed brown hair, tightly pulled back into a bun. She was wearing all black. It was the Baroness; she looked just like her brother.

"Thank you for coming, Mrs. Lundström," she said and gently touched her elbow. "Come with me. We would be pleased if you'd guide a séance for us."

A séance, that she didn't expect. Erik must have spoken of her sight too. Disappointment that he had betrayed her confidence washed over her, but she pushed it away. She hadn't actually told him not to say anything.

"I'll do my best, Baroness. But please keep in mind that the spirits come through only when they're in the mood," Anette said, hoping she sounded knowledgeable and that no one would notice that she had never conducted a séance before.

"Of course, Mrs. Lundström, I understand. I know that you recently lost your child. I want to convey my deepest condolences. I've lost a mother and you a daughter."

Anette curtsied. "Thank you, Baroness, and my sympathy for your loss."

The Baroness nodded and ushered her into a room where a small group of well-dressed people were sitting around a table, talking quietly. Anette felt the same subdued air of expectation she remembered from the gathering at Miss Ofelia's.

Erik was a sitting on a velvet-covered ottoman along the wall. He walked over and met her eyes levelly.

"I believe you've met my brother. He tells me you have a gift," the Baroness said.

Anette curtsied again and Erik looked like he was going to bow, but then he didn't.

"Everyone, this is Mrs. Lundström. She'll help us call upon the spirits tonight," the Baroness said and stepped aside to let

Anette go ahead.

She was introduced to an elderly white-haired woman named Mrs. Renault, whose face was full of wrinkles, and to Mr. and Mrs. Elvén, a middle-aged couple. Mr. Elvén wore a black suit and bow tie and had an enormous belly. His wife was also heavy and vigorously fanned herself with a dark red fan. Her forehead was pearly with sweat despite it.

They acknowledged Anette with a smile and motioned for her to take a seat next to Mrs. Renault, who touched her arm when she sat down.

"It's good to have you here, child," she said. "I hope I'll see my dear, dear Charles. He was from France, you know. Do you think you could hold the séance in French? I'm afraid he may have forgotten his Swedish by now."

"I'm sorry, ma'am," Anette said. "I don't speak French."

"Oh, you don't? That's unexpected."

"Don't worry, he'll remember," Erik said to Mrs. Renault and sat down across from Anette. He met her gaze and held it.

"Thank you," Anette said and quickly glanced away.

Then the Baroness tapped her coffee cup with a spoon. "Your attention, everyone," she said and grabbed Erik's hand. "Please place your hands on top of the table and clasp each other's hands. We must form a circle. Mrs. Lundström, you may begin."

Anette nodded and closed her eyes, trying to recall the words that Miss Ofelia had used. "We're here in peace and out of love for our dear departed. If any spirits are present, please make yourselves known." Despite her nerves, her voice was steady and clear.

At first, all she could hear was the beating of her own heart, birds chirping outside, and a clock ticking somewhere. She wished she had asked everyone to keep their eyes closed; they were probably all staring at her. Then a picture appeared in her mind's eye. "I see a man in a sleigh being pulled by a horse across a frozen lake. He's wearing a fur coat and a fur hat. There's a crack in the ice. The sleigh is falling through. The horse is being dragged down with it. It's neighing madly."

She opened her eyes, surprised to have seen something. It scared her a little. Mr. Elvén was staring open-mouthed at her.

"It was my father," he said after a long moment. "We never knew what happened. He just disappeared and we could never find him, even though there were many search parties."

"The lake must have frozen over immediately," Mrs. Elvén said.

"But why didn't the body come up in the spring?" asked Mrs. Renault.

Anette closed her eyes again and felt Mrs. Elvén's grip on her hand tighten. She tried to focus but kept hearing the awful neighing of the horse. Then it came to her. "The body is caught in a crevice."

"Dear Lord," Mr. Elvén gasped and rose from his chair.

The Baroness looked shocked. She was still holding Erik's hand on top of the table. "Where is this lake, Anette?"

"I'm sorry, but I don't know. I can only relay what comes to me."

Mr. Elvén sat back down and said, "There's a small lake on the other side of the woods. My father often took the road behind Häckeberga in those days. It was a faster route. They hadn't built the large roads yet, you see."

For the next few minutes everyone was silent. They had let go of each other's hands. Anette readied herself to stand, assuming she would be asked to leave.

But the Baroness took one look at her. "Please stay with us, Mrs. Lundström. We'll have a piece of cake and some brandy. You look a little pale."

"Thank you," she said gratefully. Her legs felt shaky, and she kept picturing the hooves scraping against the ice, the utter horror on the man's face, and his flailing arms.

"Erik, could you please ring for Edna?" the Baroness asked.

"No need, Sofia, I'll get the cake and brandy and some coffee," he said, stood up and left.

"I'll go with you," said Mr. Elvén and hurried after Erik.

Mrs. Elvén followed them with her gaze, waiting until the

sound of their footsteps had disappeared, then turned to Anette. "Mrs. Lundström, my husband's father always wore a fur hat and a fur coat in the winter. It's clear it's him. God bless you," she said and reached for her hand, squeezing it.

Anette smiled faintly, not sure what to say. It was terrible news she had brought them. Maybe it would have been better if she hadn't said anything.

"Sofia, you should see if Mrs. Lundström can ease your suspicions about that ghost you were telling me about," Mrs. Renault said.

"A ghost?" asked Mrs. Elvén.

The Baroness nodded, looking first at Mrs. Elvén and then at Anette. "It's in one of the smaller living rooms. I hear noises, and it always feels as if someone is looking at me."

"I see," Anette said. "I can try."

"Good," the Baroness said, then turned to the others and changed the subject.

Anette tried to look like she was listening politely, but she wasn't sure what they were talking about and just felt awkward. She hoped Erik and Mr. Elvén would come back soon so she could go home.

She tried not to stare when Erik and Mr. Elvén came back with the cake, but it looked so good she couldn't help it. The slices were enormous and slathered with whipped cream, fresh strawberries and powdered cocoa. Her mouth watered.

Erik sat down and looked directly at her. "You do take brandy, don't you, Anette?" He smiled at her.

"Yes, thank you," she said softly, feeling embarrassed by Erik's familiarity.

"We were just saying that Mrs. Lundström ought to come again to let us know who's haunting this castle," the Baroness said, smiling broadly at Erik.

"An excellent idea. Though you know what I think of ghosts. It's just the wind moving the curtains. But it wouldn't hurt to be sure." His eyes met Anette's briefly.

"We'll see then, won't we? I'll buy your lovely Swiss fiancée a new pair of riding gloves if I'm wrong. I know we have ghosts," the Baroness said.

Anette glanced at Erik. He rolled his eyes at his sister, but she felt him wanting to look at her. But he never did, and she averted her gaze. It was silly, but it stung to hear that he was getting married. He had been kind and sweet to her, that was all. It was just sympathy. Still, she knew he hadn't wanted her to know.

#

As she approached the statar rows, Anette could hear the others talking in the back. Before joining them, she stopped and reached into her corset. Lost in her thoughts, she had completely forgotten the envelope the Baroness had handed her on her way out. It contained ten kronor. She smiled to herself, no more thoughts about Erik. It was time to get something to drink with her own people.

Sitting around the little wooden table were Harriet, Euphemia, and her husband Lennart. They had no children, but Anette thought they had a good marriage. All three of them looked at her curiously when they saw her coming across the grass.

She ignored it and sat down next to Euphemia. "What's there to drink?"

"Harriet just made more coffee, and we saved you some brännvin. Olga and Sven drank too much and went home an hour ago."

Anette took the cup from Euphemia's hand.

"Here," Lennart said, "I'll pour you some."

"Thank you. I'm surprised to find you still up."

"We're enjoying the evening. We can sleep in tomorrow."

"Euphemia is going to church," Harriet announced.

Anette put her cup down. "You are?"

"Would you like to come?"

"No thanks," Anette said. She had had enough judgement to set foot in a church again, and church would just remind her of Ingrid's funeral.

"Me neither," Lennart said, slurring. "Come to think of it...more bramzit...brandit...bandim..."

149

"Brännvin," Euphemia said, pursing her lips.

"Just fill me up to the brim."

She poured him a half-cup. "You're a drunken fool… Maybe you should start thinking about your soul."

He burped.

"And also your body," she added. "It'll be cooler in church. The swallows have been flying low all evening. It's going to be hot tomorrow."

#

She was right. Anette woke up the next morning dripping with sweat. Edith was already awake, sitting on the little stone step outside, clutching her wooden cow and her wooden doll with hair made of sheep's wool. Lennart had carved them for her.

"Good morning, my sweet girl, have you had any breakfast?"

"No, only an apple that fell down from the tree."

"Edith," she scolded, "the apples aren't ripe yet and you'll get a tummy ache. I've told you that."

Anette patted her head, feeling a little guilty for scolding her, and went back inside to make coffee and cook the eggs she had picked up yesterday. Since she and Harriet didn't have husbands, they didn't get to have their own chickens but received eggs each week from the others. She took two and put a small log on the hearth. It seemed silly to heat up the room even more, but they had to have their coffee and eggs.

"Make me some too," Harriet mumbled from her bed. "It's so hot today. I should have gone to church with Euphemia."

While the eggs boiled, Anette buttered three pieces of crispbread and made the coffee. When the eggs were ready, she cooled them in the water bucket, peeled and sliced them, and put them in neat rows on the bread.

"Would you mind giving this to Edith? I made another one for you," she said and turned to Harriet who was now sitting up, her feet dangling over the side of the bed.

Stiffly, Harriet walked the few steps to the door, she suffered from pains in her back and legs every morning, and handed the bread to Edith, who thanked her in her sweet child's voice.

Anette stared unseeingly through the window at the apple tree outside. Some of her sadness had lifted a little. They were safe and happy here, despite everything. If she compared it to the poorhouse, it was paradise. It used to smell so bad on hot days. She would survive, Ingrid was safe in heaven with her mother. She put their breads on a plate and placed the pot of coffee on the table and smiled as Harriet limped back.

"So, what did they want last night?" she asked and sat down.

"They needed help with folding. I never saw the Baroness," Anette lied.

Chapter Thirty-one

Hanna

Vanda arrived at the Frog an hour before their meeting was to begin. Reaching into her carrying bag, she pulled out a bottle wrapped in brown paper and handed it to Hanna.

"Open it!"

There were several layers of paper and Hanna unwrapped them one by one, periodically glancing at Vanda.

"Champagne?" she asked disbelievingly when she finally had the shiny dark green bottle in her hands. "Are you leaving the temperance movement?"

Vanda laughed. "No, quite the opposite, I've gotten a legal separation from my husband." She took the bottle and kissed Hanna on the cheek. "I thought we could make an exception before the others arrive."

"Yes please, with such a victory we certainly can't be expected to drink coffee."

Vanda laughed again, and Hanna went into the scullery to find glasses. When she returned, Vanda had drawn the curtains and was beaming at her through the dimness.

"I thought it best to cover the windows," she said, pushing the cork until it popped off and flew across the room, champagne bubbling down her hand and arm.

It almost seemed symbolic; it was the same arm that her husband had broken. Touched, Hanna smiled and hurried toward her with the glasses.

"You're very wise, lest someone sees us going against our own principles," she said, and winked, then handed Vanda her glass.

Vanda looked at her warmly. "Skål, Hanna, thank you for being here for me. Without your women's group or Magnhild and Bengta, I don't know what I would have done."

"Skål," Hanna said as well, and took a small sip. It was tasty, dry and refreshing. "It's why we're here, truly. I'm glad you found it helpful. It must have been hard for you these few years. Why did it take so long to become legal?" She sat down at the table closest to the counter, putting her feet on a chair. Her feet ached from standing all day.

Vanda drank half her glass, then refilled it as she crossed the floor. "It was Alexander, he refused to meet with our parson to have that first conversation so we could go before a judge." She sighed and sat down in front of Hanna and put her own feet next to hers on the same chair. "It's been strange Hanna," she said and leaned back, "all this time he's paid for my apartment, admitting to the fact that he hurts me and that he understands why we couldn't live together."

"Really? I didn't know that," Hanna said, a little shocked. Vanda's apartment was large and modern and on one of Lund's finest streets. She had assumed that Vanda had a trust from her parents that paid for it.

"Yes, Alexander is wonderful when he doesn't drink. He's kind with an artistic philosophical mind. It's what drew me to him. I find it very attractive. It's the musician in him, I assume. And I, being a painter, relate to that side of him."

Hanna nodded, remembering Johannes telling her about his extraordinary talent. Maybe they were lovers when he was sober. If Vanda didn't keep alcohol at home, maybe she let him inside sometimes. "I'm sorry, Vanda. Do you miss him still? You're still happy that it's over, aren't you?"

Vanda raised an eyebrow, pulled her feet off the chair, and poured Hanna more champagne. "Yes, yes! I'm ecstatic. I missed him in the beginning, but every time I felt weak, I thought of his fists and there was nothing that could get me to change my mind. No number of roses sent, letters, nothing."

Hanna took another sip, feeling a little ashamed for what she had thought before.

"What made him agree to sit down with the parson? And what about your apartment, can you still live there?"

"Yes, I can, Alexander has given me money. God knows he has enough of it. He's moving to Germany." Her eyes glinted. "I'll be rid of him forever."

"That's good, Vanda," Hanna said, swirling the champagne in her glass, watching the bubbles disperse. There must be so many women who had nowhere to go, stuck in abusive marriages with no way out, with no one to give them money or apartments. Maybe some would be so scared and desperate that they killed their husbands in their sleep. What if he was so drunk that she could put a pillow over his head, would the police be able to figure out that he hadn't just died in his sleep?

"Hanna, what are you thinking about?"

"Sorry, nothing, I was just distracted." She looked at Vanda and changed the subject. "We finished the aviary yesterday. Elsa is taking over for me tomorrow and Johannes and I are going to Malmö to buy birds."

"Oh, how nice," Vanda said, looking toward the door as they heard the sound of several hands knocking on the glass. They heard Magnhild's voice. "What's Hanna doing? She's closed all the curtains. Is she renovating?"

Hanna shook her head and laughed. Renovating, Magnhild knew her well. And just when she had spoken of their newly finished aviary.

"Quick, give me the glasses and the bottle and I'll get mint leaves for our breath," Hanna whispered and then tiptoed to the counter, plucked a couple of mint leaves off her frog cookies and hid the bottle in a cupboard.

"It's open, Magnhild," she hollered as she handed Vanda her baked mint leaf.

Chapter Thirty-two

Anette

A month later, Anette was summoned back to the castle. This time, Knutsson told her to come in the afternoon directly from the midday milking. She wished he had told her in private, but everyone heard, and she saw Olga and Agneta exchange a glance. Olga's lips set in a thin line, and Agneta gave an almost imperceptible shake of her head. For a moment she considered telling them everything so they would at least know why, but then they would think she was bragging, and she left it alone.

The Baroness was standing on the lower terrace in front of the wide stone steps leading up to it. A beige hat shielded her eyes from the sun. She was pruning a cascade of blue and red flowers overflowing a large stone vase. Anette glanced at her and continued toward the back door, but the Baroness waved for her to come up the steps. She approached and stopped right at the edge of the last step, keeping a respectful distance.

The Baroness pointed to the flowers with the tip of her clippers.

"Aren't they beautiful?"

Anette curtsied. "Yes, Baroness, they are."

The Baroness cut off a bunch of brown leaves with quick, competent hands. "There, that should do it," she declared, then put down the clippers and pulled off her gloves.

"Wait right there," she said, and hurried up the next set of steps to the upper terrace and disappeared inside. A few minutes later she reappeared hatless. For a moment it seemed as if she was about to take her arm, but she walked ahead down the steps and started across the lawn. Anette followed her, looking at her back and feeling foolish.

In the shade of a large pine at the edge of the lawn, Mr. Elvén, Erik, and another man, the Baron most likely, sat around a little table covered with a white tablecloth. Mr. Elvén stood up immediately and held his hand out for Anette to shake while the

Baroness sat down next to her husband. Anette took his hand, and he held on to it for much too long. She felt dirty and worried that she was reeking of cow. At least it was fall, and she hadn't been milking in the barn; that would have made it much worse.

The Baron barely nodded. Anette curtsied, but he didn't seem to notice. Mr. Elvén pulled out a chair for her at the end of the table right next to Erik and sat down beside her.

"Mrs. Lundström, you have given our entire family closure. It was just like you said it was. They found my father's remains in a crevice between two boulders at the bottom of the lake."

"I'm very sorry," she said, hoping it was the appropriate response.

Mr. Elvén placed his hand lightly on her arm and pulled an envelope from the inside pocket of his coat. "Here, a small token…"

"Martin," the Baron interrupted sharply. "We had agreed to ask her a couple of questions first."

The Baroness frowned and Erik looked away, resting his gaze on the castle's copper roof.

"Tell me the truth, Mrs. Lundström," the Baron said disdainfully. "How did you know about Mr. Elvén's father? Did you hear about it somewhere?"

"No, Baron, I hadn't heard about it. I sense things."

The Baron leaned forward in his chair and studied her face. She caught his gray eyes for a moment before she averted hers. Immediately a thought came to her. He was homosexual, and everyone knew, but no one ever talked about it.

"Do you not recall reading about the disappearance of Mr. Elvén's father in the newspaper a few years ago?" he asked.

"Oh, for God's sake, Anders," the Baroness interjected. "She's a milkmaid. Why would she read the newspaper?"

Anette winced. She could milk cows and read at the same time if needed.

Erik stood up abruptly. "I'm sure Mrs. Lundström has things to attend to." He took her by the elbow and nearly lifted her out of her chair. She only managed a quick thank you and goodbye before he had pulled her away.

"I'll take you back this way," Erik said when they were out of earshot. "It's a nice shortcut." He stepped aside to let her walk ahead of him on a narrow, sloping trail.

"I must apologize for my brother-in-law, Anders can be a brute," he called ahead.

Before she could respond, Erik started sliding toward her on the now steeper path.

"My shoes aren't made for hiking," he laughed as she turned to face him.

Her wooden clogs remained solidly planted. They were inches apart and she could feel his warmth. She noticed how blue his eyes were. Erik tried to step back but slid even closer. Instinctively, she reached out and grabbed his arm to steady him.

"Thank you, Anette," he said and put his hand over hers on his arm. Their eyes met and they both pulled their hands away at the same time. Then his mouth was everywhere, on her lips, her cheeks, and her neck. She kissed him back and his arms went around her waist. It felt so good to feel another adult so close to her. Then a lone cow mooed in the distance as if to remind her of who she was. She pulled herself away.

"You have a fiancée."

Her words passed over his face like a shadow. "You're right. I do. She seems so far away. Antoinette is very different from you." He touched her cheek gently, keeping his eyes in hers. "You, Anette, are strong and so alive." Then he turned and went back up the slope. She was acutely aware of the moment his hand left her face.

Her heart pounding, she continued her descent, half hoping he would change his mind and come after her but relieved when he didn't. The path led through a cluster of birches and there was the bridge. She crossed it, then picked up her pace. It had been a moment of weakness only. If he came to look for her, she would have to tell him to leave her alone. Or maybe they could just talk like they had done in the woods. She might let him kiss her a little. He would leave for Switzerland soon anyway.

#

When the milk cans had been filled and the women placed

their milk stools on the wagons, Anette watched as Euphemia waved at Harriet and Alice instead of climbing up behind them.

"I want to walk today," she said and fell in beside her, then without taking her eyes off them, lowered her voice and asked, "Anette what happened yesterday? You have been so quiet all morning."

Anette grabbed her arm to get her to stop walking. "Euphemia stay here for a bit with me, I have to tell you something."

"I knew it. Does the Baroness want you to take over for Edna? Is that why Knutsson came for you?"

"Edna? Lord have mercy. No, it's nothing like that." She shook her head. "Euphemia, please, can I ask you to keep what I'm about to tell you between us?"

"Yes of course."

Anette gave a short nod, hoping she was right to confide in her, and nervous about her judgement. "I've been to the castle several times, even to do a séance. And Erik and I keep running into each other."

"Erik?"

"The brother, the man who was sitting by the fire that day."

"Oh, him?" Euphemia's eyes widened, but Anette only saw curiosity in her expression.

She told her everything, beginning with the time Erik saw her leaving the barn early and came inside to look at their hearth, the séance, and how he comforted her in the woods after Ingrid died.

"I don't even know where to begin, Anette," Euphemia said when she finished. "It's remarkable that you could tell them about someone drowning, after all that time too. And the baroness' brother, he sounds very kind, but please be careful."

"There's more. Yesterday we kissed." She held her breath.

"You kissed the baroness' brother! Anette, have you lost your senses?" Euphemia clasped her hand over mouth.

"I know. I have. And I don't know what to do. What if he, not what if, when he comes to look for me, what should I do?"

"You have to say no, Anette. You can't possibly consider taking him on as a lover. Please tell me you're not?"

"But he's been very sweet to me. It feels like he cares for me." Anette could hear how stupid it sounded. She had been through this and should know never to trust a man ever again.

Euphemia stared at her, then she slowly shook her head. "Anette, this isn't a farmer or a worker you're dealing with. Erik lives in a completely different world than us. Don't be a fool, Anette. He isn't even going to give it a second thought if he gets you pregnant."

The truth of her words stung, and she swallowed hard. "I just hoped there was a way I could make sure he *doesn't* get me pregnant."

"Anette, what are you thinking? That's a sin."

She scoffed. "There are a lot of things that are sins for women men don't need to think about because they can pretend nothing ever happened. I refuse to let myself be scared by the parson's talk of hellfire."

Euphemia gave her a surprised look, and they started to walk, continuing silently until they could see the fence-gate ahead of them. Alice's and Olga's husbands were cutting firewood on the other side. Euphemia stopped again.

"You could use sheep's wool. Mix it with sour milk and put it inside yourself before you see him. A man's seed dislikes the smell of it and runs back out again," Euphemia said and looked at her sideways. Her face was deep scarlet. Then she briskly headed toward the fence, opened the gate and turned back to Anette.

"Are you coming?"

She exhaled.

That night, Anette poured some milk into a little cup, which she placed underneath the kitchen sofa and covered with a saucer. Then she pulled off a big piece of the sheep's wool that Lennart had used for hair on Edith's doll. If Edith complained, she would tell her the doll's hair was getting too long and needed trimming.

The next morning, she soaked the sheep's wool in the soured milk, hid it in her hand and snuck out to the outhouse while Harriet and Edith were still asleep, then pushed it inside herself.

#

But Erik didn't come, and Knutsson didn't tell her to visit the castle again. Anette was more disappointed than she wanted to admit to herself, and embarrassed that she had imagined that Erik would have real interest in her, a statar woman. In her eyes, she had risen in life after years in the poorhouse, but most people thought statare were no better than chattel. She had heard the leers from people passing the farm in their fancy wagons, seen them spit in disgust while shouting after them; dirty statar packs, low lifers, or just statare in a tone of voice that made it clear what they thought.

Still, after pulling out the wool each night, she filled her cup with new milk to sour to have it ready for her outhouse visit in the morning.

And then a week later when she came back to the statar rows in the evening, having walked home alone again, she saw him approach, walking toward the barn with fast determined steps. She stopped, heart in her throat. Maybe he had an errand, a need to speak to Knutsson who usually stayed in the barn until late. She shouldn't assume he was looking for her.

Then Erik saw her and waved. He smiled; a broad, happy smile that went right through her, warming her heart, and he turned, heading straight toward her. Her stomach fluttered with embarrassment when she thought of the sheep's wool inside of her. The first day she had been scared it would fall out, but it never did. She could still go inside, just wave back politely and walk away, showing him with her actions that she couldn't let him near her. But she stayed where she was, feet planted firmly on the ground, happy he was finally coming. A door opened somewhere and slammed closed, and she heard the fast approach of clogs on the path between the rows of statar lodgings.

"Anette, what are you doing out here? Isn't Edith waiting for you?" It was Olga.

Anette faced her, first throwing a glance at Erik who had now slowed his steps, but she was sure Olga had already seen him wave at her from her window. She inhaled deeply, hoping she wouldn't blush, and decided to wave back to Erik as if there was nothing to it.

"Hello Olga," she said, then casually moved her head in Erik's direction, "Evening sir," she added and waved.

Olga's eyes were wide as she shifted her gaze back and forth between the two of them. Anette gave her a satisfied smile and looked her right in the eye.

"Edith is fine with Harriet. That's the Baroness' brother," she said, realizing that she didn't know his last name. "Euphemia and I encountered him when we covered the mirrors in the castle after the Baroness' mother's passing. I should go see what he wants. The Baroness may need my help again," she said haughtily. Olga had earned it after that sour look she and Agneta had given her the other day.

But Olga narrowed her eyes and pursed her lips. "The Baroness is sending her *brother* down here for that?"

"I don't know, as I said I'm going to see what he wants," Anette replied icily.

"You do that, Anette, and you tell me what he wanted." At that she gave Erik a sidelong glance, turned on her heels and went back to her lodging. Anette let out a long breath and walked over to Erik who had stopped by the big oak. She didn't hear Olga's door close, more likely than not she was still watching.

Erik must have had the same thought because his eyes glinted, and he looked like he was trying not to laugh. "Mrs. Lundström, my sister needs your help. Will you kindly come with me?" he said, much louder than necessary.

"Absolutely sir," she said just as loud. He winked at her, clearly knowing exactly what she was doing and that she had known why he came. There was no turning back now. They started walking, Erik keeping a respectful distance from her until they were well out of sight where the road turned toward the bridge and out of view.

There he pulled her into his arms, laughing softly and kissing her forehead. He smelled of tobacco and soap. "What was that about? Who is she?"

"It's Olga, she's nosy and just jealous. She overheard Mr. Knutsson last time when he asked me to go to the castle when Mr. Elvén came to thank me."

"Ah, I see." He grinned. "I hope it's not giving you trouble, Anette?"

She shook her head and smiled, wishing she could have seen Olga's face when she heard Erik telling her his sister needed him.

"I'm so glad to see you. I can't stop thinking about you. Would you come inside with me today? Sofia and Anders aren't home. We'll have some wine and talk." He kissed her cheek and her lips, then met her eyes and pulled back. "Only if you want to, I won't push you into anything. I'm sorry that I came on so strong the other day." His eyes were warm and kind. She did trust him, but surely his intentions were clear. He wanted more than talk.

"I don't even know your last name," Anette said shyly, then added, "It's fine, and I do want to come."

"It's Lövcrantz, I'm Erik Lövcrantz," he said, then put his arm around her shoulder, and they crossed the bridge. She wondered if he would let go of her so none of the servants would see them from the windows, but he kept his arm in place all the way to the grand entrance before letting go.

As soon as he opened the door, Anette was struck by the reality of who she was. And who he was. They were in an enormous vestibule; one she hadn't encountered with Euphemia. A crystal chandelier, sparkling with light, hung from the ceiling. Large planters with palms and ferns filled both corners in the back. In front of each were beige silk upholstered sofas, standing on red and blue area rugs. She didn't fit in here. It would be better to leave.

"Erik, I," Anette began, but he was oblivious to her discomfort and took her hand, pulling her toward a room on the left. Everything in there was covered with white sheets. They walked through it, then reached the same stairs she recognized from when she was there with Euphemia.

"My rooms are on the fourth floor, I apologize for all the stairs," he said and let her go ahead of him.

But climbing the steps invigorated her. Erik had been nothing but kind to her, and she had protection. Bless Euphemia. It had to work. She and Lennart had no children at all. When they reached his floor, she was winded but felt less awkward.

Erik's room was smaller than she had expected. There was a mahogany secretary against the wall on the right, stacked with notebooks and newspapers, and a table with three chairs on the left in a little window alcove. Straight ahead was another door, half open, the bedroom probably. Her stomach fluttered and she noticed Erik smiling at her, and they both laughed.

He went to his secretary and opened one of the doors on the bottom, pulled out a bottle of red wine and two wine glasses. Then he moved the newspapers, revealing a plate with cheese, bread, and fruit. He had hidden it so she wouldn't see at first.

"Did you want to surprise me?"

"Yes, I did," he said with a one-sided smile, motioning for her to sit while he brought everything over to the table. He filled their glasses. "I didn't know what you would think, me dragging you up here like this. I thought it would be too obvious, but then I already blurted out that I had wine, anyway. I admit I'm a little nervous about all this."

She stared at him. He was nervous? Did she mean so much to him, or did he just want to get her in bed?

Erik took several small sips of his wine while his eyes glinted with a look she couldn't read.

"Anette, I owe you an explanation. As you know now, I am engaged to be married." He drank some more of his wine. "I could pretend and tell you it isn't true, but I don't want to be dishonest. She lives in Switzerland, and we're meant to get married next year. I hadn't planned to feel like this." Erik took a couple of pieces of cheese and ate them, then bit into a plum.

Anette blushed. Her silence felt awkward, but she couldn't think of anything to say. She became aware of Erik's every breath, the way he sipped his wine and the way his hands moved. He put his glass down and looked at her.

"Anette, I have very strong feelings for you." He stood.

Before she knew it, she was standing too, kissing him while he pulled her scarf off and let it slip to the floor, freeing her hair. They moved into his bedroom and all she could think about was how good she felt, how much she wanted him. They lay down on his bed and he pulled her skirts up and undid his trousers. For a fleeting moment she was scared that he would notice the sheep's wool, but he didn't seem to, and she relaxed, enjoying his body and the closeness, grateful she wouldn't get pregnant.

Afterwards, Erik fetched the wine, fruit and cheese from the other room, and they sat wrapped in his blankets, eating and talking until it was very late. He asked her about her life in Lund and she had no choice but to lie. Telling him the same story she told everyone else, that she had been married to Jon, who drowned one night when he had drunk too much. It felt wrong, but what else could she do?

Erik told her that his family owned a Swiss watch company, which was why he and his siblings, he had one more sister, had grown up in both countries.

When she started to yawn, he walked her back. It was cold and completely dark, and she dared to let him take her all the way to her statar row, trusting that the darkness and the lateness would hide them from curious eyes.

Chapter Thirty-three

Hanna

Johannes held the door open for her, and Hanna carefully carried the covered cage with their new parakeets inside, going directly into the living room without taking off her shoes. She put the cage on the table outside the aviary. Thor, Tobias, and Selma Lagerlöf were sitting on their rope, looking at them with their little black eyes.

"I think we should put the cage inside the aviary first to see how Selma and the boys react, shouldn't we?" Hanna said and watched Johannes as he put the bag of birdseed they had bought on the floor and opened the box with new bird toys and swings. It was what the breeder had recommended, but she had been nervous all the way home on the train that Johannes would insist on just releasing the birds. He pulled out two strings with a row of colorful balls and shook them, then finally looked at her.

"Yes, I agree. I'll find places for these first, then bring the cage in." He shook the ball strings again. "We'll hang it somewhere and see how it goes."

Hanna let out a breath of relief.

As soon as Johannes stepped inside, Tobias and Thor flew over and landed in his hair, sitting there side by side while he attached a swing to one of the longer perches in the corner on the left side. The aviary had come out better than they had both hoped for. The front wall of their sunroom had been taken out and replaced with thin bars, wide enough to see through, but not enough for the birds to squeeze through. They had built a door with tinted glass so the birds wouldn't hurt themselves by trying to fly into the living room. The birds had a lot of space, even when not including the outdoor aviary that was closed now because of the chilly weather. There were perches attached between the walls, ropes hanging from the ceiling, and they had two small apple trees in giant pots with nesting boxes tied to the branches.

Hanna had given up on having ferns and other plants in

there after Professor Karlsson had explained that some indoor plants might be toxic for birds. She had been disappointed at first, having pictured a greener space, but the apple trees did surprisingly well. Her dream of having several species of birds had changed too. It could be done but might cause fighting between the birds and they had decided to stick with parakeets. Tobias and Thor were green and Selma Lagerlöf, named after the famous woman author, was blue. She was a little overwhelmed by her two suitors and hadn't settled down to nest yet like they had hoped. Professor Karlson had recommended that they get a much larger flock so she wouldn't be the only female. And today they had bought six more parakeets, three females and three males. All the boys were green, two of the girls were blue, and one was yellow.

"It's ready, the toys are up, bring them in," Johannes said and opened the door with Thor and Tobias still on his head, and Selma who had hopped onto his left shoulder. They all looked so cute, even Johannes. She picked up the cage and went inside, kissing him as soon as he had closed the door behind her. He smiled excitedly and pulled the towel off the cage. All six birds peeked up at them, cocking their heads from side to side.

"Oh, they're darling Johannes. Look at them! I love them already." Just as she said that, Selma squawked and lifted off Johannes' shoulder, landing on the cage. It sent the six inside flying around their tiny temporary space, tumbling around each other in fright. Hanna put her hand in front of Selma and pushed her finger into her belly so she would seat herself on it, but Selma just jumped over it and attached herself to the latched cage door, chirping angrily. Thor joined her and they both sat there staring at their new friends who were now squawking at them from the opposite side of the cage. Johannes and Hanna looked at each other, and Johannes shook his head with disappointment.

"This won't work. They'll be too stressed in there. Maybe we could let them out in the outdoor space. It's only September, it's not that cold," Hanna said, but wasn't convinced it was the right decision.

"I don't know, I think they'd start a territory in there and then they'd fight when they join each other. I think? I'm not sure. What if we keep half the cage covered so they can hide if it's too much, but still keep them in here?" Johannes said and put the towel over half the cage. It slid right off.

"For Christ's sakes," Hanna cursed, then swallowed her frustration and said, "We could clip it on, but the cage is so small. There won't be much hiding space."

Johannes sighed, and they exchanged another frustrated glance.

Then they both spoke at the same time, "Professor Karlsson!"

"He should be home. I'll take the bicycle and ride over there and see if we can borrow a cage," Johannes said with a broad smile of relief. "Let's cover the cage again, then we leave it in here so they can smell each other."

Hanna nodded and wiped her forehead; she was soaked in sweat. Johannes barely took time to say goodbye before he hurried out the aviary door, ran across the floor and out the front door. She stared after him, praying that Professor Karlsson would indeed be home and have a cage they could borrow. Hopefully, he didn't have any wild rescues at home that needed it.

She gently pushed Tobias, Thor and Selma off the cage, covered it, and hung it on the strongest branch in one of the apple trees. Thor flew to her shoulder and sat there watching while she added birdseed and water to their bowls. Johannes had made what they called a windowsill on the living room side, so they could sit on their couch and watch the birds eat. They had taken to have their dinners there instead of in the kitchen. Hanna usually snuck in treats for the birds before they sat down to dinner, but Johannes never noticed. She didn't have the heart to tell him about it. He was convinced that the birds wanted to eat because they were eating.

An hour later Johannes burst through the door with a large birdcage and Professor Karlsson close behind, smiling widely and clasping his hands together when he spotted the aviary.

"This is marvelous, Hanna," he said, calling her by her first name as he usually did in private. "And gorgeous parakeets, which one is the author?"

She grinned. "Johannes told you? The blue one is Selma Lagerlöf. Kurt is going to make her a writing desk. One drawer will be permanently pulled out and filled with toys."

Professor Karlsson laughed heartily and exchanged a merry glance with Johannes, who chuckled. Then all three of them entered the aviary and placed the cage on the floor. It was so large it reached Hanna's waist.

"Did you bike home with this?"

"No, Professor Karlsson's neighbor has his own horse and carriage and lent it to us, it's why I brought the Professor with me, so he could drive," Johannes said.

"That's very kind. Thank you, Professor Karlsson. I was so worried earlier, this should work better, I think. Won't it?"

He nodded confidently.

Johannes filled the little water and seed containers that were attached to the bars of the new cage while Hanna lifted the other cage off the branch. She pulled the towel up and opened the cage door, placing it snug against the already opened door of the bigger cage. The little doors were almost the same size. Hopefully, the birds wouldn't sneak past the gap. The boys and Selma were sitting on one of the higher wooden perches, too shy to fly down with the professor there. Then Hanna pulled the towel all the way off. All six birds sat tightly together on the perch, seeking comfort from each other. They stayed put.

"How will we get them to fly into the other cage?" Johannes asked.

"We'll have to wait," Professor Karlsson said, but gently tapped the bars behind the birds. They immediately jumped across to the opposite wall near the little door. He followed them with his finger and tapped again and then, as if by miracle, each of the six birds flew straight into the other cage. Johannes quickly reached over and closed their door.

"Well done for an accountant," Professor Karlsson said, and they all laughed.

"Aren't they little darlings? Look at them, I can't wait to

introduce them to their husbands and wife," Hanna said and looked at one of the males that was already eating from the seed container. They were so cute when they ate, their little beaks made such nice chewing sounds and they looked so satisfied with themselves. She made a chirping sound and all six of them turned to look at her, then out of the corner of her eye she saw Thor lift off from the apple tree.

"Come here, darling," she said, holding out her finger, and he flew right over and sat down. "Let me tell you about your new friends."

Chapter Thirty-four

Anette

"How was the Baroness last night?" Olga asked and sat down beside her on the wagon, eyes boring into hers. Anette looked back at her calmly, sensing confusion, but not malice from Olga's expression. The other women went abruptly silent.

"I didn't see the Baroness. She had put out embroidered handkerchiefs for me to stitch. Someone must have told her I used to be a seamstress in Lund," she lied, pushing down a hint of shame, grateful that Euphemia wasn't on the same wagon.

"Oh, I see." Olga looked disappointed. She braced herself when the oxen made a sharp turn. "Someone like her can't have new ones bought?"

Anette shrugged.

"That's why you came home so late yesterday, Anette? I heard you come in, I thought you had been on one of your walks again," Harriet said.

"I had planned to, but I didn't have time. It was very late when I was done."

"You walked home alone in the dark?" Olga asked, adding a tsk tsk.

Anette nodded, expecting her to tell everyone that Erik had seen fit to fetch her, but wouldn't walk her back. She couldn't well tell her that he had. But Olga said nothing.

Agneta looked at Olga for a moment, then turned to Anette. "Weren't you scared, Anette?"

"Yes, I was. Especially when I crossed the bridge and was on the road. I felt as if someone was there staring at me. Or maybe there was a wolf or a bear," she said while thinking of Erik's warm arm around her waist. She had been scared that someone would see them, so it wasn't completely untrue.

Olga narrowed her eyes.

"People like that think only of themselves," said Harriet. "I take it she didn't pay you for it? They think we should be grateful living here, but come Slack Week, then no matter what we've done for them, we'll get nothing.

#

The sheep's wool started to itch. First it was just a slight irritation, but one afternoon several weeks after she started using it, it burned and itched so badly she had to run to the outhouse. Making sure the door was latched, she put one leg up on the seat, pushed her fingers in, grimacing as her rough skin scraped against her insides, and pulled the wool out. It stunk something fierce. It couldn't be good for her. She stared at the locked door, overcome by a wave of nausea and cold sweat, remembering how the midwife at the House had explained why she had washed her hands so many times. What if this made her sick? Could you get childbirth fever even if you hadn't given birth? Another wave of nausea hit her. There was just enough time to make sure she aimed at the right place before closing her eyes so as not to have to look at all the shit and pee in the bucket below the seat, before vomiting. It made her weak in the knees, but she felt better immediately. The itching had stopped as well. Unlatching the door, she went back out into the fresh air and tossed the wool in a bush. Edith hadn't played with her doll for a quite a while. She would cut off the wool hair and simply do what the midwife, Miss Pålsson, was her name she remembered now, had explained, and wash the wool thoroughly with soap before she used it again. And if Edith became upset, she would just ask Lennart to make her new hair. They must have a stash somewhere. Anette laughed to herself. That's how he had the sheep's wool in the first place. It was Euphemia's.

It was getting colder and darker, and the cows were moved into the barn for the season. Edith usually went with Euphemia for a while in the early evenings. Euphemia enjoyed helping her with schoolwork, and afterwards Edith watched while Lennart carved figures and animals out of blocks of wood. She had a whole herd of cows now that he made for her, and the doll had new hair as well. Anette used the pretext of walking Edith over there, then snuck away to see Erik before Harriet asked where she was going.

She hurried, clogs in hand so no one would hear her steps,

171

heading diagonally across the grass behind the lodgings to Erik who would wait at the edge of the woods. The sound of branches crackling and leaves rustling in the dark, always set her heart beating until she heard his voice. Ever since she lied about walking home alone and fearing bears and wolves, she imagined them coming for her, pouncing on her at the smallest gust of wind. Today the wind was roaring, and a branch was rubbing against a trunk or something, making a squeaky sound so loud she didn't hear him until he was right beside her. She screamed aloud.

Erik covered her mouth and put his mouth close to her ear. "Shh, just stay still," he hushed.

They heard doors slam and windows being pushed open. With her heart still pounding, she leaned into him, staring toward the lodgings. There were only three windows facing their direction, but it was enough. She recognized Alice's silhouette and then her husband appeared, opened the window, and stuck his head out.

"Anyone there?" he called.

Erik kept his hand over her mouth, and she felt his breath tickling her ear. Then Alice's husband pulled his head back in and Alice closed the window and drew the curtain.

Erik put his mouth closer yet and whispered, "Let's go now, quick but quietly." Taking her hand in his, he pulled her straight back between the trees. She followed blindly until she felt the smoother ground under her bare feet and knew they were on the trail. She pulled out of his grip and bent down to put her clogs on, feeling something tug in her lower abdomen. It must be her courses coming, hopefully Erik wouldn't notice.

"That was close. I'm so sorry I screamed, I thought you might be a bear."

"A bear, at least you didn't think I was Näcken again. I have a tendency to scare you. I must improve upon myself. This won't do. What are you going to think of me next?" he said, completely deadpan.

She laughed, then told him about the questions from Olga and the other women.

"Ever since I told them, it's been on my mind. It's silly, but I can't help it." She thought he would laugh, but instead he touched her cheek with his hand, and she perceived him shake his head in the darkness.

"I'm sorry Anette, it was I who told you about bears that first time, remember?"

"No."

"Yes, when I insisted walking back with you, that time when I had been playing violin."

"Oh, I forgot." She had forgotten, not that he had scared her, but that he had spoken of bears.

Erik chuckled. "Anette, I just said that so I would have a reason to walk with you. It's not impossible, but they're more common up north, rarely seen down here in the south." He put his arm around her, and they started walking. "Anette, I wish things were different. I'm the one who should apologize, not you. Apologize for you having to sneak away to meet me in the woods like this. It's not right. Anette, I love you. I wish I'd met you earlier." He stopped walking to look at her, and she felt him waiting for her to say that she loved him back.

Her eyes had adjusted to the dark, and she saw the hope in the way he held himself. It was just so hard to admit it, painful to allow herself to love him when she knew she could never have him. He would leave soon, go back to Switzerland to his fiancée. She had been afraid to ask why he hadn't left, afraid he was staying for her, but equally afraid there was another reason, that she was just a pastime for him until he could go home.

"Anette, do tell me you love me," he prompted and kissed her so gently that she forgot her fear.

"I love you," she said, and he laughed his soft warm laugh and hugged her close. They remained where they were and she leaned into his chest, listening to the roaring of the wind in the trees above them.

"I'll figure out a way for us to be together somehow. A better way than for us to meet like this," he said after a while. She looked up, gazing into his face. There was something to his voice, something more serious, and for a moment she thought he would say that he would leave his fiancée. But of course, he didn't, he just put his arm around her again, and they walked further into the woods, into the little glen where he would put the blanket he carried in his backpack.

It wasn't until she came back inside and put the potatoes on a boil, irritated that Erik would go home and eat a fancy meal while they had their usual boiled potatoes with pickled herring, that she remembered the twinge in her belly earlier. There should be pain now. But there was none, no cramping, nothing. Counting back the weeks, her heart picked up speed. The last time she had bled was impossibly far away. In fact, it had been a couple of weeks before Erik had invited her up to the castle. She remembered it well because her rags had finally fallen apart and she had thrown them out, planning to cut new ones from Edith's old stockings next time. Her chest tightened. She hadn't had it since. It was two months ago now. The cows were in the barn already. And she had thrown up. How was it possible? She had used the wool. Not once had she forgotten. Her knees felt weak, and she felt overwhelmed with dizziness. Sinking down on the kitchen sofa, she stared unseeingly at the pot hanging on its hook over the fire. It was boiling over, but she was didn't have the strength to shift it off the flame and just watched while the water spilled out, hissing in the flames. She was pregnant.

#

It was early after the morning milking, and they lay beside each other in their glen, covered with blankets Erik had brought from the castle to stay warm.

He pulled her closer and said, "Anette, I have to leave tomorrow. It can't wait. My brother-in-law has business in Switzerland and wants me to come with him. I'll be back as soon as I can after Christmas."

"When is the wedding?" she asked, keeping her voice flat to hide her panic.

"It's not until the spring. We're… damn it, Anette, how can you be so cold and matter of fact?"

"How do you want me to behave? Would it help if I cried

and begged you to marry *me* instead?" She couldn't believe she had actually said it.

Erik looked stunned and for several unbearable moments she thought he would get up and leave, but instead he nodded.

"I'll break it off with Antoinette. I'm my own man. I should marry whom I want. I'll tell her first thing when I arrive in Interlaken. It's right that I do it in person."

This would be the natural time to tell him she was carrying his baby, but she didn't say anything. What if it scared him and made him stay in Switzerland? It would be better if she waited until he came back.

Gently, he brushed a strand of hair away from her eyes. "I'll marry *you*."

Anette looked at him as his words filled her mind. She wanted so much for it to be so, but the parson would find her name in his book and Erik would know she had lied. Learn that she had never been a widow and that his child was her fourth. And then he would leave her, just like Jon had.

"Anette, what is it?" He looked worried and disappointed.

"Erik, I'm not of your class. What will everyone say?"

His expression hardened, and he pulled himself up until he was sitting cross-legged as a tailor.

"All that concern with appearances is nonsense." He tugged at a blade of grass. The entire root came up, sending a spray of dry soil across the blanket. He didn't notice. "My sister is a prime example. Only the servants know about her husband's preferences. That's why there's no heir yet. To everyone else, it's a happy marriage."

"I could feel it, I noticed that day when I met him. But I think more people know, than you think."

Erik glanced at her briefly and then went back to pulling at his blade of grass. "I don't want a marriage like that. I want you, Anette. We'd be very happy together." He looked at her fully now and she smiled, pushing down the panic and the fear, praying that the parson wouldn't have the same information in his book. They were in a different parish after all.

Chapter Thirty-five

Erik

At breakfast, Sofia tried to engage Anders in conversation before his departure, but he only responded absently with mm-hmms while annoyingly drumming his fingers on the table. Sipping his coffee, Erik felt a sudden urge to pour the decanter of milk over Anders' head. Instead, he got up and left, confirmed in the belief that he ought not make the same mistake as his sister and marry someone just because it was expected of him.

A half hour later they were on their way. The day had started out sunny and warm, but the wind had picked up and the sky was now overcast. Erik looked longingly toward the area where the women milked when the cows were out. He had taken to riding along the pasture each morning just to get a glimpse of Anette. If she could sense his presence, she never let on. Sometimes he stopped to watch as she sat so serene and calm, leaning her head against the belly of a cow and rhythmically moving her hands up and down on the udder.

He had never met a woman like her. She seemed to know something about life. His sister and fiancée were highly literate and worldly but didn't seem to think of much more than clothes and the latest interior fashions. Antoinette was at least interested in horses, but other than that she did nothing but embroider and gossip with her friends. He sighed and noticed that Anders was staring at him.

"You're deep in thought, Erik. Is it a certain woman who's occupying you?"

Erik raised his eyebrows. Was it that obvious, he thought, then realized that Anders was referring to Antoinette, not Anette. Funny that they had similar names, for some reason it hadn't occurred to him until now.

"Yes," he said simply and looked out the window again as Anders pulled a sheaf of papers from his portfolio, letters from several factories and descriptions of the Swiss watches they were expecting to import. The carriage had gone past the empty fields now and was on the main road leading toward Lund. From there they would take the train to Helsingborg, where they would catch the ferry across the sound to Denmark and then continue by boat and train to Interlaken, Switzerland.

The carriage was passing a poor family with four small children on the right. The man wore a tattered gray sweater partly ripped at the seams. His wife and children were walking barefoot in the chilly air. Erik glanced over at Anders, but he was absorbed in his papers.

On impulse, he picked up the knocking cane and banged it hard to bring the carriage to a stop. Before the driver had a chance to get down to open the door for him, he jumped out and was shouting to the family.

"Come here for a minute, will you?" Out of the corner of his eye, he saw Anders pop his head out the window as the man gestured to his wife and children to stay back. Erik suddenly became aware of his own expensive suit and fashionable hat. The chain attaching his gold watch to his vest gleamed rudely, and he pulled his outer coat shut to hide it, then felt embarrassed. It must look as though he was afraid the man would try to take it from him.

"What can I do for you, sir?" the man asked. His wife was clutching the children tightly around her skirts.

Erik pulled several coins from his wallet, acutely aware that Anders would reproach him for exposing his wallet in front of a potential thief. "Here, please take this and buy your children proper shoes... or whatever they need."

The man stepped forward and took the money without looking at the coins. "Thank you, kind sir," he mumbled.

"For God's sake, Erik," Anders shouted, "get back inside. What on earth are you doing?"

"Good day," Erik said to the man and quickly stepped back into the carriage.

Anders looked mortified. "What the hell was that about?"

"Didn't you see them? They probably haven't eaten for days."

Anders shrugged. "If you give every hungry person a coin,

you'll soon be as poor as they are."

"Well, I'll be sure to cease my alms-giving then. At least when you are looking," he added, but Anders wasn't listening.

Chapter Thirty-six

Anette

Harriet was in the barn helping the dairy girls with something when there was a knock on the door. It was Euphemia, holding a basket of cookies and sweet breads she had made. "You need to be eating more," she said.

Anette wondered if Euphemia had noticed that she was beginning to show. Soon it would be obvious to everyone. She had been too ashamed to tell her, especially since Erik had left, afraid that Euphemia would point out that she had told her so, that Erik wouldn't even give it a second thought if she became pregnant.

"Come in," Anette said, ignoring her comment. "It smells delicious. Where did you get ingredients for all of this? I'll make some coffee."

Euphemia sat down on the kitchen sofa and handed Edith a cookie.

"Hello dear, I brought these for you and Mamma."

Edith curtsied, stuffing half the cookie into her mouth at the same time. "Thongnk you Mrs. Sschvensson."

"Finish chewing," Anette said firmly, "and thank Mrs. Svensson properly. Then run out and play."

"Thank you, Mrs. Svensson," she chirped, snatched another cookie from the basket and was out the door.

"She's such a darling, your little one. Lennart traded for it, giving away his figurines for yeast and sugar. Flour I already had, and I've made a little butter."

Anette nodded and poured coffee for the two of them. As Euphemia picked up her cup, Anette noticed her broken nails and cracked skin.

"You should pee on your hands and put some milk fat on them," she offered.

"You're right. I forget," she said dismissively, then took a deep breath. "Anette, I've wanted to ask you something for a long time. Can your sight tell you if I'll ever have children?"

Anette stared at her, the sugar-coated cookie she had just plucked from the basket, staying in midair. Was Euphemia trying to insult her? She met her eyes, but Euphemia seemed earnest, focused on her own question. Anette's heart picked up speed when she understood what it meant. Euphemia had never used the sheep's wool for herself. She and Lennart had no babies because they couldn't. How could she have been so stupid to think they didn't want any? Tears of shame sprung to her eyes, and she looked away, discretely wiping her face.

"I can try. We can do it right now if you'd like," Anette said and turned back to Euphemia, pushing down her angst.

"Oh, yes, please. Do you read in hands or in coffee?"

"Neither, let me just sit in front of you. If I sense something, I'll tell you." Anette closed her eyes and waited. And then she knew.

"It's Lennart. His seed is bad. You won't have a baby with him."

Euphemia smiled sadly. "I had a feeling."

She will go to someone else, Anette thought, and looked out the window so her face wouldn't betray that she knew what was already going through Euphemia's mind.

"I'm sorry," she said as she turned to face her.

Euphemia shrugged and took her cup in both hands, sipping noisily. "Like I said, I'm not surprised. It is what it is. How are *you*? We haven't spoken much lately. Did you ever use the…" Her eyes fell on her belly and widened. "Lord have mercy. Anette, are you with child?"

She nodded. Euphemia hadn't noticed then, after all.

"Oh, Anette, I didn't realize. And here I'm coming to you with this," she said and shook her head at herself. "I wasn't thinking. Ever since you told me you could sense things, I've been wanting to ask you, especially after you told me about the man who drowned. I'm so sorry." She squeezed Anette's arm and looked again at her belly.

"When?"

"In the late spring. I was afraid to tell you. He's left for Switzerland, but he says he's going to marry me."

"He *did?*"

Anette smiled broadly. She would let herself be happy just for one moment. For one tiny moment, she would pretend Erik would truly come back, that he had broken off their engagement, and that the parson wouldn't have her information in his book.

Chapter Thirty-seven

Erik

The train had been standing for the better part of an hour and the snow coming down was blinding. The picturesque houses they had been passing had vanished as if they never existed.

Several fellow passengers in the first-class compartments were walking back and forth in the aisle to see what was going on. The two who they shared the compartment with seemed oblivious; an old man who calmly read a French newspaper and a young girl, probably his granddaughter, who was fast asleep.

Erik jumped to his feet and started pacing. He wanted this to be over with so he could end it with Antoinette and go back to Sweden. It had been the plan all along anyway. He would take over the office in Helsingborg so his father could retire. He might as well marry a Swedish woman instead of making a Swizz one leave her country and family. In Helsingborg, no one would recognize Anette and know she had been a statare. That she was a widow with children was something they simply had to deal with.

Anders gave him a sideways glance. "It's only snow. Relax, will you? You've been restless this entire journey. I'm starting to wish you'd stayed home."

Erik glared at him, then left the compartment. He elbowed past the people congregating in the dark corridor. No one had thought to light the lamps yet.

"They're more agitated in there," a middle-aged woman said and discreetly pointed at the door leading to the second-class car. It was indeed a tumultuous scene. Through the small window he saw people standing up and arguing with each other.

Erik nodded gruffly and headed back to his compartment. As he was about to step inside, the conductor appeared.

"Sir, I want to apologize for the delay. It's unusual for a snowstorm to hit this early in the year, even at this elevation."

"When can we expect to be moving again?"

"It may be a while, sir. We won't be able to leave until the storm has calmed down and we can clear the tracks. We're fortunate to be stuck so close to a village. I advise you to stay at the inn."

"Thank you. Is there a place nearby that has a telephone, or is there a telegraph office? I must get a message to my fiancée's family," Erik said, hiding his irritation. There was nothing he could do about it, and it was certainly not the conductor's fault.

"Yes, sir, the town hall has a telephone. It's right down the hill, past the church."

"Thank you. I assume we'll be informed when the train is about to leave?"

"Of course, and as a first-class passenger, you'll be compensated for the delay."

"Thank you." Erik went back inside where three upturned faces questioned him silently. "We're advised to check in to the inn," he said in French without looking in Anders' direction.

#

They stayed at the inn for two days before they were able to continue. There was no telephone at the inn and the town hall was closed because of the storm.

When they finally arrived at Interlaken, Erik's nerves were taut with strain, only made worse when Antoinette threw herself into his arms and cried for joy in front of everyone.

She then grabbed both his hands and pulled him into an empty room while he heard Anders tell her chuckling father and brothers how annoying he had been on the train and at the inn, bursting with longing for his fiancée. If they only knew.

Antoinette beamed at him with her large dark brown eyes, and he couldn't help but smile back. She was gorgeous, wearing a dark blue silky dress that made her thick brown, almost black, hair shine. She wasn't even angry that they were so late.

"Erik, you must be exhausted after your journey," she said and pushed him down in one of the three oversized cushy recliners in front of the fireplace, then sat down on his armrest. "But we have an impromptu engagement party planned for tonight. Everyone is coming, including your sister and her husband. I'm so sorry. I hope you don't mind? Had we known it would snow and you'd be delayed we wouldn't have of course. We never expected it this early in the season. Your father is coming too." Antoinette smiled again and kissed him on the lips. He kissed her back but pulled away after only a moment, pretending it was just so he could answer her question. She was wearing a heavenly perfume, sweet with some kind of spice.

"No, of course I'm happy to see everyone, especially Magdalene. They said the same thing on the train, it's unusual so early in the winter." He needed a drink; his head was spinning.

#

The living room was full of tobacco smoke and laughter, and he was on his third glass of wine when his sister spotted him across the room and walked over. "Where is Antoinette?"

Erik shrugged. "I think she's gone out for some air," he said and gestured toward the veranda where she was chatting with one of her friends. "Actually Magdalene, can we talk?"

"Of course." She gave him a curious look. "Go ahead."

"Not here." He threw a quick glance toward the veranda to confirm that Antoinette was still occupied. She was. Grabbing Magdalene's elbow, he dragged her across the floor, past all the guests and into a small library. It was empty, and he closed the door and went to stand against one of the bookshelves.

"I've met someone else." There was no turning back now. She would tell their father, and it was done.

"What?"

He told her everything; the first time he saw Anette in Sofia's medieval hall, how he came upon her when she was running home to her sick baby, how she helped Martin find the body of his missing father, and finally, that he wanted to marry her and not Antoinette.

Magdalene put her hands on her hips and nodded as if to herself, looking down at the thick area rug they were both standing on.

"Erik, I understand that you may have romantic feelings for this woman. But she's a widow with a young daughter. It may be that she has a certain gift, though even that is highly unsuitable."

"Yes, and what else?"

"What else? Isn't it obvious? Are you truly asking me for a way to break off your engagement with Antoinette to marry a milkmaid? A statare?"

"Yes."

She scoffed. "Erik, you're not making sense."

A sudden sound made him walk over to the door. He opened it and put his head out. But things were as before. It was just loud, people were drinking and laughing in a perfectly Swizz fashion. Their father was sitting on one of the couches, deeply involved in conversation while smoking a thick cigar.

Erik closed the door again and looked back at Magdalene. "But you never cared for Antoinette. You always said she was too fragile."

"I said no such thing!"

"Yes, you did," he said, trying to keep his voice even. "Just last year when she refused to hike. Remember, she wanted to ride and meet us at the camping ground?"

"Oh, for God's sake. That doesn't mean she wouldn't make a suitable wife. This is absurd."

"Absurd?

"*Erik*," she hissed, "you'll be putting the whole family in jeopardy if you do this. Don't you realize the disgrace it would bring upon us all?"

"What about my happiness? Don't you care about me?"

She sighed and took a deep sip of her scotch. He hadn't noticed that she had it until then.

"Erik, of course I do, but you're engaged. It's too late. You're already committed. And what about Antoinette's happiness? You'd break her heart."

"Maybe. But what if I break her heart by forcing her to move to Sweden with me? Also, I don't love her anymore. I don't know if I ever did, not really. I love Anette."

Magdalene narrowed her eyes. "Erik, is there something you're not telling me? I hope you were careful. Have you gotten your Anette pregnant?"

He stared at her. Lord have mercy, what if he had? He was an idiot. It hadn't even crossed his mind.

"Erik?"

"No, no, I haven't. She's not. That's not why. I have very strong feelings for her. She's a wonderful woman and I know we'd be very happy."

Magdalene shook her head. She was visibly pale. "Erik, it'll be a scandal. You can't do this." She sat down in the only chair in the room and took another sip of her scotch, then looked up at him. "I'll tell Pappa. This isn't right. Not only will you destroy Antoinette's life, you'll destroy the business. Do you know how much Antoinette's father has invested in the Swedish office?"

"Well, I'm sure we can come to some kind of arrangement," he said.

Then the door opened, and their father entered. His smile faded when he saw their faces, and Erik's stomach churned with guilt.

He threw Magdalene a warning glance, but she took no notice.

"Pappa, you have to talk some sense into Erik, he thinks he can leave Antoinette for some milkmaid on Sofia's farm." She stood up, then marched out of the room.

"Anette is not some milkmaid, she's a widow," he called after her, but she ignored it, leaving the door wide open. He was sure it was intentional.

To his surprise, his father chuckled and put his arm around him. "Who's this voluptuous woman you've set your eyes upon?"

Erik blinked, taken aback, at the same time noticing his father's tailored suit and gold cufflinks, specially made just for him. Anette was a statare. What was he thinking? For the second time that evening, he went to the door and peeked out. This time he saw Antoinette standing alone by the piano, her hand gently playing with the keys. He closed the door.

"Pappa, I've fallen in love with someone else. I want to break off the engagement."

Chapter Thirty-eight

Anette

It was almost February and Erik hadn't returned. Her fourth child was coming and still no husband. How could she have been so utterly stupid to believe Erik? At twenty-six, she should have been wiser. Her mother was probably crying in heaven right now. It had been years since she last heard from Mother Anna or her father, but surely, they too would be horrified, and it was just as well that they didn't know where she was anymore.

Her pregnancy made sitting on her milk stool almost unbearable. Her back hurt, and it was hard to reach. One evening it was particularly bad and though she needed to get up and stretch, she forced herself to stay put to avoid drawing attention to herself. Her mouth was dry, and she was so tired. The cow hide's large white and black spots seemed to swim in front of her, blurring her vision. She closed her eyes, slumping against the cow's side.

When she opened them again, she felt strong fingers pressing into her arm so hard it hurt, and someone's hand squeezing her belly. Confused, Anette looked up, and found Olga staring at her with a stern, disdainful expression, and bending over her in the narrow stall. She must have passed out.

"Just as we feared. How dare you put our children at risk? Who's the father? And letting yourself get into this state so shortly after losing your husband. Such shame, such shame!" Olga sneered.

She knew, of course she did. Anette didn't bother to hide the tears streaming down her face. "I beg you, don't say anything. Please, if only for little Edith's sake."

"You whore! How dare you ask that?" Olga's shrieking echoed through the barn, and she heard the other women get up from their milk stools and run down the aisle.

Anette tried to stand so she could press herself past Olga, but she was boxed in and by now all the women had gathered around her stall.

"What seems to be the matter here?" Agneta asked sharply.

"This one here's a whore. What's worse, she asked me not to say anything. Can you believe it? As if I would put our little ones at risk of catching the whore sickness."

Euphemia nervously put her hands in front of her belly and met Anette's eyes briefly. At that moment she knew, Euphemia was pregnant too.

Olga spit on the ground, then stormed down the aisle and out of the barn. The others followed, even Euphemia. Anette buried her face in the cow's side and sobbed.

What was whore sickness? Had she fainted because she was sick? Remembering that she was thirsty, she decided to drink some of the milk. Pulling the bucket toward her, she scooped the warm milk into her hand and drank, repeating the procedure several times. Then she did something she hadn't done in years. She clasped her hands, placed them on top of her round belly and prayed to God, asking him to please bring Erik back to her. Begging him that somehow, they would be able to get married without anyone learning the whole shameful truth.

The others were still standing in the cold outside when she had collected herself enough to leave. She heard them clearly and stopped and placed her ear against the barn door.

Agneta's voice was loud and smug. "Olga and I had a feeling this was in the making and we took the appropriate measures."

Anette felt the baby move inside her and put her hand on her stomach. What did she mean?

"Yes indeed," Olga said, adding a tsk, tsk. "We saw her with the Baroness' brother about a year back and used the stick on her leg. We couldn't risk having a whore give our little ones bowed legs."

"The Baroness' brother?" she heard Harriet ask.

"Yes," Olga said firmly.

Anette pressed her ear more tightly against the barn door, holding her breath.

Agneta was speaking again. "Well, she's not ugly and men have their needs."

"Keep in mind," Euphemia interjected, "that Anette's been

through a lot. She lost her child and her husband died not so long ago. It's no wonder she needed someone to hold her."

Blessed friend, that's why Euphemia hadn't stayed in the barn with her. She went with them so she could defend her.

"Or maybe she's never been married." It was Olga again, her voice coming through the barn door so loudly that Anette jumped backwards. "Not only that, I saw them both again at the end of the summer. He even came down to pick her up. I confronted her about it. But Anette claimed the Baroness needed her help." She tsk tsked again, and Anette felt her cheeks prickle with heat.

Euphemia spoke more loudly this time as well. "I've no doubt she's a widow. She wears a wedding ring and covers her head too, at least most of the time. And Olga, you shouldn't make assumptions, things are not always what they seem."

Olga ignored the comment. "Her other two little ones might also be whore children. I remember…"

Euphemia cut her off. "I've heard that babies whose legs don't straighten were never swaddled properly. I don't believe it's anything to do with whores. Besides, that's an awful thing to say to somebody."

No one responded, and Anette could make out the shuffling of boots and clogs on the ground as they walked away. After several moments of silence, the door opened, and she saw Euphemia silhouetted against the moonlight.

Trembling, Anette fell into her arms.

#

Euphemia accompanied her back to the lodgings. When they arrived, Harriet's belongings were gone. She had even taken the mattress from the bed.

Edith got up from the floor where she had been drawing on a piece of wood with a chunk of coal. "Mamma, why did Harriet leave? She didn't say anything, she just came and took her things. Is she mad at us?"

"No, of course not Edith, she just needed her own place. It's late, time for you to go to bed." Anette reached for the jar of milk she kept on the windowsill. The cold was enough to keep it fresh for several days, but Edith's eyes crumbled at the sight. "I want cow's milk, not window milk!" She angrily threw the coal into the hearth. "I want cow's milk!"

"This *is* cow's milk. You know that."

"No, it's window milk."

Anette slammed the jar on the table. "It's the same as cow's milk. It's just cold. And you're embarrassing me in front of Euphemia."

"Yes, Mamma." Without saying another word, Edith sat down on the kitchen sofa.

Anette sat down beside her and stroked her hair gently, feeling guilty both for yelling at her and for having drunk warm cow milk herself and then forgotten to bring Edith her cup of milk.

"There, dear, I'll heat this up for you. Then off to bed with you, Edith. Mrs. Svensson and I need to talk."

"I've been trying to hide it Euphemia, I was really hoping he would be back by now. He said he'd be back right after Christmas. But it's almost February and I..." Anette's voice broke and she pulled her handkerchief out of her apron pocket and blew her nose. "How am I going to stand it until Slack Week? It's eight months away, and where am I going to go?"

Euphemia leaned forward and hugged her, patting her back with her hands. When she sat back up again, she looked steadily into her face. "Anette, you have to be strong. For Edith. You can do this. I'll help you. Does Erik know you're with child?"

"No, I never told him. It was stupid. I thought it would be better to wait until he came back," she said, sniffling as her nose filled up again.

"No Anette, it wasn't stupid. You did what you thought was best. This is what you're going to do. You go on as normal and I'll help you the best I can. Then when he comes back, you march right up to the castle again and you demand to speak with him. Bring your baby with you if God forbid, he hasn't come back before you have it, then insist he treat you right. He's a bastard for leaving you like this. But maybe I'm wrong, maybe he's delayed for some reason. Switzerland is very far away after all. Who knows what the reason is? But one thing is for sure Anette, whether he comes back in time and if he marries you or not, he better have a good reason."

Chapter Thirty-nine

Hanna

Hanna sat down at the end of the long row of tables at the Frog and nodded at the faces looking in her direction. She didn't know all of their names anymore. It was a good thing, she supposed. New members trickled in almost every month, often with their own ideas about how to best run a women's organization. Women's rights clubs, as people were fond of calling them, were springing up all over the country and the world. It was time that they became more organized. She glanced at Magnhild, who smiled and banged her pen on her paper to encourage her, eager to take notes.

"I better start or Magnhild here will write her own bylaws," Hanna said. Several of the women laughed, including Magnhild who nodded enthusiastically, banging her pen even harder. Hanna smiled, focused on her own paper with her notes, and began.

"Welcome everyone. My name is Hanna and as most of you know, we're sitting in my bakery and café. A few of us, Magnhild, Bengta, and I…" She paused and gestured toward them, getting encouraging nods in acknowledgment. "We started this almost seven years ago as our own temperance gro…, I mean club, believing that women would have more control of their own lives if they're not victims of domestic abuse and ills because of drunk husbands." She cleared her throat, glancing at her notes again. "We still believe that, but we must focus more on votes for women. We want to do that, it's a good must." Pausing again, she tried breathing slower. "What I mean is that we'd be lagging behind other women's organizations not only here in Sweden, but all over the world, which are all spending most of their time lobbying for our right to vote. Therefore, we've decided to refocus our efforts and organize better. So far, we've had no formal structure here, but we want to change that. How do the rest of you feel about this?" No one said anything and just looked at each other, then back at Hanna.

But then Bengta broke the spell. "Hear, hear!" she shouted, and the room exploded with cheers.

Hanna laughed with relief, noticing a couple walking past the Frog, both staring at them through the window. The woman nodded and met her eyes, but her husband shook his head.

"Phew," Hanna said and pretended to wipe her forehead. "Your silence scared me for a moment." Everyone laughed. "I suggest that we formally name Bengta, Magnhild and me co-founders. We'll form an executive board, headed by Maria and Vanda. They've been with us almost from the beginning. We also need to choose a secretary and a treasurer, which we'll decide at a later time. How does this sound?"

There were more cheers and nods, and Maria and Vanda looked touched. Maria was even wiping at her eyes. Hanna smiled at her, then reached for her water glass and drank.

It had gone well. She had rambled a bit, but it was fine. She was among friends and was getting better at speaking in front of large groups of people.

One of the new women put her hand up.

"Go ahead, Åsa?" Hanna prompted.

"No, Åsa is over there," she said and jerked her head toward a woman sitting across from her. "I'm Astrid."

"I apologize, do you have a question or a comment?" Of course, someone she didn't know the name of would ask.

"Yes, how's all this going to help us focus more on voting rights? I don't see how it would make a difference."

Hanna nodded slowly and made sure she kept her gaze steadily in hers. It was a passive aggressive way of asking, but maybe Astrid didn't intend it that way. "I'm glad you asked, Astrid. Our thoughts are that if we have a formal structure and formal membership roles, we can divvy up our work. Some of us may be more inclined to focus on temperance, while others may be more interested in voting rights. Does that explain it?"

"Yes, thank you Hanna, that sounds perfect."

Hanna smiled, feeling her body relax. Then everyone started talking at once. Vanda and Maria stood up and came over to her side of the table.

"Why didn't you say anything Hanna, thank you! We're both so honored," Vanda beamed.

"You like it then? Is this all right? Magnhild and Bengta and I were discussing it. It seemed right, but we didn't want you to feel left out not being named co-founders as well. You've been with us for almost as long," Hanna said. She had been obsessing over that fact all night.

Maria kissed her on the cheek and sat herself right down on the table in front of her, pulling Vanda down beside her. Thankfully, the café tables were made of sturdy wood.

"Of course it is, Hanna. You three were the first. Do you mind if I say something to everyone? I have a suggestion."

"No. Please do."

Maria slid off the table and turned around so she could see everyone. She looked proud and happy.

"I think what we ought to do next, is see who wants to do what. Can everyone who wants to focus on voting rights raise their hands? Magnhild write this down, will you?"

Magnhild responded with a wave of her pen. Almost everyone, including Maria and Hanna, raised their hands. Only Vanda, Lova and one of the new women kept theirs down.

"Eighteen, that's good. Who wants to focus on temperance?" Maria asked.

Vanda and Lova raised their hands, but the new woman kept hers on her lap, laughing when she noticed confused stares. "I'm sorry ladies, I don't know how to vote, I really want to do both. Can I?"

"Yes of course. Could you please tell me what your name is?" Maria asked.

"Katrin."

Hanna wasn't alone then, not knowing everybody's names. It made her feel better, and she got to her feet and watched as people rearranged themselves so Lova, Vanda, and Katrin could sit together. She picked up her chair and walked over to where Magnhild and Bengta were talking with Astrid and Ruth.

"Women in the United States have voted in one of their states already. I think it's in Wey..um, I'm sorry I don't know how to pronounce it," Magnhild was saying.

"Whiiii oomineäng, I think, it's a terrible tongue twister," Astrid said, then smiled at Hanna as she squeezed in between them. She seemed kind now and not confrontational at all. Magnhild held up her notebook and pointed to the word, Wyoming.

"I'm not going to even attempt that," Hanna said, shaking her head. "But yes, that's the state. I've heard of it too. It's actually one of the reasons we need to make this more official. If women are organizing this well elsewhere, we should too. Sometimes it feels like all we do is talk and hand out pamphlets, but nothing comes of it, just more members."

Astrid's eyes flashed to hers.

Hanna reached for her arm. "I'm not saying I'm not happy about that, just that we need to do more real work."

"Oh, I agree," Åsa said, glancing at Astrid who looked relieved. There was some tension in the air, after all. Hanna couldn't put her finger on what it was exactly. She didn't mean to trample on Astrid's toes, but it seemed as if she did.

"Let's name us the Frogs from Lund," Magnhild burst out, looking very pleased with herself.

Bengta laughed aloud, causing everyone to stop their conversation and look in their direction. Then Astrid and Åsa stared at each other, looking so perplexed that Hanna giggled.

"How about Lund's Suffrage Society? We can't call us Frogs, I have to keep my café somewhat separate from our women's meetings, at least during the day, or I'd lose my customers," she said.

"Now we're talking," Astrid said.

#

Johannes was in the aviary when she came home, and she went right into the kitchen and poured them each a glass of wine, bringing it to the aviary.

"Here comes my temperance woman after her meeting," he said and took her glass with a one-sided grin. "How was it, Hanna?"

"Well, officially we're a woman's suffrage society now. Lund's Suffrage Society. So, with that, I drink." She gave him a wicked smile and they both laughed. Mr. Blue came and landed on her hand. She pushed him onto her finger and put him on her shoulder, but he flew off and landed on one of the seed bowls. "It went very well, actually. We're all in agreement, Vanda and Lova will be focusing exclusively on temperance for now at least, and we'll see how it goes. They agreed though about the board and all that, like I was telling you about."

"Good, wine well deserved. Let's go sit, you look tired. I've swept up and fed the birds already."

She nodded and followed him to the couch, where she put her feet in his lap. Leaning back on a couple of pillows, she loosened her skirts so they weren't so tight. Her courses were coming.

"Are you feeling weak? You look more than tired." Johannes put his glass down and began to massage her feet, kneading into her arch and her heel, just the way she liked it.

"Just women's trouble. I'll be fine. I'm very glad we're doing this. Temperance is important, but sometimes I wonder what the point is. Women aren't abusing husbands because of our habits. Is it worth it to abstain just to be a good example for men?" She reached for her glass. It helped with her cramps too sometimes, but she didn't want to talk about her courses with Johannes. He didn't even know that she had visited that doctor years ago. It had just been a waste of time anyway.

He raised an eyebrow. "Is this something you women discuss?"

"No, not really, most are much more committed than me. It's only Vanda interestingly enough who actually drinks, but she won't get too involved with voting for now and will stay on temperance. For obvious reasons it's very dear to her heart."

Chapter Forty

Anette

Euphemia tried to explain what the women had meant that day when Anette fainted in the barn. Whore sickness they claimed, caused bowed legs in children. Somehow it came from not telling the truth. It didn't matter if one was an actual whore, or just an unmarried mother, something happened when things were kept secret that affected babies' legs. Euphemia assured her it was nonsense, something people had believed in the past when they didn't know any better. Babies' legs grew crocked if they weren't swaddled tightly enough, not because a mother hadn't informed people that she had never been married. Anette tried to keep it in mind, telling herself that she had nothing to worry about. Even Edith had straight legs. But she still worried, secretly studying all the statar children's legs, and panicking when she noticed that Alice's granddaughter was knock-kneed. What if it was her fault? She had lied every day since she arrived.

Whatever the case was, the others, including the milkmaids' husbands, avoided her as if she did have a disease. No one met her eyes, no one spoke to her, and they all stepped as far out of her way as possible in the barn, and Harriet never moved back.

One afternoon, Knutsson knocked on her door. He stared straight at her now seven months along belly without hiding his disgust. "You're wanted up there again," he said and jerked his shoulder backwards as if it would point to the castle. It didn't, but it was clear enough what he meant.

"What do they want?"

"How should I know," he said, turned on his heels and walked away, only to stop and look over his shoulder at her. "You know Anette, I took a chance on you that day in Lund, hiring you before Slack Week and all. Had I known that you'd go nosy yourself up with the owners in this way, I'd never have hired you. You understand? Filthy whore is what you are!"

His words slammed into her as if he had physically hit her and she grabbed on to the doorsill for support, blushing when remembering that she had asked him how the owner was to work for that very first day. And now, nosy up with the owners, he said. Did he know it was Erik's? Was he back? Maybe it was Erik who wanted to talk to her? It was a glimmer of hope, and it set her heart racing.

"Mamma, why did Mr. Knutsson call you that, it's not nice." Anette startled and looked down. Edith was standing by her side. How long had she been there?

She sighed. "I know, Knutsson is in a bad mood, just like everyone else is these days," Anette said, deciding not to use Mr. anymore when she spoke of him with Edith. He didn't deserve it. "I'm going to go up there and see what they want. Stay inside and stay away from the fire. I'll be back as soon as I can."

For a moment she considered fetching Euphemia, but this was something she needed to face alone. Erik should see what he had done. She didn't want him to hold back any emotions because they weren't alone. If he was there. She both hoped and feared it.

Walking across the lawn toward the back door, she half expected to see him waiting for her, calling out in shock when he saw the state of her body, but all was still. Then, just before she passed the front staircase to make her way around, the door on the upper terrace opened. Anette's heart caught in her throat and she turned toward it, begging for it to be Erik. But it was the Baroness, waving slowly.

"Mrs.... Lundström," she called, pausing after Mrs. "Kindly come here."

Anette cautiously climbed the stone steps while supporting herself on the wide stone railing with her right hand. Her belly was too large for her to see where she put her feet. Was Erik waiting inside? Had he told her? Finally on the terrace, Anette faced the Baroness. She nodded curtly without looking at her stomach.

"Thank you for coming. Will you follow me please?"

They entered a small room like a hallway. The Baroness briskly walked through it and stopped at the threshold to another room, motioning for Anette to walk in ahead of her. Anette's heart pounded and sweat pooled under her armpits all at once. The Baroness' face betrayed nothing as she carefully squeezed past her, begging Erik to be there. But the room was empty.

She managed to look at the Baroness, who had now walked around her and was saying something she hadn't heard.

"Pardon Baroness?"

"As I mentioned during the séance, I was hoping you'd be able to tell me if the castle is haunted, I can often feel it right here, standing just in this spot. Can you sense anything?"

Anette swallowed hard, hiding her disappointment but also relief that she didn't have to face Erik. She looked around, realizing that she was in the same room he had taken her through. Only then the furniture had been covered with white sheets.

"I'll try my best. May I sit down?"

The Baroness nodded, and Anette went to one of the couches and sat down on the edge of the seat. Closing her eyes, she waited, heard her own labored breathing and fabric against fabric as the Baroness moved her arms. There was nothing. Either she was too distraught or there was no one haunting the castle. Coming to a quick decision, she opened her eyes and looked at the Baroness.

"I'm sorry, it's rare that I actually feel something. I don't now. I'm sorry."

The Baroness shrugged. "Well, I'm not surprised. You see, I'm wondering if what I felt was Mr. Elvén's father? Then when you helped us find his body, his soul could finally be laid to rest. Do you think it might be so Mrs. Lundström?"

"Possibly. Mr. Elvén, may have been trying to tell y.. the Baroness of his plight."

She responded with a slight smile, then indicated a chair beside a small table at the other end of the room.

"I was about to eat a bowl of green kale soup. You can join me. Please sit. I'll send for the maid." She pulled on a string next to a tall, tiled heater while Anette got to her feet and made her way across the floor.

"A wedding present," the Baroness said when she noticed

Anette admiring the blue flowers painted on the heater's white surface. "My father-in-law had several installed throughout our home."

The maid appeared with a tray and placed two steaming bowls of soup in front of them. The Baroness waited until Anette had sat down opposite her, then picked up her spoon and slowly dipped it in her soup, skimming a small amount off the top, blowing on it before putting it in her mouth. She looked elegant and poised, and Anette felt clumsy and embarrassed. Knutsson had been right. What was she, a statare, doing here in a castle with nobles?

"Do try the soup. It's very good."

"Thank you." Anette tried her best to eat as neatly as the Baroness. Despite her awkwardness, she enjoyed it, and when they finished, she wished there were more. But the Baroness pulled the string again, and the maid reappeared, expertly putting their bowls on a tray along with their napkins and silverware. Then, with a disapproving backward glance at Anette, the maid left the room.

Anette was glad it wasn't Edna.

The Baroness looked at Anette silently, then for the first time her gaze landed on her round pregnant belly, staying there for several moments. "Mrs. Lundström, I'll be very honest with you. I know you haven't married again, but your condition is obvious enough. I'll not ask who the father is. It's none of my business. I *will* say this: you've helped us a great deal with your special talents, and for that I thank you. However, I must ask you to leave before the baby is born. I know you're on contract until October, but you needn't worry about that. Please understand that it's not appropriate for us to have unwed mothers on our farm, especially so close to my brother's wedding. We're to have the feast here, you see."

Anette stared at her. There was a ringing sound in her ears, and it felt as if the room was spinning. It was over then. How could she even have thought anything else? Just like Knutsson said earlier, she should never have agreed to come here. Life had been better in the poorhouse where no one threw crumbs at her, causing her to dream for things she could never have and clearly didn't deserve.

She tried desperately to conceal the tears welling up in her eyes.

The Baroness reached for one of her own embroidered handkerchiefs and placed it on the table in front of her.

"Mrs. Lundström, it's no use spilling tears over this. If your man won't marry you, he can't possibly be worth your sadness."

Anette reached for the handkerchief, then pulled her hand back and let her tears flow where they may while looking the Baroness straight in the eye. She didn't avert them, just calmly looked back at her. It was clear she didn't know. For a moment, Anette was tempted to tell her. But then she put one hand on the table for support, the other at the back of the chair, and pulled herself to stand. The Baroness didn't deserve to know that her brother's baby lay snug beneath her heart. It wouldn't be a bastard, but fit neatly into her already established lie. She was a widow, now with two children, just as before.

Chapter Forty-one

With the money she had earned from her séance, Anette rented a small room from a family which had eight children and needed the extra income. It was a chaotic household, but they were grateful for what her small rent provided them and asked no questions. In the early morning of May first, she labored alone. It was an easy birth, and Edith slept through most of it. When the last contractions came, Anette pushed the baby out and caught it with her own hands. It was a little girl. She slapped her on the back the way her midwives had, and she cried loud and clear, waking Edith. As they had talked about, Edith proudly fetched the scissors from Anette's sewing basket, ran outside to the water pump with their soap and washed the scissors thoroughly. Then Edith cut the cord and chose a name for her little sister, Ester.

\#

Euphemia had written a letter to an aunt of hers who milked cows on a farm in Östra Vemmenhög, asking her to put in a good word for Anette with the owner. She was lucky. A few days before Slack Week, Anette received word that there was space for her.

It wasn't a grand place like Häckeberga was. The paint on the manor house was chipped and windows were boarded up where the panes had broken. The only protection from the constant wind was a row of Scania Willows leading up from the narrow main road. There were two statar lodgings, small and run-down. The walls had been painted red, but the wood came through in most places, leaving just a faint tint of color in the corners and under the windowsills.

The owner, or the patron as he was called, was in his fifties, lean and weather-bitten. He helped Anette with her valise and led them to their sleeping quarters, a small alcove in a room already occupied by a family of four. It only had space for a small bed. She would have to keep their belongings underneath it, there was simply no other place for them.

The patron put the valise down. "Have yourself a little rest.

You can start milking tomorrow. I'll tell Agnes that her niece's friend has arrived."

Anette curtsied and he was out the door with a quick nod.

Edith looked around and grimaced. "Mamma, where will I sleep? The bed is too small."

"If we sleep with our heads at opposite ends, we'll both fit."

"What about Ester?"

"She'll fit beside me near the wall," Anette said just as the door swung open.

A very tall and skinny woman was standing there. Her grayish blonde hair looked like it was attempting to escape from under her scarf.

"You must be Anette. Oh, my dear child, look at your new baby. What a jerk to leave you all alone with a baby. Is it a girl, or a boy?"

"A girl," Anette replied, astonished at the bluntness.

The woman rushed across the room and embraced her.

"Euphemia didn't betray your confidence, but I imagine it's the truth? She didn't mention a husband, dead or alive. There's no need to pretend anything with me. We who have Yggdrasil and the three Norns in our hearts need not judge each other. Just don't mention it to the patron or his wife, she's a deeply Christian woman."

#

Anette kept a basket in the barn where she let Ester sleep while she worked. The patron had objected at first, but when she explained how she had lost little Ingrid while milking her cows at Häckeberga, he relented.

She was about to start on her fourth cow when she heard the barn door open and the patron's voice calling for her. "Anette, there's someone here who wishes to speak with you." He closed the door, leaving it cracked slightly, and continued on his rounds.

Bewildered, Anette left the warmth of the stall and stepped outside. Forgetting about the wind, the door flew out of her hand and slammed into the wall, and she heard a horse neighing and tapping its hooves nervously. Then she recognized the voice trying to calm it down, and her knees buckled beneath her. It was Erik.

He was wearing a long brown coat that was flapping in the wind; the horse's ears moved back and forth each time it flapped. Later, Anette would wonder how she could have noticed such a thing at that moment. But she did, just as she noticed that Ester's nose looked like his. Erik dismounted, let go of the reins, and walked toward her.

"Anette...I'm sorry."

"What are you doing here?" Her voice sounded angry and harsh, but she couldn't help herself. He was sorry? After saying he wanted to marry her but hadn't even had the decency to tell her he wouldn't. It was too late for apologies.

"I'm here to see you. I've been trying to find you for a long time. It wasn't until I thought to ask Euphemia that I found out you were here."

"I take it you want to see your daughter then," Anette said bluntly. "Come, help me with the door... so it won't scare that horse of yours again."

For the moment it was munching contentedly on the brown grass where the wind had scattered the snow.

When they opened the door, the women looked up curiously, but Anette said nothing. She met Agnes' eyes briefly, then lifted the sleeping Ester out of her basket and went back outside.

"I'll milk your last one," she heard Agnes say just before Erik closed the door behind her.

His face crumbled when he saw Ester, but he collected himself and pulled off his gloves, tenderly touching her little face. Her heart softened. He cared. No one else ever had. Then she saw his gold wedding ring, and she pulled back, hugging Ester against her chest.

"It's cold out here. I need to take her inside to our room."

She started across the windswept field without looking back. He followed her, and she saw out of the corner of her eye how his big horse trailed after them and nudged his shoulder from time to time. Then Erik picked up his pace until he caught up with them.

"I do love you."

Her chest tightened, but she ignored him. When they reached the lodgings, he left the horse loose and slipped through the door behind her.

"Love me? Aren't you married now? People usually marry the ones they love," she said when they walked through the front room to their alcove. She hoped he took note of how small and poor it was.

"No," he said. "People marry the ones they *have* to marry."

Anette sat down on the bed and hugged Ester to her chest. She wasn't sure how to answer that.

"I tried to break the engagement off," Erik said and sat down beside her.

"But you didn't."

"No, I had to do what was expected of me."

She tried to meet his eyes, but he was looking at the baby.

He reached out and put his hand on her little bald head.

"She's beautiful," Erik said, then quickly pulled back his hand. "Why didn't you tell me I got you pregnant?"

He looked right at her now, boring his eyes into hers. She loved him. Why had he left?

"I wanted to wait until you came back, you said you'd come back after Christmas. You said you'd marry me. Who told you?" Tears were filling her eyes. If she blinked, they would fall.

"No one. I looked for you, but you had already gone. I didn't think to ask Euphemia at first. By the time I thought of it, it was too late, I was already married."

She inhaled sharply.

Erik leaned forward and placed his palm on her forehead, then let his hand slide down over her eyes, and she felt his skin wipe the tears that now fell beneath her eyelids. He had looked for her and she hadn't been there. Her heart cracked open.

"I'm so sorry. Please let me help you."

His words startled her, and she felt confused for a moment. "Help me?"

"Yes, let me find an apartment for you in Helsingborg. We could see each other."

Gently, he took her free hand in his. She noticed how clean his fingers looked. The nails were cut short, and the skin underneath was pink. She pulled hers away with their dirty, broken nails and rough skin and hid it under Ester.

Helsingborg, the thought was dizzying. She could have a different life, an apartment with curtains and maybe even a special room just for the girls. Maybe her parents and the rest of her family would speak to her again when she was settled. But it would all be a lie. She could never measure up to a wife, and he might leave her again.

She took a deep breath. "No, Erik, I have my life here. I won't be a kept woman. You're married."

His eyes widened for the briefest of moments, and he opened his mouth to say something, but then he closed it again and nodded. He looked hurt, and a part of her regretted saying no.

Several minutes passed and they just sat together in silence. Finally, he reached into his vest pocket and handed her a small card. "I've written down the address to my office. If you only knew how many letters I tried to write you. But I didn't know how to explain myself without hurting you."

His voice sounded hoarse and thick, and she got a fleeting picture of him throwing crumpled papers into an enormous fireplace.

"Thank you, Erik," she said softly, then smiled at him. "Do you want to hold her? Her name is Ester."

"Ester, that's beautiful, yes, please." He held out his arms, and she placed her in his arms.

He held her so tenderly that her eyes filled with tears again. Blinking them away, she looked at the card he had given her. It had a Swedish address. His office was in Helsingborg.

"You work in Sweden now? I thought you said that your...she lived in Switzerland." She couldn't bring herself to say it aloud.

"We've moved. We're living in Sweden permanently now. I've taken over the Swedish office after my father." He carefully handed Ester back to her. Then, once she was secure in her arms, he leaned forward and kissed Anette on the cheek. "May I please still visit you?"

"Yes."

#

The next morning, the patron came to speak to her. He looked ill at ease and kept scratching his chin.

"I never flat-out asked you, but I assumed you were a widow." He paused and glanced at the ring on her left hand, then at the scarf covering her hair. "But this gentleman...'

The thought of once more being cast out to face an uncertain future with her daughters filled her with dread, but she knew she couldn't lie now, things were too obvious.

"It's true, sir. We're not married."

The patron nodded. "Say nothing to my wife."

Chapter Forty-two

Hanna

December 1899

As the new century approached, Hanna closed the café for a few days to have it painted.

At dawn, after it had snowed all night, she skied to the Frog. The air smelled as fresh as it did in the countryside, with the snow covering all the horse manure and the old soot on the streets. Snowflakes carried by the wind swirled around the two towers of the cathedral. She had never paid it much notice, but today when the world was silent and she was gliding past it on her skis, it seemed magical.

A solitary horse-drawn sleigh went past her, its driver waving just as she arrived at the Frog.

Mr. Johansson, the foreman painter, opened the front door while she was shaking the snow off her skirts and mittens. "Good morning, Mrs. Agnell, you've come to look in on us, have you? Just some touch-ups left to do."

"Wonderful! Do you think you'll be finished today?"

"It depends. If your husband is satisfied, we should be able to finish by this afternoon."

Hanna frowned. "My husband? I'll have a look myself and let you know." It was annoying. She was the one who had signed his contract last week. Why did he think Johannes would need to approve it?

"Certainly." He stepped aside so Hanna could pass but didn't apologize.

She sighed, not caring if he heard. Then stopped and clasped her hands together with excitement, forgetting his disrespect. Gone were the white walls; replaced with bright red. The moldings, which were green before, were now painted gray. It looked incredible. One of the painters was standing on a ladder, finishing the moldings near the ceiling. He smiled when he saw her expression.

"Is it to your liking, Missus?"

"Yes, very much, thank you," Hanna said, grinning from ear to ear.

She stayed for a moment, ignoring the overwhelming smell of paint, picturing how it would look with tables and chairs. She had ordered new sets, dark brown chairs and matching tables. Pale green wouldn't do in a red dining room. Then an idea came to her. She would ask Vanda to paint an automobile on the wall.

Smiling at the thought, she walked back to the foreman. "It looks fine. What time will you be done?"

"By four o'clock, Mrs. Agnell."

"I'll see you then," Hanna said. To give him credit, he did seem a little regretful.

#

Two days later, Hanna, Magnhild, Bengta, Maria, and Elsa watched as Vanda applied the first brush stroke.

Hanna handed Magnhild the small photograph with an automobile she had given Vanda as a model earlier. "Hold this. I'll go make a pot of coffee."

Vanda waved her hand behind her back. "*All* of you, go. Leave me alone so I can concentrate. Go have your coffee and don't come out until I call you. Just hand me back that photograph."

As they piled into the scullery, Bengta laughed and absently stroked her newly cropped hair. It was cut just below her ears, which made her wavy blond hair seem thicker than usual. "I like your hair, Bengta," Elsa said and glanced at her mother. "I want to cut mine short too."

Maria looked warily at her daughter. "Men like women's hair long. Don't you dare give your sisters any ideas by cutting yours."

"Ideas, Maria?" Hanna grinned. "Weren't you the one who brought Elsa to our very first temperance meeting here at the Frog, when she was a wee thirteen-year-old?"

"I was twelve, actually," Elsa said pointedly.

Magnhild grabbed some cups from a shelf. "When are your other daughters going to join us, Maria? And, Hanna, why is the paint smell still so strong in here?"

"It's the snow," she responded, somewhat defensively. "The painters said it'll take time since the air is so humid. I should've waited until the spring. But I was inspired by the new century and wanted to renew the place. It's going to take at least another week before I can open."

"Don't you worry, Hanna," said Maria. "You'll get so many customers that it'll be worth it. Kurt says it's a great idea. He's over at the smithy trying to get someone to make him an automobile-shaped cookie cutter."

"Really? I like that," Magnhild said.

Elsa tossed her head impatiently. "Mother, Magnhild raised a good question. When are my lazy sisters going to join the fight? I don't understand how they can be so blasé about it. Especially now when the Fredrika Bremer Association is going to petition for votes for women. I thought that would get them interested, but they don't care."

Maria turned an empty bucket upside down and sat on it. "You know how they are. They're romantic and want a man to take care of them. Emily isn't even interested. Can one of you please talk some sense into my daughters? I didn't raise them like that."

"They're just being rebellious," said Hanna. "Give them some time."

"Right, they just need some time," Maria said, but she didn't sound convinced.

Hanna filled a tray with spoons, coffee, crème, and a jar of chocolate covered cookies that were layered with raspberry jam. "Come sit, Magnhild, bring the cups."

They seated themselves on the floor in front of Maria's bucket, and Magnhild poured coffee for everyone.

Bengta placed her coffee on her lap and plucked a cookie from the jar. "These are delicious, are they new?"

"Yes, and it's my recipe actually. Thank you." Hanna smiled proudly. "Kurt made them though as usual."

"So good," Elsa said, grabbed a second cookie while chewing vigorously and talking with her mouth full, getting a frown from

Maria. They all laughed, but then Hanna brought the subject back to voting.

"If I understand this correctly, the petition will be presented to Prime Minister Boström at the end of the month and we Fredrika members will deliver it ourselves."

"That's what I've heard too," Magnhild said.

Hanna bit into her cookie and nodded, picturing the women in Stockholm heading to parliament on their own. If the petition was taken seriously, it would make a difference in all things, not just voting. Men couldn't just dismiss their opinions and ask women to check with their husbands like that foreman had done. It still irritated her. Thinking of painting, Vanda should be finished by now. Maybe she should ask her to add a frog to her automobile. It might be nice to have one on the hood with her coffee cup just like the one on the sign outside.

"Hanna?"

She looked up, finding them all staring at her. "I'm sorry, I was just daydreaming. I'm feeling anxious about the painting out there," Hanna said and gestured toward the dining room. "I must take a look." She got to her feet and headed over, then stopped at the threshold. "I'm going to ask her to paint a frog somewhere."

"I heard that Hanna," Vanda called from the other room. "Come here all of you."

Hanna turned toward the wall and let out a gasp. The automobile was finished, wheels and all, done in a shiny black that popped from the red walls without being too loud, even as it covered the whole back wall. But the best part was inside the automobile. Vanda had sketched a frog with a woman's hat at the steering wheel. Hanna laughed aloud as the other women lined up around her. They both had the same thought, she and Vanda.

"I wanted to check with you first, but I do have green paint, and I think it would look very nice with a green frog driving it. That way we'll stay on your frog theme, Hanna. What do you think? If you don't like it, I'll erase it, it's just chalk."

"It's perfect. Yes, please do, I mean, please paint it."

"Great friends think alike," Magnhild said, and put her arms around Bengta and Hanna. "It'll drive us right into the new century and toward the voting booth."

Chapter Forty-three

Anette

The snow was melting rapidly, and small bundles of crocus and snowdrops sprouted where the ground was bare. Erik was waiting for her, leaning against a large boulder set back in the trees. He was smiling so sweetly that Anette felt herself go warm and instinctively patted her swelling belly, hidden beneath her wide skirts and winter shawls. Erik embraced her silently, then gently pushed her against the boulder, pulled her scarf off, and let it slide to the ground. Completely lost in her hair and breasts, he didn't seem to notice her condition. When he finally pulled himself out of her arms, it was only to shrug his coat off. After a quick glance over his shoulder, he spread it over the melted snow and lay her down upon it. Murmuring her name, he embraced her from behind. It was over quicker than she wanted.

"I'm cold, Erik. Everything is getting wet," she said and pulled herself up to sit.

"Let's walk a bit, shall we?" He put his arms around her and slowly got up, raising her with him.

She pulled herself free so she could wrap her shawls around herself again. And then he finally noticed.

"Is there going to be another?"

Erik sounded so surprised; he made her smile. "Yes."

"When?"

"In the summer." There wasn't much else to say. She had expected it. Erik came to visit her at least once every month and most of the time they found a place to make love. She hadn't bothered with the sheep's wool. It did nothing for her last time, and besides, there were no sheep near here where she could get wool.

He spun her around so she was facing him. "Please accept my offer. You can't live here with another one of my babies. I could provide for you. You and the children can be comfortable."

"No. What would my neighbors say if I had a baby every year without a husband? I'll have the baby and then I'll move to another farm," Anette said casually, taking his hand so they could walk. She had already thought about what to do and was going to ask to rent that room at the same farm again, like she did when she expected Ester. They would be fine. They had Erik now, bringing clothes and extra food for them. She turned to smile at him, but it faded when she saw his face.

"That's ridiculous. You can't be moving around all the time, at least stay here then."

"The patron's wife will never accept my staying here, Erik."

"Why?" he said incredulously, as if there was nothing to it.

"Surely you understand that, Erik. You know what good Christians say about women who have babies when they're not married," she said, feeling irritated now. They only had a few hours, and she didn't want to spend them arguing.

"But you had our Ester here."

"No, I didn't. I had her in the village. I came here when she was a tiny baby. I let everyone think I was a widow, just like last time." As soon as the words were out of her mouth, she realized what she had done, and her heart started pounding.

Erik let go of her and stepped back, staring at her with his head cocked to the side. "What did you just say?" His voice was full of anger and disdain. He reached for her hand and tugged at her ring.

Despite the pregnancy, her fingers were slender and in the cold the ring was loose. For a moment she thought he would pull it off, but he let go and it slipped back into place.

"Whose ring is this? Are you a widow or not?" he barked, then abruptly let go of her hand.

"No," she whispered, heart still pounding. He would leave her now, surely he would.

"You told me your husband's name was Jon and that he drowned in a ditch when he was drunk. You've lied to me?" His voice was softer now, and so full of surprise and hurt that she wanted to look away, but she kept her eyes in his, overwhelmed with guilt and shame.

"Who *is* Edith's father then?" he added.

"It's Jon, like I told you."

"He's not dead?"

"No."

Erik let out a slow breath and his shoulders relaxed. "Why didn't you marry him?"

"He abandoned me. I had nowhere to go." Who was he to talk? He who was married to someone else. She exhaled, her panic easing and shifting to annoyance. "Erik, you of all people have no right to come here and judge me."

He looked stunned. Without a word he went back to the boulder, braced himself on his arms and hoisted himself up to sit on it.

Birds chirped loudly, and a door closed somewhere. And then she knew what he was going to ask next. She tried to think of something to say to distract him, but he spoke too soon.

"I don't understand. Why didn't he ask to marry you, especially after you got pregnant the second time? Ingrid was his too, wasn't she?" There was a shadow of fear in his expression.

"Yes, of course," she said, praying that he couldn't see the lie in her eyes.

"Anette, how could a man have two children and not marry? I still don't understand."

She didn't even hesitate. Moving her shawls, she flattened her skirts and blouse to expose her bump, then lifted her head and looked at him.

When it dawned on him, his expression was almost comical. At first his eyes widened, then he laughed nervously, and then he blushed. It was the first time she had seen a man blush.

"Was he married too?"

She nodded. Another lie made no difference. The fact that she had had three children with three different men before she met him wasn't something he could ever know. She could barely admit it to herself. Still, she felt guilty for lying to him.

"Anette, I'm so sorry."

"You're the brother of the Baroness. If you'd told her, I could've lost my employment. I did what I had to do. Just like I do now. I have children to feed.”

Shamefaced, Erik slid off the boulder and came to her, touching her stomach and kissing her. “I’m so sorry, my love. But please let me take care of you. You don’t have to live like this.”

“I’ll think about it,” she said, but knew she wouldn’t. She had been shamed too many times to stay in one place with eyes of judgement upon her.

#

The patron took Anette aside one afternoon in the beginning of May and told her she would have to leave. He shuffled his feet and spoke without looking her in the eye.

“You may stay here until the baby is born, but my wife doesn’t want you milking anymore. People might see you from the road. But you’ve been here for almost four years.” He glanced at her enormous belly. “Obviously we can’t force you to leave at this stage. It wouldn’t be Christian of us.” He scratched at the stubble on his chin. “I know a couple of people at Dybäck’s farm, not far from here. They have a very large dairy herd and always need help. I’ll put in a good word.”

“Thank you, sir.”

“No need to thank me, you’ve been a good worker here. My wife will make sure the little one gets a proper baptism,” he said, then lifted his hat and walked back across the yard. At that moment Edith came back from school, carrying her books and slate with Ester in tow.

“What were you and the patron talking about, Mamma?” Edith asked.

Anette pulled her close. “We have to move again.”

“Why?”

“Because of the new baby.”

“Is it because you’re not married?”

Anette winced. “Yes.”

“But Mamma, why aren’t you married? Everyone else’s mother is.”

Anette sighed, then took Ester by the hand and placed her arm around Edith’s shoulders. She didn’t remember Jon being very tall, but Edith was already as big as a teenager.

"I suppose you're old enough to know now that Erik is married already. It's one of those things you'll learn more about when you get older. He had no choice. You should know he does care for you and he'll help us the best he can. But you shall never speak of this to anyone. Do you understand?"

"Yes Mamma."

Ester was looking at her, eyes narrowed with consternation. It would be a few years before she had to explain things to her too.

#

On the twenty-fourth of June 1900, Ebba Elvira was born. The patron's wife took Anette to the parson to confess her sin. Reluctantly, he gave her the Eucharist and spoke of the flames of hell if she didn't mend her ways. Then he baptized little Ebba Elvira. At Anette's request, Erik wasn't named in the church records.

Chapter Forty-four

The patron drove them to their new home. The farm where Anette would work belonged to Dybäck's castle, an enormous white mansion surrounded by a cluster of buildings, lush trees, and a moat. The oldest structure dated back to the fifteenth century; the others had been added through the first decades of the seventeenth.

In the early years, the patron explained, the noble Bing family lived at Dybäck. During the 1480s Count Bing had a dispute with his neighbors, the Beddinge brothers, over who owned the land. According to legend, Count Bing put soil from the farm into his shoes and walked around the disputed property so he could claim he had been stepping on his very own soil. It was said that he still walked around the farm at night, taunting the Beddinges.

With Ebba sleeping against Anette's chest, they sat on a fallen tree by the crossroads between the farm and the castle, waiting for the patron to fetch the farm manager who would take them to their new lodgings. But it wasn't a man that came running down the road toward them. It was a woman, waving her arms wildly. Anette stood up slowly, shielding her eyes from the evening sun. Then Edith jumped to her feet and ran to greet the approaching figure.

"Euphemia! Euphemia!" she shouted and threw herself into her arms.

Anette let out a gasp when she recognized her, and Euphemia loosened her grip on Edith and laughingly embraced her.

"I overheard your former patron talking to the farm manager, and heard them say that an Anette Lundström and her daughters were here." She stepped back and glanced down. "This must be Ester? Oh, my sweet Jesus, she's a big girl already. I believe my son is the same age, four, isn't she?"

It was as she had thought then, Euphemia had been pregnant.

"Yes, she's four too. Euphemia, what are you doing here?"

"The three Norns didn't watch over me as I had hoped. Lennart must have suspected he couldn't sire any children, and when I told him I was with child... well, let's talk of it another time. What's the little bundle's name?"

"Her name is Ebba."

#

Anette couldn't believe her luck when she saw where they would be living. After years of occupying the little alcove in the same lodging as Agnes and her family, they had their very own cottage all to themselves. There was a large bed, a small table with two chairs, a free-standing cupboard, a hearth of her own to cook on, a counter with a washbasin, and a dried-out fuchsia on the windowsill. She would water it to make it thrive.

The girls were exhausted from the journey. After playing a bit on the bed, they fell asleep. Anette covered them with a blanket and was about to go to bed herself when she heard a knock on the door. It was Euphemia, her face beaming as she held up a small bottle of brännvin. Anette embraced her and pulled her inside, feeling as if they were back in Häckeberga.

Then she went to her new cupboard and opened it, looking for glasses, but there was only a stack of coffee cups all the way back in the corner. She pulled two out, disturbing a nest of black bugs that scurried down the door, disappearing between the floorboards. She stifled a gasp and wiped the cups off with her skirt, deciding to give everything a thorough cleaning in the morning.

"Tell me everything," she said and handed the cups to Euphemia.

She filled them up and handed one back.

"I will, but first I want to hear about you. Did Erik find you? He came down to the farm to ask me about you. I hope you didn't mind that I told him where you were?"

Anette shook her head. "No, I'm glad you did."

"That man loves you, Anette. He was so grateful when I told him I thought he was going to cry. Is Ebba his?"

"Really?" Anette smiled, picturing Erik holding back his

tears. "Yes, she's his." She took a long sip of brännvin and swallowed it with a flicker of guilt for not having gone to Helsingborg like he wanted.

"I left Häckeberga when I began to show. Lennart kicked me out when he figured I had another man's baby in my womb," Euphemia said.

"How could he be so sure it wasn't his? Who *is* the father?"

Euphemia lifted an eyebrow. "One of the traveling peddlers that frequented the farm."

Anette shook her head with a chuckle, and Euphemia laughed.

"How Lennart was so sure, I don't know. Maybe because he was married before and didn't have any children with his first wife either. I only know that he threw all my things on the ground outside the statar lodgings for everyone to see... then he locked the door on me. I waited out there all night. The next morning, he tossed his wedding ring out the window... and then I left. When I arrived here, I told everyone I was a widow."

"I'm sorry, Euphemia. I was going to do the same, but Agnes understood I wasn't. The patron and his wife assumed it, but then when Erik came to visit me, the patron figured it out," Anette said, wondering what Euphemia would think if she knew she had never been a widow at all.

"Don't be sorry, Anette. I got what I wanted so badly. A baby. He's the joy of my life."

Anette glanced over at her three sleeping daughters. They were her joy too; she was just so tired.

"What did Olga and Agneta say when I left and then when Lennart kicked you out?" she asked, pulling her eyes away from the bed.

Euphemia reached for the bottle and refilled their cups.

"Let's begin with you. The rumors began as soon as you left. Olga claimed she had heard that Edith and Ingrid were Erik's as well, and that you and Erik once had such a horrible argument that he divorced you and then you became a statare on his sister's farm just to aggravate him. But Agneta disagreed, she said that Erik had saved you from your first drunken husband and now you had finally fled to America together."

Anette laughed coldly. "Didn't they find out that Erik married Antoinette?"

"I don't know, probably not."

She sighed, somewhat relieved. Whichever story they believed, it served them right. She hoped they were jealous.

"This is a good place, Anette. People are kinder here. I thank Yggdrasil that the three Norns connected the two of us again," Euphemia said. "Does Erik know where you are?"

Anette reached for her arm and squeezed it. "I do too. Yes, I've written to him. I'm not sure what to say when he'll visit."

"Tell them he's a sailor. Pretend you're married. You have your ring."

Their eyes met, and Anette nodded. They both carried rings now that told stories that weren't true.

Chapter Forty-five

Hanna

Hanna had fallen asleep on the couch when she was awakened by voices and the front door closing. She sat up and wrapped her robe tighter around herself, moaning when the movement caused another cramp. Then Magnhild strode in, waving a letter in her hand. When she saw Hanna, her face fell.

"Are you ill? Johannes let me in. He didn't say anything."

"No, it's the time of the month," Hanna said and felt tears coming into her eyes. Embarrassed, she wiped them off with the back of her hand.

Magnhild immediately rushed over and hugged her close. "I've never seen you cry in all the years I've known you."

"I'm sorry, Magnhild. It's just that every month I hope… I feel like a failure every time." This month she had been five weeks late. It had never happened before, and they had cautiously celebrated last night. Then this morning, her courses came, and she had to tell Johannes there was no baby. He had been wonderful, given her breakfast in bed and assured her he was happy with just her and their flock, but it hadn't helped. She had cried all day.

"Oh Hanna." Magnhild put the letter on the coffee table and squeezed her arm. "You're not a failure. You're the envy of all the other women in our group, married and still independent, with your own business."

"I'm not. Secretly they all wonder what's wrong with me because there are still no babies."

"No one thinks that Hanna, it's just how it is sometimes."

Hanna nodded, but the tears were still flowing. "I even saw a doctor for treatments a few years ago, but nothing came of it."

"Who did you see?"

"Doctor Andersson, he has an office near the pharmacy."

Magnhild held her gaze for a moment. "I've heard of him."

"Let's not talk of it anymore. What's in the letter you brought?" Hanna pulled a handkerchief from her robe pocket and blew her nose.

"A lot, you're not going to believe it. It's from Alva. You know her, she's active in the Fredrika Bremer Association in Stockholm."

"Yes, of course," Hanna said and placed a hand on her stomach to still the pain.

"Carl Lindhagen sent a motion to the King about voting rights for women," Magnhild said as she reached for the letter, then pulled it from the envelope and unfolded it. "Yes, on the 11th this month. We should write this date down actually, April 11th 1902."

"Yes, we should." Hanna sat up straighter so she could see better. "Lindhagen is a real ally for us women."

Magnhild nodded enthusiastically and traced her index finger along the words as she paraphrased. "Fredrika Bremer has officially put out a statement of solidarity for his motion. And they've formed a women's suffrage committee too."

"That's wonderful, finally!"

Magnhild threw a sidelong glance at Hanna and grinned, finger still holding her spot in the letter. "Just wait until you hear the rest. I should write about this. On the 20th, they had a huge demonstration for general voting rights in Stockholm. But then the next day people went back, and a woman was arrested!"

"Arrested?"

Magnhild nodded gravely. "Yes, she was. Her name is Anna Maria Engström, Alva writes. She was waving her arms in the air, shouting about voting rights and women's rights. The police asked her to leave, but she refused, and they arrested her."

"Lord have mercy. Is she still in jail?"

"I don't know."

"Is she one of us? A Fredrika Bremer member, I mean?"

"Hanna, that's a good question, I don't know that either." Hanna shifted in her seat, feeling the flow fill the rag in her undergarments. She abruptly got to her feet.

"I'll be back," she said to Magnhild and hurried out to the water closet.

Finding a clean rag in the drawer, she replaced the wet one

and put it in the basket for washing later. The first few weeks she had been too scared to hope, but when she went days over the following month as well, she was sure she was pregnant. It was pure joy. And now it was over. Pouring water over her hands to rinse the soap away, she was overcome with an urge to crack the porcelain pitcher against the mirror. She held it in her hand, gripping it so hard her knuckles whitened. She almost did it, but then put it back down and dried her hands on the towel, resolving to get back to the conversation and ask Magnhild for more details about the arrest and the suffrage committee. But when she opened the door, Magnhild was standing outside. Without a word, she pulled Hanna into her arms. Johannes must have told her.

"Hanna darling, I'm so sorry."

She let herself go, sobbing into Magnhild's shoulder while her round arms held her in a sturdy grip. When she finished. Magnhild gently stroked her cheek.

"Johannes has gone to get sandwiches for us from the Frog, and now you and I are going to sit down and relax. Unless you'll allow me to go visit your lovely birds?"

Hanna laughed, surprising herself. She did feel better. "Of course I will, and thank you Magnhild."

She shook her head. "We're friends. That's why we have each other."

They went into the aviary and sat down on their pin-chairs. Blue and Selma flew over and landed on Hanna's lap while Tobias and Jonathan sat themselves on a perch next to Magnhild, staring shyly at her.

"Thor left us a few months ago, I think I told you?" Hanna said.

Magnhild nodded.

"Selma and Tobias are old, but they're doing so well still." She patted Selma's soft wings, then changed the subject. "Magnhild, it's a little annoying that Lindhagen has to take our cause to the king. I'm glad he did, but I wished Boström had got it done when we women petitioned ourselves."

"I know. I was thinking the same thing. Still, it's good to have men on our side," Magnhild said.

Hanna glanced at her. Sometimes she wondered how she and Bengta did it with no men by their sides.

Magnhild raised an eyebrow. "I know what you're thinking, Hanna." She laughed, but then gave a serious nod. "Bengta and I are very happy together, but sometimes I wish we didn't have to hide it. It's hard sometimes. Especially now when we have more members at the Frog. Ruth and Åsa would never come if they knew."

"Ruth?"

"Yes, Ruth, I overheard her and Åsa speak of us, not me and Bengta personally, but women like us. We're repulsive according to her, and she's upset that homosexuals are joining the suffrage movement."

"Magnhild, I'm so sorry. What are we going to do? We should…"

Magnhild interrupted her with a wave of her hand. "No, there's nothing to do. Just ignore it."

Hanna nodded hesitantly. It was very upsetting. How could Ruth, one of her closest birder friends, think that? She, if anyone, with so much knowledge about the natural world should understand that things weren't always as they seemed. Magnhild averted her gaze, looking down at her lap. Bengta's and her lives weren't perfect either.

Chapter Forty-six

Anette

Euphemia was right. Life was better at Dybäck's farm.
People were friendlier and didn't gossip as much. Nor were they
bothered by the fact that Erik visited as often as he could get away.
Anette told everyone he was a sailor, just like Euphemia had
suggested. If they could tell by his smooth skin and fine clothes that
he wasn't, they never said anything. Each time Erik came, he took
her to the inn nearby. He always insisted on getting the dinner sent
to their room so as not to be seen with her, but she didn't care. If
anything, it added excitement that they had to sneak around. It was
a luxury to spend the night at a real inn and she took what she
could get.

In the early spring, the birth of their third child was getting
close.

Her legs were swollen, and her back ached as soon as she
sat down on her milking stool. Some afternoons, Euphemia offered
to take her cows so she could rest. And today, she was lying
comfortably on her bed with one pillow beneath her knees and
another behind the small of her back, resting and reading one of
the books Erik had brought her.

She was alone, Edith and Ester were taking their time
coming home from school. Ebba was out playing with the other
children as usual, staying outside until the evening milking was over
and all the statar children were called back in to eat.

Later, Anette would ask herself how she had failed to sense
what was to come. But she was dozing peacefully when the door
burst open. It was Edith, pointing in the direction she had come
from without saying a word.

"What is it Edith?" Anette asked as she with great effort
pulled herself up, swung her legs to the floor, shrugging when Edith
didn't answer, and followed her.

Three of the milkmaids' husbands stood outside, hats in
hand, and eyes lowered. She blinked, trying to understand what

was happening. Then she felt Edith take her hand and let go again.

"Mamma," she whispered.

Anette took hold of the doorsill and walked out, and the men respectfully stepped aside. There was a small wagon behind them. An empty flour sack was neatly spread out, covering something. Her heart started to beat fast.

"What's the meaning of this?"

One of the men nodded. It was Emma's husband Nils, she saw now.

"There's been an accident. I'm so very sorry, Anette." He lifted the edge of the sack and she saw Ester's face, cold as marble. Her hair was wet.

She screamed and fell to the ground, hearing her own voice echoing between the statar buildings.

Anette didn't know how she got back inside, but she was sitting on the bed again and everyone was around her. Edith was by her side with Ebba in her lap. Euphemia and her son Rolf were there, Nils and his wife, and the two other men who had brought Ester, and their wives. She couldn't remember any of their names. Ester was inside too, lying on a makeshift table that someone brought in. She looked peaceful, as if she were asleep, and her hair had dried. She had drowned. In the moat. Edith was on her way to go after her, but Nils had stopped her. If he hadn't been near and heard the screams, she could have lost them both. Then Nils tried to get to Ester, but it was too late. No one would tell her anything else. Though Euphemia had told her it was March 23, 1903 today, as if that was important. It meant that Ester would have been seven years old in a couple of months. Anette felt cold and shaky, but she hadn't cried. She couldn't.

"I need to tell Erik," she managed. Everyone turned toward her and stared.

Then Euphemia nodded. "We'll take care of that for you, Anette," she said and gestured toward Edith who put Ebba in the crook of Anette's elbow and slid off the bed.

Chapter Forty-seven

Erik

Sofia and Anders had been taking the waters in Ramlösa and were having dinner with him and Antoinette before traveling back to Häckeberga in the morning. They had just been served their coffee and cognac in the drawing room when the maid appeared to announce a visitor.

"Who is it?" Antoinette asked.

"It looks to be a worker of some kind." She frowned slightly and addressed Erik. "He insists on speaking to you alone."

Erik glanced at his pocket watch, 9.36 p.m. It was certainly an odd hour for a visitor.

The maid had left the man standing in the cold. By the light from the vestibule, Erik could clearly make out his face. He had never seen the man before. His clothes were frayed, and he didn't look all too clean.

"How may I be of service?"

"Sir, may I speak with you in private? It has to do with your daughter."

"My daughter?" Erik frowned; he had tucked his girls into bed just an hour ago.

"Sir… I'm afraid I have bad news… please come down to the sidewalk." The man glanced toward the window. Erik followed his gaze and spotted Antoinette's silhouette.

"Maybe you should come inside and speak to both me and my wife."

"That wouldn't be advisable, sir. I need to speak to you alone."

"Wait here." Erik went back in the house, told the maid that he had to go outside for a few minutes, and asked her to apologize to the others. She handed him his coat, and he hurried down the stairs. His coffee would go cold.

Out on the street, the man went straight to the point. "My name is Nils. I've been asked to inform you that there's been an accident. Ester was walking across the ice on the moat, trying to retrieve the mittens she dropped, but it wasn't strong enough and she went through. She… Ester drowned yesterday afternoon. Anette is not herself."

Erik tried to comprehend, feeling his knees give way and then Nils' hands on his shoulders as he helped him sit, rather than fall, to the ground.

"No, that can't be right. There isn't any ice now," Erik said, looking at Nils who was crouching next to him.

"There is, but it's thin, sir."

An image of Ester falling through the ice flashed before him, and it was as if he could hear her scream.

"Please come as soon as you can," said Nils. His face, visible in the faint light from a streetlamp, was full of concern. "I'm sorry to come with bad news, and so sorry for your loss."

Erik started getting on his feet, and Nils held out his hand for support. He grabbed it gratefully.

"If you're able, can you come with me now? I have a carriage down the road." Nils looked back toward the house. "I've been made aware of the delicacy of your situation," he added.

"I can't, but I'll be there as soon as I can," Erik said, his voice breaking.

Nils clapped him on the shoulder, then lifted his hat and hurried down the long path bordering their neighbors' villas and made his way toward the main road.

Erik stared after him without seeing. He would have to make something up, find a reason for leaving the next day. If only Anders and Sofia weren't staying over tonight. Antoinette wouldn't be a problem. She had grown accustomed to his excuses. But his sister and brother-in-law would never let it be. They would bombard him with questions. He decided to pretend everything was fine tonight and announce his departure tomorrow when Sofia and Anders were safely back at Häckeberga. Surely he could do that. He felt strangely calm.

As soon as he stepped back inside, it became clear that it wasn't going to be that easy. Antoinette was pacing back and forth in the vestibule, wild-eyed. Sofia walked beside her, trying to calm her down. It took him a few moments to understand that they had overheard him talking with Nils on the steps before they went out to the street.

"Erik, what did that man want with our daughters? What did he mean?"

He stared at Antoinette but couldn't bring himself to answer.

Sofia gave him that piercing look he knew so well, the one that always told him he was in trouble when they were children. "Erik, what's happened?"

"There's nothing wrong. Our daughters are fine." He pushed past both women and headed down the hall to his study.

As he closed the door behind him, he could still hear their questioning voices. But he couldn't deal with it. Lighting the lamps, he poured himself a large whiskey and fell into his leather recliner. His hands shook so much that he had to hold his glass with both hands. Drinking deeply, the warming alcohol calmed him, and the tears came, falling into his glass.

The house was quiet when he stopped crying, and that's when it hit him. He had never told Anette where he lived. How did she know to send Nils to his home? What if it was a ruse? He went ice cold, but then shook it off. Nils would have nothing to gain by making it up. He hadn't even asked for money. Ester was dead.

Somehow, he must have fallen asleep because he was startled awake at the sound of the curtains being pulled aside and a window being opened to allow the cold spring air inside. Then Sofia was standing in front of him, studying his face.

"Erik, Antoinette has gone to bed. You can talk to me. What happened?"

"Oh, for God's sake, Sofia, leave well enough alone. It was a mistake. Our daughters are fine."

"It certainly doesn't seem as though it was a mistake from the way you're acting. If you don't think there's anything to explain when some ragged fellow comes calling in the middle of the night, there's no point to this conversation. I'll go to bed now."

He glanced at her but didn't have the strength to say anything. Waiting until she had gone back out and closed the door behind her, he put his head in his hands and sobbed once, then clasped a hand over his mouth to stop it. But Sofia had still heard and came back into the room.

"Erik, *please*. Tell me what this is about."

He swallowed several times. "My daughter is dead."

"What? Your daughters are safely in bed. I saw them myself. Have you lost your senses?"

Sofia took the empty whiskey glass out of his hand and went to the bar and refilled it. She took several large gulps, then handed the glass back to him and sat down in the other recliner.

"Yes, I suppose I have." He took a long drink. "I see that Pappa and Magdalene have guarded my secret well. I have more children than the ones upstairs."

"What?"

"Do you remember Anette Lundström?"

"The milkmaid with the sight? I don't understand..." She stopped, staring at him as her eyes widened with shock. "Oh my God Erik, she was pregnant with *your* child when I fired her?"

"What did you just say?" He shot out of his chair. "You bloody bitch!"

"*Erik!*"

He ignored it. With one long step he was back at the bar, refilling his glass even though there was still some left. Remaining with his back turned to Sofia, he closed his eyes and held on to the table for support. He should have known that Anette couldn't have left before Slack Week unless she was fired. All this time he thought Anette had been angry with him for not getting back after Christmas like he promised. Had he found Anette and learned she was pregnant before the wedding, he would never have gone through with it, not then. It was Sofia's fault that Ester was dead.

"Jesus Christ, Erik, what was that for?"

"Did you *know?*" Maybe she had done it because Magdalene or Pappa had told her to. Why else would she personally fire a milkmaid? Wasn't that Knutsson's job?

"Know what?"

"You bloody well answer truthfully."

"Erik, you have to stop cursing at me. It's very unlike you. I didn't know that Mrs. Lundström was carrying your child, if that's what you're asking? How could I have known that you were down at the lodgings fraternizing with the farming staff? Please."

He relaxed, seeing the truth in her eyes. He lifted his glass to his mouth and took a big swallow, and again, the tears came as soon as he drank. Sofia got to her feet and put her arms around him.

"She drowned, Sofia," he said, clinging to her and soaking her shoulder with his tears.

Chapter Forty-eight

Hanna

Hanna and Magnhild looked at each other and smiled as the women filed into the Frog. Somehow they were able to squeeze in, and soon every chair was occupied while others gathered around the tables or leaned their backs against the walls. On the counter were stacks of pamphlets. All the plates, cups, and saucers had been moved to the scullery. What a difference from when they were four or five people gathering in Helga's storeroom.

Hanna met Magnhild's eyes again, grinning with excitement at what she was about to say, then banged their gavel on the counter to get everyone's attention.

"The meeting is now in session. I barely know where to start. First, let me comment on how large our group is. It's wonderful. Look around you!" Scattered applause. "Who said women can't organize?" Loud cheers. "Which brings me to a special announcement."

Only a few of them nodded knowingly, and Hanna felt another jolt of excitement that she would be the one to tell the rest. "As we're all well aware, last year the Organization for a Woman's Political Right to Vote was formed in Stockholm. And now they've joined forces with us local groups in the National Organization for a Woman's Political Right to Vote, LKPR. We finally have a national organization. Local organizations can accomplish a lot, but now we're all under one umbrella. The politicians will have to listen." She waited for it to sink in.

Then the room exploded in applause and cheers. Hanna grinned as Bengta and Magnhild came to stand beside her, clapping her on the back and hugging her while the room broke out in another loud applause. Hanna let out a breath and kissed first Magnhild, then Bengta on the cheek, overcome with happy tears. She was doing this. *She* little Hanna, an only child who had been small and unassuming as a girl, too shy to play with the other children in her neighborhood. And here she was at *her* café, leading all these women.

"Let's talk among ourselves for a while. I didn't know I'd get this emotional about this. I'm just so happy that we're all here," she said and wiped her tears with a broad smile, feeling herself again.

"I counted to forty-four," Bengta said, and exchanged a happy glance with Magnhild.

Maria, who was talking with her daughters and three new women, beckoned Hanna over. "Please come and meet Mrs. Karlsson, Mrs. Andersson and…" She hesitated and looked at the third woman. "Mrs. . . . I'm sorry, I didn't catch your name?"

"Miss Kline."

"Kline?" Hanna said as she extended her hand. "That's an unusual name."

Miss Kline grasped it lightly. "My father is American."

"Ah, I see. Where did you grow up?"

"I actually grew up here in Lund. My father met my mother on one of her trips overseas, and then he moved to Sweden to be with her. My cousin is involved in the movement back in America. The whole world is beginning to realize the potential of women."

Maria took Hanna's arm and squeezed it proudly. "Hanna is the owner of this café. My husband has been her baker since she opened it."

"It's a very nice place," Miss Kline said. "I love the lady frog in the automobile. Very clever." She glanced briefly at Maria, who had gone back to her conversation with the other women, then turned back to Hanna. "What do you think LKPR will do about the men?"

"What do you mean?"

"Well, as you know, according to our current law, only men of a certain class have the right to vote. Wouldn't it be wise if we worked together?"

"What do you propose, Miss Kline?"

"I'd say we should start out by working with them. If we ensure that all men can vote first, then we can work toward the goal of all citizens, all men and women, having the right to vote."

"So you're saying that we ought to drop our own fight and

work for the rights of men?" Hanna asked, irritated that she could think to bring this up now. Was she criticizing her?

"Yes, for the time being, we'll never get a consensus in the country if we try to win the right to vote for all women before every man has it."

Hanna tried to keep her voice level. "I'm not sure I agree. Especially now when we finally have a national organization for women with a proper voice for us."

She and Magnhild had been planning this meeting for the entire past week. They had fantasized about how encouraged everyone would be and how they would all work together. It had been brought up before, but today she wanted to celebrate women, not bring back that old conversation.

"In my opinion," Hanna continued, "it would be a grave mistake to alter our approach now when we've come this far. Think of why we're here today."

Miss Kline nodded once, then again, a little faster. "That's a very good point. Perhaps, we should focus on ourselves. The fact that LKPR was formed means we're moving in the right direction either way." She smiled apologetically. "I was touched by your speech, Hanna. I didn't mean to dampen your happiness. I was just curious about what you thought."

"It's absolutely fine. It's a concern. I've often wondered if we'd have the vote now, if all men had already been able to." Hanna smiled, happy to have turned the conversation around.

"They do in New Zealand and in Australia already, but I don't know about the men there," Miss Kline said, just as Vanda came over.

"We should've brought champagne," she said, wagging her finger at them.

Hanna and Miss Kline laughed, causing Maria to turn around to see why.

"Yes, we should have. Votes for women need no temperance. At least not for us women," Hanna said and winked.

Chapter Forty-nine

Anette

She felt familiar arms around her and familiar hands stroking her hair.

"I'm here, Anette."

She opened her eyes and looked into Erik's face. It was swollen and he was pale and gray. His breath stunk. What if he was angry with her for not watching Ester properly?

"I'm so sorry, Erik. I didn't know they were playing by the moat. I was... my back hurt from the baby." She put her hand on her belly. "I didn't know. Edith was with Ester. She would have gone in after her if Nils hadn't stopped her at the last moment. My little girl is gone. My little..." Her voice broke into sobs.

"Shush, shush, it's nothing you could have known. I'm the one who is to blame for all this, Anette."

Surprised, she tried to sit up, but the baby pressed on her and the way he was sitting on her bed made it impossible to move. "It certainly isn't your fault, Erik. You weren't even here."

"I know."

His voice sounded odd, but she was too tired to understand what he meant. Euphemia had given her something that made her sleepy, saying that she had to rest up for the baby's sake.

They were still holding each other when Edith and Ebba came home. Ebba ran to Erik, shrieking with excitement. He scooped her up and held out his other hand to Edith, who took it with a nod. She tried to look brave, but Anette could tell that she too, was afraid that Erik would be angry with her. She waited until Edith let go of his hand and went to make coffee, then whispered so she wouldn't hear.

"Edith blames herself. She told me she wished they hadn't gone up to the castle, but she says that all the statar children like to sit at the edge of the moat in the back and pretend they're royals. Ester didn't understand how thin the ice was this late in the year. It was a miracle that Nils happened to walk by just at that moment."

Erik narrowed his eyes. "Edith isn't to blame. It was an accident."

Anette glanced over at Edith who was placing coffee and several cookies on a tray. They had an abundance of food for a change, meats, jams, pastries with whipped cream, and cheeses from the castle. As if eating would make you feel better after your child had drowned. She hadn't tasted any of it.

Erik left the bed and went to sit down at the table with Ebba on his lap, taking one of the cookies for himself and handing one to Ebba. She ate it and chewed slowly, wrinkling her nose with consternation. Then she said, "Pappa, Ester fell in the water. Her body doesn't work anymore. She's dead."

"Yes, darling, I know," Erik said, and exchanged a glance with Anette.

She pulled herself out of bed and joined them. Ebba told everyone just like that. It was a child's way to process it. She understood that. Still, it rendered her heart into pieces every time.

"How did you find me? I don't think I've told you where I live, have I?" Erik asked, and reached for her hand.

To Anette's surprise, Edith blushed deeply. "Erik, I lied to your colleague. We didn't know what else to do."

"Lied?" Anette exclaimed.

"Mamma, do you remember how Euphemia said she would take care of letting Erik know?"

She nodded.

"I looked in your bag and found Erik's card and the letters with the address to his office. Then Euphemia and I went to the castle and asked to borrow a telephone. At first they didn't want to let us inside. The housekeeper or the maid or whoever she was almost slammed the door in our faces. But then Euphemia explained who I was and that it was my sister who... who died," she said. Her voice broke, but she continued anyway, crying and talking at the same time. Erik handed her a black handkerchief. Maybe it was for mourning.

"We didn't know how to use a telephone, but I remembered what my teacher had explained about it and I managed to reach a man in your office. I had hoped you'd answer so I could just tell you, but you'd already gone home. I should probably have waited until the next day, but I didn't want to." Edith looked at them both, blushing even deeper now. It reminded Anette about herself at that age.

"I told your colleague that I was fourteen years old and would very much like to send a little gift to your daughters who had kindly picked up my pocketbook filled with confirmation money that I'd dropped near church. I said that they had run after me to return it, but I was so stunned that I hadn't even thanked them. I asked if it might be possible to get your home address so I could send them something. He gave it to me and then we fetched Nils and he offered to go all the way to Helsingborg to get you."

"Edith, this isn't what I meant," Anette said sharply.

"It must have been Jonas you spoke with." Erik laughed a strange dry laugh, then he took Edith's hand. "I thank you. It was the right thing to do. I'm so sorry that you had to do that. But I'm very glad that I was told in person. It was for the best. Nils was very kind."

Edith's shoulders slumped in relief. "I'm glad you're not angry. Can I take Ebba outside now, please?"

Anette and Erik both nodded. As soon as the girls were out the door, Erik turned to her.

"Anette, please reconsider my offer of living in Helsingborg. This is outrageous. I'm not... I can't... I cannot protect you like this. Please. I'm begging you."

"I don't know Erik. Please stay until the funeral, then I'll see. I can't talk about it now."

"I have a room at the inn."

She met his eyes. This fully pregnant, she couldn't stay with him there. It would be too obvious. And Erik wouldn't stay here. He would blame it on the fact that she had only one bed, but she knew that the walls with old dirty paint and the acrid smell bothered him.

#

Erik wanted to buy mourning attire for them for the funeral service. Anette refused. No one else would wear it, at least not the full mourning attire Erik had in mind. People would think she was putting on airs. Besides, it would make them question why she was a statare instead of living in the home a sailor clearly could provide for his family. It was enough that Nils had been told the truth. In the end Erik just bought them black shawls, and he wore the black coat he had come with.

Anette kept staring at the casket lid covered in the flowers the castle had sent, trying to make up for the fact that a child had drowned in their moat. She felt removed from everything, numb. Even crying felt fake, as if she were someone else pretending to have lost a child, again. Erik was stoic, but had tears continuously flowing down his cheeks. Ebba was silent and Edith sobbed.

#

Anette gave birth to a girl. Euphemia and Edith helped her, and she came before the midwife arrived. Born on May first, the very same day of the same month as Ester, seven years earlier. It seemed meant to be, and she named her Ester in memory of her dead sister. They called her Little Ester.

#

A month after the birth, Erik came to see his new daughter. They walked together behind the pastures to have some privacy. Anette with Little Ester tied tightly to her chest with her shawls, and Erik silently beside her. She knew what he was about to say.

"Anette, why? Why can't you let me get an apartment for you? Why? I keep asking, but you never say yes. I don't understand. You may have your own little cottage here, but it's dilapidated and nasty. It's bloody outrageous. Someone I love shouldn't have to milk bloody cows just to feed my children."

She glanced at him, but he was looking straight ahead, scowling angrily. Erik never used to curse, but he had done that during the week of the funeral too.

"Your sister doesn't have an issue with bloody cows for people. I don't see what's so wrong with it."

He turned to her, shaking his head slowly. "Because all those women at Häckeberga have husbands that love them, even if they're all poor. It's the same here, isn't it? But I'm not poor and I can provide for my family."

"But you're not my husband," she whispered, but he didn't hear it. Looking down at Little Ester's head, she put her nose to her fuzzy blond hair and sniffed. Ester had drowned, there was no need to struggle anymore, it would be all right to say yes. She looked back up. He still looked angry.

"You know Anette, do you know what I had to do to cover for Edith's lying?"

"No."

"Well, I'll tell you. I had to explain to Jonas, my assistant, that it wasn't true, pretend that it had been some kind of ruse, like a dare, to get access to my address so someone could send a prankster letter. Just so Jonas wouldn't ask my other daughters about it. Not to mention how mortified Jonas was. Then I had to pretend I was angry that he gave out my address, even though I was thankful. You hear?"

She couldn't believe it. He was upset because he had to give an excuse? And she who lied to protect him, just most recently at the baptism, just to protect him and his other family. It was the same parson as last time, and again she kept Erik's name out of the church books.

"You have the gall to complain to me about having to make excuses for my existence, when you're the one who's married to someone else?" she screamed angrily. It woke Little Ester who let out a loud ear-piercing howl. Anette ignored it. "I lie, I lie all the time for you, to protect our love even as I carry your babies."

Erik's head jerked backward as if she had slapped him, but he didn't answer.

She had been so close to say yes. But he answered it for her. If something happened that gave away their secret, she would be on her own again and have to drag their children back into statarhood. She wouldn't be able to bear it. At least now she knew what they had. She went to sit on a tree stump and pulled out her breast to feed the baby. Erik followed, hugging her close before she sat down, murmuring apologies in her ear. But something had broken between them.

Chapter Fifty

Hanna

1905

Two red splotches were forming on the woman's cheeks as she pointed at Hanna's cakes with green marzipan.

"That one there looks delicious. Is it filled with crème?" she asked, cooling herself with a large black fan.

"Yes, slightly sweetened. Would you like a sample?"

"Oh yes, thank you."

The woman looked so excited that Hanna instinctively pulled a chair over for her. "Please sit. Do you have a big occasion planned?"

"My daughter's engagement. We're having a reception next week. Soon she'll give us grandchildren."

"Congratulations, I'm happy for you," Hanna said, suppressing a twinge of jealousy at the mention of children. She felt like telling her not to take that for granted.

The woman nodded and picked up a forkful of cake and put it in her mouth slowly, taking time to savor it. "I like this. I think I'll take four of them. Will that be enough for thirty people?"

"It'll be just enough if you serve thin slices. Perhaps you could offer something else as well," she suggested, gesturing to a plate with her automobile cookies. "These are popular."

Mr. Larsson, a regular customer at a nearby table, signaled that he wanted more coffee, and Hanna excused herself. As she poured his coffee, he pointed to his newspaper that lay opened on the table. The headline read, Norway Declares Union with Sweden Dissolved.

Hanna stared at the words, trying to remember what the issue was.

"What else does it say? Is this about the consulate?" she asked, leaning over the table, careful so as not to spill coffee over his newspaper.

"Yes, the Norwegian government had wanted its own, separate from us, remember?"

Hanna shook her head. She should have, but she didn't actually remember it.

Mr. Larsson pursed his lips and pointed to the text below the headline and paraphrased, "The Norwegians wanted to resign, which of course King Oscar declined since he can't form a new government now because of this. But look here," he tapped his finger on the second paragraph, "Norway says that since the King can't form a Norwegian government, the union is dissolved."

Mr. Larsson turned to Hanna with his eyebrows raised. "But the King didn't say he *couldn't,* he said he couldn't *now.* It's outrageous, an insult. Imagine breaking up a union that has stood fast for nearly a hundred years? We may have to go to war," he added loudly.

"I hope not." Hanna poured him a little more coffee and left him to his reading. He must surely be exaggerating. War couldn't be an actual possibility, could it?

When she returned to the counter, her customer's face was as pale as a ghost's.

"I heard what you were saying. I must... my daughter's fiancé is in the army." The woman looked out the window as if she expected to see troops in the street. "What are we going to do?"

"For now, have a seat." Hanna pointed to the chair she had brought over earlier. "Let me get you a cup of coffee."

"Oh, dear... my husband, I have to talk to him. Do you have a telephone?"

"No," Hanna said, deciding at that moment that she would get one for the Frog.

The woman nodded with resignation and sat down. Hanna pulled the table closer to her chair, moved the other two chairs over and went to get her a cup, bringing one for herself as well.

"Mr. Larsson," Hanna said as she sat down. "Will you join us?"

He nodded, looking pleased that she asked. Pushing his chair out behind him, he balanced his coffee and sandwich in one hand

and the paper in the other and walked over.

"Thank you, Mrs. Agnell."

"Of course. Do you really think we'll go to war?"

"Maybe not, but we're likely headed for some tense negotiations," he said, glancing at her customer who was fanning herself vigorously again.

"Ma'am, would you like me to walk you home?"

"Would you, sir? That would be most kind."

They both stood at the same time and Mr. Larsson picked up his paper and put it under his arm, leaving his sandwich half eaten on his plate. He only had time to throw a glance at Hanna before rushing after the woman to open the door before she did. Hanna stared after them, wishing she could call him back so they could discuss it more. He had looked so happy that she invited him over to sit with them. But of course, when a woman fanned herself with distress, men fell over themselves to be of assistance. Sighing, she went to get a dishrag to wipe down the tables. It was almost closing time anyway, and the Frog was empty now. She would get her own paper on the way home and talk about it with Johannes over dinner. Hopefully, it would be resolved peacefully. A telephone was a good idea though. They ought to get one for home as well.

Chapter Fifty-one

Anette

Anette had heard about King Oskar and the military troops assembled on both sides of the border between Sweden and Norway. Then on October 26 the foreign ministers of both countries signed a peace agreement and the union dissolved peacefully. It was a relief, but she hadn't had much time to worry about it. Everything was changing. She hadn't seen Erik for almost two years, and though they never said anything to each other, she had known it was over. It wasn't just the arguing. It felt as if their relationship was surrounded by grief and death. They met when his stepmother died, then when Ingrid died, and now Ester was dead too. It was unbearable and she resented grieving alone when he went home to his wife and children. Edith was almost fourteen already and was leaving Dybäck's farm. She had been offered a position as a laundress at a fine house nearby. She would have her own room and live inside the home. It was a great opportunity for a statar girl. Anette had a feeling that the Dybäck owners had recommended her as a way to help after Ester's death, but she wasn't sure.

Euphemia had met a new man and was moving with him to his torp-cottage in Beddinge. The torp had its own plot of land leased to him by the landowner in exchange for work two or three days a week, depending on the season. Euphemia only needed to help out on occasion. It was when she told Anette about all this, that she offered to take Ebba for a while, saying that Anette needed time to herself after everything that had happened. Ebba would have a better life with someone who could look after her most of the time, someone who was not in the barn or out in the fields milking all day. Most importantly, Ebba and Euphemia's son were inseparable, and Rolf treated her as his little sister. Reluctantly, Anette agreed to let her go. Surrounded by memories of the funeral and Ester's traumatic death, she decided it was time for her to move on as well. When Slack Week arrived, they all went their separate ways, and she left Dybäck's farm with only Little Ester in her arms.

#

Tjute Farm looked impressive, not like a farm at all despite the name.

Two pillars, each taller than a man and wide as a cow, stood at the entrance to a long grove of large trees which led to a garden with neatly trimmed hedges. Beyond it was a majestic white house. It had a grand entranceway that beckoned visitors inside, but Anette knew she wasn't expected to use it and kept walking.

There was a door at the back of the house. It even had a clearly marked wooden sign on it that read Farmhands and Maids Knock Here: Don't Enter. She knocked and stood waiting while Little Ester nodded off on her shoulder. The only sound was the wind blowing in the trees. Anette shivered in her thin coat and shawl and hugged Little Ester closer. When no one answered, she peered through a window but couldn't make anything out. Even though it was late in the afternoon, no lamps were lit.

She left her valise on the ground in front of the door and looked around. Two barns were very close to the main house and had a large yard between them. Perhaps people parked their carriages there when they had parties, or even automobiles. She had seen one driving up to Dybäck's castle once, looking very odd the way it drove all by itself, but Erik said that they were becoming more and more common.

Little Ester was now sound asleep and growing heavy in her arms. Looking around again, she found a large tree stump and had just sat down on it when she heard a shout.

"Hello there, ma'am!"

A man was coming from behind the barn on her left. He looked to be around forty. His clothes were of excellent quality but splattered with mud and dust. Something wasn't right about it, and she sensed that he wasn't supposed to be there.

"Good evening, sir," she said and quickly stood up, curtsying as best she could.

"No need for such displays as that, ma'am," he said with a laugh. "Are you looking for the mistress? She isn't here today. No one is. They're all at the Nilsson auction."

"The what?"

"The Nilsson auction, you've never heard of it?"

"I came from afar." Anette sat down again, not caring if he thought her rude. She had traveled for two days with three other statar families that were also relocating. The farm where she had hoped to find work didn't have room for her, but the owner had dropped her off here, assuring her they needed milkmaids.

The man glanced over at her valise on the ground. "Are you here to work with the cows?"

"Yes, sir."

"Call me Ludvig Svensson. You're a widow I take it since I see no husband about?"

Anette nodded, relieved that he had offered his own explanation.

He picked up her valise. "It's a bit of a haul. I'll take you over to the statar lodgings. I have my cart around back. Wait here, please."

He started walking, but then he turned and let the valise slip to the ground. "It's nonsense to carry this when I'm coming back," he said.

Anette exhaled. She had worried that he was going to walk off with it. Not that she had left any valuables in there; those were well-hidden in her corset.

She didn't know what to think of the man. He seemed nice enough, but something about his manner told her to be careful. From the way he spoke, she would have thought he was one of her own class, but his clothes, albeit dirty, said otherwise.

He returned in a wagon loaded with sacks of grain. Maybe he had stolen them. That may be why he had come around to the front without his carriage, just to make it wasn't the owners that were coming back. It might be better if she waited for someone else. But it was getting dark, and the air had grown colder. She took Svensson's hand and let him pull her up beside him. Then he whistled loudly to his horse, and they were off.

When they reached the bottom of a small hill, he reigned in

the horse. "It's up there, not far," he said, pointing toward a trampled path. Then he jumped off, got her valise, and helped her down. "I can't get up there with my wagon, but that's where the milkmaids live," he said and climbed back up.

"Thank you, Ludvig Svensson."

"You're quite welcome, ma'am," he said with a grin and whistled to his horse, which broke into a trot. Anette watched as he drove off, then picked up her valise with her free hand and walked the way he showed her. As soon as she started up the little hill, she could see two statar lodgings. Each was painted gray with a black roof and had only one door and two small windows. There was a well close by. That was certainly an improvement. At Dybäck she had to walk to the barn each day to get water.

Anette was balancing Little Ester higher on her shoulder when the door of the closest lodging opened, and a woman poked her head out.

"Good evening," she said and smiled. She was young and wore a beige dress with washed out blue cornflowers, barely visible anymore. "You must be new."

Anette drew closer, heartened by the friendly welcome. "Thank you. I'm Anette and this is Ester, my daughter," she said, deciding to not use Little Ester anymore so she wouldn't have to explain that she was named after her older dead sister.

"Oh, what a darling and sleeping she is already. Has it been a long journey? Where are you from?"

"I worked at Dybäck's Farm."

"Oh, I've never heard of it. Come in, come in."

Warm air greeted her, along with the scent of coffee and something cooking. There were three beds on one side, a table in the middle with two chairs, a threadbare rug on the floor, and a rather small hearth with a kettle and a cauldron competing for space on the fire.

"My mother will be here soon. She went to get a couple of eggs," the woman said, then stopped, smiling apologetically. "I didn't introduce myself. My name is Anna."

"Nice to meet you, Anna." Anette pointed to a bed that

looked as though no one had slept in it. "May I put Ester down?"

"Oh, of course, she must be heavy, and you can have that bed if you wish. No one has claimed it yet. Is this little one your first?"

"My third," Anette lied. "Her sisters are big enough to be on their own." At least that was somewhat true. "What about you, do you have any little ones?"

Anna giggled. "No, of course not, I'm not married." She glanced at the ring on Anette's left hand. "Where's your husband?"

Anette looked Anna straight in the eye. "He died when Ester was a couple months old," she said, then regretted it. She shouldn't tell people that Erik was dead. It wasn't right. She loved him still, and he didn't deserve that. What if he found her again? Though it was near impossible. No one knew where she had gone, and Euphemia wasn't there to tell him anything anyway. But what if he still did?

"I'm so sorry."

"Thank you," Anette said awkwardly, nodded at Anna and put Ester on the bed. When she turned back around there was another woman in the room. She placed a small basket of eggs on the table, then faced Anette with a broad smile.

"Oh dear, a new person already? We didn't expect anyone for a day or two," she said and wiped sweat off her forehead with her sleeve.

"This is Swea, my mother," Anna announced.

Swea extended her arm and shook Anette's hand. "Welcome to our humble abode. Glad to have you and the little one too, what a darling," she said and smiled warmly at Little Ester, who was snoring softly with her arms flung above her head.

"Have a seat and relax yourself. I was just about to make us something to eat. Are you hungry?"

"I am," Anette said, relieved by their kindness. "Thank you."

Chapter Fifty-two

Hanna

November 1905

Hanna squeezed Vanda's and Maria's hands, looking around herself excitedly. They were in a lecture hall in Stockholm, waiting for the author Frida Stéenhoff to come on stage. She was a women's rights activist, feminism she called it, and Hanna's heart was beating with anticipation. The hall was filled with women, each as excited as she was, though some tried not to show it. A woman sitting nearby opened a small embroidered handbag and pulled out a notebook and pencil. As if on cue, several other women in her row did the same.

Hanna nudged Vanda with her elbow and whispered, "Who *is* she? People are staring at her."

Vanda leaned forward. "It's Kerstin Hesselgren," she said. "I can't believe it!"

"Who?" Maria asked.

"Kerstin Hesselgren," Vanda whispered. "I've heard a lot about her. She just returned from England. She studied Industrial Inspection at Bedford College. Fredrika Bremer gave her a scholarship and... look, look who's sitting in the row right behind her to the right."

Vanda waited for them to spot her then said, "It's Kata Dalström!"

Maria squeezed Hanna's hand. "Oh, dear, it is. I heard she helped organize the voting demonstrations here in Stockholm."

Hanna grinned, wishing Magnhild was with them. She was still talking about the demonstration where that woman had been arrested. Knowing Magnhild, she would go speak to Kata and ask if she knew her, then asked to be introduced.

"Now the Social Democrats think she's become too radical," Vanda added.

Then Frida Stéenhoff walked in, and everyone stopped

talking. Smiling, she walked across the stage and stopped in the middle. Her thick blondish hair was tied in a bun on top of her head. Several strands had escaped and hung down on the sides and across her forehead, framing her large eyes and full lips. She looked wonderful. Hanna smiled at Vanda and Maria, but their eyes were glued to Frida, and they didn't notice.

"The women's movement and the movement for voting rights, like all movements, is a response to a problem. It comes from a common wound caused when those who are stronger exploit or take advantage of those who are weaker. . . ." Frida began, and Hanna looked forward as well, forgetting everything else.

"A woman's existence depends on her serving a man, therefore she may not speak of things that are not interesting or pleasing to the man; maybe it would push away her future provider. . . .

"This is understandable, but not an excuse. I don't understand those who say women have not yet given the movement enough time and effort, therefore they should not yet have the right to vote. Men have expended a great deal of time and effort on achieving the right to vote for men of every class. Can we not build upon their work? . . .

"It is said that women are not yet mature enough to vote, that they are not ready. But women work and pay their taxes as well as men, working side by side with them to earn their daily bread. Women work in factories, universities, schools... They have no voting rights and therefore are not equal to the men. . . .

"And what about those times when the government discusses laws that have to do with women's issues? Shall we women not have a say? Why should women wait? And for how long? Five years? Ten? Twenty?"

The question remained suspended in the air, and Hanna and Maria exchanged a glance. God forbid it would be more than five years.

Frida continued speaking, keeping everyone focused on her words. She was a wonderful speaker and Hanna wished she had brought a pencil and notebook too. When Frida was about to conclude, she paused, looked out at her audience, and said,

"During times of uncertainty, one would hope that the government would be wise enough to provide women with the assurance that fairness is not dead."

She bowed her head and stood silently for several moments. Then the audience broke into applause, and Maria and Vanda grabbed Hanna's arms and pulled her to her feet. The clapping went on for so long that her hands hurt. Still, she couldn't stop. Frida had been incredible. She was right. Why should they wait?
When they finally stopped clapping, Maria put her hand to her chest.

"Oh," she breathed, shaking her head. "I don't even know what to say."

"Truly inspirational," Hanna said, grinning at Vanda who was already waiting at the end of their now empty row of chairs.

They worked their way through the crowd. The hall seemed more packed than before as people were standing in the aisles. Once outside, they remained on the steps of the building for several minutes while the other women poured out and swept past them. The city lights were glittering like stars in the moist night air. Large snowflakes flickered in front of the streetlamps and carriage lanterns as the horses trotted past. It was beautiful. Maria touched Hanna on the shoulder. "I won't ever forget this night," she said.

"I won't either," Hanna said and shifted her gaze from the view to look at her. "I loved how she brought up the times when the government is discussing laws that have to do with women's issues. It's perhaps the most important reason we should be able to vote. Men shouldn't sit around talking about what concerns us when we're not present."

"Indeed," said Vanda, nodding for effect, then stopped when a woman wearing a dark fur coat approached them.

"I hear from your accent that you're from the south. Did you come all this way just to hear our Frida?"

"Yes," said Hanna and smiled, happy to make a connection. Maybe she was a member of LKPR. But the woman didn't return her smile. She was frowning.

"So, I take it you're not married, or you wouldn't be able to travel so far just for a speech."

"We've come from Lund for the speech and my friend here and I do happen to be married," Hanna said and nodded toward Maria, feeling confused.

"I stand corrected. But what about your children?"

"I have six children, daughters all. I've traveled here so they can have a better future," Maria said proudly.

Hanna met Maria's glinting eyes gratefully. Why was the woman so nosy? She seemed to have thrown herself at them just to ask personal questions.

"That's one way to look at it," the woman said, then turned back to Hanna. "And you, missus, how many children do you have?"

"I don't... we don't have any," Hanna said, then wished she had told her it wasn't her concern.

"Oh, recently married and still fighting for the cause?"

"No."

"So, how long *have* you been married?"

Hanna sighed, knowing what would come next. She would look pain-stricken and start going on and on about how sad it was. Her evening would be ruined.

She straightened her shoulders. "My husband and I have been married thirteen years."

"You're a radical."

It was so unexpected, Hanna thought she misheard. "Pardon me?"

"You know, the movement opposes contraception. It's why men don't want to give us the right to vote. If they think we'll stop having children, they'll never support it. I knew it. Shame on you!" she said angrily, then hurried down the steps.

Hanna's mouth fell open. "Bloody hell!"

"How dare she?" Maria said, almost shouting. "I'm going to have a word with her."

Vanda grabbed her arm. "Don't bother. That woman isn't worth it."

Hanna stared after her as she reached the bottom step and ran toward someone waiting for her by a streetlamp. It was easy for Vanda to say, but the woman had ruined a wonderful and inspiring evening. Why did she always have to be reminded of her infertility?

"People who prejudge like that are never worth it, Hanna," Vanda repeated, then linked arms with them both. "Come, ladies, it's a beautiful night. We don't need a carriage. Let's walk. Then we'll be hungry when we get back to the hotel."

Hanna nodded and let it be. There was no reason to ruin their evening as well.

An hour later, Hanna, Maria, and Vanda were sitting in the hotel restaurant with glasses of wine and a plate of fruit and cheese.

Maria cut off a piece of brie. "That woman was crazy. To accuse Hanna of willfully refusing to have children."

Vanda took a long sip of wine. "I know you mean well, but quite frankly it pains me to see you so bothered by the idea. You see, I *am* one of those radicals the woman was talking about. I'm not ashamed to admit that I've used contraceptives."

"You *have?*" Maria put her wine glass down and tried to exchange a glance with Hanna, but she averted her eyes. In Vanda's case it must be a blessing. Just imagine what her husband could have done to a child.

Maria gazed down at her glass, picked it up again, and finished it. "Of course you're entitled to your point of view, Vanda. But if women didn't get pregnant, men would just have relations and then leave. They'd have no reason to marry. Then the poor girl would never find a husband. No man wants to marry a woman who isn't a virgin. It's the law too, women are supposed to be virgins at their weddings." She gestured to the waiter, asking him to bring more wine.

Vanda waited until he had refilled their glasses. "Yet there are women who become pregnant, and the man leaves anyway. Haven't you heard Bengta speak of the babies she's delivered who aren't wanted? Besides, I for one was married when I used it. You both know the reason," she said, looking straight at Maria who was becoming visibly uncomfortable.

Hanna drank silently, glad that Maria had at least relaxed her views on absolutism a bit. This evening clearly needed wine.

"Well, I have many things to say about all this," Hanna said. "First, my activism and passion for suffrage has nothing to do with if I have children or not. I should have told her, but I was too stunned. The woman was very odd. I shouldn't have let her treat me like that. I got a bad feeling in my stomach as soon as she started asking all her nosy questions. She was smug from the beginning, and Vanda, I wish you hadn't stopped Maria from going after her." She exhaled deeply, then took another sip of wine. "I want a baby so much, with all my heart, but women aren't all the same. Bengta and Magnhild don't have babies, you don't have any, and we seem quite capable to fight for suffrage without destroying the movement. Don't we?"

Maria reached out and touched her hand. "You're right Hanna, I'm so sorry. This is a sensitive topic for me because," she lowered her voice, "I love all my daughters, but before the last two came I had hoped not to have any more. I was so exhausted from my pregnancies, and when I became pregnant again, I was disappointed at first. Still, I have trouble picturing doing something that would've prevented them. I love them so."

Hanna nodded, remembering that day when Kurt told her how surprised they were that Maria was expecting again.

Vanda was silent. The waiter was looking at them. He probably couldn't hear anything but must see that it wasn't the appropriate time to ask them if they needed anything.

"It's nothing to be ashamed of Maria. Six children are a lot," Vanda said after a moment. "And Hanna, I'm sorry. I shouldn't have told either of you what to do or how to feel, especially not you Hanna, I apologize."

"Thank you both, apologizes accepted," Hanna said and smiled. Maria looked relieved.

"But something else that I think often," Vanda said, "is the babies who must live with people who don't love them. People who might have them without being able to care for them properly. I've seen parenting that gives me nightmares for weeks, just after overhearing a conversation between the parents and the child. I've seen harsh hands too, and I'm not talking about myself here, but others. And God knows a baby wouldn't be safe in the home I had with Alexander." Her hand went to her knobby arm.

"Yes Vanda, you're right about that too. I can be very conservative sometimes and I don't always think about every side of an issue," Maria admitted.

Hanna took another sip of wine, then reached for a piece of cheese and a pear wedge. Their words became muffled and something warm came into her chest. It was what Vanda had said about Bengta delivering babies that weren't wanted. Why hadn't she thought about this before? At the House, some of the women didn't want to keep their babies.

She reached for her wine glass again, but her eyes teared up and instead of grabbing the stem, she pushed it and the glass fell over, spilling on the white tablecloth. Had it been red wine, it would have been very symbolic. She chuckled and smiled into Vanda's and Maria's concerned faces.

"Hanna? What's happening?"

"I've been an idiot, really. It's been so many years. I'm going to speak with Bengta. Thank you, Vanda."

Vanda narrowed her eyes. "What did I do now?"

"Adoption," Hanna laughed, then burst into tears.

Chapter Fifty-three

Anette

Anette wiped the sweat off her brow and opened the door to let some air into the dairy.

"It's too hot today," she said to Anna. "I wish we didn't have to deal with the milk ourselves. I used to work at Häckeberga Castle and we milkmaids never went to the dairy, we had what they called dairy girls do that for us."

"Really, dairy girls? That must have been much easier."

"Yes, it was," Anette said, then heard hooves outside and a man's voice talking to his horse.

Moments later, he poked his head through the door, his face lighting up when he saw them. It was Ludvig Svensson.

"Mornin' Anna, Mornin' Anette, I wanted to come by to introduce you to my new horse."

Anna looked at Anette and laughed, and Anette chuckled. Ludvig came by every so often. He was a strange man, but as far as she knew, he hadn't stolen anything since that first day almost a year ago.

Anette closed the lid on her milk can and put her bucket on the floor. "Why not? We'll come out," she said.

As soon as they stepped over the threshold, they were awestruck. The horse was enormous. It had a black mane and a light brown coat that made the muscles gleam in the sunshine. It was wider and thicker than any horse she had ever seen. It made Erik's horses seem spindly.

Ludvig nodded with satisfaction at their expressions.

"It's a new breed, a workhorse. Some say they'll replace oxen one day," he said. "I just got him. Come pet him, he's friendly."

Anette went up to the horse, and he turned his big head and looked at her, reminding her of the cow she had milked at Häckeberga that first day. Everything was reminding her of Häckeberga lately. She put her hand under the thick black mane, feeling that moist warmth that all horses had under their manes. She always loved petting them there.

"I've named him King. Do you think my fiancée will like him?"

"I'm sure she will," Anna said. "When is the wedding?"

"Soon." Ludvig stared at something at the horizon. "I should go," he added and grabbed the reins. "May I borrow a bucket so I can mount?" he asked with a half grin.

"Yes, of course," Anna said and hurried inside to get one. As soon as she disappeared out of sight, Anette felt Ludvig's eyes boring into her side, but she didn't turn around. When Anna came back out, Ludvig placed the bucket upside down next to King, then stepped on it and hoisted himself up on the saddleless back, lifted his hat, and was off.

"I love horses," Anette said as they walked back into the dairy. She missed Erik and their rides to the inn, and the horse he used to rent so he could get from the train station to her.

When Anette saw Ludvig again a week later she was alone, taking a shortcut across a fallow field on her way to the statar lodgings. Walking briskly, he crossed the road and jumped over the ditch to get beside her.

"Ah, there you are, my dear woman. I was hoping to see you. I've heard that you're a very good seamstress."

Dear woman? He had never called her that before. It made her uneasy. She stopped and looked around to see if Anna was behind her, but the field was empty.

"I am, yes."

He looked relieved. "I'm in a real predicament. My suit is worn at the elbows. Could you help me with it?"

"What color is the suit?

"It's gray."

She breathed a little easier. "I do have gray thread. I'll see if I can alter it for you. Bring it to me tomorrow."

"I thank you kindly, but could you please do it today? I'm meeting with my fiancée's family tomorrow for an engagement feast. I'll drive you to get whatever you need." He pointed across the field at his carriage and new horse, which was whipping its tail around to shoo away the flies.

"Very well, but I can't stay long. I must get back to my daughter."

"Of course."

He helped her across the ditch to the road. Moments later, they were sitting behind the horse. It made it up the hill with no effort.

Anette had hoped Anna would be there to accompany her, but the room was empty. Not even Stina, the eight-year-old girl who watched Ester while she milked, was there. Disappointed, she grabbed her little mending basket and went back outside. Ludvig was standing next to his horse, patting his head. For a moment she wondered if she should tell him to go home and fetch the suit instead, but it would just seem strange, they had already decided.

Ten minutes later they reached his home. It was red with white trimmings and looked new. It was only a bit down the road from Tjute Farm.

"Your house is nice," Anette said.

"Thank you. I built it more or less myself. I'm eager to hear your opinion once we get inside, to see if it's fit for a woman." His eyes passed briefly over her bosom as he took her hand and helped her down. She ignored it, pushing down the same uneasy feeling as before.

"So what do you think?" he asked as they stepped through the doorway. "Any suggestions?"

The place was neat but dusty, with bare hardwood floors, a table, four chairs, and a fireplace. A door to another room was closed.

"Your fiancée might like a rug to warm the place up a bit."

"That's a good thought," Ludvig said, then reached for the suit hanging from a hook on the wall. He gestured to one of the chairs by the table, and she sat down as he handed it to her. Just as he had said, it was worn at the elbows, and she relaxed a little.

Anette turned the sleeves inside out. "It's been taken in at the arms. I can cut there to make patches."

"That'll do. As long as it looks right."

"It will."

She set to work and by the time she finished, Ludvig had placed a flask and two cups on the table. He took the suit from her and hung it back on the hook with barely a glance.

"Have a drink with me for your trouble," he said, then sat down and filled each cup. He swallowed his, then refilled it. Flask in hand, he looked expectantly at Anette and said, "Skål!"

She drank half of hers and he promptly added more, then swallowed his own and refilled it again. He raised his cup in a toast and they both drank. Leaning over the table, he refilled her cup again. It was delicious and warmed nicely in throat.

"Anette, can you tell me what else I may need to make my fiancée like me? Not about my house, just in general, if you understand what I mean?"

She did, but said, "When is the wedding? And what kind of alcohol is this?"

"You like it?" He refilled her cup again. "It's whiskey. The wedding is a year away."

Ludvig didn't say anything after that, and she hoped her comment about his wedding would make him stop with his uncomfortable flirting.

She looked around, sipping slowly and biding her time until it seemed that a polite length of time had passed. When she stood up, her legs felt wobbly, and she grabbed the edge of the table for support. In the next moment, he was by her side.

"Here, let me take your arm. Before you leave, come see the bedroom. You might be able to suggest an improvement there too."

Maintaining his grip on her elbow, he guided her across the floor and opened the door. The room was small, just big enough for a bed. She hadn't meant to enter, but he put his arm around her waist and swished her inside as if they were dancing. Then his lips were on top of hers. She pulled away, noticing that she was perfectly calm. Her legs felt strong again too.

"Don't be so unfriendly," he grunted. "Stay a little longer."

"I need to go," she said, and now her heart started racing

out of control. She had to get away from him.

"Don't be so pious." He put his arm around her waist again. "You're a beautiful woman, such unusual eyes."

She struggled against his grasp, but he kissed her again, this time shoving his tongue into her mouth. It tasted sour. She pushed his face away with her hands and moved her own head as far backwards as she could.

"I need to go home to my daughter. Swea and Anna will be worried," she said. It didn't sound the way she meant it, just slurred and weak.

He pulled her closer.

"Let go of me!" She was screaming now, pulling and scratching at his arms, sitting like heavy ropes around her waist. They didn't budge. This couldn't be happening. She should never have gone with him. Why hadn't she listened to herself?

Ludvig ignored her and pushed her down on the bed. It happened so fast that she didn't have time to react. He cursed under his breath, pulled her skirts up around her waist, pulled her drawers down, spit on his hand, and rubbed her roughly between her legs. She tried to get her knee up to push him away, but he was too heavy, and with the blood pounding in her ears, she closed her eyes and prayed for it to be over soon.

When he was finished with her, she rolled off the bed and stumbled through the house and out the front door. Then her drawers that she had forgotten to pull back up, slipped down to her feet, and she tripped, falling headlong on the ground and scraping her right knee. She pulled her drawers off and got up and ran, holding them in her hand. Out of the corner of her eye, she thought she could see his silhouette in the window, and she shifted her drawers into her other hand so he wouldn't see them.

Anette ran until she reached the bottom of her hill. There she stopped, smoothed her hair, and straightened her underskirts. She picked up a leaf from the ground and blew her nose in it, glanced up at the darkening sky, and said a prayer that her courses would come as they should in a couple of weeks. Then she walked the rest of the way to her door. She would pretend it hadn't happened, push it deep down in her mind to that secret place where she kept Carl and Jon hidden.

#

But as soon as she opened the door, both Swea and Anna dropped their knitting on the floor and the look on their faces pulled everything out again.

"Anette, what happened?" Anna screamed, crossed the floor in two long steps, then grabbed her by the waist. Instantly the feeling of Ludvig's heavy arms squeezing her came back, and Anette pushed her away before she knew what she was doing. Anna looked surprised, but not angry.

"I'm so sorry, I didn't…" Anette stopped. Her voice was so sore and hoarse that she didn't recognize it. Suddenly she remembered that she had been screaming at Ludvig when he was inside her, screaming the entire time even while closing her eyes. She thought she had been silent, but she hadn't. And he had laughed while she screamed.

Swea came close and gazed searchingly into Anette's face.

"Anette, what happened, did someone hurt you? Where's your headscarf and why is your face dirty? And you're bleeding."

"I am?"

Swea pointed to her skirts. There was blood on her clogs and the outer skirt was torn in several places, exposing her underskirt, which was red with blood.

"He forced himself on me. I.. I couldn't stop him." Anna clasped her hand over her mouth, but Swea grimaced calmly, eyes still locked with Anette's.

"Who?"

"Ludvig Svensson," Anette whispered.

Anna's eyes widened, and she turned away and walked over to the hearth, then spit in it. When she came back, her eyes were blazing. "That brute of a miscreant! I knew there was something not right with that man."

Anette remained where she was, swallowing the shame Anna's words confirmed. Ludvig wasn't a good man, and she should have known and never gone with him.

"Anette, may I take your hand and help you sit?" Anna asked and slowly walked toward her.

She nodded.

Anna grabbed her hand as gently as she could, and Anette resisted the urge to jerk it back as Anna's warm skin enclosed around her ice-cold hand. Then they made their way across the floor.

"Wait here," Anna said, and went to get a blanket from her own bed. She folded it, then placed it over the seat and backrest. Anette sat down, grateful for the softness. She glanced at her own bed where Ester lay asleep with her back turned toward them. Thank God she was asleep at least.

Swea sat down in front of her. "I'm going to lift up your skirts now so I can wash your legs. Then tomorrow we shall head to the constable."

"No, I went to his house willingly. They'll never believe me," Anette said and shook her head.

"That's not a reason for him to do what he did," Anna said angrily. "He had no right, no right. You're a widow."

Anette closed her eyes, feeling the room spin slightly. Maybe if she hadn't lied and Ludvig thought she had a husband that could come to kill him, he would never have done it.

Chapter Fifty-four

Erik

Enormous snowflakes floated to the glistening white ground. Erik wished that Christine Marie were awake to see it, but she had fallen asleep in his arms as soon as their sleigh moved.

Antoinette sat quietly between Emelie and Sigrid, warm in her deep blue coat with its white fox collar that seemed to shimmer in the faint lantern light. She looked beautiful. He smiled at her, and she returned it warmly. Maybe it was just the Christmas spirit, but it felt almost like it used to feel between them before she found out.

"There it is," Sigrid shouted, snapping him out of his reverie. The clouds had drifted away from the moon, revealing Häckeberga lake ahead. It was covered with ice and snow.

Antoinette's smile widened and Emelie pointed toward Häckeberga castle. "Look, Pappa, we can see Aunt Sofia's Christmas tree in the window."

Erik squinted until he could make out the flickering triangle of candles. "You have good eyes." Then, with a wink, he added, "I can't believe we're here already, especially since we were picked up from the train by a sleigh instead of an automobile."

Sigrid giggled. "Pappa, what makes you think you'd be able to travel in those noisemakers in the middle of the winter? It's too cold. The tires would get stuck in the snow and if you stopped, the motor would go out and you'd have to wind it up again. You'd freeze to death."

"While several highwaymen robbed you," Antoinette said.

"Yes, before making their getaway in a horse-drawn sleigh," Emelie said. They all laughed, and he scoffed, mockingly shaking his finger at them. It sent Sigrid and Emilie into a giggling fit, and he exchanged another warm glance with Antoinette.

The horse slowed down and cantered over the bridge leading to the front of the castle. Sofia and Anders had placed torches on either side of the entrance and in the empty flowerpots on the upper balcony. The thick wet snowflakes made a spitting sound as they hit the flames.

Sofia appeared in the doorway and hurried down the steps.

"Oh, little Christine-Marie," she said, taking her from Erik's arms while beaming at the others. "Come in, come in. Anders has the brandy ready in the medieval room. We have a tree there too. Come, Sigrid and Emelie."

Erik hid a sigh as he took Antoinette's arm and helped her down. Of course, it would have to be the medieval room, the very room where he met Anette for the first time.

It had been years now since he last saw her. Where did she and the girls celebrate Christmas? Did they sit in her drafty one-room cottage or were they in Euphemia's room in the statar row with Rolf? Little Ester would be almost the same age as Christine Marie. He pulled their suitcases and the bag with Christmas gifts from the sleigh and followed the women inside, pushing his guilt aside.

"Hello, dear boy, come in and warm yourself by the fire." Anders hugged him and gave him an exaggerated manly clap on the back, then smiled at Emilie and Sigrid who were busy admiring the Christmas tree. In their excitement, they had dropped their coats where they stood.

"Girls, pick your coats up off the floor," Erik said sharply.

Anders just laughed. "Here, have a scotch. Or perhaps you'd prefer a brandy? It's the best libation for getting someone in the mood for Christmas."

Erik chuckled. "It certainly is. But I'd still prefer a scotch, thank you." He took the glass from his brother-in-law and sank down on the fur-covered bench, putting his feet on the log that served as a footrest. Sofia and Antoinette ushered the girls up the stairs and ignored the coats and the drinks.

Erik shook his head at them and raised his glass. "It's nice to have a couple days away from the office." He took a long, warming drink and gazed at the flames engulfing the Yule Log in the fireplace that Edna must have lit just before they arrived. It smelled like Christmas.

"Yes, finally," Anders said and yawned, leaning back against the seat.

Erik poured himself another glass of scotch. "Let's go join the women." He stood up and walked to the door, then stopped at the threshold. "Come. Bring your drink."

"I will shortly, you go on. I may close my eyes just for a moment," Anders said and yawned again.

Erik considered talking him out of it, but then he shrugged and went to look for his wife and sister.

He found them all in the library. Sofia sat with her feet wrapped in a multi-colored, crocheted quilt, and smiled when she saw him.

"Ah, there you are," she whispered, pointing to Sigrid and Emelie who were dozing in the armchairs, long legs splayed out at odd angles. "I put Christine Marie to bed."

He took a seat next to Antoinette on the couch. She waited a moment, then got up.

"I think I'll retire now, if you don't mind?"

Erik glanced at his watch, 8.30 only. "It's early yet, Anders is napping out there as well. Why is everyone so tired? We just got here."

"It's the country air," Antoinette said. Then she gently shook Sigrid and Emilie. They followed her, their feet pitter-pattering across the floor as they held on to their mother with their eyes half-closed.

Erik watched them until they were out the door. "They act like little women most days, but as soon as they get sleepy they become little babies again."

"They're simply darling," said Sofia. "I wish you had a dozen. And who knows? Maybe you do."

"What?" He leaned forward and placed his scotch glass on the coffee table. "I think it's time for me to go too."

"Erik don't leave. That was uncalled for."

He leaned back in his seat with a nod. There was no point in telling her he still only had five girls.

"Have you seen her lately?"

"I broke it off." His eyes narrowed. "Didn't want to do the

same as Anders." He knew it would hurt but didn't care. She was ruining his mood.

Sofia grimaced almost imperceptibly.

He glanced toward the door Antoinette and the children had exited. Then, picking up his drink, he swallowed what was left.

"I'm sorry, Erik. And again, please forgive me for what I said." Her voice sounded soft and apologetic.

"It's fine. I'm sorry too, we shouldn't be arguing. It's Christmas Eve tomorrow." He picked up his empty glass, then put it back again. "I begged Anette to move closer to me. I would have paid for it, of course. But still, she refused. Each time we had a child she moved to another farm, and I had to chase her down. The places where she lived were wretched. Still, I couldn't persuade her. Then Ester drowned, and even after that she wouldn't move. I finally gave up."

"Did Antoinette ever find out?"

"Yes, I told her after Ester's funeral. It was never the same between us after that."

That was an understatement. Antoinette had lost her mind, screaming and throwing things, even hitting him. But it had been nothing compared to watching her heart break into pieces when she understood how he had lied; that all those business trips hadn't been business trips at all, and that their whole marriage had been a lie.

Sofia smiled sadly, then reached over to touch his arm. "Anders and I were unhappy for years. You saw how it was with us. It was a charade. Then, about two years ago I think it was… yes, two years. We had an awful fight. It ended with both of us sobbing in the kitchen after I threw a fork at him."

"A fork?"

"I wanted to throw a knife, but at the last second I decided a fork would do."

"Good thinking."

She laughed. "That's when he opened up for the first time. We spoke for hours and he told me everything. About his lover. That man. It's not such a bad life now that all the lying has stopped."

Erik nodded, listening for a moment to make sure Anders or Antoinette weren't joining them after all. But the castle was quiet.

"It's not the same for us. You can understand why Anders can't love you in the same way, but Antoinette cannot. I should be able to, and I do, but it's not like it was with Anette. She's the love of my life. A cliché I know."

Sofia looked as if she was about to say something, but then just smiled sadly again. Maybe she thought of how she had fired Anette that day. What if he had been sitting here right now, but it had been Anette and his other daughters who had gone upstairs? Then Ester would have been alive, and Little Ester would have been named something else. But then the three girls upstairs wouldn't exist.

"I should go to bed," he said, and stood. As he did, his gaze fell on the mirror between the bookshelves and for a moment he thought he saw Ester's face reflecting in it.

Chapter Fifty-five

Anette

Anette knew something was different this time, and it wasn't only because of what Ludvig had done to her. She was larger and her back hurt constantly. She couldn't sit on her milking stool anymore but was allowed to perform other tasks like cleaning out the buckets or sweeping the floor. She was grateful for the understanding. Thankful that despite of what was now obvious, the other milkmaids didn't shun her. They understood. Even the owner turned a blind eye, which made her wonder if it wasn't the first time Ludvig Svensson had raped someone. It ought to make her angry, but she was just numb and exhausted. It was as if she didn't feel anything at all anymore.

Anna watched her closely while they were finishing the milking for the day. "It's not too late to go to the constable, you know."

Anette shook her head. "I went to his house willingly and even stitched his suit. They'd just laugh at me."

"I wish I could kill him myself," Anna said and spit in the straw. Then she took Anette's broom and finished sweeping the floor for her.

#

Anette recognized the midwife as soon as she stepped inside. It was Miss Pålsson, the same one who helped her at the House. She who had wanted to hide what Ludvig did to her in the very place in her mind where Carl was, and then it was the same midwife. What were the odds, and why?

Anette followed her movements as she took her coat off and hung it on the hook by the door, then placed her black bag on the floor next to the chair Swea had placed at the foot of the bed. By the light of the lantern and the candles on the table, she looked about the same, though her body was stouter, and her wavy blond hair was cut short.

"My name is Miss Pålsson," she said and shook Anette's

hand.

Nothing in her expression indicated that she recognized her, and Anette let out a breath, praying it would stay that way.

"Good day," Anette said simply. Maybe if she could keep her name from her, Miss Pålsson wouldn't remember and start talking about things she didn't want Anna or Swea to know.

"Is it your first?"

"No, my fourth," Anette lied. "That's my third over there," she said and gestured toward Ester who was sitting next to Anna at the table.

"Where's the father?"

"He…"

"She was taken advantage of by a very evil and ugly man," Swea interrupted. "He's not here."

"I see," Miss Pålsson said. "Was a report made to the constable?"

"No," Anette said.

Miss Pålsson looked at her for a moment, then turned to Swea and Anna and said, "Please boil some water. I brought my own soap."

Anette looked away, recalling how ignorant she had been the first time when she thought Miss Pålsson was taking too long with all that scrubbing of her hands.

When Miss Pålsson had washed, she sat down on the chair and smiled encouragingly. "I'm going to feel how far along you are," she said and put her hands on her belly, firmly pushing and prodding. "It seems to me that there's more than one baby. Does it seem that way to you?"

"It's been feeling very different and I'm much bigger than I was with my daughters. But do you really think so?" Her heart sank. She knew it but hadn't wanted to admit it to herself. It was all too much.

Miss Pålsson chuckled. "We'll find out soon enough."

#

Twins. A tiny boy and a tiny girl. Anette couldn't deny it, they were beautiful. Both fit well in her arms, but it felt odd that

270

there were two of them. Only the girl had Ludvig's nose, and the same eyebrows. The boy looked more like her, and a little like Carl. Maybe just because he was a boy too. Anette didn't cry. Just felt numb as before. Miss Pålsson sat down beside her and asked Anna and Swea to take Ester outside. Anna looked disappointed, but she scooped Ester up and walked out with Swea close behind her.

Miss Pålsson didn't say anything at first. She just sat there, looking at her and the babies. She seemed preoccupied. Then she straightened her shoulders and put her hand on the boy's tightly swaddled stomach; he was on her right arm and closest to Miss Pålsson. She met Anette's eyes.

"I wanted to give us a chance to speak in private and make sure I understood what Swea meant. Was I correct in my assumption that you were raped?"

She said it so calmly. Nothing that hinted at anything shameful. Somehow it was comforting.

"Yes, I was," Anette said, surprised at the strength of her own voice. "First, he asked me to stitch his suit. And then he pushed himself on me and pulled me into his bedroom. I should never have gone with him, but he said he had a fiancée. He's an odd man, and I should've…" Anette tried to swallow, but her mouth was parched. Miss Pålsson handed her a glass of water and held it for her so she could drink while still holding the babies. They were sound asleep. She felt disconnected from them. Almost as if they weren't there, even as Miss Pålsson had to hold the glass for her.

"I tried to push him off me, but he was too heavy."

"Miss, you don't need to defend yourself. I understand you tried everything you could to get away and did what was safest for you in that situation."

Anette inhaled deeply. Her innards hurt from it, but it felt good anyway, and some of her numbness eased a little. She had felt so guilty that she hadn't managed to push him off of herself, and that she had closed her eyes. Afraid her screams made him think she liked it. But she had done what she could. She exhaled.

Miss Pålsson nodded. "Miss, you're not alone. It happens every day to women all over the country, all over the world. Even wives are raped by their husbands sometimes. I'm not saying this to minimize what you're going through, but you should know that it was never your fault. None of it was. What happened is always the man's fault. Always."

Anette let out another breath. The relief was painful.

Miss Pålsson nodded once and smiled gently. "Are you going to stay here?" She made a sweeping movement with her hand, indicating their little room with only three beds, hers and Esters, and Anna's and Swea's. How would all four of them fit in her narrow bed?

"I don't know. I'm not sure what I want to do with..." Anette looked at the little faces in her arms. She had considered an orphanage, but it seemed so cruel, and she was afraid they would ask her to stay to feed them in.

"You have considered not keeping them." It wasn't a question.

"Yes."

#

Anette wanted the churching and baptism over with and arranged for a stable boy to drive her to church.

"Their father's name is Ludvig Svensson," she told the parson. "He's getting married soon; to someone else. I feel sorry for his wife-to-be."

The parson was not stern and judgmental as the others had been. He calmly went about his task, smiling as he made sure the babies were comfortable. It was the first time she had told a parson who the father was.

Chapter Fifty-six

Hanna

Hanna handed Johannes his cup of coffee as she sipped hers. "Good morning You're still here?"

"Yes," he yawned, "I have no meetings until ten."

She gestured toward the kitchen window. "Look at that cloudy, dark sky. It's such a dreary morning. Can you come with me to the Frog for breakfast?"

"Sure, I'll go with you," he said, and ran his fingers through his messy morning hair. "I'd better wash up."

Johannes disappeared to the water closet while Hanna drank her coffee at the counter and looked over the newspaper.

The telephone rang in the study. It sounded especially shrill at this hour of the morning. She put her cup down and went to answer it.

But Johannes got there first. "You don't say… oh." He grinned at Hanna as he spoke into the receiver. "I see… I… that's wonderful news, wonderful. No, we don't need to discuss anything. Today? Yes, we'll leave this morning. You're where?" He scribbled a few words on a pad of paper. "Thank you, Bengta."

As he placed the receiver back in the cradle, she noticed his shirt was open and his unbuttoned trousers were slipping down. He must have run to the telephone while holding them up.

"Hanna, my dear, dear wife, Bengta has found us… actually she found us two!" He grabbed his trousers at the waist.

"Two?"

"Yes, two babies, a boy and a girl… they were born last week. The mother is a statar milkmaid, a widow with three other children."

"Babies?" She stared at him, trying to take it in but not daring to believe it. "Are you certain? Who was it? Who called on the telephone?"

"It was Bengta." He grinned from ear to ear. "I told you already. Bengta found us babies," he said, then his grin became a sob and he let go of his trousers and reached for her as they slipped to the floor.

Hanna threw her arms around him and held on tightly as her tears mixed with his. Her heart was racing, and thoughts came at her from every direction. Two babies, it had to be twins then. Could they take two babies? Where would they get milk? Could babies drink cow's milk? How could the mother have babies if she was a widow? Why didn't she want them? Had her husband died after he got her pregnant? She looked up at Johannes' face, still close to hers. He was beaming with the tears drying on his cheeks.

"Oh, Johannes, where are they?" Hanna asked and let go of him. "Bengta said she had to be out in the countryside for a couple of weeks."

"She's in Tjutebro. The midwife who usually delivers babies there hurt her back." He pulled up his trousers and buttoned his shirt. Then, with a look in his eye that told her not to question him, he cranked the telephone handle to reach the operator, and asked her to connect him to his office. Giving Hanna a quick smile, he started talking.

"Good morning, it's Johannes Agnell. I'm going to have to ask you to cancel my meeting at ten. Yes, and all of them after that." A tear fell down his cheek as he met Hanna's eyes. "No, thank you. I'm not sick, but I'm going to have to take the day off. Perhaps tomorrow as well, I'll explain more later." Long silence. "Yes. Thank you. Goodbye." He placed the receiver back in the cradle. "Come here, my dear mother-to-be. Let's go get our babies."

Hanna nodded, overwhelmed with nerves and happiness. "Yes, lets, Elsa can run the counter today. I'm not even going to telephone them. Johannes, we need to go now."

Then she hurried to get their coats.

Chapter Fifty-seven

Anette and Hanna

Anette had told Ester that a nice woman would come with her husband and bring the babies home. Explained that the woman was sad because God hadn't been able to find her a baby, and since Anette already had her, Ebba, and Edith she would let the woman and her husband love the babies for them all. Ester understood. She didn't remember Edith and Ebba and was used to having siblings somewhere else, and Anette left it at that.

The day was sunny and unusually warm for April. Swea and Anna helped Anette into a chair in the yard out front. The babies were sleeping in a small basket on the ground, wrapped and snug and covered with a blanket that Swea had knitted. Ester solemnly held Swea's hand as she stood beside Anette's chair.

They waited.

Finally, they heard the rumble of wheels and the sound of hooves on gravel as a horse strained to get up the hill. It whinnied as if it could sense the emotions of the people waiting in the yard, and perhaps of the passengers it was hauling as well.

Miss Pålsson was at the reins. The wagon was scarcely more than a milk cart, and the couple was sitting on a bench crudely fastened behind the driver's seat. Anette threw a worried glance at Anna. Were they poor? What if they were another statar family? Then she noticed how they were dressed.

The man was wearing an expensive frock and shiny shoes. He jumped to the ground and turned to face the woman, who was wearing a beautiful moss green coat with a tan collar. She took his hand and stepped down gingerly. Anette inhaled sharply as the woman's feet touched the ground.

As she came closer, her face seemed to melt into that of a younger woman wearing a beautiful brown dress and matching shawl. For a moment they were back in Lund and Anette was hurrying back to the House with her sausage and wine. It was as if she could still hear the thump when the sausage fell out of her bag onto the porch and rolled underneath the hems of the woman's skirts. It was her.

Hanna held Johannes' hand as hard as she could and looked at the scene in front of her. Three women and a little girl were waiting in front of a gray low house with a black roof, one in a chair and the others standing around her. Was she the mother? They were all wearing black threadbare shawls over their shoulders and beige dresses that didn't look very clean. One of the women was heavyset and older than the other two. The girl's dress was made of a checkered red and green fabric and wasn't as dirty, but it had been stitched in several places. There was a basket on the ground. Hanna took a step toward it, holding her breath. Her little babies were in there. Their tiny little heads were sticking up under a bright yellow blanket. Her chest constricted, and she squeezed Johannes' hand harder. Then the woman in the chair, it must be the mother, stood. She hesitated for a moment and looked right at her. There were dark shadows under her eyes and her face looked drawn. Something about her seemed familiar, yet different.

"Have we met before?" Hanna asked, and out of the corner of her eye, she saw Bengta's eyes widen. Then the mother bent toward the basket and picked up one of the babies.

Anette held her daughter to her chest and breathed in the scent of her warm baby skin. It was as if everything fell into place. The three Norns didn't plan for Ludvig Svensson to rape her, but when it happened, they connected everything together, the same way Yggdrasil's branches and roots did. That was why Miss Pålsson was her midwife again, and why the kind temperance woman would be the mother. Her husband would be considerate and sober.

The memories from that day at the House washed over her. How embarrassed she was, but how kind the woman had been when she picked up that sausage, her warm laughter and the gleam in her eye, how she never said anything about the wine, even though she must have seen the bottle. It was the week before she gave up Carl, her only son. She had always regretted it.

Anette looked at the temperance woman and her husband. They stood close together, still holding hands. And she made her decision.

With strength coming from deep within herself, she handed her little baby girl to the woman. "Call her Linnea. That's all I ask. I'm keeping the boy. His name is Helmerth."

The wind made the bare branches in the trees around them rustle.

She went inside, leaving Swea and Anna to deal with Miss Pålsson and the couple as they had already arranged. Sitting down on the bed, she hugged Helmerth tightly and finally cried.

Hanna brought the tiny baby into her arms as carefully as she could, while Johannes put his hand below hers as if he was afraid she would drop her. Or maybe he just wanted to help. Her eyes were tightly closed, she had a little bent nose with half-moon nostrils, and her skin looked a little yellow. She was the most beautiful being Hanna had ever seen.

"She's keeping the boy? What happened? What made her change her mind?" Hanna tore her face from the baby and looked at the others. It was the younger woman who had spoken. The basket was empty, and the mother had gone inside. It wasn't until then she fully comprehended what she had said. Johannes looked stunned, and Bengta was narrowing her eyes and staring toward the statar house. Then the little girl pulled her hand out of the older woman's hand and ran toward the closed door, reached for the handle that was well above her head, pulled the door wide open, and ran inside without closing it.

"My brother can stay?" she hollered happily, and the last thing Hanna saw was her little checkered dress before it was absorbed by the darkness inside.

Johannes looked at Hanna, and when she met his eyes, she knew he had the same thought as her. They both nodded at the same time. "It's good as it is. If this is what she wants, we can't tear a baby from a mother's arms," he said.

Chapter Fifty-eight

Hanna

Tears of happiness and worry were streaming down Hanna's face when they left the mother and Linnea's twin brother behind. There was a part of her that was relieved that she only had one baby instead of two. It would certainly be a lot easier, especially for a new mother like herself. But even though she had never even held the little boy in her arms, she wondered if she would always think something was missing. Should they have insisted to take both? Holding the little baby girl safely against her chest on the rickety wagon, she looked up, searching Bengta's and Johannes' faces. They looked calm, and she didn't read anything in their expressions that seemed like regret. Insisting would have been unbearable, and the sister had sounded so happy.

Bengta drove them to the parish house she was staying in while covering for the midwife who had injured her back. The parson and his family lived there, but Bengta had her own private door which led to a little guestroom with a small bed, a table, and three chairs. Only two chairs were matching. Bengta must have borrowed one for Johannes. Touched, Hanna went to her, leaned close as if she were hugging her while still holding Linnea with both arms.

"Thank you, Bengta. Johannes and I owe you a debt we can never repay you. Thank you from the bottom of my heart."

Bengta's eyes glinted warmly, and she gave one quick nod, looking almost embarrassed at the compliment. Johannes put his long skinny arms around her and hugged her and wouldn't let go, smiling at Hanna and Linnea over her shoulder. Finally, Bengta grabbed his arms and pried them off herself.

"It's my honor to help my dearest friends become parents, but now I need to get something for that baby of yours so she doesn't starve," Bengta said and hurried out. Just before she closed the door, Hanna saw her wipe at her eyes.

Johannes stared after her and pulled a handkerchief from

his pocket and blew his nose. They were all crying today. It felt like her eyes were in a constant stage of flowing wetness.

"We have a child, Hanna, a beautiful baby girl," Johannes said, and put his hand on Linnea's head. There was no hair, just thin baby fuzz. She would have to get her a hat.

"I like the name Linnea. We'll keep it won't we?"

Johannes nodded, looking as if he was about to cry again, but then they heard the door open, and Bengta strode back in, carrying a glass with what looked like thick milk and a big piece of bread, and he swallowed his tears.

"Hanna, sit here," Bengta said and pointed to the chairs. "You too, Johannes," she added, and then sat down herself next to Hanna.

Bengta expertly tore off a piece of bread and dipped it in the milk. Then she gently stroked Linnea's cheek while bringing the bread close. It made Linnea open her mouth and Bengta squeezed the wet bread, creating a steady, slow stream of milk dripping into her little mouth.

She nodded somberly in the way she always did when she had something important to say. "This is how you'll feed her today. Tomorrow when we get back to Lund, we'll see if Helga has a mother that might spare some milk and can nurse her for you. I'll also show you how to make a proper combination of milk, flour and sugar that you'll feed your daughter." Bengta smiled broadly as she said the word daughter, eyes still on the baby. "Are you happy, Hanna?"

"Yes, so very happy," she said, smiling at Johannes who was shaking his head with disbelief, his eyes gleaming with joy.

"I am too," he said. "I can't believe she's ours. She really is, isn't she?"

"Yes, the baby is all yours, Johannes and Hanna. Your dreams haven't only come through, but you've helped that woman more than you know. She's not had a good life, that one. It pained me to see her."

"She looked familiar. It's as if I've met her somewhere," Hanna said.

Bengta looked away from Linnea for the first time, throwing Hanna a sharp glance.

"You have?"

"Yes, I couldn't put my finger on it, but I recognized her face. I was trying to think if she'd come to one of our meetings, but I don't think a statare would ever have a chance to."

"No, not a statare," Johannes agreed, then added, "Poor woman, widowed before giving birth to twins. I wonder what her husband died from, maybe a farming accident?"

Bengta didn't respond. She pushed the milk and bread from the edge of the table. "Put her on your shoulder Hanna and see if you can get her to burp."

Hanna carefully moved Linnea and gave her back two light little pats. She burped right away, and Hanna exhaled, jolts of happiness bursting through her chest. She looked at Johannes, and they both grinned. Bengta was still silent. She seemed thoughtful.

"What is it, Bengta?" Hanna asked, suddenly concerned. Was there something wrong with Linnea? She looked so peaceful with her little head on her shoulder, already sleeping. What if it wasn't normal?

Bengta sighed, then threw an eye at the door as if to make sure that there was no one overhearing them. "You must promise to never say anything. Hanna, you know how seriously I take confidentiality. But you're her parents now, and I think you have the right to know."

Hanna's heart skipped a beat, and Johannes reached for her free hand and took it. They looked at each other, then spoke at the same time. "Of course, we'll keep this between us."

"She stayed at the House with Helga when we had our meetings there. It's probably where you saw her," Bengta said.

"She was one of Helga's mothers? When?" But as Hanna asked it, it came to her. It was the girl with the wine she had encountered when she had gone out for some air, that day when she was going to tell them about the Frog, when the woman, she couldn't remember her name now, had cried because her husband wouldn't let her come to meetings anymore.

"I remember her! She's the one who smuggled in wine. Remember?"

"That was her?" Bengta chuckled. "I'm glad to hear that there's some spunk in her." She stopped smiling, growing serious again. "It's hard to believe that this weather bitten, tired woman was that shy girl. I didn't even recognize her in that little dark hut of a house they live in, but then outside in the daylight today, and when you asked her if you had met before, Hanna, I realized who she was. I'm not sure what her husband died of Johannes, but he wasn't the one who fathered her twins. I can't tell you more than that."

Hanna patted Linnea's tiny back. Her hand covered it completely. "Will they be all right without each other? Did we do the right thing?" she asked.

A shadow crossed Johannes' face, and he looked first at Hanna, then at Bengta, who nodded calmly.

"It's always the mother's decision, not yours. You have nothing to regret. Let's focus on the joy of your beautiful little girl instead."

Johannes looked relieved, and he smiled at Hanna.

There was a knock on the door. Hanna's heart went in her throat. What if the mother came to ask for her baby back? But then the door opened, and the parson stood there in his collar and frock, next to a woman who must be his wife, holding a shoebox. They were both beaming.

"We apologize for barging in like this," the parson's wife said. "But we wanted to see if your little one would fit in this?" She lifted the shoebox in the air. "And my husband would like to give your baby a blessing."

Hanna let out a sigh of relief. Her emotions were all over the place. It was normal, she supposed. How could it not, when from one moment to the next, she had become a mother.

The parson's wife entered first, smiling when she saw Linnea in Hanna's arms. Then, without a word, she put the box on the table and stepped back so Hanna could put Linnea inside. There was room to spare.

"I'll go and get a sheep's skin and a blanket," the parson's wife said.

"She's so small, she fits in a shoebox!" Hanna exclaimed.

"Not for long," Johannes and the parson said at the same time, and they all laughed.

#

The first weeks were a whirlwind of activity and happiness. When they arrived home, they were greeted by Maria and Magnhild who on such short notice had managed to collect baby clothes, bottles, diapers, and blankets, even two bottles full of breastmilk from the mothers at the House. Hanna had no idea how they got the milk into the bottles, but she was grateful, Linnea was screaming when they came home. The next day,o

two of the mothers from the House came and stayed with Hanna, taking turns to breastfeed. They came every day for the first week, but then Linnea became used to the milk combination that Hanna learned to make, and they left. Linnea was thriving.

#

Two years later

Hanna took Linnea by the hand and helped her down the front stairs. Just as they reached the ground, Johannes came home.

"Pappa!" Linnea shouted, pulled herself out of her grip and ran to hug his legs.

"Hello, my little sweetbun," Johannes said, put down his briefcase and scooped her up as he kissed Hanna on the cheek.

"Where are you two going?"

"Well," she lifted an eyebrow. "We've been on our way out for about an hour, but Linnea was very busy today. Tell Pappa, Linnea."

"Birds, I feeden birds. They eat seesds," she explained proudly. Hanna's heart melted each time she mispronounced things. Linnea was two now, had a head full of blond hair, so pale it looked perfectly white, and talked more and more every day. Today she was especially adorable, wearing her little red coat, white stockings, and black shoes.

"Ah, so that's what they eat, sweetbun." Johannes chuckled,

then looked back at Hanna. "Where are you going?" he repeated.

"We were going to have an early dinner with Magnhild and Bengta. I left you a note. I didn't expect you home for another couple of hours. Care to join us?"

"Gladly." He glanced at her curiously. "You haven't heard then, have you?"

"Heard what?"

"There's a newspaper in my briefcase. Actually, could you take it inside first, please?" He lifted Linnea by the waist and perched her on his shoulders. Hanna brought the briefcase into the house, placed it on the hall table, and pulled out the paper without looking at it, then hurried back outside.

"Unfold it," Johannes said. "It's on the first page."

General Voting Rights Extended to All Men Over Twenty-four, the headline read in big bold letters. She sighed silently. It must have been why the telephone had been ringing several times today then. She had heard it when they were in the outdoor aviary and earlier when they came home from a walk, but by the time she answered, it had been too late.

Hanna peered over the top of the page at Johannes. Without saying a word, he started to walk through the gate and out to the sidewalk. She followed, glancing at the newspaper as she walked.

"Just think, after all the work we've done they're only extending the vote to the men," Hanna said.

"Had you expected it to be different?"

"No, and it's not all men anyway. If a man has received welfare, or has been to jail, he can't vote. What they've done though…" She paused to make sure she didn't step on anything and kept reading. "Yes, it says here that there's no longer a requirement that men have to be above a certain pay grade to vote. That's annoying, if men don't have to, then they can't use the mother argument."

"Look, horse!" Linnea shouted and pointed as a carriage drove by.

"What do you mean?" Johannes asked, acknowledging

Linnea by squeezing her foot.

Hanna folded the newspaper and stuck it under her arm as she caught up to them.

"What I mean, is that some argue that women don't earn money and shouldn't vote because of it. But if money isn't an issue anymore, then they can't use that argument. Not only that, women do work and own businesses as well. Frida Stéenhoff brought this up at her lecture. It holds even more true now then."

Johannes nodded. "But this must be a good first step. You can use what you just said as leverage."

"I know, but I can't help but wonder if LKPR had worked for general voting rights for all, men included, then it might have been different now. It's what Miss Kline had wanted to do at first." Hanna sighed. They would have to see. For now, she was going to enjoy her walk with Johannes and Linnea.

"Sweetbun," Hanna said, and reached for Linnea's little chubby hand. "Are you happy we're going to visit Aunt Bengta and Aunt Magnhild?"

"Yes," she shouted.

Chapter Fifty-nine

Hanna arrived at the Frog at the same time as Magnhild, just as Elsa was closing for the evening. Hanna inhaled deeply, savoring the scent of coffee and the morning's baking. She missed it, wishing she could take on a shift for Emily or Elsa, who now ran the Frog entirely without her.

Magnhild kissed her on the cheek, then patted the canvas bag she carried slung over her shoulder. "I have Bengta's and Vanda's notes from Hinke Bergegren's lecture in here," she said and lifted her eyebrows with an excited shake of her head.

"Oh boy," Hanna said and threw an eye at Elsa who was looking at them both questioningly. Apparently, she hadn't read anything about it in the papers. The lecture had been quite controversial, Bengta told her, and she and Vanda had requested to lead tonight's meeting. She couldn't wait to hear more about it.

"What is it?" Elsa asked.

Magnhild put her canvas bag on a chair and started dragging a table across the floor, speaking at the same time. "Hinke Bergegren is a socialist who held a lecture on precautionary measures to limit unwanted children. It was in Stockholm a little over a week ago and Bengta and Vanda were there."

Elsa's eyes widened. "Birth preventatives?"

"Yes, contraceptives. Bengta said it was incredible. People were lining up along the street to get into the People's House to listen to him. Supposedly there were seven hundred women from all social classes there. And," she paused when Hanna and Elsa dragged another table over and waited until they had put the short ends together, "Bengta isn't going to bring this up tonight, but there was a police report made the next day when he held the same meeting for men. He held it for just women first. It was so no one would get embarrassed."

"No wonder if he was talking about those sorts of things," Elsa said.

"Indeed." Magnhild nodded, trying to look somber, but then

she threw her head back and laughed.

Hanna dragged the last table over to the row and sat down, smiling at Magnhild. She was so passionate. It was like the first time they met at that snotty women's reading group that kicked Magnhild out. It was over twenty years ago now; it was hard to believe.

Magnhild pulled out her leaflets and placed three neat stacks of them on the tables.

"I can't even picture it," Elsa said. "I hope my mother won't be too upset. She has very strong views on these things."

"I know, but she won't be the only one. It's one of the reasons Bengta and Vanda want to lead our meeting tonight, so we can discuss all this. It's going to affect suffrage and LKPR I'm sure," Hanna said and glanced at the wall clock. Five more minutes, then the other members would arrive.

"Well," Vanda said. "It's certainly been an interesting week." She folded her hands in front of her as she addressed the group. "As some of you know, Bengta and I were in Stockholm and attended Hinke Bergegren's lecture on Malthusianism. It was quite enlightening."

"Yes, it truly was," Bengta agreed. "He first had a lecture for us women on April 7th, then the next day he held the same one for men. He called it his Love Without Children lecture."

"That must have been something. I don't want to imagine how it went during the men's lecture," Lova said dryly.

Bengta laughed. "You could say that."

"Take a leaflet so you can read the notes Bengta and I took during it. We've compiled them and made carbon copies for you," Vanda said and pointed to the stacks Magnhild had put out. "Bengta would like to read through them point by point and then we can discuss what to do about it."

"What to do about it? What do you mean by that?" asked Ruth.

"We need to decide how we feel about birth prevention, and where we as a group stand on it," Hanna said.

"Where we stand on birth prevention? We certainly can't be

for it. We're a suffrage group. Why would we even think about it?" Ruth said, then pursed her lips and put her arms over her chest.

Hanna and Magnhild exchanged a quick glance.

"We feel differently Ruth," said Bengta. "Like Vanda said, I'm going to read through our notes point by point and then we'll discuss." She held up her hand to stop people from talking.

"Hinke Bergegren," she began, "said that the working class often have more children and live in small, crowded spaces, and can't always provide for their children." She looked up briefly. "This is something I can attest to. I've helped many a mother labor who live in those conditions. Bergegren spoke of the hypocrisy that women are supposed to be married, chaste and faithful, but men aren't expected to. He also questioned the fact that only men have sexual feelings. Questioning if it's really true that only men have them and not women." Bengta looked up from her notes, but everyone had their faces glued to their own leaflets, except Ruth, who still had her arms crossed over her chest and was looking out the window. Hanna glanced at Maria. She was blushing and looking like she wanted to leave.

"He certainly kept us alert by that statement," Bengta said, her eyes gleaming. "But he lectured very well, pointing out how often men are making women pregnant without taking any responsibility for it. He also mentioned hereditary disease that can affect children, and spoke of innocent children born out of wedlock, questioning if we have the right to bring children into the world if we can't take care of them. He said children are being born into such poverty that they die. And he pointed out that a hundred children out of a thousand die within the first year, two hundred in the poorer Stockholm neighborhoods." Bengta looked up from her notes again, looking very serious now, and sat quietly for a moment before she continued.

"He ended like this, love without children is better than children without love. Love without children is better than children without love," she repeated and looked at Vanda. They held each other's gaze.

"After that," Bengta said, "he spoke of specific birth

prevention methods. We've listed them here in the leaflet. Please take a look at those yourself. Then we'd like to discuss all of this, like Hanna mentioned. We feel it's time that all women's groups form an opinion on the subject of birth prevention."

"We do," Vanda agreed. "You should've heard the way people were talking after the lecture. Some of them said that prevention will lead to the extinction of our population." She rolled her eyes.

Hanna wished she hadn't. It was rude. She looked down at her leaflet and read the list of preventative suggestions. There were balls with cocoa butter with boric acid that women should put inside themselves, elastic things like the finger on a glove, called a condom that men would put on themselves, or something like little sponges for women. It made her feel embarrassed and uncomfortable.

"I agree wholeheartedly," said Pernilla. "The true purpose of intimacy is procreation. It's the natural order of things that lovemaking leads to family. Using these unnatural contraptions could very well lead to human extinction. Not only that, but if a man didn't have to think about this risk, he'd never look for a wife, just for a vessel where he could rid himself of his seed."

"Right," Maria said. "That's *exactly* what would happen. It's something I speak of often."

Agneta got to her feet, visibly upset, picked up a leaflet and waved it in the air angrily. "Yes, it would sterilize love, make it something you do just for pleasure."

"Why is that so bad?" Magnhild asked and looked at Bengta, who met her eyes and smiled.

"Well," Agneta said, "It's what Malthusianism is about and why it's called sterile love. I read about his lectures in the paper. I find it grotesque. And I'm quite surprised that you and Vanda would go sit and listen to such indecency."

"It was certainly not indecent," Vanda said curtly.

Hanna leaned forward in her chair. She had to say something, they had never had a meeting get this tense before. Clearing her throat, she put her hand up to get their attention.

"I'm not sure how I feel about this, but something to keep in mind is that anti-voting people may take this opportunity to argue that we're trying to become men. That we would stop having children so we can take over the world. As you all know, it's an argument they like to throw at us quite often."

Maria nodded at Hanna and took Agneta gently by the arm, "Sit down, dear." Then she turned to the others. "I agree with Hanna. Motherhood is what defines me. My greatest strength is to create life. It's one of the reasons we women should be able to vote, because we have that ability. We can add a mother's perspective to our society."

"What about those of us who don't have any children," Bengta said icily. "Or women whose uterus is falling out because she's giving birth for the fourteenth time. Women who have children without any support from the father. I've birthed many who were taken advantage of by men who promised to marry them, only to leave them pregnant and alone. Do you believe these women are thinking of the motherly strength they can add to the voting booth?"

"Indeed," Magnhild added, "Women have had no control. What about all these years we've worked for temperance so a woman can have more say in her marriage?"

"Yes, as a matter of fact, Bergegren brought up temperance in his lecture too, and how women can't say no to their drunk husbands and then get pregnant. If they used preventatives, then that wouldn't be an issue at least," Bengta said.

"Don't you two gang up on me," Maria shouted angrily.

"No one is Maria," said Vanda. "You know as well as I that we've never been able to agree on this."

"No, that we have not. But we're a temperance group, it's outrageous that you're promoting something like this instead of temperance in the first place."

"We're not Maria, we're discussing it," Vanda said with a sigh. "You could also argue that we're more of a suffrage group now."

"I agree with Maria," Pernilla said. "And if a woman

suggested to a man that he put on one of those condoms, she'd be called a whore, married or not. I have a friend who…"

Bengta held up a hand to stop her. "Maybe, but there are other ways that the man needn't know about. That was his point, too. Look at the list in the leaflet."

Hanna stayed silent, letting them argue. She understood both sides of this. Intellectually she was on Bengta's, Magnhild's, and Vanda's side. It was horrible that children died when they were just babies. Linnea's mother had been dirty and tired, and the little statar house where she lived had been so dilapidated that it looked like it would fall apart at any moment. But what if Linnea hadn't been born because of one of those devises on the list? Or what if her twin brother had died because they were too poor? He might not be alive anymore. It was on her mind more often than she wanted to admit. She folded the leaflet so as not to have to look at the list, then rolled it into a tube.

"What are you arguing for?" Astrid said, startling her. Hanna stopped fidgeting with the leaflet and looked at her. Astrid was standing with one foot on her chair, looking exasperated. "I don't understand you at all. I think the lecture sounds wonderful. I agree with everything Bengta read and I'm glad you both went. To hear a man defending our feelings during intimacy instead of agreeing that we must stay chaste while men enjoy themselves is very refreshing. And yes, I agree it's much worse to have a child you can't take care of than to use precautions."

Hanna smiled. She couldn't disagree with that either, despite everything. She was very torn. Bengta and Vanda looked relieved.

Magnhild got to her feet, smiling broadly. "Thank you, Astrid. Let's take a vote. Who's in favor of Lund's Suffrage Society supporting Hinke Bergegren's lecture, and of birth prevention in general?"

Bengta, Magnhild, Vanda, Elsa, Lova, and Astrid along with four other women raised their hands. Hanna wrote down ten, hoping they would let her abstain. She felt Magnhild boring her eyes into her but ignored it.

"Who is against Lund's Suffrage Society supporting Hinke Bergegren's lecture, and of birth prevention in general?" Magnhild asked.

Maria, Pernilla, Agneta, Ruth, and eight others raised their hands, and Hanna wrote down twelve. Magnhild looked disappointed.

"I'm assuming that some are abstaining then?"

Hanna and the rest of them raised their hands. Including her, they were seven.

"Hanna, how many?"

"Ten support it, twelve are against it, and seven are abstaining. We don't have majority. I'm sorry, I'm usually surer of myself. But I can't vote either yes or no for this. I also feel that it's wise of us to wait to see what happens. See how our sister suffragists feel and where the discourse goes. I don't want to formally support this right now."

"We understand," Vanda said. "Meeting adjourned."

#

Several months later, in June, Hanna was having breakfast and reading the paper. It was on the first page. Hinke Bergegren had received a two-month prison sentence, and a new law against sexual education had been put into place.

PART THREE

Chapter Sixty

Erik

Helsingborg, 1915

Erik sighed loudly, prompting a laugh from his secretary, Eva, who was leaning against the doorpost brandishing a cigarette in a long holder.

"Have you heard there's a war going on? We have Russian and German ships chasing each other in our Swedish waters, there's a major food shortage, and here you are complaining about a pile of Swiss invoices."

"You sound like my wife. Of course, I'm aware there's a war going on. That's why we have all this extra paperwork."

Eva was an excellent secretary, but she wasn't at all like Jonas, who retired a couple of years ago. Jonas worked quietly and never disturbed him unless he had a specific question. Eva, on the other hand, seemed to find a reason to come into his office every hour. She somehow still managed to get her work done, but Erik lost his focus each time she came in.

He had just gotten back to the task at hand when she appeared again.

"Yes? What is it now?" Bloody hell, why couldn't she just leave him alone, he had ten pages left to do.

She took no notice of the irritation in his voice and smiled brightly. "You have visitors, two young ladies."

"I do?" The only young ladies who ever visited him were his daughters, and they always came in unannounced.

"Yes, shall I let them in?"

"By all means." There went his focus. He would have to start all over again.

They stepped inside as Eva walked out and closed the door behind her. The older of the two looked like she was in her early twenties, and the younger must be around fifteen or sixteen. They were both skinny and wore coats that were clean but threadbare. There was something familiar about them. Maybe he had seen them at Signe Bergqvist's, but he wasn't sure.

Then the younger girl extended her hand. "Hello, Pappa," she said as the other said, "Good day, Erik."

It was Ebba and Edith, his own daughter and Anette's oldest.

He was so stunned that he just stared at them. Ebba was only a child when he saw her last, but he should have recognized her. Ebba's eyes had the same turquoise color as her mother, and the hair escaping from beneath her hat was fine, silky, and blonde like Anette's. His throat constricted, and he wanted to pull her into his arms and hug her. But he got to his feet and just grabbed her hands in both of his. He was at a loss for words for what to say.

Edith had blossomed into a young woman and was very tall. He wouldn't have recognized her on the street. He put his hand out to her, but she didn't take it. She just looked at him with a steady gaze. He should have expected this. She had told him she had found his office address on the letters he wrote to Anette, or maybe it was his business card, he couldn't remember which. Why had it never crossed his mind?

"Please have a seat," he said. "I'm very happy to see you both. Just a little surprised."

Erik was about to sit down again when he became paranoid that Eva might be standing out there, listening. "Excuse me for just a minute, will you?"

He went to check and had to give her credit; she was working at her typewriter. He exhaled with relief.

"Eva, you may go home. I won't need you for the rest of the day."

"I have the second account to finish. Shouldn't I…?"

"No, it can wait."

She nodded and got her coat from the hook on the wall next to her desk.

"Have a good day, Erik. I'll see you in the morning."

"Indeed," he said, and went back to Ebba and Edith, relieved that she didn't ask who they were. Eva really was a good secretary.

Jonas would have asked a lot of questions.

They were sitting where he left them, Ebba on one end of the sofa and Edith on the wooden chair that Eva used when she had work to do by his desk. He swallowed something thick in his throat.

"How's your mother?" he asked and sat down. Suddenly it occurred to him that they might be there because something had happened to her.

"Mamma is fine," Edith said. "I received a letter from her the other day."

"A letter? Where is she?"

"She's near here, at Pålsjö Farm."

Thank God, she was well. Then their words sunk in. Pålsjö Farm was practically within walking distance from his home. How in the world could she be so close to him?

"And where are you girls staying?"

"Ebba moved in with Euphemia and her new husband several years ago. I found placement as a laundress. But I've since moved up. I'm a housekeeper now," Edith said and smiled proudly.

Sigrid and Emelie were studying at Lund's University now. Was this what was in Ebba's and Little Ester's futures too, happiness about housekeeping positions?

"How's Little Ester?"

"She's fine," Edith said with a hint of anger in her voice. "We just call her Ester now. So is Helmerth."

"Helmerth? Is your mother married?" A picture of Anette with a husband and a new child by her skirts appeared in his mind, and he suppressed a rush of jealousy.

"No, Erik." There was something odd in the way she said it.

"I see."

"Why did you stop coming to see us?" Edith asked.

"Well," he began, taken off guard, then decided to be honest. "I don't know what I can say in my defense. I'd understand if you're angry. All I can say is that I loved your mother... I still do. I tried to get her to move to a better place. I wanted to get an apartment for all of you, but she always refused. When Ester... when Ester drowned," he took a deep breath, "I tried again, but all it led to were arguments. We kept them from you, but that summer when she died, Anette and I just weren't good together. And my wife finally figured it all out when Nils came to tell me what happened."

Edith flinched.

He reached across the desk and touched her right hand, which was resting on it.

"Edith, you did the right thing, you know that. I told you as much then. It's not your fault that I'm married to someone else. I'm the one who was lying to my wife. That's my responsibility." But if she hadn't sent Nils, he would never have needed to tell Antoinette.

"Why didn't you marry Mamma in the first place, Pappa?" Ebba asked.

He took a long look at her and then at Edith. "I didn't dare go against my father's wishes." He managed a slight smile. "An old excuse, no doubt."

Neither of them responded. It was getting dark in the office as the sun was setting, but he hadn't noticed. He turned on the electrical lamp on his desk.

"All these years I've been angry with you for not marrying her. I didn't know you had wanted to, or that you had tried to get us to move," Edith said, her voice thick with emotion.

Erik reached for her hand again and patted it, not sure what else to do.

Ebba hadn't said much. Maybe she was angry too. He was her father.

Erik rose to his feet and turned to her. She was still sitting silently with her hands in her lap. "You both have every right to be angry with me. I should have stood up to my father. And I should have insisted more strongly that your mother move. If I had, our first Ester would still be alive."

"I'm not angry, Pappa," Ebba said and smiled genuinely. "Mamma has been through a lot, but she keeps a lot to herself instead of asking for help, making everything harder for everyone, including you," she added, sending a wave of relief through him.

He nodded, took his papers from the top of his desk, and

placed them in a drawer. Ebba was right. Anette did keep a lot to herself, and he never truly trusted her again after she told him she had lied about being a widow.

"Please, dear daughters, let me take you to dinner and then take me to your mother. It's time I talked to her about all this."

They smiled and when he held his arms out, Ebba came to him and then Edith did the same. He hugged them both.

Chapter Sixty-one

Anette

Anette had just managed to get Ester and Helmerth to bed when there was a knock on the door. Thinking it was her neighbor coming in for a nightcap as usual, she didn't bother getting dressed but opened it in her warm woolen nightgown and coarse stockings.

It was Edith and Ebba! What were they doing here? She hoped Edith hadn't gotten herself fired.

"Come in, come in. What are you doing here on a night like this?"

They both stepped inside but left the door ajar. Anette closed it.

"I just put the little ones to sleep. Are you hungry? I can make you something."

Edith shook her head and glanced at Ebba, then said, "Mamma, there's someone waiting outside who'd like to talk to you."

"Who?" Anette went to the window and peered through the curtain. Was Euphemia with them? That would explain why Ebba was there too.

"It's too dark to see and I'm not dressed." But she slipped her feet into her dirty barn clogs and threw her coat over her shoulders. Before going out, she turned back to them and smiled. There was something in the way Edith was looking at her.

"Edith, do you have a boy with you? You both look like you're up to something?"

"Go, Mamma," Ebba said.

A man was standing out there in the dark with his hat in his hands, looking down at the ground. She hesitated, not sure what to do. Then he stepped into the little square of light coming from the window and her heart started to beat so fast that she put her hands to her chest as if she could still it. It was Erik.

"Erik, lord have mercy you scared me," she cried, and he grinned in that familiar warm way she used to love so much.

"May I come in?"

"Yes, of course." She stepped aside to let him pass. He had changed. His hair was thinner and almost completely gray, and he had deep lines on both sides of his mouth, yet the glint in his eyes was the same. She looked into them.

"You go ahead. I'll be in shortly," she said, her own eyes filling with tears. She didn't blink until he had closed the door.

Anette stood on the little stoop in the cold and looked out into the darkness. The sky was full of stars and there was no moon. She couldn't sense why he had come but supposed Ebba or Edith had telephoned him and arranged to meet them here for some reason. Ebba was his daughter, after all. Anette pulled out a milk rag from her coat pocket, blew her nose in it, and went back inside.

Erik was sitting at the table between the girls. His shirt was a dazzling white against the rest of the room, and Ebba and Edith who had looked so smartly dressed just a few minutes earlier looked ragged beside him. She looked down at her nightgown. It was stained and patched where she had mended it. "I wasn't expecting such grand company," she said quietly.

"It's just me, Anette. I'm not very grand."

Without a word, Edith motioned to Ebba to come with her, and they left.

Anette sat down in front of Erik. His eyes widened when he saw the remnants of tears on her face but didn't say anything.

"Won't we wake them?" he asked instead, glancing over at the two heads sticking up through the blankets on the bed in the corner. His own daughter whom he had never gotten to know and her small, sweaty-headed little brother.

"No, they sleep like logs."

Erik placed his hand on the table in front of her, close but not touching, and looked at her silently for several moments before speaking. "I won't have any more of this. No more. You're coming with me. I'll rent you an apartment near my office. It should have been done a long time ago."

"What?"

"You heard me."

"Erik, you can't show up here after twelve years and demand that."

"Yes Anette, I can."

His face was open and vulnerable, his blue eyes looking at her in a way she had seen before but never acknowledged, sincerity. She swallowed. Erik always came for her, even now, after all this time and all her lies and pride. She who had refused for so long, pretending to be independent and insisting to do it alone, when all she had to do was tell him the truth. That she feared the parson's judgement as well as his. If she hadn't been so afraid, she would have tried to stop him from marrying Antoinette, told him she was pregnant and prepared him for what he could expect from those church books. She could have just told him the whole truth.

By the time Ebba and Edith returned nearly an hour later, Anette had agreed to go with him.

It would take some doing; she was a statare on contract. But the next day Erik went to talk to the owner. A few weeks later she moved with Ester and Helmerth to their new apartment in Helsingborg.

The first week, she did nothing but sleep.

Chapter Sixty-two

Helsingborg, Early May 1915

The apartment was spacious, with tall windows that allowed the sunlight to flood in. It had two large rooms with pale wooden floorboards and a kitchen, which was covered with black and white stone tiles in a checkerboard pattern. It was cool to the touch and made her think of the dirt floors in Östra Vemmenhög and the old wood in her little cabin at Dybäck's farm that left splinters in her rag whenever she spilled something.

There was a real water closet with a porcelain bowl big enough to stand in, and a jug for rinsing herself off. Erik had placed a beautiful bar of soap on the adjacent shelf. It smelled heavenly and Anette washed both her hair and her entire body two times a week, an unimaginable luxury.

There was a telephone on a small table in the front room with a directory beside it. On the first page, Erik had written the number to his office. Helsingborg had a new system where each subscriber was assigned a number. The telephones themselves worked differently now, too. All she needed to do was pick up the receiver. She didn't even need to crank the handle, and an operator would connect her call.

Erik had telephoned her on it twice. He sounded as if it was the most natural thing in the world, but to Anette it felt a little spooky. Part of her couldn't accept that he was in his office and not in the same room somewhere. Not that there was anywhere to hide, she didn't even own curtains yet.

This morning, she had telephoned him for the first time. The operator connected her to Erik's office where a woman's voice answered, who then asked her where she was calling from. Anette wasn't sure how to answer and just said that she was calling from Helsingborg. The woman chuckled, and then Erik's voice was suddenly in her ear. It seemed complicated to talk to all these people when she could just have gone to his office, but she supposed she couldn't do that. They arranged to meet at a café called Signe Bergqvist nearby. It was named after the woman baker who owned it, Erik told her.

It was warm and sunny outside. It had to be around May third or fourth, she assumed. As she walked, glittering Öresund was to her left. A boat was making its way across to Denmark toward Kronborg Castle on the shore. To her right, across the street, the medieval fortress Kärnan stood high atop a hill, majestically overlooking the sound.

She found a boy selling newspapers near the café and bought one. May 7, 1915, she had been off by several days. Directly below the date was a photograph showing a group of soldiers. She quickly folded the paper without reading the headline.

Out of the corner of her eye, she saw Erik approach.

"Good morning, you smell so nice," he said when he got close, and she was glad to have used the soap before she left.

He took her by the elbow and guided her to a table at the back of the cafe. She wondered if he had picked the back because he didn't want to be seen with her, but he seemed relaxed, so maybe not.

When the waitress came, Erik ordered coffee, sandwiches and two kinds of pastries each. "Anette, I remember the first time I met you at Häckeberga when the cook had just given you a plate of food. I love women who enjoy food."

Anette was suddenly conscious of the large piece of bread with cheese in her mouth. She could tell him it was because they never had enough food at his sister's farm but decided to not ruin the mood.

"She was supposed to bring me brandy too, but she never did. And I thought you had fallen asleep by the time I started eating."

"With you there?" A grin spread across his face.

She laughed, then glanced around the room. The café was empty except for a man absorbed in his newspaper and two women in matching white dresses engaged in a lively conversation. Watching them for a moment, she decided not to let being in public bother her. She had nothing to be ashamed of. Erik would have met her in her apartment if he was trying to hide anything. She took another bite of her sandwich, and a sip of her coffee. It was delicious. Everything seemed to taste better in Helsingborg, and everything was so clean and luxurious.

"Erik, I'm overwhelmed by all this. The apartment is enormous. It's too much for you to do this for me. We're not together anymore, and Helmerth isn't yours." There she said it, it was better to get it out of the way.

Erik had already finished his sandwich and was biting into a chocolate pastry with cream. He looked amused.

"Well, it seems like a lot to you. But really Anette, it's not something you need to worry about. I can afford it."

He said it so easily, as if he had bought her a pair of shoes. Imagine that she could have lived in that apartment all these years. He must really have loved her to keep coming to spend time with her on the farms. She had judged him harshly because of her own mistakes.

"What will Antoinette say, Erik, and what if someone sees us here?" She gestured with her head toward the other tables.

"Then I'll tell them you're one of my closest friends, Anette. A widow I befriended years ago at a séance my sister was holding. It's the truth, isn't it?"

She exhaled. "The séance part is at least."

He laughed and his eyes were so warm. It felt like they had never been apart.

"And our friendship?"

"Of course."

Chapter Sixty-three

Two years later

Anette spent part of each morning reading the newspaper. She hadn't realized how much she was missing when she was a statare. Bits and pieces of news mixed with rumors had come her way, but never more than that.

The Great War was still going on. Food was often in short supply, but in the past they had gotten by on even less, and she still felt they ate in luxury. Meanwhile, women all over the world were demanding to be heard. In every Scandinavian country except for Sweden, women now had the right to vote. In Denmark, suffrage had been won two years ago.

More and more, Anette was noticing women on the street who were active in the fight. She could see it in the way they held themselves. They seemed so confident, so strong, and many had attached yellow and white ribbons with the words Votes for Women, to their lapels.

One day she was even pulled aside and handed a flyer about secret meetings on birth prevention. Anette quickly shoved the paper deep into the pocket of her coat, wondering what the woman had seen in her that emboldened her to take such a risk. Surely it couldn't be legal?

#

Anette and Ester were relaxing in the kitchen, drinking surrogate coffee made from roasted acorns. Real coffee was rationed because of the war. Ester handed her the newspaper she had been reading and pointed to one of the articles.

The Angelmaker from Bruksgatan, the headline read in thick black letters. There was a picture of her, sitting on a chair and staring calmly into the camera. Her hair was dark and straight and was parted to the side, and she had an annoyed, or perhaps even defiant, look on her face. Anette flashed Ester a horrified glance. Bruksgatan was a small street, only blocks from them. They walked through it often, especially when going to the little market square in front of the church.

The Angelmaker, Hilda Nilsson was her name, had been arrested for the murder of no less than eight infants, Anette read. She and her husband Gustaf were very poor, so Hilda tried to make ends meet by fostering children from women who had their babies out of wedlock. She was paid for it, but to her dismay the money didn't cover as much as she had hoped. Fearing that the little ones would eat them out of the house, she decided to murder them. Hilda placed the baby in a washbasin and covered it with a board, which she weighed down with a bucket of coal. Then she left the house and didn't return until several hours later. Anette stopped reading and put the paper down on the table with a slap, staring at Ester.

"That's horrific! Thank God they caught her, Ester. Imagine if we had lived here, instead of at Tjute Farm back when…" she couldn't even finish her thought. What if she had been one of those mothers? She could have given Linnea to Hilda Nilsson instead of the nice temperance woman who had taken her, maybe Helmerth too, her little darling boy.

Ester shook her head. "No Mamma, you wouldn't have."

"No, of course not, you're right," Anette said, more for Ester's sake than her own. Then she opened the paper just to see the horrid face of Hilda Nilsson one more time.

What if the mothers read the article? How would they ever live with themselves, learning they had given their babies to a murderess?

It wasn't until she went to bed that night that she remembered the flyer in her coat pocket. She would go to their meeting on Thursday.

Chapter Sixty-four

Anette walked up a rather steep hill, the flyer snug in her pocket, then stopped at a well-kept, three-story building where the meeting was to be held. Red pelargoniums were blooming in the windows, and the few people walking by didn't give the place any particular notice. She took a deep breath, pulled the entryway door open, and walked up to the third floor. When she found the right apartment, she knocked. No one answered, so she knocked harder several times and then she heard a woman's voice from inside.

"Who's there?"

"My name is Anette Lundström."

The door remained closed.

She raised her voice and added, "A woman gave me a flyer a few weeks ago. I want to attend…"

Before she could finish the sentence, the door opened and a thin woman with long blonde braided hair pulled her inside.

"Don't mention the flyer so loudly in the hallway. We can't have the neighbors know."

"I'm sorry. I didn't realize."

"It's fine. Come with me. We're about to start the meeting," she said and threw a glance at the hallway, then closed the door firmly and led Anette down a long, unlit corridor to a room at the end.

Five women turned to look at them when they entered, all seated on chairs that were arranged in a semicircle. One of the chairs had a stack of booklets with the title, The Society for Humanitarian Procreation, on the seat.

A woman in the adjacent chair picked the booklets up and placed them on the windowsill behind her. "Please sit," she said, and looked searchingly into Anette's face. "How do you feel about what we stand for?"

"I agree. I agree fully. After reading that article in the newspaper about Hilda Nilsson, I decided it was time to do something."

The woman grabbed a booklet from the windowsill and handed it to Anette. "Better not to get pregnant in the first place than to give your babies to someone who might drown them," she said, pursing her lips angrily. "That's why we dare to call for preventive measures. Women are constantly being abandoned and left with babies to care for."

"And everyone calls them a fallen woman or a whore," Anette blurted out, regretting it as soon as the words were out of her mouth. Clearly, she had revealed too much.

But the woman nodded enthusiastically. "Yes, yes, that's another reason the laws need to be changed! Thank you for your candor. Now we can introduce ourselves. My name is Märta. This is Anna, Jenny, Vanda, and Ingegerd. Vanda travels all the way from Lund to attend our meetings," she added.

Vanda acknowledged her comment with a shrug and a smile.

"I'm Märta as well," said the woman who had opened the door when she arrived. "Märta Carlberg, everyone calls me Märta C."

Anette noticed Jenny was staring at her. "I'm Anette, she said when she turned to her, Jenny returned a shy smile.

Then Ingegerd leaned closer to Anette. "I'm glad you're here," she said. "I read an article a while ago where a Norwegian writer proposed that people who mistreat children should be sent away to an island. A woman author, I can't remember her name."

"Her name was Elise Ottesen," Märta C said. "An island would be too lenient for a murderess, in my opinion. I heard they might put Hilda Nilsson to death. It's just what she'd deserve, I say."

Anette nodded uncertainly. She felt a little intimidated by them. They were so sure of themselves. But she had resolved to do this. The past was gone. She gathered her courage and said, "Could you please tell me a little about what you do here. I want to be involved, but if I understand correctly, this isn't legal." She didn't blush.

"That's correct," Vanda said. "But like you do, we feel it's important." She glanced briefly at Märta C, who gave a quick nod. "We're careful, but we feel it's worth the risk to inform people about how to prevent pregnancy, women especially as I'm sure you can imagine. Mostly we gather here to discuss ways to reach those who might need it, and to see if we can find politicians who may be swayed. That hasn't been easy so far."

"We also sometimes stand near the pharmacy, or doctor's offices, and more often than not, we can tell why a woman is there and may be approachable," Märta C added.

Anette wanted to ask why they had given *her* a flyer, but she felt too nervous to ask something so personal and just let it be. The woman who gave it to her wasn't there anyway, which felt like a relief.

She listened mostly after that but felt more comfortable. The women were friendly and welcoming, and she was very impressed with what they had to say.

Shortly after noon, Märta C passed around flyers which announced the next meeting agenda, and then everyone said their goodbyes and hurried down the stairs and out the entryway. Anette assumed it was so as not to linger in the stairways and draw attention from the neighbors. She did her best, but all those years of milking had taken their toll on her lower back and she wasn't able to handle stairs too well, especially on the way down. As she exited the building, Jenny was waiting for her.

"Anette, which way are you walking?" she asked.

"North."

"I'm headed that way too. May I ask you something?"

"Of course."

"Do you know of a place in Lund called the House, and a woman named Helga?"

Astonished, Anette took a closer look at her face. The jowls were heavy and there were deep creases around the eyes, but it was a face she knew.

"Jenny! Little Jenny from Stockholm? We used to sew together." How had she missed it?

Jenny laughed as a solitary tear rolled down her cheek. "I recognized you immediately, you and your turquoise eyes."

"I can't believe this. It must be close to thirty years." Anette embraced her tightly, overcome with both surprise and memories she hadn't thought of in a long time. "Please, come with me. Let's go to Signe Bergqvist."

They took each other by the arm and walked in silence all the way to the café, savoring the closeness and wanting to save their conversation until they were sitting down.

They picked a table by the window, but before they took their seats, Anette spoke to the waitress and paid handsomely for real coffee.

Jenny's eyes widened. "You must have done well for yourself after you left Lund, Anette. You didn't need to do that. I'd be happy with the usual."

Anette glanced around. The café was empty except for the waitress who had already left and was wiping tables on the upper floor. She could lie again or tell the truth for once. Jenny was the only person who knew about Carl.

"Jenny, are you married?" she asked, her heart racing just a bit.

"Yes, I met someone a few years after I had the baby and we've been married almost 25 years now. We've been living here in Helsingborg since ten years back."

"Did you apply for your banns?"

Jenny narrowed her eyes and leaned closer. "Why do you ask that?"

So she told her. Everything. How she met Jon, how happy she had been, and how the parson had destroyed her chance to start over, about Jon's anger, her years in the poorhouse, and then finally how she met Erik. They were both crying when she came to that part. Anette felt shaky, but something was lighter in her chest.

"If I'd known that there were methods I could use to protect myself with, I could have moved to Helsingborg a long time ago. Part of the reason I didn't was that I was afraid of what my neighbors would do when I had new babies without a husband." She lowered her voice. "I tried sour milk in sheep's wool, but it never worked."

"I imagine not. I'm sorry."

Anette nodded, feeling a little embarrassed, and changed the subject. "Those church books ruined my future."

"And Jon did. Have you ever looked for him? He ought to be ashamed of himself for leaving you like that. Honestly, Erik sounds much more the man than him."

Anette smiled. "That he is. No, I haven't looked for Jon, not since the day after that day in church. He wasn't ashamed for leaving, he was ashamed of *me*." An image of Jon's stony face when he opened the door and handed her the money and that brand new valise came before her. Maybe she had been lucky after all. Erik *was* much more a man than him. Jenny was right about that.

"I've been very angry with Helga for not warning us. Do you think she knew we'd never be able to keep our first babies a secret? And could you? That's why I asked."

"Yes, I gathered as much." Jenny sipped some more coffee, while glancing at the waitress who was still cleaning tables upstairs. "Well, I don't know. The parson didn't look us up in the church books the way you described it. At least he didn't check our addresses like that. But knowing my parents, they may have paid him not to say anything. Or maybe it was because I lived so far from Lund."

"I was under the impression that each parish shares information with each other so they can keep track of where people move. I'm not certain, though. But the parsons do take down all the information during the baptisms. Helga may have thought I would have realized that."

Jenny stared at her, and Anette knew what she was about to ask.

"Does Erik have children? I mean other children. What did his wife say when they...?"

Anette splayed her fingers on both hands in a shrugging gesture. "I've never told the parsons about him, so it's never been an issue."

"Does he know you've done that for him?"

"No."

"You should tell him, Anette."

Her words hung in the air, and Anette looked at her silently. She had wanted to, but she was afraid of the questions it might bring up, and there was so much Erik didn't know.

"Maybe," she said finally. "But enough about me, please tell me how you are?"

Jenny looked as if she was going to ask something else, but then she smiled and said, "Knut and I have two boys. He's quiet, a banker. Not what my parents had hoped for, but he's a very good man."

Anette reached across the table and squeezed her arm. "I'm very happy to hear that Jenny," she said, while noticing that it had started to rain heavily, and passersby were hurrying down the street with their umbrellas.

Chapter Sixty-five

Hanna

Göteborg, June 2, 1918

Hanna could hear the cheering before they reached the square. "Votes for women, votes for women!" With emotion tightening in her throat, she rolled out her flag, watching as the three stripes, yellow on top and below, and the words Votes for Women in yellow on a white stripe in the middle, unfolded against the sky.

"I see them. Hurry!" Maria exclaimed and pointed forward.

"Where?" Hanna asked, squinting to see, then felt Bengta take her arm and drag her forward. And as they turned the corner, she saw. The square was full of women already, and more were coming from every direction. Her heart skipped a beat.

Vanda rolled out her flag and held it high. She was grinning from ear to ear.

The five of them, Vanda, Bengta, Magnhild, Maria, and Hanna had taken the train to Göteborg to protest the parliament's latest refusal to let women vote. Hanna had expected a crowd, but not like this. It was packed. This must get them to change their mind. It had to. She lifted her flag and waved it in the air along with Vanda, who was holding hers in both hands and moving it back and forth with big strokes. It looked like a sail in the wind.

"I'm happy to have another grandchild, but I wish Elsa wasn't eight months pregnant just now. She would have loved this," Maria said, and beamed at two women holding a huge yellow and white banner with thick yellow fringes at the bottom. GÖTEBORGS FKPR VOTES FOR WOMEN, it read in large embroidered yellow letters.

"Why is it FKPR not LKPR? Aren't we a national organization now?" Maria asked when the women were out of earshot.

"It's because we're in Göteborg and Göteborg was one of the local suffrage associations that formed LKPR with Stockholm,"

Hanna said and waved her flag in the air again.

"Thank you, Hanna!" Maria shouted. "I'm glad my husband impressed you all those years ago so you could drag me into this. Look where it got me."

Hanna laughed. "I'm not so sure you're not the one who's dragged me places," she said as the wind caught her flag and snapped it in the air.

"Votes for women!" Magnhild and Vanda shouted and waved their flags high above their heads. Bengta walked silently, then whispered, "Yes, votes for women."

Hanna put her arm around her shoulder. "Votes for women!" she repeated and looked across the square, now full of what must be thousands of women, most wearing dark coats with wide beige or white hats, and large white collars. They were congregating on the left side. Men passed them by, turning their heads curiously as they continued on their way, but some joined in. In fact, there were a lot of men in the square as well. A woman with a white coat over a black skirt and a dark hat was standing in the middle of the square. The crowd was splitting in two on each side of her, with mostly women on her left and mostly men on her right.

"This is beyond anything I could have imagined," Bengta said as a group of at least fifteen women passed them.

Hanna followed them with her eyes, then discretely pointed to the woman in the crowd. "Do you see that woman in the white coat? She's alone, but she looks so confident."

Then the wind picked up again and the woman's hat blew off and landed right in front of a man. He looked first at the hat, then at the woman, waved his hand at her and said something, then turned around and walked off.

Hanna's jaw dropped. "He didn't pick it up."

"That he did not," Bengta said curtly, shaking her head. "Did you see that Magnhild?"

"No, what happened?" Magnhild responded with a broad smile on her face. Clearly, she hadn't seen it.

"Let's go speak with her," Hanna said as Bengta explained to the others.

They hurried into the crowd, pushing themselves between everyone. The woman was easy to spot in the sea of mostly black except for the hats and collars. Only a few others wore all white, but none like her with a black skirt.

"It's very chilly for June, isn't it?" said Vanda, just as they caught up with her.

"Good Day," Hanna said and extended her hand. "My suffrage sisters and I saw what happened and wanted to come over to talk to you."

The woman took her hand and shook it, looking a little confused. She was young and pretty, with brown eyes and curly, light brown hair. "I'm not sure I understand," she said.

"We happened to notice that your hat flew off and landed right in front of that man who wouldn't pick it up. I hope he wasn't rude?"

"Oh, *that's* what you thought?" she threw her head back and laughed just like Magnhild always did. "No, no, that's my brother. He was born with bad hips and can't bend down. But it's very nice to meet you all, anyway. Where are you from?"

"Oh lord, here I was prejudging. I'm so sorry," Hanna said, making a note to herself to be more careful with her assumptions. "We're from Lund's Suffrage Society," she added proudly.

"Don't worry about it. I'm glad you came to introduce yourselves. Please come join us. I'm with Göteborg's FKPR," she said warmly. "The organizer is right over there; come, I'll introduce you."

#

That evening they boarded the train back to Lund, carrying sandwiches and chocolate bars, along with addresses and telephone numbers to several of Göteborg's suffragists, including the woman who had introduced them to FKPR. Her name was Stina.

They ate in silence, just smiling at each other, too exhausted to talk. While the train chugged along, Hanna finished her sandwich, watching the towns and trees speeding by. The clouds had cleared, and the landscape was shining in that gorgeous warm evening light that only came on summer evenings.

Hanna hadn't felt so encouraged since the day LKPR was formed and they had their celebratory meeting at the Frog. She had been so sure then that it would only be a year or two until they got what they wanted. Never could she have imagined it would be 1918 already and they still couldn't vote. But today she felt hope and encouragement. Seeing so many fellow suffragists together, so calm but determined, in that square, moved her. The Iron Square, it was called. It was fitting. They were the iron women. She smiled to herself at the thought, feeling her eyes droop at the same time. Soon she was dozing.

When she opened her eyes again, Bengta and Magnhild were sound asleep. Magnhild's head was resting against Bengta and they were holding hands under their hats on their laps. Maria's hat was pulled down over her face, and she was snoring softly. Vanda was smiling at Hanna.

"Are you going to stay awake?" she whispered.

Hanna stretched and pulled her watch out from under her blouse, then snapped the lid shut. They still had almost two hours left, but she didn't think she would sleep anymore. "I'm fine. I think I'll eat my chocolate now."

"There's an empty compartment next to us. Can you come with me? I could use the company, and there is something I've been meaning to tell you for a while," Vanda whispered. The way she said it made Hanna take a second look at her. She seemed nervous.

"I'll come with you." She got to her feet, grabbed her purse, and placed her hat on the seat.

Vanda closed the door of the new compartment, then sat down and patted the seat next to her. "Come sit here, Hanna."

She did as bid and pulled her feet up so she sat cross-legged, turning herself sideways to face her. "Is everything as it should, Vanda?"

"Yes, but there's so much I've never told you that I've been wanting to. I wasn't going to say anything today, but when the others are sleeping and we have all this time to ourselves, I thought it might be the best time after all."

Hanna broke off a piece of chocolate from her chocolate bar

and ate it. Vanda always confided in her. What was there she hadn't yet?

Vanda exhaled audibly. "Do you remember the first time we met and Bengta introduced me as her friend?"

"Yes, of course, it was back when we still had our meetings at Helga's."

"Did Bengta ever tell you how she and I met?"

"No, she never has," Hanna said and put the rest of the square in her mouth, then folded the wrapper over the bar and put it in her purse.

"I met her when she came to my house when I gave birth."

Hanna turned her head sideways in confusion. Had she and Alexander had a child?

"I see your surprise, Hanna. No one knows about this except Bengta, and she doesn't even know everything. I was seven months along when Alexander went into a drunk frenzy and beat me so badly that I went into labor. She didn't make it."

Hanna clasped her hand over her mouth, then put it back down. "Oh, Vanda, I'm so sorry."

"No one knows everything," Vanda repeated. "Bengta was wonderful. She stayed with me for several days until he stopped drinking. Helped bury her and took care of me. What I didn't tell her though, was that it wasn't the first time. Years earlier I lost two other babies, but they weren't so far along that we needed to call a midwife. He went into frenzies when I was pregnant. It's not uncommon I've heard. Some men get uncontrollable jealousy when…." She took a steadying breath. Hanna tried her best to look like she was listening calmly, but she really wanted to scream. Lova had been right that time when Vanda first told them. They should have gone to the constabulary.

"After that I used precautions, except they didn't work that night when our daughter was conceived. It's for this reason I'm so adamantly in support of Hinke Bergegren and have always been for it, even long before that."

Hanna shifted her gaze to the window. The train was speeding past a lake with the evening sun setting over it, making it sparkle with warm light. It was beautiful, but it blinded her, and she couldn't see Vanda's face when she looked back at her.

"I'm so very sorry, Vanda. I know how it is to lose a child, I think anyway, I'm sorry, I know it's not the same." She shouldn't have said that. It was almost insulting. She had only missed her courses once, which may or may not have been an early miscarriage.

"No, I understand Hanna, and it's part of why I wanted to tell you, because you do understand how it is to want a child. I did too, you know." Her chin quivered once. Then she took another breath and said, "Hanna, there's a lot more."

"More?" Vanda had a strange expression on her face. Almost as if she was both excited but frightened at the same time. "Please tell me Vanda, you're making me nervous," Hanna said, then stopped talking. There were footsteps approaching and someone looked through the little window in their door, then walked off.

Vanda waited a moment, keeping her gaze on the door, then turned back to Hanna. "I will. When we voted not to take a stand on the contraceptive issue, after Bengta and I went to Hinke's speech, I decided to take it on myself. I've been traveling to Helsingborg every week to attend meetings with the Society for Humanitarian Procreation."

"What? Why haven't you said anything? We knew what you thought."

Vanda chuckled. "Well, I may have been helping them to hand out flyers with information about us and then given women instructions on how to protect themselves. It's illegal, at least the part about informing women about what to do."

Hanna laughed and shook her head, picturing Vanda on a little side street somewhere near the harbor.

"Well, I'm glad you're laughing Hanna because there's more."

Hanna raised an eyebrow. "Do tell me you haven't been arrested?"

"No." Vanda reached for her hand. "Hanna, what's Linnea's

birth mother's name?"

Hanna's heart picked up speed. Why would she ask that? "I only know her first name. It's Anette. I just found out recently, actually. It was to be somewhat anonymous, but since we met her briefly when we picked Linnea up, I begged Bengta to at least tell me that much. I always thought of her as the mother, but it started to bother me. *I'm* Linnea's mother. Why do you want to know?"

Vanda didn't answer.

"It was twins, wasn't it?" she asked instead after a moment. "Her brother was a boy? Do you by chance know his name?"

"Oh yes, that I'll never forget. It was Anette who named both Linnea and her brother. It's Helmerth. I just hope he's... they were very...." She stopped when she noticed that Vanda was crying.

"What is it?"

Vanda was hesitating for too long.

Then finally she smiled through her tears. "I've met them, I've met both Helmerth and Anette. Anette is also a member of the Society for Humanitarian Procreation."

The hairs on the back of Hanna's neck stood up. "You *know* them?"

"Yes. I've even been to her apartment; it's how I know about Helmerth."

A wave of both relief and disappointment washed over her, and she shook her head. "Then it's just a coincidence. Anette is a statare, she lives out in the country in Tjutebro."

"I know she did, but not anymore. Please Hanna, bear with me and let me tell you everything."

"Sure, please do."

"Anette showed up at one of our meetings sometime last year. It was right when the horrible story about the Angelmaker from Bruksgatan was in the papers. Anette had read about it and decided to become involved. She's a very nice woman, Hanna, a little shy and cautious, but she's been more open and comfortable lately. She invited me and another woman from our group to her home about a month and a half ago. We were having coffee in her kitchen when her children came home. A teenager named Ester and an eleven-year-old boy named Helmerth who looked exactly like Linnea, Hanna."

Her body reacted before her mind did, and she was suddenly sweating and feeling ice cold at the same time. How could Anette live in an apartment in Helsingborg? She had been a statare, dirty and so poor that she had been afraid that Helmerth hadn't survived. He was alive.

Vanda patted her hand.

"Is this a ratty apartment she lives in? Did she tell you she'd been a statare?" Hanna asked, barely able to keep her voice steady.

"No, not at all, it's a fine place, simple, but large and clean. She didn't tell me about being a statare, but said she'd been very poor and had worked on a farm in Tjutebro just like you said. I recognized the name, but I didn't put two and two together until Helmerth and Ester came home. She has two other daughters as well but they're older and don't live there."

Hanna laughed nervously. "It doesn't make sense. You should've seen the way they lived. No father from those circumstances could afford a fine apartment. Are you really sure it's her?"

"Yes, they even have the same birthday, Hanna. It has to be her."

Hanna uncurled her legs and got to her feet, then walked over to the window and looked out. It was completely dark now. She crossed her arms over her chest. One of the older daughters who didn't live with Anette must have been born when she stayed at the House with Helga. It would be better if she didn't mention that to Vanda.

"Tell me how she looks," Hanna said, turning her head toward her.

"She has blond hair that's graying a little, interesting eyes with an unusual pale bluish color. She's round with a full bust. And her back troubles her a lot, from milking cows on that farm where she worked, she says."

"Lord in heaven! It's her then." Hanna turned back to the window and wiped at her eyes with the back of her hand. Then she sat back down, but on the opposite seat across from Vanda.

"Was I wrong to tell you, Hanna? I wasn't sure, I've been debating it with myself, but I thought it would be worse not to."

Hanna hesitated. Part of her wished she hadn't but the truth was always better. She nodded. "No, I'm glad you did, even if it's hard to hear. I've been so worried about Helmerth and it's a relief to know he wasn't one of those babies Hinke spoke of who died within his first year."

"Did you worry about that?"

"Yes, especially after you told us about the speech and those horrific statistics. I had nightmares," Hanna admitted.

"I'm so sorry."

"It's not your fault. Anyway, what I want to know is how the father could have let her give only one of the babies away and then get her an apartment like that? I can only assume she's not paying for it herself."

"I was wondering that too, but I get the sense that it's not Helmerth's father who's paying for it. She says she's a widow, but she's not saying much else. It's all a little strange I admit."

"When did she tell you she had been poor and worked on a farm? I think it's something I may have kept quiet about if I were her," Hanna said.

"It was fitting with the context. We were sharing a bit. I told her about the loss of my daughter, and that's when it came up. She said she'd been very poor but received some help after her husband died."

"I see. Johannes thought her husband had died from a farming accident while she was expecting, but Bengta said that it wasn't the husband who was the father. I wasn't supposed to tell anyone that, so please don't tell Bengta I told you."

Vanda nodded.

"Could she have met someone else? Maybe that's why she wants to use those devises," Hanna said, feeling a little horrified at the thought. How many men had Anette had?

Vanda's eyes glinted. "Maybe, she would deserve some love."

"True, of course, she does." Hanna paused, then said, "Anette gave us the joy of our lives. I'll always be grateful for it."

She hadn't even thanked her. It had gone so quick that day. From one moment to the next she had Linnea in her arms, and then both Anette and Helmerth were gone.

Hanna let out a long deep breath. Helmerth was fine, and he didn't live in that dark dilapidated house anymore.

#

Saturday May 24, 1919

Hanna hurried down the stairs and answered the telephone. At first she only heard excited shouting and didn't recognize the voice.

"Who am I speaking to?" she asked when there was a pause in the enthusiasm.

"It's Stina Johansson," the woman said, and then Hanna recognized the voice and put a face to the name. It was Stina who they met at the demonstration last year.

"How nice of you to telephone me. What happened? You sound so happy, but I'm afraid I didn't hear what you said."

"I'm in Stockholm. We won! They announced it just now. We did it, Hanna! We did it."

"We won??? They said yes?"

She must have screamed because both Johannes and Linnea came running in.

"Oh, my Lord, we've won! I can't believe it. Well, I should believe it. We've seen it coming, but... I can't believe it," she said to Stina while grinning at Linnea and Johannes.

"I know, same here, I can't either. Oh, Hanna, I wish you were here with all of us. We came up two days ago. I must go now. I just wanted to let you know." The connection ended.

Hanna put the receiver back in its cradle, tears of happiness streaming down her cheeks. Johannes embraced her, then reached for Linnea who was still standing by the door and pulled her close too.

"We did it, Johannes, after all this time. Finally, it's done," Hanna said, leaning into him and sagging for a moment. She felt him sniff her hair, but he didn't respond, just squeezed his arms tighter around her. Thoughts and memories raised through her mind out of order. There was the time when they made Lund's Suffrage Society official, and she had been nervous speaking in front of everyone at the Frog but felt she had handled it well. The time when they had hot chocolate in that cute little café and was overheard by a man who got so angry, he hit his head on the door when he rushed out. Or when she spoke with Mrs. Kjellberg at grandma's, and when they listened to Frida Stéenhoff's speech in Stockholm.

"Mamma, are women really going to be allowed to vote?" Linnea asked, interrupting her thoughts. Her eyes were full of disbelief.

"Yes, in the next election, my wonderful girl. They've just decided to change the law," Hanna said, laughing and crying at the same time and pulling herself out of Johannes' arms. She grabbed Linnea's hands and started to dance around the room.

"We're going out, I'm getting the Ford," Johannes said, and left the room. She could tell he was about to cry.

With Johannes at the wheel of their new Model T, the three of them headed out for a drive. Hanna and Linnea had tied white and yellow scarves in their hair that made a snapping sound in the wind, reminding her of the banners and flags they had waved in Göteborg. She would never forget it now.

Their little street was quiet, but as Johannes turned toward Lund's center, they heard voices. The closer they got, the louder it became. Hanna drew a sharp intake of breath. The street was filling with women, some wearing white and yellow, carrying suffrage flags and Swedish flags, running, laughing, and pouring out of shops and private homes. Linnea burst out laughing in surprise, and Hanna grabbed her hand and kissed it, unable to think of what to say.

"Mamma, I've never seen anything like this. I didn't realize until now how important this is."

"I know Linnea." Hanna looked at her profile, watching her round face flush with excitement. Linnea would never understand how hard they had fought. In the future, people wouldn't question the rights of women, and they would look back on this time and wonder what all the fuss was about. But *she* knew, and she would savor this moment.

Johannes slowed down and entered a side street, following four middle-aged women who were skipping arm-in-arm like a group of schoolgirls.

"Johannes," Hanna said, turning to him with a broad grin. "Drive to the Frog, I'm sure everyone will congregate there."

"Already on my way, darling," Johannes said, then added, "Linnea, your mother did this not only for herself, but for you."

Emily had opened the doors wide and was standing on a ladder, placing a suffrage flag by the frog's hand. There was a hole behind the cup, and the little handheld pole fit perfectly.

"Bravo, Emily," Linnea shouted, jumping out as soon as Johannes stopped.

"Get champagne," Hanna said as she followed.

Johannes put his hand to his hat. "Yes, ma'am," he said and drove off.

Emily laughed and climbed down. "What do you think, boss?"

"It's wonderful. I can't believe it. I'm so overwhelmed I feel shaky, my legs are wobbly. Is anyone else here?"

"No, but the telephone has been ringing constantly. Pappa is here too still, he's taking on a second shift. Assuming you don't want to close?"

"Close?" Hanna lifted an eyebrow. "We're celebrating. Let me go talk to him."

She left Linnea with Emily and went into the scullery. Kurt was just pulling out a tray with three large pound cakes from the oven. He looked up at the sound of her coming in and placed the tray on the table, then went to her and hugged her close, patting her back with his warm oven mitts. He didn't say a word. He didn't have to.

"Kurt, it feels unreal, doesn't it?" she asked when he let go of her. "Thank you for staying."

"Of course, Hanna. I'm making our special chocolate layered cakes for us." Kurt gestured to the pound cakes on the tray. Then he looked at her mischievously and waved her over to the cabinet, pulled out a drawer, and pointed into it. "I've been saving these," he whispered ceremoniously.

Three cookie cutters lay neatly displayed on a yellow napkin, one in the shape of Goddess Justicia and her scales, another cutter with Goddess Justicia inside a flag, and lastly a flag shape.

"Oh Kurt, you had these made in secret? You're incredible."

"Well," he said with a wink. "I was superstitious and didn't want to show you until today. I had them made when you ladies went to Göteborg. I knew it would happen after that." He winked again. "How could I not? We have frogs and automobiles already, I had to have suffrage cookies."

"I can't say I disagree," she said and hugged him again. Then they heard familiar voices from the dining room, Bengta and Magnhild.

"Viva la Justicia!" Hanna shouted, picked up the little Justicia cutter, grabbed Kurt by the hand, and dragged him out of the scullery.

By that evening, everyone had arrived. Maria and her and Kurt's other daughters with their families, Vanda, and all the other women in their group, nearly fifty in all. As they had done for meetings in the past, they put the tables together to form one long one. Only now, instead of papers and lists, it was filled with glittering candles, lanterns, champagne bottles, and Kurt's new cookies and cakes. Astrid brought her guitar and Maria's daughters sang while they filled the dining area and spilled out into the street carrying flutes with champagne.

Chapter Sixty-six

Anette

1923

"I want to show you something," Jenny said. They were sitting on Anette's couch, facing each other. She reached into her pocketbook and pulled out a small clipping from the newspaper.

"Ottar is giving a lecture next week."

"Ottar, who's that?" Anette asked.

Jenny nodded knowingly. "Do you remember the first meeting you came to, when Ingegerd spoke of that Norwegian article she'd read?"

"The one where the writer wanted to put criminals on an island?" She hadn't thought of that day in a long time. It was right after Hilda Nilsson had murdered all those babies. She had hung herself in her jail cell some time after that, but they hadn't known that then.

Jenny handed her the clipping. "Yes, it's the same woman. Ottar is her pen name. She's involved with a man and even though they're not married, she goes by Elise Ottesen-Jensen now, even Mrs. Jensen."

Anette stared at her. "Truly?" She threw a quick glance at the clipping, but the text was too small to read without her glasses.

"Yes," Jenny said, and smiled. "They live in Stockholm now. She has a column in the Worker called The Woman and the Home. Ottar is one of us, Anette. She's for birth prevention. And she's traveling around the country speaking out against the sex laws."

"Publicly?"

"Yes, she is." Jenny put her pocketbook on the floor and stretched her legs toward Anette on the couch. "She's a very interesting woman. Her dream was to become a dentist, but her hands were injured in an accident. So she became a journalist."

"Good, we could certainly use her skills in our movement. But I want to learn more about why she's calling herself Mrs. Jensen when they're not married. Why aren't they?"

Jenny shrugged. "I don't know."

"Maybe she had a child that she gave away, like we did Jenny. She might be making excuses, so he won't find out what the church books says."

Jenny furrowed her brow, then shook her head. "I don't think so. Knowing her views, I think she would just say it if that was the case. It may be more like you and Erik. Maybe he's married."

Anette smiled. Imagine if she had called herself Mrs. Lövcrantz.

"Her lecture is in Malmö. She had one in Grängesberg, and this is supposed to be one of the first ones down here in the south. I want to go and I want you to come with me. Please?" Jenny looked ready to burst with excitement.

Anette laughed and grabbed one of Jenny's feet and squeezed. "Of course, I'll go with you." She reached for their wine glasses that they had left on the sofa table and handed Jenny hers. "I better not tell Erik, she added, then sipped slowly, savoring it. It was delicious. And expensive. Erik had brought her two bottles last week. Yesterday she had gone into a store and asked for it just to see how much it cost and almost fainted when she heard how much he had paid for it.

"He won't approve?"

"Well, yes, but no. He feels as I do now. But he's nervous about me drawing too much attention to myself, and since it's illegal, it's just better not to say anything." She smiled wryly. Drawing attention to herself used to be her worry.

"How are you two, these days?" Jenny asked, then reached for the bottle and poured them both more wine.

"We're doing very well. He still visits on Mondays and Tuesdays. Antoinette thinks he works late after the weekend." She chuckled. "His wife has nothing to be jealous about these days. I cook dinner and we talk. It's ironic, isn't it? Now when I'm both too old and would have access to protection, we have no need for it." Anette took another sip of her wine. They had made love only once since she came here. It hadn't felt the same after all those years apart, and they had relaxed into a deep friendship instead. Erik had shown her a softer side of himself. There was a sensitivity and kindness about him that she wished she had known of earlier. They never argued anymore either.

Jenny nodded. "Yes, life always is ironic."

#

Ottar entered the stage of the auditorium. She held up her hands, prompting a sharp intake of breath from the audience. Anette's first thought was that someone had said something inappropriate and quickly turned around and scanned the room. Some were leaning forward in their seats, but everyone looked calm. Jenny was smiling.

"As you can see, dental school ended dramatically for me. It's not easy pulling teeth without certain vital digits, I'm sure you'd agree. An explosion in the laboratory. Somehow I can't forget it." She turned her hands this way and that to show them off from different angles, and Anette realized several fingers were missing. Slight dizziness came over her, and in her mind's eye she saw Ottar's fingers smashed to pieces. Breathing deeply to clear the vision, she looked around the room again. Some people were laughing at the joke. Others seemed as uncomfortable as she was.

"There, now we can begin," Ottar said with a gleam in her eye. "Now we can speak about our genitals instead."

Anette covered her mouth with her hand to hide a burst of laughter, but she was not the only one laughing. Ottar sure knew how to capture an audience.

"First, I'd like to tell you my motto: Every child should come welcomed into this world. Welcomed and loved. My own dear mother had eighteen children. Can you imagine what that does to a woman's body?"

Eighteen, ten more than her, no she couldn't imagine. Hers had been quite enough. She had been so tired, always tired. And her back still troubled her.

Ottar took a sip of water from a small table to her right. "Do you think these women enjoy their husbands' lovemaking? It's not easy when you're exhausted and afraid of getting pregnant again.

326

And what of the fallen women, the ones who become pregnant out of wedlock?" She was looking across the audience and seemed to be focusing right on her face. Anette's cheeks burned. There was something in the way Ottar said it that seemed very personal. She could sense it.

Ottar took another sip of water, then started talking about the various methods of prevention that she and Jenny were familiar with already. The audience leaned forward to catch every word. Jenny and Anette exchanged a glance and smiled. Clearly, this was new for most of them. Ottar concluded in a strong voice, her hands clasped tightly in front of her. "I dream of the day when every newborn child is welcome, when men and women are equal in every respect, and when sexuality is an expression of intimacy, joy, and tenderness."

Anette was silent as she and Jenny stood up to leave. Never before had she heard someone speak so openly about something so private in such a large setting. She pulled Jenny close and whispered into her ear, "I'll meet you outside." Then she headed back toward the stage, pushing past people on their way out. There was a hallway on her right. At the far end, a light was coming through the bottom of a door.

She knocked and when no one answered, she pressed down on the handle and walked in. A small group of women surrounded Ottar who was leaning against a desk, speaking softly, while holding a round rubber item in her hand, a diaphragm. Ottar stopped talking when she noticed her coming in and smiled warmly.

For the rest of her life, Anette would wonder how she summoned up the nerve to step forward and say what she did, especially in front of all the women in the room.

"Mrs. Jensen, I myself have been marked as one of these fallen women you were speaking of. I'd be honored to assist you in any way I can."

At first Ottar didn't say a word, just straightened up and scrutinized her. No one else said anything, and Anette's heart picked up speed. But then Ottar smiled again and held her hand out for Anette to shake. It felt odd to touch a hand with missing fingers, but she was careful not to show it.

"I'm a member of the Society for Humanitarian Procreation," Anette said, feeling both embarrassed and proud. Ottar didn't seem shocked or surprised by it at all.

"Do you own a telephone?" she asked.

"Yes."

"Good, telephone me next week, I'll be home in the evenings." She took a small notepad from the desk and jotted her number down. Anette held the piece of paper for a moment, then slipped it into the pocket of her coat.

Epilogue

Three years later

Anette sat down in her plush armchair by the telephone table and opened the envelope which had arrived that day in the mail. It was a card with a beautiful illustration of two women walking together across a beach, their skirts and unbound hair blowing in the wind. She recognized the handwriting immediately.

Dear Anette,
I write these words in a spirit of friendship and gratitude. Many women have come my way because of you, women who have been nervous but eager to learn how to protect themselves. Together, I know we can change the lives of women for the better.
With deepest affection,
Ottar

She smiled to herself and remained in the chair as darkness fell outside, pulling her shawl tightly around her shoulders, and watching the moon rise across the sky.

APPENDIX

The Real Anette and the real Hanna

While this book is a novel, there was a real-life Anette Lundström. She was my great-grandmother, my dad's father's mother.

When I was growing up, stories were told about her from time to time. I remember hearing that she had lived in several castles and had experienced various hauntings and paranormal events there. This inspired me to give the Anette the gift of clairvoyance.

It all sounded so romantic. I imagined my great-grandmother as a young woman walking the halls of these castles dressed in beautiful gowns and fantasized that I might even be descended from royalty. But the real truth was quite different and never spoken of in my family. My great-grandmother occupied one of the lowest rungs of Swedish society at the time. She was a statare (see glossary below).

My novel takes us through the towns and farms where eight of Anette's nine children were born—all out of wedlock. The father was listed as unknown each time, except once. In that instance, the man married another woman a year later. The babies he had with Anette were the twins born in 1907, one of whom was my grandfather, Helmerth. His sister Linnea was to have been small enough to fit in a shoebox, according to family lore. I don't know the circumstances of how Helmerth and his twin sister were conceived, but I do know my grandfather didn't think kindly of his father. According to my dad, my grandfather went to see him once as an adult and was invited in for coffee. He declined the offer and would not even leave his car. It was quite enough, he said, just to get a look at him. (The name Ludvig Svensson is fictitious.)

Two of Anette's children died, Ester and baby Ingrid. I don't know the circumstances of their deaths, but I am assuming an older child may have died in a tragic accident and that the baby may have died of an infection. No matter the circumstances, each loss must have been devastating.

Anette had a ninth child, a daughter, born 1910, and again listed the father as unknown. For the purpose of the narrative, she doesn't play a role in my story.

As in this book, the real-life Anette grew up in Hardeberga and gave birth to her first child in Lund, a town well known for its cathedral and its university. Her father and stepmother adopted Carl and relocated to the town of Södra Sandby.

Helga and her sewing shop, and the other mothers living there, are a product of my imagination. But I imagine Anette stayed in a nicer place the first time she became pregnant, and since her parents adopted her first child, I'm assuming she tried to start over, not knowing that one "mistake" would haunt her for the rest of her life.

Just as in the story, the parson would have known about Anette's first child. Birth, death, and residency information were meticulously logged in church records and shared. In fact, it is because of this record taking that I could follow Anette's footsteps today.

The law about women being virgins until their wedding day was abolished in 1921.

Anette lived in the poorhouse in Lund for a couple of years. It had a sign warning people they wouldn't eat if they didn't work. Residents were given their own fly swatters, and it was known to be full of lice. The buildings are still there, but the sign is gone. She had two daughters while living there, then found employment at Häckeberga farm. In the years that followed, she moved each time she had a baby, always to a large estate or castle. This pattern intrigued me, and after some digging, I started to understand why. In the traditionalist Swedish society of that time, a smaller farm would never hire an unwed mother. It would bring dishonor to the owner. Large estates typically had an extended workforce of statare, and an unwed mother could get by relatively unnoticed.

But for every class of Swedish society, pregnancy out of wedlock was unacceptable, and the source of much superstition. As shown in this book, for example, people believed that an unwed mother could give rickets to other people's babies by her mere presence, but only if she didn't admit to her "sin." Those of a more modern orientation viewed this belief with disdain and thought that rickets was because of improper swaddling. Rickets, we now know, is caused by vitamin D deficiency or malabsorption syndromes.

Something tells me there was more to Anette's story than getting pregnant, moving to a new place, meeting someone new, and getting pregnant again. Although Erik is a product of my imagination, I would like to believe there was someone who she loved and was in a longer relationship with. Sofia and the other inhabitants of Häckeberga Castle are likewise fictitious. The castle itself, however, is real and can be visited to this day. Anette did work as a milkmaid on its farm, but it is unlikely that she ever set foot in the castle.

Anette lived in Helsingborg at the end of her life. If she became involved with the birth control movement, I don't know, but I imagine that Elise Ottesen Jensen must have made quite an impression on her. Here in my story, their relationship is a product of my imagination.

Dybäck's Castle, Tjute Farm, Pålsjö Farm, and the farm in Östra Vemmenhög are also actual places where my great-grandmother lived. But, as with Häckeberga, the specific events and characters depicted exist only in these pages.

While there was a woman named Hanna, who adopted my grandfather's twin sister Linnea, the Hanna portrayed in this book is invented. A business owner and early feminist, she embodies the dramatic changes unfolding in Sweden and the world during the decades of the late nineteenth and early twentieth centuries. Just as in my novel, the long fight for suffrage began with the temperance movement and was a complicated process that also involved general voting rights for men.

And finally,

Dear Gammelfarmor (Great Grandma), I proudly share your last name, and think of you often, wondering what you would have thought if someone had told you that your great-granddaughter would move to New York City and write a book about your life.

Glossary

Angelmaker - from the Swedish Änglamakerska. Women who killed newborn babies and thereby turned them into angels.

Brännvin - strong clear alcoholic drink, like vodka.

Gata/n - street or the street, as in Lilla kyrkogatan- Little Church Street, or Bruksgatan-Workshop Street.

Headscarf- from the Swedish huvudduk-"Head Cloth" were used by married women well into the 20th century, especially in farming communities. Fashionable women often chose to wear hats, like Hanna and Helga did.

Hysteria treatments - in my research, I've never come across anything that surprised me more than this. In the nineteenth century, doctors in Europe and in the United States thought women were often hypersensitive, weak, or too emotional because of congestion in the uterus. This, they thought, also led to hysteria, a label doctors used to explain a broad variety of troublesome conditions, including telling people what you thought, laughing too loudly, crying, having strong opinions, shortness of breath, nervousness, infertility, and fainting spells. A common treatment was massaging the clitoris until the "uterus expelled the blockage." At that time, it was not acknowledged that women had orgasms. Sex meant penetration. Massaging the clitoris, therefore, was regarded as purely therapeutic. When women became aroused, it was assumed to merely be the uterus getting ready to achieve "paroxysm," relieving the congestion that caused the unpleasant symptoms described above. The vibrator was invented to address the problem of doctors getting tendonitis or carpal tunnel syndrome because of the strain of massaging clitorises all day in their offices. In fact, most doctors with a staff had their nurses perform this menial task until the vibrator was invented. They were happy to resume the practice themselves once the bulk of the work could be done with machines. Take special note of Rachel P, Maines' book, The Technology of Orgasm in the resource list below.

Kitchen Sofa - a wooden sofa covered with a thin cushion and a lid opening to a storage space, or even sleeping space, under the seat. There aren't many things that are more Swedish than a kitchen sofa.

Kronor – Swedish currency.

Löndahora - "Hidden Whore," an unwed mother who didn't explain that she wasn't married. (The term Löndahora itself isn't used in the story, but added for context here)

Näcken - a strikingly handsome mythological man who played his violin naked in streams and small rivers. He used the music to lure passersby into the water, whereupon he would drown them. A woman who had recently given birth was especially vulnerable if she hadn't yet been "churched" — received her first post-birth Eucharist. (Visit my website *helenerwin.com* and follow me on social media to learn more about my next novel in which Näcken is the protagonist.)

Parson - a Lutheran pastor

Scania-Willows - willow trees with their branches cut short, planted on fields to protect the soil from erosion. Very popular in Scania, Sweden's southern province.

Skål - Cheers

Statare - there is no word in English that adequately describes this agricultural system. Statare were laborers, usually consisting of entire families, who lived in cramped workers lodgings belonging to large farms and manors. They were paid in room and board—cash stipends were rare and only minimal—and bound by yearly contracts; a worker leaving prematurely could face arrest and fines. Statare had one week off each year—the last week in October—at which time they were free to look for a new position. This was known as slankveckan — "slack week." The statar system was abolished in 1945.

The Three Norns - female nymphs that sit by Yggdrasil's roots and guard the Well of Wisdom.

Torp - a small cottage with a plot of land, rented to workers in exchange for labor on the landowner's farm and land.

Torpare - the person, or persons living in the torp.

The Underworld - the place where certain paranormal or otherworldly creatures live.

Wise Woman - from the Swedish Visekvinna, or klok gumma. When the midwifery education became the norm, there was some pushback from midwives who were not officially educated. As of 1819 midwives studied six months, and as of 1856 midwives studied nine months. Sweden's Midwife Association was founded 1886.

Yggdrasil - from Norse mythology, a tree which roots extend deep into the underworld. Also known as the World Tree."

Real-life Characters, Organizations, Publications, and Places

Kata Dalström - socialist lecturer and author. She is known as the mother of laborers and socialists.

Hinke Bergegren - a prominent birth control advocate. As a response to his controversial 1910 lecture, Love Without Children, the Swedish government made it illegal to distribute information about birth control or promote its use. What became widely known as the "Lex Hinke law" was finally revoked in 1938. The notes Bengta read at the meeting at the Frog are based on his actual words.

Erik Gustaf Bernhard Boström - Prime Minister of Sweden 1891–1900 and 1902–1905.

Anna Maria Engström - an activist who was arrested in Stockholm on April 21st. 1902. After appearing in court, she was given a fine.

Kerstin Hesselgren - Sweden's first female industrial inspector.

Elise Ottesen-Jensen – also known as Ottar, was a pioneer in sexual education. She founded and headed RFSU Riksförbundet för Sexuell Upplysning, translation: National Organization for Sexual Information. She also co-founded International Planned Parenthood Federation and became an honorary Doctor of Medicine (1958). After holding her first lecture in 1923, she traveled around the country lecturing about sexuality and birth control. She fitted women with diaphragms afterwards, sometimes behind curtains in lecture halls or even in outhouses and in the back of cars.

Carl Lindhagen - a politician working for women's suffrage. He was on the board of The Fredrika Bremer's Association's Law Committee.

Hilda Nilsson - known as the Angelmaker from Helsingborg or the

Angelmaker from Bruksgatan. She murdered eight babies by drowning them in a bucket and was convicted of murder in 1917. Hilda Nilsson was sentenced to death but hung herself in her cell before she was executed.

Emilie Rathou - linked oppression of women to alcohol use. She advocated that sober men would be less likely to abuse their wives. This would also give women the ability to reason with their husbands, plan the spacing of their children, and have more money for their households if money wasn't used for his alcohol consumption.

Frida Stéenhoff - feminist and advocate for women's suffrage. She spoke in Stockholm on November 23rd, 1905. Her speech in my novel is derived from a portion of this speech. She's known as the first Swedish woman who used the word feminism.

FKPR Föreningen för kvinnans politiska rösträtt - translation: The Organization for a Woman's Political Right to Vote, established in 1902. It joined forces with LKPR and became a national organization. The banner held by the women in the Gothenburg Suffrage March had these initials. See in link-list below.

LKPR Landsföreningen för kvinnans politiska rösträtt - translation: The National Organization for a Woman's Political Right to Vote. Established in 1903.

The Fredrika Bremer Organization - a Swedish women's rights organization. Established in 1884, still actively working for women's equality today.

The Society for Humanitarian Procreation - an organization for family planning.

Places

Altona - an inn in Lund, popular during the 19th Century, a city block is now named after it.

Dybäcks Castle - now a cultural site.

Folkets Tidning - The People's Paper, a liberal newspaper in Lund.

Häckeberga Castle - now a hotel and conference location.

Karolinska Institute - a medical university in Solna, Stockholm

Kronborg Castle - a Danish castle, and the inspiration for Hamlet.

Kärnan - a 14th century tower in Helsingborg.

Lund's Cathedral - built around A.D. 1100. It is the seat of the Bishop of Lund, one of Sweden's 13 dioceses.

Lund University - one of Sweden's main universities, founded in 1666.

Ramlösa Hälsobrunn - Ramlösa Health Spring. A natural spring with a surrounding park which is now a residential area and a public park. The mineral water Ramlösa, has its source here.

Signe Bergqvist - a café in Helsingborg, founded in the 1880's. It used to be my own favorite café, but it sadly closed in 2018.

Resources

For clickable links to these resources, visit
https://helenerwin.com/resources/

Hinke Bergegren, Kärlek utan barn EOD books2ebooks.eu
Ungsocialistiska partiets förlag.

Höjeberg, Pia, *Jordemor: Barnmorskor oc barnaföderskor i Sverige
(ett stycke gömd kvinnohistoria).* Carlsson förlag, 1981.

Hultgren, Inger, *När barnmorskan kom till byn.* Books on Demand,
2010.

Frykman, Jonas, Horan i bondesamhället. Carlsson, 1993.

Levin, Hjördis, *Masken uti rosen: nymalthusianism och
födelsekontroll i Sverige, 1880-1910.* Förlag Brutus Östlings
bokförlag Symposion, 1994.

Maines, Rachel P, *The Technology of Orgasm: "Hysteria," the
Vibrator, and Women's Sexual Satisfaction.* The John Hopkins
University Press, 1999.

Ottesen-Jensen, Elise, *Ovälkomna barn.* Brand, 1926.

Ottesen-Jensen, Elise: https://www.rfsu.se/om-rfsu/om-oss/rfsus-
historia/ottar--pionjaren-i-svensk-sexualupplysning/ Lena
Lennerhed

RFSU Swedish organization for Sexual Education
https://www.rfsu.se/

Stockholmkällan-Sällskapet för humanitär barnalstring Source on
The Society for Humanitarian Procreation
https://stockholmskallan.stockholm.se/sok/?q=S%C3%A4llskapet+f
%C3%B6r+Humanit%C3%A4r+Barnalstring

Stéenhoff, Frida, *"Hvarför skola kvinnorna vänta?"* (pamphlet), Björck & Börjesson, 1905.

Stéenhoff, Frida:
https://stockholmskallan.stockholm.se/post/27055

Swedish Labor Department: https://www.arbark.se/sv/

Voting rights for Swedish men and women:
https://stockholmskallan.stockholm.se/teman/demokratisering/rostratt/

Women's Suffrage http://www2.ub.gu.se/kvinn/portaler/rostratt/

The original Suffrage banner from the Suffrage March in Gothenburg 1918
https://www.svt.se/nyheter/lokalt/vast/goteborgskvinnorna-som-kampade-for-rostratten

The photo with the woman in the white coat and black skirt that Hanna and her friends introduced themselves to at the Suffrage March in Gothenburg. Gothenburg's Suffrage Organization FKPR
http://www2.ub.gu.se/kvinn/portaler/rostratt/databas/public.xml?id=24&detail=1 (*Reproduktion: KvinnSam, Göteborgs universitetsbibliotek*)

Josefin Rönnbäck PH.D: https://demokrati100.se/landsforeningen-for-kvinnans-politiska-rostratt/

http://www2.ub.gu.se/kvinn/portaler/rostratt/historik/

https://demokrati100.se/den-enda-gatudemonstrationen/

Lund's Poorhouse: https://kulturportallund.se/sjalabodarna-fran-fattighus-till-rosa-radhus-och-kyrka

Häckeberga Castle: https://www.hackebergaslott.se/sv

Dybäcks Castle https://dyback-slott.business.site/

Signe Bergqvist Café https://www.nyakultursoren.se/?p=9280

Ramlösa Health Spring https://www.guidebook-sweden.com/en/guidebook/destination/ramloesa-brunnspark-former-spa-gardens-helsingborg

Statar museum http://statarmuseet.com/

Life as a statare, this link in particular has excellent photos and info and is worth putting into google translate
https://popularhistoria.se/vardagsliv/arbetsliv/statarnas-harda-liv